Kissed by a
Dark Prince

Felicity Heaton

ETERNAL MATES SERIES

Kissed by a Dark Prince
Claimed by a Demon King – Coming February 2014

Find out more at: www.felicityheaton.co.uk

CHAPTER 1

Olivia had never seen anything like the male specimen on the inspection table in front of her.

Her heart raced. She hadn't experienced this explosive combination of uncertainty, anticipation and enthusiasm in a long time, ever since her superiors had stripped her of her rank and sent her to this satellite facility in London, taking away her high-level privileges and forcing her to work on studying demon and fae species already extensively researched. It still felt as though they had shoved her out of sight, burying her in the Archangel equivalent of a basement to punish her for her mistake. She had lost all hope of removing the taint it had left on her name in the organisation.

Until now.

The specimen lying right in front of her was her chance to prove herself again, a gift that some higher power had literally dumped on her doorstep.

Blood stained his neck and splashed across his jaw, and pooled at the left corner of his mouth too, luring Olivia's gaze to firm sensual lips that had her staring blankly, lost in their perfection. She blinked herself out of her trance. Time was of the essence. She needed to get her study underway before her guest woke up or one of the other doctors belonging to the facility barged in and tried to take over.

She shook her hands to steady them, pulled her digital recorder from the pocket of her white coat, and turned it on. She set it on the silver trolley filled with all the equipment she thought she might need to complete her inspection of their unconscious guest.

Olivia tugged on a pair of latex gloves and ran her fingers over the scalpels and tools, and settled on a pair of shears. It had been a long time since she had been able to work on a live specimen and she wanted to start by getting his vitals monitored.

She picked up the shears and cut down the middle of his long black tunic style jacket. Red stained her cream gloves.

"Specimen appears to have suffered severe injuries, worse than at first thought, resulting in a high level of blood loss." She reached the end of his jacket and peeled the two sides back. She paused, her eyes widening at the impressive display of taut honed muscles under tight bloodstained and bruised skin. "Specimen also isn't wearing anything under his coat."

Completely unprofessional of her but she had expected at least some sort of undershirt, and she certainly hadn't anticipated a body like this. She drew in a shaky breath, mentally told herself to get it together, and cut upwards along each of his sleeves. She peeled the two sides of his ruined jacket away from his body and set them down on the tray.

"Multiple lacerations and abrasions on his torso and arms. Many appear to be claw marks. Possible demon attack. Subject wears matching black and silver metal bands on each wrist." Olivia spread her fingers and stroked along the lines of four long slashes over his left deltoid. She gasped. "Specimen has markings on his body that hadn't been visible prior to interaction with him."

Olivia tracked the symbols with her fingertips, following them as they formed a curl over his deltoid to his shoulder. Whenever she moved along the line, more symbols appeared, luring her fingers. The colourful swirls and glyphs shimmered through the blood staining him. They swept over his shoulder and under his collarbone, and suddenly she was caressing his left pectoral, chasing them as they followed the shape of his muscle downwards over his heart and around across his torso, and then curled under his nipple to end in a point there.

She had never seen anything like this. It fascinated her. The ones that curled around his deltoid were already fading, disappearing into his skin.

She had made it her business to study the written languages of the fae and demons, because many non-humans bore markings like this and it made it easier to identify the species of the owner. Incubi were born with lines of symbols on their skin that not only changed colour to show their mood, but also detailed their lineage, proudly displaying their heritage in the paternal line. The symbols inked on this male's skin weren't that of the common fae language though. They were new to her.

"Specimen's markings seem limited to his upper torso." She leaned over him and swept a single finger across his right pectoral, and sure enough, markings appeared there too, perfectly mirroring the design she had followed. Olivia used the shears to cut through the waist of his black trousers and froze when more markings shimmered over his hipbone. "Correction. Specimen's markings continue on his lower body, notably his hips."

Olivia flicked a glance at the front of his trousers. If this lean, unusual male didn't wear an undershirt, what were the chances he wasn't wearing underwear too?

She curled her fingers into fists and stifled the blush that crept onto her cheeks. She had seen plenty of nude men during her years as a doctor and in her personal life too. He was just a specimen. Her gaze roamed to his handsome face, taking in its sculpted perfection. A very gorgeous specimen.

Her heart beat harder and she rolled her shoulders. She had to get a grip. This was her chance. If she had never seen anything like this man, then there was a chance neither had the other scientists employed by Archangel. All those scientists that were currently enjoying a soiree at headquarters, leaving her as the only medical staff in the building. If she could document everything about this male, and figure out what species of demon or fae he was, then her superiors would have to give her some credit, and maybe she could get back to doing what she loved most—studying new species.

So, she had to do this. He was just another subject.

Olivia cut away his trousers, running the shears straight down each long, toned leg. She removed the central part and swallowed as her gaze betrayed her, darting to his groin. No underwear. Her face flushed. Oh my. The man was built like a god with not an ounce of fat on his lithe body. All powerful muscle.

She set the shears down and took another steadying breath before touching the fading marks on his left hip. They brightened again and she followed them.

"Specimen's markings curl over his hip from behind. Cannot risk moving specimen without harming him to investigate them. They move down past his... groin... and then sweep back around to curl over his hip." Her heart ran away with her again, her blood rushing through her ears. She hadn't needed to follow the marks all the way to make the ones that arced around towards his buttocks appear. Her fingers had brushed the ones closest to the dark thatch of curls around his genitals and they had appeared.

His hip twitched beneath her fingertips.

Olivia quickly pulled her hand back and froze. He didn't move again. The breath she had been holding rushed out of her.

"I am going to proceed with monitoring the specimen's vitals." She picked up several of the pads used as contacts for the machines and stuck them to his chest and below his ribs on the left side. If he had a similar physiology to a human as many fae species did, chances were high that she could pick up and monitor his heart rate this way. She connected the wires, switched on the machine, and placed a clip over his index finger. The heart rate monitor beeped slowly but everything else was off the charts. "Specimen shows extremely high levels of oxygen in his blood, beyond normal parameters. What are you?"

She ran her gaze over him. He had taken a severe beating before they had found him unconscious outside the building, as if someone had wanted them to find him.

Sable, her friend and demon hunter extraordinaire, had taken one look at him and her gift had told her that he wasn't mortal.

The hunters who had helped her bring him in had believed he had crawled to them or had made his own way to their doors. Sable didn't believe that and neither did Olivia.

No demon or fae in their right mind would place themselves at the mercy of Archangel.

No. Someone had dropped this male on their porch and left him there, wanting Archangel to bring him inside. Why?

It could be a trap and it would be just her luck if it were.

"Specimen appears mortal. Markings on his skin appear fae possibly." But they hadn't captured a fae in years and he was nothing like the fae she had read about in the database or seen firsthand. "Specimen is male, estimated six-feet-six, one hundred and eighty to two hundred and twenty pounds. Black hair."

Olivia inspected his stomach, pressing in to feel his organs. He felt human but something about him, something other than his mysterious markings, told her that he wasn't. She peered closer at the severe wounds on his stomach and chest.

"Specimen appears to have advanced healing ability. Age of blood around the wounds is indicative of a recent injury, but the wounds in question are already closed and beginning to scab over." Many demon and fae species had heightened healing. He could be any number of them. Olivia carefully pulled his upper lip back and studied his teeth. "No fangs. Canines appear normal."

She drew back and something caught her eye. She parted the wild strands of his short black hair and traced the pointed tip of his ear. Was he a demon? They had pointed ears.

Olivia hovered over him, looking down at his handsome bloodstained face. She had never seen a demon as beautiful, mysterious, or deadly as he was.

Deadly.

She could feel it like an aura around him.

He was dangerous.

And waking up.

Olivia scooted backwards and reached for the call button on the wall near the head of the bed. She didn't make it. His eyes slowly opened and she froze in mid-swing for the button, transfixed by them. They were incredible. She had never seen eyes like his. His irises were the most amazing shade of purple.

His gaze slid towards her but he didn't move.

"What are you?" Olivia whispered it again as his eyes began to change, shifting to a normal shade of blue, and then his ears changed too, the points dulling until they appeared human. Adapting. He was studying his environment and her, and he was adapting.

It was incredible.

Fascinating.

She lowered her hand to her side and stared at him.

"Specimen appears able to blend into his environment, changing his appearance to conceal himself."

She had never seen a demon do this. Many of them did it and she had heard the tales from the field agents, but she had never witnessed it.

"You are being held in a secure facility and no harm will come to you." She hoped he understood English. His blue gaze narrowed with his frown, locked on her mouth as she spoke. Maybe he didn't understand her.

He sat up in one fluid motion, swinging his legs over the edge of the inspection table, the movement so swift that it startled her and she shot backwards, distancing herself. Her heart thundered in her throat. She should have pressed the call button.

She should have strapped him down.

Stupid.

Her gaze darted to the red button off to her right. Could she make it there and sound the alarm before he attacked?

"Where am I?" The sound of his deep voice sent a fiery tremble through her. It was at odds with his lithe figure. The commanding edge to it had her forgetting the call button and automatically answering him, because he didn't sound like the sort of man you could piss off and live to tell the tale.

"At a secure research facility in London." She hoped he didn't ask what she had been doing to him while he had been unconscious because now that he was awake, very awake, that sense of danger he radiated had only grown stronger. Her shot at resuscitating her ailing career looked as though he might kill her if he didn't like any of the answers to his questions.

His blue gaze moved around the room, cataloguing everything, a keen edge to it. Strategising. He had adapted to blend into his environment and now he was plotting a way out of it.

"How did you do that?" she said, unable to get her voice above a whisper. His attention snapped back to her.

"How did I do what?" He could definitely grasp her language.

"Your eyes... your ears." She pointed a shaky finger at them.

He planted his hands on the edge of the table on either side of his hips and she struggled not to look down. Her guest didn't appear to have any qualms about being naked in front of a stranger. He sat on the table, frowning at the equipment in the room. His gaze caught on the wires attached to the machines and he followed them to his chest. He raised a single black eyebrow and pulled the sticky pads off his body.

"Strange to ask me how and not why," he said at last and looked up at her through his long black lashes, his blue eyes holding a glimmer of curiosity.

"I'm a medical doctor... a scientist." She pulled at the chest of her long white coat, drawing his attention to it.

He glanced at it and then back around the room. His gaze lingered on the tray of tools to his left, narrowed, and then slid to her. A threat. She had enough experience of the world to know when someone was silently threatening her. He didn't intend to use the scalpels and other implements on her. No. He meant to warn her that if she dared to attempt to use them on him, she would come off worse.

Olivia held her hands up in front of her. "Listen, I'm just curious about your species, and the things you can do. I wanted to help you."

He grimaced and his grip on the edge of the table tightened until his arms shook. He ground out dark words in a foreign tongue and paled further. The edges of his irises turned purple.

The heart rate monitor still linked to his finger went crazy. He scowled at the machine and tried to move to take the clip off. His hands trembled violently.

"You're not well." Olivia reached out to steady him, instinct telling her to help him. She caught his upper arms and gasped. He was burning up, shaking beneath her fingers, his skin clammy. "You need to rest."

"I will be fine... with a little fluids." Pain grated in his deep voice and he swallowed hard.

"I wasn't sure what to give you." Olivia pressed her palm to his forehead. A fever? Was it part of his healing process or was his condition deteriorating? "I wasn't sure what would harm or help you."

He leaned forwards and his breath skated over her bare neck. She shivered, a hot rush sweeping through her.

"I know what fluid I need," he whispered low, his voice barely there and teasing, stirring unbidden heat in her veins and quickening her pulse.

"Tell me and I'll get it." She tried to draw back and his hands shot up, fingers closing tightly around her upper arms.

"Oh, you already have it."

He struck hard on the left side of her throat and her eyes widened. Shock stole her senses for a second before reality came crashing back. He was biting her. He was drinking her blood. Dark memories surged to the surface and she fought his hold on her, struggling like a wild thing. She wouldn't let it happen to her again. She shoved at his chest, clawing with her short nails, and pounded her hands against it, striking as hard as she could.

He pulled her against his chest, caging her there, his arms steel bands across her back, pinning hers between their bodies. She wriggled, desperate to escape him, fear pounding down on her and making her heart stutter. He was going to drink her to death.

Tears streamed down her cheeks and her head spun, wooziness threatening to pull her down into the darkness.

"Please," she whispered, breathless and weak, barely clinging to consciousness as her panic and fear overwhelmed her. "Release me... don't kill me."

He immediately pulled his fangs from her throat and she crumpled, only his arms around her keeping her on her feet. His heart beat wildly against her palms, strong when hers was weak, a timid thing that barely beat at all.

Olivia managed to find the strength to look up into his eyes.

They were different again, amethyst and dazzling. He wobbled and shimmered, said something she didn't hear over the whoosh of blood in her ears. Ears. His were pointed now, more so than they had been before. All his markings were shining too, colourful and beautiful.

Olivia wrestled her right hand free and absently raised it, the action seeming to take forever. She touched his bloodied lips and they parted to reveal his fangs. Her blood. He had stolen her blood. Her head turned and twirled, the bright white room spinning with it. He spoke again, his beautiful mouth moving against her fingertip. She stared dazedly at it, captivated, lost, feeling not quite herself in the presence of this man.

He continued to hold her, cradling her against his body, keeping her on her feet, and stared down into her eyes. His shimmered with something she couldn't decipher through the haze in her mind. The fog refused to lift and part, even now that her strength was slowly beginning to return.

Olivia grazed the point of one of his fangs with her fingertip. He remained very still and she had the strangest feeling that he was letting her see him like this.

"You're not... like any vampire... I've seen." Her words swam in her head, disjointed. Was she making sense to him?

His lips quirked.

"Not a vampire," he whispered and drew her closer, and her gaze lingered on his mouth. Decadent. Profane. A mouth made for kissing. She wanted to kiss him. Olivia shook herself. It was just the blood loss talking. He frowned, a flicker of concern in his purple eyes, and then his expression turned guarded again. "Perhaps I am a forefather of that species."

He leaned down and she didn't resist him. His cheek brushed hers, cooler now, and he licked her throat. The gentle sweep of his tongue over her flesh sent a shudder through her and the achy heat returned, making her skin feel too tight.

She lost herself again in that caress, each stroke of his tongue cranking her temperature up another ten degrees, until she was burning inside.

His words swam around her cloudy mind.

"Forefather." She frowned and the fog began to lift, bringing with it too many questions, all of them centred around the gorgeous male clutching her against his naked body, licking her throat. "How old are you?"

He lifted his head and stared down into her eyes.

Alarms shrieked and the room spun in a blur across her eyes, and suddenly she was behind him, her bottom against the empty inspection table, and he was in front of her. He reached behind himself and grabbed her arm, pulling her closer to his back. Bottom. Oh my. She stared at it, blaming the blood loss for her shamelessness. He had a fine backside. The markings swept above it, meeting on his spine and drifting up his back to his shoulders.

She dazedly reached out to touch them.

The doors burst open and the man jerked her closer, smashing her against his back. She peered past him, touching him forgotten. Two men were there and she didn't recognise either of them.

The men she worked with didn't wear black armour like these men. It was like a second skin on their bodies, covering them from jaw to toe. Their helmets were fashioned to cover all but a V across their eyes and rose back into two dragon-like horns. She gasped when the part that swept downwards to conceal their nose and mouth opened, each slat sliding beneath the next.

The man shielding her said something in his foreign tongue.

Olivia pressed herself against his back and eyed the tools just a few feet away from her. A scalpel wasn't a weapon, but it would suffice in an emergency. This was definitely an emergency.

Were these the men who had harmed the one in front of her?

The alarms continued to shriek and she prayed the resident hunters reached her before it was too late and these men attacked.

She dived for the tray of tools, but wasn't quick enough. The man grabbed her right wrist and pulled her back to him, the swiftness of the action too much for her in her weakened condition. Her legs gave out and she hit the pale floor of the medical room, her left hand catching on the trolley and sending it crashing into the monitor stands.

One of the other men spoke.

In the same language as her specimen.

He answered them and she looked up at him, on her hands and knees on the floor. The men pressed their hands to their chest in a sort of salute. They were with her specimen. Here to take him from her. He reached for her and voices sounded outside in the corridor. The two men rushed forwards to grab him. The male snarled something dark and looked at her with striking purple eyes that spoke of anger, confusion and regret.

And disappeared in a brief flash of violet and blue light that left a flickering outline of him behind that lasted barely a second.

Olivia stared at the space where he and the two other men had been, blinking slowly, trying to get her head around what had just happened.

Hunters raced into the room, her friend Sable leading the charge. She rushed over to Olivia and helped her stand. He had wanted to do that. He had tried to protect her from men who clearly served him.

Olivia rested against the inspection table, confused and dizzy.

What was he?

She tugged the collar of her white coat up to conceal the marks he had placed on her throat, her fingers lingering over them.

He had bitten her, but said he wasn't a vampire. A forefather of that species.

Olivia turned her head and stared at the remains of his clothing, replaying everything that had happened after he had bitten her. He had taken care of her, sealing the puncture marks, and then he had protected her.

And then he had held his hand out to her.

She had the weirdest notion he had meant to take her with him and had been angry because the arrival of the hunters had stopped him from doing so.

"Are you alright?" Sable bobbed around in front of her to get her attention, her golden eyes shining with concern.

Olivia focused on her friend and nodded.

Lied.

She didn't feel alright.

She wasn't sure she would ever feel right again.

Not until she knew what he was.
Not until she saw him again.
Not until she gave him hell for biting her.

CHAPTER 2

Loren curled his hips, driving himself into the female's supple body, tearing another sweet moan from her lips. Her fingers tangled in his black hair and she kissed him, her mouth hot and teasing, her tongue sweeping along his. He took control of the kiss, mastering her mouth and forcing her into submission. Her tongue danced with his, her lips soft and yielding, her taste addictive. He caught the nape of her neck with one hand and held her in place, taking her mouth as he took her body, his kiss as aggressive as his thrusts.

Her feet tightened against his backside, a silent plea for more, and he clutched her hips, dragged her to the edge of the black-rubber-topped table and pumped her harder, thrusting as deep as he could go. She tipped her head back, causing the soft waves of her chestnut hair to spill around her shoulders, a beautifully wanton and wild look in her rich brown eyes. Loren growled and took her harder, driven by a need to claim all of her. He grunted with each thrust, each meeting of their hips, lost in how warm and wet she was, tightly gloving him and driving him crazy with a need for more.

A fine sheen of sweat slicked her flushed cheeks and dappled across her bare breasts, some drops gathering on her beaded nipples.

Another growl escaped him. He wanted to taste those exquisite buds as he took her.

He leaned over her, pressing her down into the table and rising above her without breaking his rhythm. Her white coat parted, falling away from her body and revealing all of her to his hungry eyes. He snarled possessively and swooped down to claim her left nipple, tugging the hard pebble into his mouth. She mewled, clawed his shoulders and dug her fingers through his hair, clutching him against her. Her body clenched his, drawing him deeper, heightening his pleasure as he thrust into her with long measured strokes, feeling all of her.

Loren still needed more. It wasn't enough. He needed to know she was his and she knew it.

She rocked her hips, countering his movements, taking him as deep as her body would allow. The tip of his length struck deep inside her and he withdrew almost all the way out of her before he plunged back in, striking her again. He moaned and curled his hands around her shoulders, settling his weight on his elbows. He dragged her against him with each thrust of his hips, desperate for more, needing to take her harder and deeper, ruining her to all other males. His legs quivered but he didn't stop. Couldn't. He wanted to possess her. He wanted to stamp his mark on every inch of her.

Loren rammed harder into her, making her feel him, wanting her to know she was his now.

She groaned and arched her breasts into his mouth, and he sucked harder on her nipple, teasing it with his blunt teeth as he continued to drive into her, relentless and hard, unable to ignore his need to take her so thoroughly she would never want another male and would never forget him. He lightly bit down on her nipple and her husky moan went straight through him. His fangs descended in response and he rose off her again, bracing himself over her as he plunged into her, bringing her towards her climax with savage relentless strokes. She thrashed her head and arched upwards, her body tightening around his, ripping a groan from his throat. Her feet pressed into his buttocks, forcing his hard length into her each time he withdrew. Her dark eyes pleaded him for more, her breathless moans his guide, telling him that she was close.

Loren wanted to feel them climax together.

His lips peeled back off his fangs and she obeyed, turning her head to one side, revealing the marks he had placed on her before, in this same laboratory. He struck hard again, burying his fangs into her soft warm flesh and pulling hard on her blood. She cried out and her body quivered around his, her pleasure racing into him through her blood, bringing him to climax. He shuddered and jerked, growled into her as he came, pumping his seed into her hot core as he pulled her blood into his body.

Loren shot up in bed, breathing hard and shaking, his senses reeling with the intense pleasure boiling in his veins. His cock ached, the brush of the silk covers pooled around his waist agony against his sensitive flesh. He rubbed his palm down it and heat shot through him, sweeping outwards with his groin at its epicentre. He groaned and flopped back onto the bed, struggling to catch his breath.

It had been two days since he had woken a captive of a mortal organisation and taken the female's blood. Every time he had closed his eyes to catch some sleep and speed his healing, she was there waiting for him in his dreams.

Erotic, intense, incredible dreams.

Loren palmed himself again and then dragged his hand away. He was only inviting the dreams if he pleasured himself because of them. He dug his hands under the soft pillows beneath his head, caging them there, and stared at the wooden ceiling of his rooms.

Why couldn't he get his mind off her?

She haunted him every waking hour and every sleeping one, filling his head with thoughts that had him needful of her and aching, hard at some extremely inappropriate times.

Loren sincerely hoped that his clothing had concealed the erection he had sported during a council meeting. It had refused to go away, dragging his mind through the gutter, making him imagine taking the female right there on his throne. He hadn't heard a word his trusted advisors had said as they had gently berated him about his lack of caution that had led to him being injured and left at the mercy of demon hunters.

He scrubbed a hand down his face and then shoved his fingers through his black hair, yanking it back hard enough to hurt.

He hadn't experienced lust in forty-two centuries, not since he had gone to war with his brother. He also hadn't thought of anything other than Vail and their war in that time. He didn't like it. He needed to focus on his brother now that he had re-emerged from hiding.

Searching for his brother had occupied most of his days since their war had begun. Vail cloaked himself, making it impossible for Loren to find him through the link between their blood, so all searching had to be done manually, using scouts and his dwindling army to follow up rumours and find clues.

His brother had been gone without a trace, clue or rumour to follow for almost four centuries.

Loren's guard had been down three nights ago when walking the castle grounds, needing the space from his aides so he could think. Vail had defeated him before he had even managed to rally his senses and begin to defend and retaliate.

Somehow, he had ended up in the mortal realm. Was Vail there now?

It unnerved Loren. Vail had never taken their battle to the mortal realm and the council were concerned that he intended to reveal the existence of his kind to the humans.

Loren's people were already low in number as it was, weakened by attacks resulting from his brother's nefarious plots throughout the centuries. He wasn't sure they would survive should the mortals discover a way into this realm and send in their armies.

The council were using this latest attack, and almost successful attempt on Loren's life, to force him to agree to drop his attempts to capture Vail and end him instead. Loren closed his eyes, his chest aching at the thought of killing his brother, his only family. He was still convinced that Vail could be saved, but he was the only one who felt that way. Everyone else, even his second in command, Bleu, believed that Vail was a tyrant and deserved to die in exchange for the lives he had taken on the battlefield, both by his own blades and by underhanded tactics.

Loren had a duty to his people.

The council took great pleasure in reminding him of that and Loren could never argue against it. His duty was to his people and he would do all in his power to protect them.

Even kill his brother.

He wasn't sure he had the strength to do it though. Whenever he saw Vail, he wanted to capture him and bring him home. He wanted to save him and he hesitated because of it, allowing his brother to escape.

Now, Loren feared that it was a fool's dream and that he would live to see his kingdom fall and his people suffer because of his love for his brother.

Because of his inability to place his people before his only family.

The council weren't on the battlefield to see what he witnessed. Whenever he met Vail in battle, they dealt each other blows, but it had always felt as though they were toying with each other, neither of them desiring the death of the other.

The times when Vail's female were present were different though. The witch had been present at many of their fights over the centuries and each time Vail had been a savage, wild man, focused and determined. The sight of his brother like that left Loren with the feeling that his brother had completely lost his mind.

Whenever they had crossed swords without Kordula present, Vail still seemed crazed, but not savage or mindless. He flitted between attacking and retreating, as though he was split between them, his mind torn in two.

Loren heaved a sigh and pinched the bridge of his nose.

He still ached. No longer the ache of arousal. The wounds on his body were healing but sore, a lingering reminder that Vail was dangerous and had almost killed him this time.

Why now?

He couldn't recall everything that had happened. There were pieces missing and he had a strong urge to return to the female doctor and finish finding out how she had come across him.

Not a wise idea.

Common sense warned that he really wanted to return to her because he had another strong urge, the one that occupied his dreams and had him rising beneath the sheets again.

Loren sat up and shifted his legs over the left edge of his expansive mattress. He shed the dark purple sheets and rose from the bed, stretched and tried to ignore how hard he was again. It was no use. He had ignored it for two days and it wasn't going to go away until he found release. Many in his court would suggest finding a female to slake himself on but he didn't want a stranger in his bed, a female who would be there under orders no doubt, doing her duty for the kingdom.

He hadn't bedded a woman since long before he had gone to war with Vail. He wasn't going to start now. He wanted his *ki'ara*. His fated female. He wanted the one destined to be his forever.

He crossed the room, heading towards the arch to his right, beyond the wardrobes that lined the opposite side of the wall to his bed. His bathing room was half the size of his bedroom, all dark stone on the floor and walls. A beautiful crystal chandelier hung above the bathing pool that was set into the floor. The crystals shone in different colours, casting them around the room.

Loren bent and swept his hand through the water in the large square pool. It was warm. He stepped down into it and sunk under the surface, holding his breath and letting the water heat every inch of him. Coloured light rippled and danced across the surface above, and a sense of peace flowed through him. When the need to breathe became urgent, he broke the surface and moved to the side of the pool closest to his bedroom. He leaned back against it and closed his eyes, resting the back of his head on the edge.

Thoughts of the female instantly invaded the darkness behind his closed eyes. Loren focused on the warmth surrounding him and how peaceful he had felt while under the surface, trying to shut them out. His cock ached again, rigid beneath the water. Loren ignored that too. He would soak to ease his tired muscles and sore body, and then he would rise and dress, and would speak with Bleu.

The female danced back into his mind, wearing the parted white coat and very little beneath. He pictured her standing across from him, at the edge of the pool there, her brown eyes dark with desire as she raked them over him.

She cocked her head to one side and ran her fingers down her chest, circling her breasts with them, shifting the two sides of the white coat and flashing her dark nipples. He groaned and she smiled, hooked her fingers into her coat and slowly opened it, revealing all of her to his eyes. She let the material slide down her body and pool around her bare feet, and then stepped into the water.

Loren swallowed hard, transfixed by her as she waded towards him, her hips swaying with each leisurely step, teasing him.

He ran his arms along the edge of the pool, waiting for her.

The female stopped before him and he held one hand out to her. She slipped hers into it and he lured her down to him. She pressed one knee beside his thigh and straddled him. Loren swallowed again and eased lower in the water, took hold of her hips, and brought her into position above his hard length.

The head of him nudged into her hot sheath and she moaned, easing down onto him, taking him deep. Loren clutched her hips and groaned as he raised her off him and then brought her back down, setting a slow pace this time. She held on to his shoulders, causing his markings to shimmer brightly, and began to ride him, seizing control of their lovemaking. Loren let her, laying back and enjoying the feel of her taking him into her body, squeezing and releasing him, making him buck beneath her. She smiled whenever he thrust upwards, unable to help himself, and rode him harder and faster, until they were both panting and moaning, lost in the moment.

She arched backwards and cried out her release. The feel of her quivering around him pulled him over the edge. He growled as he grasped her hips, slammed her down onto him, and spilled himself, pleasure rushing through his veins and stealing his senses. He breathed hard, trying to bring himself down, his thighs trembling.

Loren didn't want to open his eyes.

He didn't want to witness the result of the erotic acts of his dreams becoming fantasies that invaded his waking hours too.

Loren peeled his hand away from his still-throbbing length, reached under the water and pulled the chain on the large stone plugging the bottom. The water immediately began to rush down the drain. He stepped out of the pool, dried himself off with a square of thick purple cloth and growled at his lack of self-control.

He padded silently across the dark stone floor to the elegant wardrobes lining the wall of his bedroom, drying his hair at the same time. All eight doors were black wood decorated with a beautiful inlay made of precious stones and shells, depicting dragons and his kind, living in harmony with all the kingdoms. Life had been like that once, thousands of years ago. Now, many of the demon kingdoms wanted him dead, blaming him and his people for his brother's ruthless attacks on their villages.

Only the first and second demon kingdoms kept the other five from razing his lands and murdering his people. He had signed a peace treaty with them a thousand years ago. The kingdoms didn't tolerate any individual demon from outside their realm passing through it without permission, let alone an army.

He took a pair of black tight trousers from the stack and slipped them on, fastening them over his hips, and then jammed his bare feet into his black leather riding boots.

His markings flared, a hot shivery feeling that always made him tense. They had done that too often since he had taken blood from the female, unsettling him.

It wasn't the only anomaly.

He wasn't healing as quickly as he should have either. It had been two days. His wounds should be gone by now, but they lingered, and he felt weaker than usual. His brother's attack had been severe, but he had taken blood from the female and had drunk stored blood since returning to his world. He had eaten too, devouring the plates of nourishing vegetables and fruits that Bleu had pressed him to consume even when he hadn't felt hungry. He should have healed by yesterday.

Perhaps he needed more blood.

Loren raked his fingers through his damp black hair and crossed the expansive bedroom. Daylight flowed in through the tall arched windows lining the wall to his right, where his bed was. Someone had been in while he had been resting and opened the twin arched doors that led onto his balcony. A breeze swept in through them, tousling the sheer blue curtains, carrying the scent of flowers.

He stopped at the long black low cabinet that lined the shorter side of his bedroom and opened one of the doors. Someone had topped up the icebox too. The small triangular metal containers of blood in the dark stone box smelled faintly of Bleu. Loren smiled to himself and took one of the canisters out.

Bleu had been livid with him when he had come to take him from the female doctor's laboratory. Loren had received more than an earful. Bleu had practically scolded him, sounding much like the mother Loren had lost almost five thousand years ago.

His second in command had never learned how to express his feelings. Whenever he was concerned, it came out as angry. Loren appreciated his friend's concern though, and that he had managed to track him to the mortal world before the humans had, well, he still wasn't sure what their intention had been.

Studying him.

The female had said she desired to study him.

She had desired to help him.

Loren groaned at the memory of what he had done after that. He had bitten her. He had felt weak and shaky, on the verge of passing out from the pain of his injuries. It had been instinct. She had smelled divine and had been so close to him, so warm and beautiful. He hadn't been able to stop himself.

He pulled the cap off the canister and swiftly gulped the contents down. He closed the cabinet door and set the empty canister down on the top, and walked across the room, passing his bed and heading for the double doors beyond them that stretched twenty feet high. The light blue fabric caressed his bare torso as he moved through the curtains. The blood would kick in soon and then he would feel better.

His stomach cramped, pain vibrating through his body. He shot a hand out and grasped the door to his left, clutching it for support. Something was wrong. He should be growing stronger but he felt as though he was getting weaker.

Loren's eyes shot wide and he held his stomach, fighting a wave of nausea.

Cold fingers danced down his spine, chilling his blood in his veins.

The female was more than a source of sustenance. She was different. Not just a normal human. Did she know it? Did Vail?

Loren had a terrible feeling that his brother knew.

Ki'ara.

His knees weakened. She couldn't be. It wasn't possible that the human doctor was his fated female. His ki'ara.

Loren growled, his frustration getting the better of him. He had wanted to find his ki'ara for almost fifty centuries but he didn't need this now and he certainly didn't need her to be a member of some sort of demon-hunting organisation.

Icy claws drifted down his back again and curled around his heart.

He feared that it wasn't fate that had brought him together with his eternal mate now.

It was his brother.

He needed to know exactly what had happened the night he had met her.

Loren pushed away from the door and stumbled across the room, aiming for the bed. He had to be careful though. If he was right, and he had bonded the female to him, returning to her might not be a wise move.

Bonded males could become extremely aggressive and dangerous in the presence of their female.

16

Vail was proof of that.

The completed bond with the dark witch had changed him and Loren felt certain that it was responsible for his brother's madness and thirst for violence. If he had taken the first step in binding himself to the female doctor, he couldn't afford to let it change him as it had changed his younger brother. He could never complete it, no matter how long he had waited for his ki'ara. The fate of his people rested on his shoulders.

He needed to find a way to shatter the fragile bond.

If she was his ki'ara.

There was one way of finding out.

If she were, he would be able to use the bond between them to locate her. His knees hit the mattress and he collapsed on his front and rolled onto his back.

Loren closed his eyes and focused, turning his thoughts inwards, towards the female and her blood. He found a slender thread of her within him and held on to it, using his psychic abilities to enhance it, until it grew into a thicker ribbon of colours that swirled like his markings, iridescent and beautiful. His breathing grew laboured, the strength it took to use his abilities weakening him further. A room shimmered into focus in his mind, a place with cream walls and soft brown furniture, and technology he had never seen before.

The female walked into view, dressed in her long white coat and dark tight trousers beneath them, her chestnut hair twirled into a knot at the back of her head.

Loren stood and willed his personal portal to appear. Violet and blue light chased over his body, outlining it, and he commanded it to take him to the female.

He appeared behind her in her small apartment. He had been to this building before. It smelled familiar. She lived in the place where she worked.

He had wanted to speak with her here, where familiar things would surround her and she wouldn't feel threatened, but he couldn't risk her raising the alarm.

Loren grabbed her from behind and covered her mouth with his hand. She instantly began wriggling in his arms, rubbing her backside against his groin, reigniting the desire he had barely managed to leash back in his bathing room. He ground his teeth together and caged her against his body, and willed himself to return to the portal in his room.

The moment his rooms appeared around him, he released her and she turned on her heel and smashed her fist into his mouth.

Loren stumbled and fell on his backside, the impact with the cold stone jarring his spine.

His female stood over him, a fiery glow in her dark eyes, her lips compressed into a thin line of fury.

She was beautiful.

But she could never be his.

No matter how long he had waited for her, had dreamed of having his ki'ara, he had to do the right thing for a change. He had to place his people first and he had to defeat his brother.

There was only one way he would be strong enough to battle and kill Vail.

He looked up at the female towering over him, his heart beating in synchronisation with hers, his body weakened by their incomplete connection.

He had to find a way to break their bond and let her go.

He had to sacrifice his dreams.

CHAPTER 3

Olivia's knuckles burned.

The man she had planted on his backside didn't look as though she had dealt much damage with her blow though. She had the feeling she had caused herself more pain than she had inflicted on him. She stood over him, letting him see the full extent of her anger in her eyes. It was a little over two days since he had tried to take a chunk out of her throat and her fury over it hadn't dropped from a boil to a simmer. The twin wounds on her neck were still sore, irritating her, a constant reminder of what he had done.

She had thought about how this meeting would go many times during the course of the past fifty hours, considering all the scenarios, but she had never once imagined it would actually happen and she would see him again.

She had definitely never imagined he would kidnap her from her apartment.

Where the hell was she?

Her gaze darted between him and the room, trying to take it all in without giving him a chance to attack her unawares.

If he tried anything funny, she was aiming lower and with her foot. He was anatomically similar to a human male and that meant she could deal him a blow he would definitely feel, all without causing herself a single ounce of pain.

The room around her was dark and grim, the walls and floor made of stone that verged on black, and the ceiling made up of a rich sort of timber. The arched windows at intervals along the wall to her right and the tall arched door a few metres behind her on the same wall let in a large amount of light though. The world outside was bright. Far brighter than it should have been. He had taken her in the dead of night. Were they on the other side of the world now?

The man picked himself up off the floor and she scooted back a step, brandishing her fists in front of her. He cocked an eyebrow at her and rubbed his mouth with the back of his hand, his purple eyes darkening. She knew that look. She had pissed him off. Not what she had aimed to do, but it was satisfying nonetheless.

"You have a hell of a lot of nerve, Mister. You take liberties with my vital fluids and then you kidnap me?" She stood her ground when he rose to his full height, reminding her just how tall he was, the honed muscles of his bare torso stretching with his action.

Olivia refused to let her eyes drift down and take in that delicious body. He had hurt her. He was some kind of demon and he had bitten her, and she'd had enough damn men in her life like that. She wasn't looking for a repeat performance with the tall, dark and deadly slice of sexy standing before her. No way.

She really wasn't.

"Do you intend to hurt me?" She was sure that he wasn't likely to be honest and tell her if he was, but she had to ask.

He shook his head. "No. To hurt you would be to hurt myself."

That sounded rather noble and romantic. She glanced around the room again. It was huge, and the furniture was solid wood, possibly ebony, and very ornate. Was she in a castle? This was how she had imagined castles looked. Why did he live in a castle?

"Female, tell me everything about how we met." That commanding tone again. He was a man used to getting his way, issuing orders and having people obey, and he seemed to live in a castle on the other side of the world to her offices in London.

Her mind supplied that perhaps he was a knight or a prince. He had a regal bearing and was handsome enough to be someone of noble blood. He acted like a stuck up bastard too.

He took a step towards her and Olivia moved back one, keeping the distance between them steady. She wasn't sure whether he had other powers besides the ability to teleport, but she wasn't going to risk letting him close the gap. He had already bitten her once. There was nothing to say he wasn't going to try that trick again and drain her dry this time. She bristled at the memory of him attacking her and clenched her fists.

He halted and quirked an eyebrow at her. Maybe he had good senses like many demons and had detected her anger.

"Listen. I'll answer your questions but if you come near me, I won't be held responsible for the damage done to your private parts."

He backed off a step. It seemed that even demons had preservation instincts when it came to their balls.

"Better." She moved a step too, enlarging the gap, giving herself more space and ending up closer to the doors. The rich blue sheer curtains billowed on a warm breeze that smelled like blossom. Southern hemisphere? It was early autumn in the northern. "The patrol team found you close to the facility."

"How close?" He frowned, his eyes darkening.

"That was the weird thing. You were practically dropped on our doorstep... like a gift."

He cursed in his foreign tongue, his expression turning pensive, which was not good for Olivia because he was even more handsome when the black slashes of his eyebrows drew together, his sensual lips pursed, and his purple eyes flashed with keen intelligence.

"I knew it," he muttered, his bass voice still at odds with his lean athletic figure. He paced, his boots making no sound on the floor.

How could he move silently like that? The dark floor was solid stone and his boots looked heavy, the soles made of layers of leather and possibly wood.

He should be shaking the foundations with each determined stride, but he wasn't.

She had a thousand questions she wanted to ask him, most of them about whether she was getting out of this alive, but couldn't find the courage to voice them when he looked so dark and troubled.

Olivia settled for tracking him as he paced, sure that he would have another question for her soon, because he was thinking hard. He was pale too, maybe even more so than he had been when she'd had him on her inspection table. Was he still sick?

His purple gaze flitted to her, and then away, and then back again. Whenever it landed on her, he looked lost for a moment, bewildered, as if he had forgotten what he was supposed to be doing but had a suspicion he had been doing something before setting eyes on her.

Olivia's body betrayed her every time his gaze landed on her, flushing with fiery heat and that shivery achy feeling that had come over her when they had first met. She cursed herself. She was not going to go through this again. At least the first time she hadn't realised that she was dealing with a demon until he had tried to take down the central headquarters of Archangel. She knew this time and she had her barriers up and locked in place. There was no way he was going to break them down.

She was not going to lust after another demon.

He wheeled around to his right and her eyes shot to the arched door near the other end of the room, close to a low long cabinet.

It was one of the men from the other night. The one who had spoken. She recognised his face. He still wore his suit of armour, but his helmet was gone, revealing black-blue overlong wild hair. Did all of their species have the same hair and eye colour? He stared at her, purple eyes dark and cold, but laced with a touch of surprise.

"I sensed your agitation." He switched his focus to the man who had bitten and kidnapped her. "Is everything well, my prince?"

Prince. Oh my. She had been right on the money. Her kidnapper was a prince. A prince of what though?

The other male's eerie gaze slid back to her and narrowed, and Olivia had the dreadful feeling that he would be all too willing to kill her if she was upsetting the man he had referred to as his prince.

The prince in question shook his head and waved regally, dismissing the male. "That action will not be necessary, Bleu. The female is not a threat to me."

Olivia bristled at that. She could have killed him when she'd had him unconscious on her inspection table. Not a threat her ass.

Both men slid deadly looks her way and Olivia realised she had said it all aloud. She shrank back, trying to make herself look as small and nonthreatening as possible.

The prince dismissed the male again. This time, he obeyed and left. Olivia waited until he had closed the wooden door before she moved her attention back to the prince and relaxed a fraction. The man in the room with her had bitten and kidnapped her, but had said he wouldn't hurt her. If she had to choose between him and the one he had called Bleu, who had looked at her as if she were a pest to be eradicated, she would choose her blood-drinking captor over the homicidal maniac.

"Continue," he said and she half expected him to use that regal wave on her. If he tried it, she might be inclined to relocate his testicles after all. She might be human, but she wasn't going to let anyone order her around, not even a powerful immortal prince. She had enough of that from her superiors. "What condition did you find me in?"

"You'd taken one hell of a beating... don't you remember fighting?" she said and he shook his head and sat on the edge of his bed. Rumpled purple covers. Barely dressed male. She could do the math. He had woken and come to take her shortly afterwards, because he couldn't recall the fight and how he had ended up at Archangel. He looked like the sort of man who liked to be in control and hated weakness, and not remembering the events that had seen him dumped unconscious at a demon-hunting organisation were probably driving him mad. "It must have been epic."

The light in his eyes faded and he looked off to his right, staring at the foot of the row of wardrobes.

"My battles with this particular enemy always are." Something drifted in his rich purple eyes, a shadow of remorse that left her feeling he would rather not fight this enemy.

He cursed again, pushed to his feet and paced, taking long agitated strides up and down the room.

Olivia leaned back against the wall and studied him in silence, giving him time to think and beginning to relax.

He was beautiful, his tall lean figure shifting sensually with each stride, working his muscles like a symphony. Every so often, the markings she had followed with her fingers would flash into existence and he would growl, seemingly irritated by them, and glare at her, as if she were to blame.

Olivia lost track of time, her fear melting away and her guard dropping with it. What was he thinking? He looked melancholy at times, pained, but angry at others. Feelings flitted across his handsome face, rapidly changing his expression, drawing her to him all the more.

He seemed sad for some reason, a terrible sorrow that shone in his eyes, fathomless and painful. Mixed in with that sadness was a sense of lethalness though, the danger she had originally felt in his presence, a feeling he exuded like an aura. It should have warned her away from him. Instead, she found herself moving away from the wall and towards him, lured by an inexplicable need to comfort him and ease the pain she swore she could feel in him.

"Are you okay?"

He stopped dead and looked across at her, his expression open and blank, as though her question had caught him off guard. His look hardened again a second later and he pivoted on his heel and crossed the room to her. He halted inches from her, towering over her, making her feel nervous and unsure of herself. The longer he stood there studying her with those intense purple eyes without saying anything, the more on edge she felt, until her insides had twisted into tight knots and she couldn't bear it anymore.

"Have you finished questioning me now?" she blurted out.

He nodded.

"I can go home?"

"I am sorry but I cannot allow that to happen." He looked beyond her left shoulder, towards the blue curtains and the doors. "My enemy has made you a target, a well played move on his part and one I did not predict or even consider."

Her anger came back to a rolling boil and she opened her mouth to give him hell, but he stole her voice. His eyes came back to meet hers and he lifted his hand, slowly reached towards her and brushed aside the collar of her white coat. He caressed the marks on the left side of her throat, sending a hot achy shiver through her.

"I have made you a target." Those words sent a different sort of shiver through her. This one not at all pleasant.

She raised her hand to touch her throat and ended up covering his hand instead. His skin was cool beneath hers. His nostrils flared, his eyes brightened and the pointed tips of his ears extended and sharpened. He bared his fangs at her and shifted back, pulling his hand away from her touch.

Olivia's heart leaped into overdrive, thundering against her ribs, and her hand shook, fear freezing her feet in place.

The prince looked ill but, at the same time, there was an unmistakable spark of desire in his eyes.

It might have flattered her if she hadn't been clinging to what he had said, repeating it in her head and growing increasingly angry with each cycle. She was a target for a maniac who had beaten this immortal male close to death?

"What the hell is going on here?" she snapped and advanced on him, surprised when he actually retreated, as if he feared her. No way a powerful male like him would fear a little woman like her. He hadn't liked it when she had touched him. He had reacted strongly to it. Maybe he feared she would touch him again if he let her get close enough. She wanted to touch him alright. She wanted to crack his nose with her fist. "I want to know what's happening because I have the feeling my life is on the line and I didn't sign up for this shit. You bit me... I damned well didn't ask you to violate me... and I want to know how your abuse of my body and my rights has made me a target."

The prince held his hands up and she halted, breathing hard to settle her volatile feelings. Getting angry with him probably wouldn't solve anything. If she was in danger, she was probably going to need his help. He had dragged her into this. He could damn well get her out of it unscathed.

"The reason your comrades found me so close to your facility is because my enemy left me there... it is a twisted game... he could have killed me but I would not have suffered." He sounded too damn calm and he looked it too.

Olivia couldn't see how he could be so relaxed about all of this. Some psychopath had beaten him close to death and dropped him on her doorstep, and it was all a game? That wasn't a game. That was sick.

"And he wants you to suffer... why?" She couldn't hold the angry note from her voice. He had wanted answers and had brought her here. Well, now she wanted some damn answers of her own.

"It is not for you to know," he said quietly.

It damned well was. "Why did he dump you with us? Did he think Archangel would torture you?"

He shook his head, the solemn look returning to his eyes. "No. He knew *you* would torture me."

Olivia frowned. "I don't get it. What do you mean? I said did he think we would torture you and you said no, and then you said he knew we would... that doesn't make sense. I warn you, I am liable to relocate your testicles if I don't start getting some straight answers."

He took a step back. "It was a straight answer. Not we... you... he knew you would torture me."

"Me?" Her eyes shot wide and indignation joined the ranks of her feelings. "I'm a doctor. I know I work for a demon-hunting group, but that doesn't mean I would torture one."

He glanced down at his boots and then back at her, his expression troubled. He growled, exposing his fangs, and shoved his fingers through his black hair.

"He knew what you were when he dropped me there and he knew what I would do," he barked the words at her, his expression wild and desperate, the look of a man firmly on the edge. He stepped towards her and reached for her, and then let his hands fall to his sides and cursed.

"What... bite me?" She touched the marks on her neck, feeling the pronounced bumps where his fangs had punctured her. What had he done by biting her?

The prince closed the distance between them and she tipped her head back, holding his gaze. He frowned and she gasped as his fingers settled against her jaw. He slid his hand along it to cup her cheek, his eyes locked on hers, drawing her into their purple depths until she felt lost.

"Bind you to me."

CHAPTER 4

Olivia couldn't breathe, and it wasn't only because she was drowning in his eyes and lost in the feel of his gentle touch.

Bind. Her. To. Him.

Bind her. To him.

It gradually sank in, leaving her feeling numb and dazed.

The man had beaten him unconscious and dumped him on her doorstep. Specifically. The prince had come around, injured and weak, and had bitten her. That bite had bound them together.

His enemy had known the whole thing would happen.

He had orchestrated it to make the prince suffer and make her a target.

Olivia changed her mind. It wasn't sinking in at all.

"What the hell do you mean?" she snapped and glared up at the prince.

His hand was still against her face. Dangerous. She pulled her barriers up, more afraid of him now than she had ever been. She was bound to him. That couldn't be a good thing. It sounded distinctly intimate and she was not doing intimate with a demon. Never again. She had learned her lesson. You couldn't trust a demon.

"Under normal circumstances, my biting you would not have been a problem. Your blood would have restored my strength, you would have healed, and your life would have gone back to normal."

"You keep saying normal." She always had been perceptive and he might be talking in a very practiced calm and rational voice clearly designed to placate people and keep them calm and rational too, but she was so far beyond calm and rational that she couldn't even see it in the rear view mirror. "If that's the normal version of events... what crazy one really happened?"

His fingertips caressed her ear, distracting her.

Olivia knocked his hand away and glared at him. "Answer me."

He lowered his hand and his shoulders slumped. "Very well. Your blood carries a specific gene that is rare amongst humans. It marks you as a potential mate for my species."

"Vampires." She threw it at him like a barb.

He neatly deflected it. "You know I am not a vampire... a forefather of that kind, yes, but not at one with the darkness as they are."

He was right and it wasn't only because he had told her before that he wasn't a vampire that she knew. She knew better than most that he only bore a passing resemblance to a vampire because she'd had firsthand dealings with one, a memory she had buried deep and would rather not recall because it hurt worse than the memory of the bastard demon who had used her.

"Female?" His deep voice pulled her out of her dark thoughts and back to him, and she stared up at him, lost again but for a different reason this time. Her heart ached. She rubbed the spot on her chest and stifled the tears that threatened to come. "Are you unwell?"

Olivia shook her head, touched by his concern and the gentle way he brushed his knuckles across her cheek.

She sucked in a deep breath and squared her shoulders, shoving the pain away and locking it back within her heart.

"What kind are you then? Just what species are you a prince of?" Would he finally give her the answer to the question that had plagued her from the moment she had set eyes on him? He owed her a little honesty since he had pulled her into a messed up war.

"Elvenkind."

Olivia's eyebrows shot up. "Elves? The elven species are supposed to be extinct... little more than myths... and you expect me to believe you are an elf?"

He had pointed ears, sure, but he also had fangs and was darkness made flesh. She had always imagined elves would be fair-haired and nature friendly, not black-haired with a penchant for drinking people to death.

He was beautiful though, and tall. She was overly aware of his stature as he closed the gap between them again and she had to tip her head back to keep her eyes on his.

"We are not extinct. We merely left the mortal realm and for good reason. Mankind had become increasingly violent, waging war against demonkind and the fae." His expression blackened, as if he were recalling the bloodshed he spoke of. "They hungered for violence, butchering our kind until many of the weaker harmless and defenceless species were extinct. We withdrew from the world, fearing the cruel acts would taint our souls."

And turn them wicked no doubt. Had the vampires stemmed from the elves who had remained behind, their souls blackened by the violent nature of mankind?

"How long ago was that?" she said, her curiosity getting the better of her again.

"Close to fifty centuries have passed since I lost my father and withdrew my people from the mortal realm. I have not set foot in that world since forty-two centuries ago, when I went to war with Vail."

Olivia couldn't take that in. Almost five thousand years since he had moved his people and over four thousand two hundred years since he had been in her world. He was old. Very old. Damn ancient. Was Vail the name of his enemy?

"Why were you here this time?" she said with a frown.

"I did not consciously move from my realm to yours." He averted his gaze and it picked up that conflicted edge it had whenever he was thinking about his enemy.

The man had injured him, rendered him unconscious, and then dropped him into her world.

Olivia paused. "Wait... what realm is this?"

"It is not your world." His smile was wicked.

It did a funny thing to her insides that should have been illegal.

Olivia's gaze slid off to her left, towards the tall arched doors and the flowing curtains. Not her world. Her eyes slowly widened.

The scientist in her found that fascinating.

Beyond the walls of this building, there was another world, one filled with creatures she might never have heard of before.

The woman in her was petrified.

"I want to go home now."

"I cannot allow that."

Olivia snapped her attention back to him and fixed him with a scowl. "Why not?"

"Because you are bound to me... my mate."

He didn't have to say it like that, in a deep husky voice that sent another unwanted hot shiver dancing over her skin, making it ache for his touch. It didn't matter what had happened. She was not staying here and she was not being his mate.

"Why did he do this?" There had to be a reason. The prince had said his enemy had done it to make him suffer.

"Vail sought to bond us to weaken me and make me vulnerable, and therefore grant him a shot at killing me."

That wasn't right. His logic was screwy and he was hiding something.

Olivia folded her arms across her chest. "Your enemy could have killed you rather than dump you at my door. I still don't get why you haven't just killed him before. You've been at war for four thousand years. There must have been opportunities."

"I almost succeeded once." He began pacing again, long strides eating up the stone floor with ease. The man couldn't keep still whenever he felt agitated and watching him pace only served to agitate her. It showed off his body in far too good a light and gave her a terrible excuse to stare. "I came close to killing Vail's ki'ara... it would have given me a chance to capture him."

Olivia didn't miss that he had said capture him. Not kill him. Now she knew why they had been fighting for so long. The prince couldn't bring himself to kill this psychopath. Why not?

"What's a ki'ara?" She figured it was safer than probing about his reasons for not killing his enemy.

He glanced across at her. "It is our term for our fated female... our eternal mate. You are my ki'ara. The dark witch named Kordula is Vail's ki'ara."

So his enemy was another elf, and he had a fated female too, and the prince had tried to kill her.

"Do you get like a harem of them... or is it a one-time deal?" She hoped he didn't say that each elf only got one ki'ara, but the solemn edge to his purple eyes warned that he was going to shatter that hope the moment he spoke.

"We have one fated female." He looked away from her again, his head lowered now, his focus on his knee-high black boots.

Whatever this ki'ara thing was, she had the impression that elves placed a lot of value on it and it wasn't something they gave up lightly. She couldn't imagine having just one shot at true love. The prince was five thousand years old and now he had found his ki'ara, in her, and he didn't need to say it aloud for her to know that he was thinking about giving her up. He didn't act or look like a man who was happy to have found his soul mate and was going to fight to keep her.

"What happened with Vail and his ki'ara?" Olivia said and he stopped pacing, his gaze on the floor and his eyes widening.

He frowned and spat out what she could imagine was a vile curse.

"I am a fool. I have been looking at this all wrong." He threw his head back and growled, his fangs sharp and ears pointed again. "Vail will seek you out and torture you to drive me to the brink. He is seeking revenge and desires me to suffer as he had. He will use you to hurt me."

Olivia's blood chilled to sub-zero temperatures and she stared at him, struggling to get past the part about this madman torturing her.

She managed to reach the end of what he said and realised that what he had told her earlier hadn't been something romantic or noble at all. He had meant it literally. If someone hurt her, then he would feel it. He would share her pain.

Olivia couldn't comprehend that. It was too much. She couldn't breathe as the weight of it pressed down on her and the thought of being tortured closed her throat. Her head spun, the room viciously turning with it.

"Calm yourself!" he bellowed, a dark commanding snarl.

No. She was damned well going to have herself a major panic attack and he could damned well deal with it. She was sure that a panicking woman wasn't on his list of things he enjoyed dealing with, but he had just announced that someone was out to torture her and considering this man had beaten the crap out of the prince, she felt her demise at his hands was somewhat inevitable.

"Female," the prince gritted out and Olivia tried to focus on him.

He wobbled into focus and she frowned when she saw he was clutching his chest and was paler than ever, on the verge of collapse too.

Oh my God. He didn't only share her pain.

His knees gave out, sending him crashing to the floor, and he whipped out a vicious curse in English this time, his handsome face contorting, revealing how much he despised what was happening to him. Olivia rushed to him and crouched before him. He inhaled hard, his shoulders heaving with each breath, struggling for air just as she had been a moment ago. She laid her hand on his shoulder. He was shaking like a leaf.

Olivia ran her hand along his jaw and lifted his chin, and studied his eyes. She tilted his head towards the light and away, monitoring the responsiveness of his pupils.

"What's wrong?" She checked his pulse, pressing her fingers against his neck. It was fast, far quicker than it had been when she'd had him hooked up to the machines in the lab.

She dropped her hand away.

It matched hers.

"Not used to the pace," he ground out. He was talking about his heartbeat. Her heartbeat. She swallowed, stunned by the reality before her.

The bond between them was so deep that it affected him physically. It linked them right down to their hearts.

Incredible.

He sat back in front of her and drew in slow breaths and her eyes widened when her pulse began to slow. He was the one making it happen.

Olivia tried to help him, seeking calm amongst the raging storm of her feelings, but it was hard. She was in a strange environment, felt threatened and overwhelmed, and someone was out to torture her. Just thinking about that had her pulse picking up again.

"Calm yourself." He was back to commanding her again.

"I'm trying... it's... I can't... it's too much." Olivia's panic spiked, her hand shaking against his face.

He looked deep into her eyes and then she was in his arms, held close to him, and they were kneeling together on the floor.

Familiar scents swirled around her and she instantly felt more relaxed. "What did you do?"

He drew back from her and she found that he had taken her home and they were kneeling in the middle of her small living room on the cream carpet, between the beige sofa and the TV.

The prince brushed cool fingers across her brow. "You feel better now."

She nodded, her heart levelling out again, the soft feel of the carpet beneath her knees and the familiar surroundings making her feel comforted and safe.

He sighed.

"I cannot remain here... and that means you cannot either... but I will not rush you," he said in a low voice, one laced with a solemn note.

She appreciated that because she could see how difficult this was for him. He was a man used to issuing orders and having someone instantly obey. He was a man unused to having a weakness and she knew that was what she was. She didn't want this bond between them either. She wanted it undone or broken or just gone somehow. She didn't care how.

"Is there a way to undo it?" she whispered, afraid to hope that there was.

"It is possible it may fade if we do not complete it. I will have my men look into it and we will know soon enough if it is possible to break the bond. If it is possible, you will be free to go."

She didn't like the sound of that. "And if it isn't?"

"If it is not possible, then my only choice will be to complete the bond. Completing the bond will restore my strength, because it will make you immortal, stronger." He held her gaze, unflinching as she glared at him, thinking about giving him another piece of her mind. "You must understand... I must defeat my enemy and to do that, I need to regain my strength, whether that is through breaking or completing our bond."

In other words, she wasn't getting a choice. He was just going to make that decision for her.

"I don't want this bond. I'm stating that for the record. I didn't ask you to bite me and drag me into this mess. I don't want it completed. I want it gone."

"I will do all I can. I will have my best researchers on it as soon as we return."

Olivia shook her head. "I'm not returning. That's another thing. I want to stay here until we know for certain."

His black eyebrows pinched together. "I cannot allow that. You will be vulnerable here."

Olivia held her ground, refusing to give an inch. "Can't one of your men stay with me, like a bodyguard?"

His expression darkened and his ears went pointier again. His voice was a thick growl as he spoke, his fangs brushing his lower lip. "You wish for another male to keep you company?"

Not what she had said at all but clearly that was what he had heard, and he didn't like the idea one bit. Was the dark possessive snarl in his deep voice a result of the bond too or was it because he felt attracted to her? She hadn't failed to notice the desire that shone in his eyes at times either. Was that the bond at work? A fragment of her heart hoped it wasn't. Olivia squashed it.

"Listen, Buddy, you don't seem to want to stay with me and you won't let me stay alone, so what other option do we have?" She prodded his chest, driving her point home so he wouldn't be able to miss that she wasn't going to roll over and do whatever he commanded.

"You will come with me." Clearly, he hadn't got the message at all.

"I damned well will not," she snapped and he leaned back, frowning at her. She could tell he wasn't used to people speaking to him like that but he was going to have to get used to it if he was going to be hanging around her. Maybe if she were caustic enough, he would let her have her way. "I have work to do and I don't need another boss in my life. One is enough, thank you very much. You caused this mess and that means you have to do some major sucking up... starting with allowing me to continue my work."

He snarled and Olivia bravely stood her ground. Or sat it. She realised that they were still sitting together with his arms around her. He hadn't made a move to release her and she didn't think he would. For all his growling, he clearly felt possessive of her. Because of her blood and the bond?

Olivia didn't like it. Not one bit. She didn't like how her feelings towards him were mercurial either, swinging from anger one moment to desire the next. The last time she had felt attracted to a man, she had ended up duped and then disgraced, and she wouldn't let it happen again.

"I cannot allow you to continue your work, because... because..." The demanding prince lost for words? This was a new one.

"Because what?" she barked, trying to force him to spit it out. She really wanted to know his insane reasoning so she could rip it apart.

"Because that would mean you desire to take one of my men into your laboratory." His expression hardened, his purple eyes verging on black. "Men there would desire to harm them."

She couldn't rip that one apart. If he had spouted the answer she had anticipated, stating she desired one of his men, she probably wouldn't have had the heart to rip that apart either. At this point, if he looked at another woman, she would probably go all growly too.

What the hell was wrong with her?

It was the bond. She was blaming the bond. She had been wrong the night they had met. It hadn't been blood loss that had made her feel attracted to him, hazy and hot whenever he touched her or looked at her. It was this stupid bond.

"We would want to study them, not hurt them." Although she could see why he had reservations about it. He wanted to protect his men. "If a demon or fae isn't a threat to mankind, then Archangel doesn't hurt them. Besides, I would like to run some blood work and see if there is something I can do about this bond. If I have a sample of your blood and my blood, and perhaps some blood from an elf who isn't bonded, then I might be able to see how we're connected."

He arched an eyebrow. "I highly doubt that."

Olivia sighed at the incredulity in his tone and then reminded herself that he was five thousand years old and hadn't been in the human world in four of those. He might not have a clue about the progression science had made in those four thousand years.

"Listen... I'm a scientist. Studying demon genetics and physiology is what I do for a living, and I'm very good at it. I know a lot about demon and fae, as well as human, genomes. If this bond is somehow physical... a change at a base level in our bodies... I might be able to find it and find a way to reverse it. At least let me try."

He stared blankly at her for long seconds, as though trying to decipher what she had just said, or maybe he was impressed that the little human female knew things he and, probably, his people didn't have a clue about. Finally, he released her and rose to his feet in one effortless fluid movement.

Olivia used the couch and scrambled to hers. Her feet tingled, numb from the awkward kneeling position. She scrunched her toes, trying to clear the pins and needles so she could walk without making a fool of herself.

The prince paced a short distance away from her, his handsome face locked in a troubled expression. He still looked too damn gorgeous for his own good whenever he turned pensive. Olivia looked anywhere but at him, thinking about how she could convince him to let her do her thing while his men did theirs. She was sure that the answer to the bond lay in their blood. It had to be something like that. A change on a molecular level.

"What is your name?" He turned to look at her and she lifted her chin. His eyes captured hers again, their incredible colour still fascinating her.

"Olivia." It was on the identity badge pinned on her left breast pocket but she didn't mention it. Making a prince look like a fool when he was already on the edge would probably tip him over it and she preferred him calm. And pensive.

He padded towards her, his steps silent on the carpet, but she knew he wouldn't have made a sound had he been walking on solid stone. He held his hand out to her. "Loren."

Loren. A very noble sounding name. One that suited him. Prince Loren.

Olivia slipped her hand into his. A shiver of current shot up her arm as they came into contact. The way his pupils dilated, swallowing his purple irises, told her that he had felt it too.

"Olivia," he said, his foreign accent and deep voice combining to make her name sound exotic and sensual, leaving her wondering how it would sound if he husked it close to her ear. She shook herself out of her dirty thoughts. She wasn't going there. Never. His fingers closed around hers and he drew her closer, and she lost awareness of the world again, falling back into his eyes. "I will escort you to your laboratory."

She blinked. He was going to let her continue her work and was going to be the one to stay here with her? That surprised her until it dawned on her that he would sooner risk himself than one of his men.

She could see he was a prince as he stood before her, tall and beautiful, noble and willing to step into the lion's den to protect his men from those he believed would seek to harm them, offering her a diplomatic solution to their problem and patiently awaiting her answer.

Olivia felt as though he had just offered her a second shot at regaining her status within Archangel too and she wasn't going to waste it.

She nodded and shook his hand.

"Agreed."

CHAPTER 5

Loren appeared in his rooms in the castle and desire to return to Olivia flickered briefly in his heart. She would be safe without him for now and had to speak with her superiors about allowing him access to the building. It had been hard to agree to the time apart, but Olivia needed some space to take in everything he had told her and he had already pushed her too firmly on the subject. If he had tried to force her to agree to allowing him to remain in her small home while she went to speak with her superiors, she would have demanded he leave and refused to cooperate with him again.

He didn't want her demanding that another male take care of her.

Loren growled at that. No male would go near her.

He stilled, freezing right down to his marrow. What if she already had a male?

He hadn't smelled the scent of anyone male in her apartment. He had smelled only his female.

Olivia.

She smelled sweet like blossom.

He rubbed his thumb across the pads of his fingers, remembering how they had interacted, both verbally and physically. He had touched her soft skin too and felt each meeting of their flesh like a hot current going through him. She had reacted similarly, her pupils instantly dilating and her breath hitching whenever they touched. The increase in her heartbeat had spoken to him of desire, forcing his to obey the rapid beat and follow suit. Perhaps it had been desire on his part too and both of them were responsible for the increase in the speed of their combined hearts.

Loren crossed the dark stone floor to his line of wardrobes and opened one near the door of his apartment. He took out a long black jacket and paused.

His pain was gone.

He looked down at his bare arms. The wounds on them seemed more healed now than they had been before he had taken Olivia, the red marks faded to pale scars. He felt stronger too. Being around her, close to her, had restored his healing ability and had given him back a fraction of his strength. Fascinating.

Loren focused on her. It was still very fuzzy, but he could sense her more clearly now, even over the enormous distance between them. He no longer had to exert his powers to the point that they drained him in order to feel her.

The distance between them diminished the effect of the bond though. If her heart rate increased, it wouldn't affect him. He could feel a glimmer of her emotions, but not as clearly as he could before.

Was this boost in his strength and abilities temporary? If he remained away from her, would his strength fade again and his abilities weaken?

He knew much about bonds, but had never read anything about a bond between a mortal and an elf. He couldn't risk remaining here in this realm long enough to discover the answers to his questions. He had to speak with his men and then return to her.

Not only to protect her and help her find a way to break the bond.

He wanted to see if spending time in her presence would give him back more of his strength or whether it had been something else, something more dangerous, that had restored his healing ability and a sliver of his strength.

Not closeness in the sense of proximity, but closeness on an emotional level.

He couldn't allow himself to fall for her.

He couldn't bear the pain of parting with her if that happened.

He slipped his jacket on and buttoned it down his bare chest. He straightened the stand up collar that almost reached his chin and did up the purple metal fastening across the front of it.

He had been wearing something similar the night he had met Olivia. When he had come around, it had lain shredded on the table beneath him. He hoped that this one fared better.

Loren smoothed the flat ends of the tails over his knees and studied the purple embroidery that depicted dragons locked in battle.

What had Olivia made of his clothing?

It must seem strange to a modern human. He doubted any of them wore a long coat such as his, fitted flush to his chest but looser at the waist, and then flowing down in four long rectangular tails, all outlined with fae symbols and with a beautiful depiction of fae life at the base of each panel. Would she think him handsome in it?

Loren pushed that thought away. Considering such things would only cause him pain. It didn't matter what she thought of him. He would find a way to undo the bond, she would be safe from his brother, his full strength would return, and they would never see each other again. It had to be this way. She had said herself that she didn't want this bond.

The way she looked at him when she thought he wasn't watching said differently though.

She had studied his body, lingering on his bare torso, and he had reacted fiercely to the heat of her gaze, his markings flashing violently in response. Her eyes had roamed back and lingered on him whenever he had begun to pace, trying to get his thoughts into order. She was afraid to look at him when he faced her, but couldn't help herself whenever he left her to her own devices and lost himself in thought.

Her behaviour confused him.

He would call her shy, but she had stood up to him, fiercely at times, challenging him and even putting him in his place.

Loren couldn't recall the last time someone had dared to do that.

Bleu tried from time to time, but his attempts were always weak, held back because of Loren's position as his prince.

The last person to put him in his place was probably Vail, all those millennia ago.

Loren shoved those memories out of his head too because only pain lay down that road and he didn't want to go there. Even the happy memories he had of his brother had become sources of sorrow for him.

He switched his thoughts back to Olivia. She hadn't mentioned how long she would need to convince her people to allow him to come to the facility in an official capacity. He would go and speak to his researchers about finding a way to undo the bond and then he would return to her.

Loren closed the black wardrobe door and turned towards the main arched door of his rooms.

Bleu leaned there, dressed in similar garb to him, with rich blue embroidery on the jacket. The collar and top few buttons were undone, revealing the three jagged scars that slashed diagonally down the left side of his neck.

Loren shifted his gaze up to Bleu's face and grimaced.

His second in command did not look pleased.

He waited, staring into his friend's cool purple eyes as they slowly narrowed with the increasing frown that joined his black eyebrows.

"You reek of mortal female," Bleu said, his bass voice suiting his slightly larger build and the darkness in his expression. "What business had you bringing her here?"

Loren exhaled slowly. What business indeed? Bleu suspected that Loren had brought the female here to make love with her and that was enough to have him ready to lecture him on his safety, the safety of their kingdom, and a myriad of other things. If his friend didn't like entertaining the idea of him risking his neck and those of his people to get a taste of a pretty human female, then he was going to hate the truth.

"It is not what you think," Loren said and waited until Bleu's expression began to soften before he added, "It is worse."

"Worse?" Bleu shoved away from the door and came to stand in front of him. They were equal in height but that didn't stop Loren from feeling as though Bleu was towering over him, attempting to show him how angry that one word and the involvement of the human female made him.

Loren moved past Bleu and headed along the long stone corridor. Coloured crystals lit it at intervals, casting shadows in the intricate carvings across the barrel-vaulted ceiling.

"The female doctor... is my ki'ara." Loren kept one step ahead of Bleu, not wanting to see the thunderous look he could feel directed at the back of his head.

"What do you mean... she is your ki'ara?"

Loren sighed. "Exactly that. Vail left me outside the Archangel facility on purpose. He knew that the female was my fated one and conspired to throw us together."

"He ensured you would need blood the moment you awoke... believing you would be in the presence of this female." Bleu stopped dead and Loren halted too, and slowly looked over his shoulder at him. Bleu stared straight ahead, his eyes wide and eyebrows lodged high on his pale forehead. He remained motionless for almost a full minute and then his purple eyes slid to Loren and he frowned. "You bit her and unwittingly bound yourself to her."

Loren nodded. "Unfortunately. In doing so, I have made her a target for my brother and have weakened myself. I have no doubt that Vail will seek her out and torture her, inflicting her pain upon me, having his revenge for what I did to Kordula."

Bleu swore an oath under his breath and started walking again, his footsteps silent in the hall. Loren waited until he was in line with him and then began walking, keeping pace beside him this time.

"What will you do?" Bleu said in a low, cautious voice.

His second in command wasn't sure what to make of this or what Loren would do. Loren could sense it in him. His emotions were all over the place and fear laced all of them. Not fear for Loren or the female. Bleu feared saying the wrong thing, inciting the wrath of a bonded male.

That sagacity was the reason Loren had made him his second in command four thousand two hundred years ago when Bleu had been one of the few to make it back from the first attack by Vail. The male had been born for the role of commander of Loren's legions, a first rate soldier and strategist, and a man who would speak his mind without fear if he felt the kingdom was making the wrong move.

"I will not be completing the bond if I can help it," Loren said and felt his friend's emotions immediately settle, the fear drifting away. "I go to speak to the researchers about it now. They will find a way to undo it."

Bleu cast him an unconvinced look. "What if there is no way?"

"I will complete the bond to restore my strength." He didn't let the emotions that swirled inside him whenever he thought about laying claim to his ki'ara colour his voice. If Bleu detected that part of him wanted to complete his bond with Olivia and finally have his eternal mate, he would speak out against her and remind him of his position and his duty, and his war with his brother. All good reasons to let Olivia go, but it wouldn't stop him from turning on Bleu. Loren wasn't sure he would be able to control himself.

He felt irritable just talking about her with Bleu, half of him expecting his friend to turn against her, the other half expecting Bleu to attempt to steal her from him. Would he feel like this around all males until the bond with her was broken? He was on the edge and close to losing his cool, scenarios running amuck in his mind, most of them involving beating any male who dared look at her into a bloody pulp.

If this was how he felt now, he didn't want to think about how he might feel if he completed the bond with Olivia.

No wonder Vail had gone insane.

"I will kill the female."

Those five words turned Loren's blood to fire.

He fought to contain the explosive rage that ignited within him and calmly said, "She must not be harmed."

Bleu cast him a suspicious look, eyeing him closely. "Because it would hurt and weaken you."

Loren couldn't lie to his sole friend. "No. I will not allow her to come to harm because she is my responsibility. I brought this upon her."

Bleu snorted and folded his arms across his chest, stretching the thick black material of his jacket. "She is nothing but a mortal. She is expendable. If we kill her now, you will regain your strength before your brother can attack again."

Loren whirled on his heel, grabbed Bleu around the throat with one hand and slammed him against the dark stone wall. He shoved Bleu up it, until his feet dangled above the floor, and tightened his grip until the male choked and grabbed at his arm, desperately trying to prise Loren's hand off him.

He felt his markings flash, the buzz of them appearing adding fuel to the fire, pushing him closer to the edge.

"That is my ki'ara you speak of so ruthlessly. My female." Loren squeezed harder, his fangs sharp points against his lower lip and the tips of his ears extending. He growled, exposing his fangs, and his ears flattened against the sides of his head. Bleu's face turned red, veins popping out on his forehead and temples. He gripped Loren's hand, scrabbling against the wall, pulling at Loren's fingers. "Watch your tongue, Bleu. I will not hear another word against Olivia."

Loren sucked in a harsh deep breath, struggling to tamp down the emotions running riot inside him, demanding Bleu's head as payment for his cruel words regarding Olivia. He shut them down one by one, his grip on Bleu's throat easing at the same time. The colour drained from his friend's face and he breathed hard, wheezing and relaxing in Loren's grip.

"Olivia?" Bleu rasped, his hands going lax against Loren's arm.

Loren lowered him to his feet and peeled his hand away from his throat. He forced himself back a few steps, giving Bleu some room, still battling his heightened emotions. He didn't want to hurt his friend, but he would if Bleu dared to speak of killing her again. He wouldn't be able to stop himself. He might want to break the bond, might not have been looking to form one with Olivia in the first place, but he was still a slave to the effects of it. He would defend Olivia from anyone who sought to harm her, male or female, and he would kill any male who dared to attempt to take her from him.

"My female is called Olivia," Loren said and Bleu bent over, grasping his knees and wheezing as he tried to breathe normally. "It is a good name. Beautiful."

Bleu looked up at him, his black hair strewn across his forehead and wild around his pointed ears. The look in his purple eyes told Loren that he was dying to ask if he truly wanted to break the bond, but that sagacity that Loren admired in him won out, and Bleu held his tongue.

Loren knew he didn't sound as though he wanted to undo what had happened. He could understand Bleu's difficulty believing him. He would put his friend's mind at rest.

Bleu straightened, swept his hair back out of his face, and exhaled hard.

"Sorry about that." Loren wasn't used to issuing apologies and he had done it twice this day. Once to Olivia and now to Bleu. Maybe the bond changed him in ways other than awakening his lust and making him volatile.

Bleu casually shrugged. Loren continued along the hall, banking left when he reached an intersection and heading down the stone staircase to the next level. This one was made of paler stone that glittered in the white lights, far brighter than the level where his rooms were.

"Olivia is going to work on finding a way to break this bond too, so you see, you have nothing to worry about, Bleu." Loren turned right at the bottom of the pale staircase, heading along the grand hallway, past towering white statues of the former kings and queens of his bloodline. Vail had a statue once, opposite his at the end of the hallway, close to the throne room.

Someone had destroyed it.

"How is the female able to help?" Bleu sounded sceptical again.

Understandable.

Loren had felt the same way when the female had offered to help, but his lack of belief in her had frustrated her and then she had said a lot of words he hadn't understood. They had all sounded very technical. He had also felt her belief in herself and her abilities, and that was the reason he had decided to grant her request. She felt she could find a way to break the bond by studying their blood. It sounded fascinating and he was almost looking forward to being with her while she worked on it.

"Olivia is a scientist. It would appear modern science is rather incredible. She is apparently able to study our blood and something to do with things called genomes, and other things I have no clue about. She is confident she can discern from it whether our link is a physical change that she may be able to reverse." It still sounded incredible, even when he still wasn't quite sure what those things were.

Bleu raised an eyebrow.

"You know they have cloned things... creating a duplicate of a living creature." Bleu motioned with his rigid index fingers, holding them with their full lengths pressed against each other at first, and then moving them apart but keeping them identical. "Some of their science seems dangerous to me."

Loren frowned. "How is it you know about things I do not?"

Bleu smiled at last. "The benefits of being able to travel freely to the mortal world whenever the mood strikes me. I think I had relations with a doctor once... or a journalist who was writing about cloning. I cannot remember."

Loren wasn't surprised. Whenever the 'mood' struck him, Bleu took off for a night to the mortal world to satisfy himself with loose women all too willing to give up their bodies, and their blood. The mood struck Bleu often, at least three or four times in a lunar month.

He was probably the most well-versed in human affairs of all of Loren's staff, yet he was also the one with the lowest opinion of that species. Perhaps spending so much time in the company of females who slept freely with strangers affected Bleu's opinion of the species in general.

"I am looking forward to discovering more about the advances in science when I spend time with Olivia at Archangel." Loren banked left, past the statue of his mother, and pushed the first set of arched dark wooden doors on his right open.

"What?" Bleu reached for him, stopping just short of grabbing his arm, the volume of his voice causing the five males in the library to stop their work and stare at him.

Loren looked across his shoulder at Bleu. "I mean to spend time with Olivia in her world. She needs laboratory equipment in order to do her research."

"Bring it here. We will build her a laboratory." Bleu had that look again. The one that Loren had often seen in their four thousand years together. He thought Loren crazy.

"I cannot. I brought this upon her—"

"You will be too vulnerable there," Bleu interjected, shocking the five males in the room and Loren too.

Bleu had never dared to speak over him before.

They were friends, but Loren was still a prince. The flicker of nerves in Bleu's purple eyes was apology enough for Loren. He knew his friend meant well, but he couldn't speak to him in such a way in front of others. He didn't want to have to punish Bleu for such a thing. He valued what they shared and never wanted the difference in their statuses to come between them. If the council heard of Bleu's disrespectful behaviour, they would demand Loren punish him.

"Forgive me." Bleu lowered his head and Loren placed his hand on his shoulder and gently squeezed it to let him know that he forgave him. Bleu lifted his head. "You will be vulnerable there... both to your brother and to an attack from the hunters within that place. You know I cannot allow you to venture there, and neither will the council."

Loren intended to visit them next. The moment he had agreed to Olivia's plan and had offered to be her escort, he had known he would need to convince the council of elders to agree to it too. They were not going to be happy with him. He was going to pull rank on them.

"I will speak with them and make them see that my mind is made up on this matter and I will not be swayed." Loren stepped into the expansive double-height room that served as the library. There were two levels, although the upper floor didn't cover the entire length of the room. There was an open rectangular space above him with a balcony running around it. White oak bookshelves lined every inch of wall space and elegantly carved stacks filled the area to his left on both floors.

Above the open area, rainbow colours swirled across the sheer crystal roof, softly illuminating the room.

"I still believe you should bring the female here." Bleu wasn't going to let this one go, was he?

Loren sighed. "Olivia needs her laboratory to conduct her research and I cannot leave her alone and vulnerable." He held his hand up to silence Bleu when he went to speak. "And I will not bring her here, where she feels afraid and unsafe, or allow any other to protect her in my stead."

He turned to face his friend, wishing for all of his kingdom that Bleu would see in his eyes that his mind was truly made up and no one was going to change it.

"I disrupted her life, Bleu. I caused this problem for both of us, and I will deal with it."

"Your brother is to blame here." Bleu's frown returned, turning his eyes cold and dark. "Meaning your brother plans to attack her. I cannot allow you to place yourself in danger—"

"What do you suggest then?" Loren shoved his fingers through his black hair, his frustration mounting and getting the better of him.

He was going in circles with Bleu and he wanted to break the cycle almost as much as he wanted to break his bond to Olivia. His heart whispered that was a lie and he knew it. Loren ignored it and stared at Bleu, his gaze narrowed and demanding the male offer a solution that would stop him from constantly harassing Loren about his plans.

Bleu looked deadly serious. "I will go with you."

Some of Loren's frustration faded on hearing those words leave Bleu's lips. Loren appreciated his friend's support and his desire to protect him. The council would be more likely to allow him to go to the mortal world to assist the female if Bleu were with him and he would be safer from his brother too.

The only downside Loren could see was that Bleu would be hard to control around people he evidently viewed as a threat to Loren, but even that wasn't dampening Loren's spirit. He would be glad to have Bleu with him.

If only to keep Loren in check and stop him from fulfilling a desire that had seized him with both hands several times this day.

He wanted to kiss Olivia.

CHAPTER 6

Olivia wasn't making any progress at all. Mark stared back at her from behind his large black wooden desk, his grey eyes narrowed, causing crow's feet to form beside them. She had known him for almost ten years now, and he had been caring towards her, taking her under his wing and giving her so much freedom and opportunity within Archangel. That had all changed the night she had royally messed up and her demon boyfriend had gone on a rampage, attempting to bring down Archangel's headquarters in London. Since then, Mark had held her at arm's length and rarely agreed to meet with her. He didn't even acknowledge her if they passed each other in the hallways or were present in the same meeting.

Mark leaned back in his mahogany leather executive chair, the deep red colour setting off his crisp black suit and almost matching his silk tie. He tunnelled his fingers through his sandy hair, a tell that she knew well. He was having difficulty taking in what she was asking him to do, and even more difficulty bringing himself to find a shred of the trust he had once shown to her.

"Please. You've read my report on the specimen that the team brought in." Olivia leaned over the black desk, planting her palms on the surface. She struggled to keep her voice smooth and level, hiding her mounting hurt and frustration from Mark. "He's a rare fae and when I spoke to him about how I would like to have the opportunity to study him, he offered to come in and willingly subject himself to it. All I'm asking is that you call a meeting with the higher ups and we can come to some agreement about this opportunity and they can issue an order to the hunters stating that he's not to be touched."

Mark steepled his fingers in front of himself and frowned at her. "Your report about the male intrigued me, Olivia, and I agree this appears to be a good opportunity, but I don't need to remind you that having living fae or demons in the building as guests is not allowed."

He really didn't need to remind her. He didn't need to remind her on the rare occasions he did speak to her, but that didn't stop him. He was still punishing her for her mistake.

"Mark... please? I know the risks and I'll take full responsibility for him. He isn't a threat to us. This is a once in a lifetime opportunity to record data and study a species hitherto unknown to us." Olivia dug her fingertips into his desk, her patience slipping.

He dropped his gaze to his laptop and tapped a few keys. "You know that you can't judge whether he is a threat or not. What you're asking for is a leap of faith, Olivia. I'm not sure my superiors will agree to it. Not after last time."

Her shoulders sagged and her hope deflated. If Mark couldn't get her clearance to work with Loren in her laboratory, perhaps she could go to the prince's castle and work with him there. He had teleported her there. Could he teleport the equipment she would need too or was his ability limited to living objects within specific parameters?

"I'll call the meeting... but on one condition."

Olivia jerked back to the room and stared at Mark through wide eyes. "Name it."

"You work in a team and you have armed escorts at all times."

Loren would never go for that. Neither would she. If she had a team working with her on this, they would ask questions about what she was doing and how was she meant to explain that Loren had accidentally bound them and they were really looking for an out clause?

Never mind the fact that they would realise what Loren was. If they realised he was an elf, and a prince of that species, they would kick her off the team and hand it over to those still in Archangel's good book.

She was damned if she would let someone steal Loren away from her.

Olivia didn't want to consider how that sounded. She was talking professionally, not romantically. Never romantically.

"We'll convene in meeting room three in fifteen minutes. I suggest you prepare." Mark's tone made it painfully clear that he knew her thoughts and also believed that their superiors would try to hand this over to someone more worthy of the opportunity to study a new species of fae. If she didn't make a good case, she would be off the team.

Her only choice then would be to have Loren kidnap her again.

If she went back to his castle, separated from her world and everything here that kept her grounded, it would only be a matter of time before she gave up the fight against the sparks that exploded along her nerve endings and heated her blood whenever she was in Loren's presence.

Olivia straightened and curled her fingers into fists. That wasn't going to happen. She would find a way to make her case watertight so Archangel couldn't remove her from the team or make this about a team at all.

"Thank you." She picked up the scattered papers of her report from his desk and swiftly left the roomy cream office, heading along the pale corridor to the elevators.

She pressed the call button. She would start with her report and her findings, and then she would state her case, embellishing a few things. If she said that Loren had agreed to the tests on the basis that only she would be involved, and they would be left in peace during them, would her bosses go for that? She wasn't a great liar, but she was sure that Loren had only agreed to come to Archangel and work with her because he thought they would be working alone.

He wouldn't want others at the facility finding out what he was. He had taken his people away from the mortal world to protect them. If Archangel discovered that elves not only existed but lived in a whole different realm, accessed via teleportation, they would want to go there and investigate it.

Olivia knew that for a fact because it was what she wanted to do.

She headed down to the next floor, found the meeting room and set herself up at one end of the long oval beech table. She opened the folder and spread her report out in front of her, scanning over Loren's vitals and the transcription of her voice recording. She could do this.

No sooner had she thought that than the doors opposite her opened and several senior staff members filed in, together with four hunters, one of which was Sable, and some of the top medical staff. Mark was the last to enter. He took the seat at the other end of the table.

Olivia glanced at Sable. It was nice to have a friendly face amongst a sea of scowling ones. No one looked happy to be here and Olivia changed her mind.

She couldn't do this.

All three grey-haired men on her left, the senior members of Archangel based in this facility, looked as though they had already made up their mind about her request and she was going to be off the team. Two male doctors in white coats sat opposite them to her right, a smug look on their faces. They knew the deal. Let her speak, indulge her, and then watch as her superiors crushed her hope and gave the fae to them.

They had probably all scanned her report in the last few minutes, taken a look at her findings, and then her request, and thought she had gone crazy to even think about asking to lead the study.

Olivia's hands shook as she shifted her papers around and then sharply raised her head and threw herself onto the tracks of the last train for La-La-Land.

It took her less than fifteen minutes to outline her findings and field some very personal questions that she definitely hadn't anticipated, and a few disdainful remarks, and then all Olivia could do was try to prove that she hadn't gone insane and that she believed that the test subject wasn't out to blow up the building.

One of the doctor's made a very snide comment about it being a male specimen and her report about his body. Olivia's blood boiled and she pressed her hands against the desk, fighting to keep her anger below their radars. The chatter amongst the hunters, her superiors, and the doctors verged on an argument.

"What she's suggesting is crazy. A healthy fae male of unknown origin cannot have free run of the facility. At the very least, he should be contained during the study." The oldest male hunter's brown eyes had a twinkle in them that looked a touch sadistic to Olivia.

"The male in question will not subject himself to containment. You're talking about forcibly restraining him. Doing such a thing to a guest of Archangel is not going to help us improve our image." Olivia's words fell on deaf ears as the doctor who had remarked on her relationship with a demon spoke over her.

"Of course we would contain the specimen. He should have been contained when he had first come into the lab. Then we could have carried out a full study on him, without this debacle."

Oh, he didn't. Olivia almost growled. "He is willing to come in and let us study him. Surely you can't expect him to agree to being strapped down while that happens? I want him here as a guest, not a prisoner. He must be free to come and go."

"As he pleases? That sounds dangerous to me." The grey-haired man in the middle of the three superiors raised an eyebrow at her and the other two nodded in agreement.

Olivia drew in a breath to stop herself from saying something that would probably get her the same treatment as they were offering to Loren. She had spent a few days in the cells at the containment centre before. She didn't want to go there again.

"Perhaps we should have a break?" Mark smiled at everyone, defusing the bomb that had come close to exploding.

Olivia nodded and exhaled slowly. Everyone rose from their seats and the doctors immediately made straight for the senior staff members, schmoozing them with false smiles and talk of how they would handle this study. Sable caught Olivia's arm and pulled her away, towards a table lining the cream wall.

"Don't kill the other doctors," Sable said, her voice light and airy. Her friend was deadly serious seventy-five percent of the time. The rare times Sable let her sense of humour out, things were normally dire and about to get worse.

"They're going to take this away from me." Olivia knew it. They were going to pull rank on her and take her off the study completely, and then they were going to strap Loren down and do God only knew what to him. "I can't let that happen."

"So don't let it." Sable's logic was sound but also full of holes.

"And how do you propose I don't let it happen? I have zero standing with the five most powerful people in this room. Even Mark doesn't want to let me have this chance to redeem myself. I can see it in his eyes." She looked across the room at him where he was talking to the three male hunters.

The air between them shimmered and Olivia gasped as Loren appeared right before her. The air behind him wobbled too and the other one appeared, the one who had looked ready to kill her the few times they had met.

Sable drew her short collapsible crossbow from the belt of her black uniform and had it aimed at Loren before Olivia could react. The other three hunters sprang into action too, drawing their weapons and aiming them at the two elves.

Loren stood before her, dressed in complete black scale-like armour that hugged every inch of his lithe body like a second skin. A black helmet covered most of his head, the top flaring up from a point above the bridge of his nose, sweeping back into serrated curved spikes that almost resembled a crown. The black metallic material obscured the lower half of his face, but she would recognise his blue eyes anywhere.

His fingers flexed around the black sword he had drawn. His armour turned them into long jagged claws with sharp pointed tips that looked deadlier than the blade they gripped.

Loren's blue eyes met hers, a touch of warmth in their silent greeting, and the lower part of his helmet folded back to reveal his face, stopping when it had cleared his cheeks.

She had forgotten how tall he was, but she hadn't forgotten how beautiful. He stole her breath.

The hunters behind them called for assistance on their communication wristbands and the alarms in the building wailed, dropping the room into red flashing light.

Loren's sensual lips peeled back and he bared his teeth. All blunt. He was masking what he was and she couldn't blame him.

He raised one hand, his claws flashing menacingly in the red strobe, and the alarms went silent and the lights came back on.

Everyone stared at him, surprise written across their faces. She probably looked the same way. What powers did Loren have? Just the abilities she had seen him use so far were incredible and she had the feeling they were just the tip of a very big iceberg.

Loren turned on her, his blue eyes cold now, his voice little more than a thick snarl. "Is this the greeting I was to expect?"

Olivia raised her hand and lowered Sable's weapon for her, and indicated for the other hunters to do the same. They didn't. This wasn't going to go well. If Loren felt threatened, his friend would attack to protect him.

The male tossed an emerald green glare at the men around him, disgust written in every line of his handsome face.

Olivia stepped towards Loren. "No, but we hadn't settled the details regarding your visit and your arrival was unexpected... and you're not exactly dressed in the friendliest way."

"You expected us to walk into this trap without weapons... pitiful mortal." The man behind Loren sounded just as gruff and vicious as he had the time he had barged in on her and Loren back in the castle. He went to draw the black blade hanging at his waist.

Loren placed his hand on the male's arm. "We are not here to do battle, Bleu. Remember that. Our quarrel is not with these mortals."

He sheathed his own sword and released Bleu.

"I apologise for the manner of our arrival, Olivia. We had not agreed a time and I had concluded my business, so I felt it provident to come here so that we might begin our tests."

Olivia stared up at him. No one in this world spoke like Loren. He sounded antiquated, a constant reminder of his incredible age. A cute sort of reminder. She liked how he spoke all formally and rigid. All noble and princely.

Her bosses came forward, the three male hunters flanking them, leaving the doctors to stare at Loren and Bleu from across the room.

It struck Olivia again how tall the elves were, towering four inches over the tallest of the men in the room. They were slighter than two of the male hunters, but Olivia knew that didn't mean a thing when it came down to their actual physical strength. These two elves probably had the strength of twenty powerful human males.

"I apologise for the way you were greeted." The senior staff member who had said it was dangerous to allow Loren to come and go as he pleased held his hand out to the man he wanted contained and Olivia wanted to tell Loren not to take it. It turned out she didn't need to. Loren just stared at the man's offered hand and then into his eyes, a cold edge to his blue irises. The man shifted nervously and lowered his hand. "We are not a threat to you."

Bleu smiled grimly. "At least you are aware of that."

Olivia had the feeling he wanted to squish the man like a bug, and there was a tiny part of her that would pay to see it because he was being an almighty ass.

She cleared her throat, bringing all eyes to her, including Loren's. They burned into her, setting her body aflame, making her yearn to look up into his eyes and lose herself in them all over again.

"Now that we've established that the fae I want to study is real and he's not a threat to us and we're not a threat to him, will you send out the notification that he and his comrade are off limits to all staff?" Olivia smiled, figuring that it wouldn't harm her chances.

"I believe our top medical staff should handle this case," the grey-haired man said and the other two backed him up again. The smug doctors in the corner exchanged a glance and sized up Loren and Bleu.

Olivia opened her mouth to protest.

Loren stepped forwards to tower over the man. He tilted his head and narrowed his gaze on him. "I believe Olivia must have mentioned that I will only work with her, and the data from our tests will remain private until she sees fit to make it available to others. I am a busy man, and I do not have time for this delay. It is very simple. Olivia is to work with me, alone, and if anyone seeks to harm myself, Bleu, or the female, they will answer to me."

Olivia might have omitted the threat at the end, but all in all, he had perfectly captured what she had wanted to say.

The senior staff members scurried off to a corner with Mark, talking in low voices. The irritating doctors cast thunderous glances her way. Bleu eyed them and the three male hunters as though he was already dismembering them in his head, and was enjoying it.

Loren stared at her. "It will work out, Olivia. There is no need to be anxious."

Anxious. Elevated pulse. Increased hormone levels. Everything that Loren was probably experiencing just because she was feeling it. She nodded and breathed slowly, settling her racing heart. She didn't want to make him ill again.

Her superiors returned to them and Mark came forwards. "We have agreed you can work alone with the fae, but on the proviso that they are not allowed to roam freely without supervision and you run thorough tests, including those requested by other medical staff, and document everything."

Loren looked reluctant to agree to that and hair-trigger boy looked as though he was going to draw his sword and cut her boss into tiny bite-sized pieces.

Loren's blue gaze slid down to her and he spoke softly. "I will subject myself to whatever you believe is necessary."

Olivia nodded. "It will be simple tests. Stamina, strength, abilities. That sort of thing."

Loren still looked uncertain. He leaned closer, bringing his lips down to her ear. His breath tickled her neck and his proximity did funny things to her insides, making them quiver and heat. She ached for his touch, her body curving towards his against her will, drawn to him.

"My results may not be the most sensible to record," he whispered and Olivia's eyes widened. He was right. His bond to her had affected him physically, weakening him because of their link.

He was weaker because of her.

Was she stronger?

She was curious about that and wanted to run a few tests on herself too. Loren drew back enough that she could see his eyes. The moment they met hers, she was lost in them again, fighting the current in the torrent of desire that flowed between them and feeling as though it was already pulling her under and she was going to drown before she could save herself by breaking the bond.

CHAPTER 7

Loren much preferred the location Olivia had led them to compared with the one they had arrived in. She had been quick to make her excuses and usher them from the room, leading him to suspect that the males who had stated they were not a threat to them had lied. He would have to be on his guard while they were here. It wasn't only his life at risk now. It was Bleu's too.

Bleu had been twitchy from the moment they had arrived, refusing to remove his armour and vehemently stating that he wouldn't allow Loren to either. Loren had kept his armour on to placate his friend while they had walked from the meeting room down to the laboratory where Olivia was to study them.

His second in command had also muttered dark things about the tests that Olivia had to run on them, giving Loren the impression that he wanted to refuse. Olivia would need Bleu's data though. In desiring to keep Loren safe from the mortals, Bleu had inadvertently offered himself as another test subject. She would desire to record Bleu's data in order to compare it with Loren's so she could understand how they differed now.

Bleu paced to Loren's left, along the front of a table which held a row of three machines he had learned were computers. The brightly lit white room they were in was smaller than the one Loren had come around in when he had first met Olivia and there was no bed or any of the equipment that had been present.

Olivia sat in a black swivel chair in front of him, closer to the glass door off to his left, and patted the seat of a tall chair beside her. It was different to the one she sat on, made of white metal with black leather padding, and bolted to the floor. It had a plate for the occupant's feet and a headrest too.

Loren removed his sword belt from his waist and set the weapon down on the long table with the computers. He crossed the room to Olivia and sat in the chair.

Bleu cast him a curious but dark glance. Loren could almost read the doubts crossing his friend's mind and hoped to allay them by allowing Olivia to test him first, showing Bleu that she could be trusted and was not out to harm them.

Bleu's fingers rested around the hilt of his sword, his green gaze monitoring Olivia as she took her dark hair down, neatened it and twirled it into a messy bun, pinning it at the back of her head. She brushed a few rogue strands from her forehead, glanced across at Loren, and smiled. His heart beat harder, a familiar rush of heat racing through his blood. Not her feelings. His. She was beautiful, her deep brown eyes bright with excitement that he knew was because she was going to study him, unlocking secrets about his species, learning about him.

Loren wanted to study her too. He wanted to unlock all her secrets, learning her sweet spots and her taste, how she would feel beneath him, around him. How she would sound as he made love with her.

Her cheeks flushed crimson and he cocked his head to one side, intrigued by the blush of colour. Did her thoughts run along the same lines as his were, imagining them together, touching and kissing, learning each other?

Her eyes darted away to settle on the white table to her left and then crept back again, the colour on her cheeks rising as they edged towards him and her pupils slowly dilating. Her heartbeat picked up, a flood of hormones surging through her blood and through his in response. He breathed hard, a slave to the feelings she awakened in him, his body aching with a need to have her in his arms again, pulled flush against him, feeling every inch of her pressing against his flesh.

Bleu cleared his throat.

Loren snapped his gaze away from hers and fixed his eyes straight ahead on the glass doors, focusing to eradicate the out of control emotions that threatened to have him thinking about kissing her again.

Humans slowed as they passed the doors, glancing in at him with curious eyes. Some were dressed as Olivia was, in a long white coat. Others wore black combat trousers and t-shirts. Hunters.

He recognised one of the males dressed in white. This one stopped at the doors and stared at him. He had been present in the meeting. One of the doctors who had looked at Olivia with disdain in his eyes. Loren gripped the ends of the armrests, his claws slicing into the metal as though it was as soft as flesh.

He wanted to slice into this male like that, rending his flesh, spilling his blood.

Loren's fangs emerged and he felt his ears shift, the points extending beneath his helmet. He fought the change, aware that if he allowed it to continue his eyes would change next, switching from a normal shade of blue to a colour no other fae or demon had.

He felt Bleu's gaze on him and then his second in command moved towards the doors, no doubt to see what had disturbed him. The doctor glanced towards Bleu and left. Bleu looked over his shoulder at Loren, his green gaze dark again, speaking volumes about his dislike of this place, the people here, and Loren's predicament.

"Loren?" Olivia's soft voice coaxed his eyes away from Bleu and the door, drawing his attention back to her. The world faded away again, a sense of calm washing over him, startling in its intensity. He was falling deeper into the bond already, when he was meant to be clawing his way out of it. He was coming to rely on Olivia's voice, scent and presence to soothe him.

She smiled and his heart thudded.

"Can I draw some blood?" She held up a needle attached to some sort of cup and a glass vial that looked as though it might fit into it.

Loren nodded and focused, mentally commanding his armour to recede. Olivia gasped as it raced down his head and his neck, the helmet and scales disappearing, and cleared his chest and back, and then his arms. He halted it there, keeping it in place from his stomach downwards. It was hard to hold it like this, but he wanted it partially out so it would be quicker to come if he needed it. Besides, elves wore nothing beneath their armour.

"How does it do that?" Olivia absently touched the black scales across his stomach. He sucked down a sharp breath when her fingers accidentally brushed his skin too, sending a wave of sparks skittering across his flesh and causing his markings to flash.

Bleu drew his sword. Olivia yanked her hand back, turning fearful eyes on his friend. Loren held his hand up to stop him and turned back to her.

"I issue a mental command and it obeys," Loren said and she looked even more curious. He focused to materialise his trousers from his wardrobe onto his body, covering his legs beneath the armour. Everything an elf owned became connected to them, giving them the ability to call it to them via the teleportation side of their psychic gifts, no matter how great the distance between them and that possession. He stood. "I will show you."

He issued the command and the remaining scales of his armour shifted, swiftly rising up his body and down his arms, disappearing into the black and silver bands of metal around his wrists.

"Fascinating." Olivia stared at them and he held his hands out, allowing her to inspect the bands. The brush of her fingertips across his flesh was too much, stirring his body, and he withdrew from her touch.

Loren used another mental command to bring his armour out again, so it covered him from the waist down, and took his seat.

"It's incredible." She looked from him to Bleu. "Yours is the same?"

Bleu shifted uncomfortably. Loren tossed him a look designed to warn him to answer whenever Olivia spoke to him. The last thing Loren needed was Bleu treating Olivia in the same manner as the other humans. Loren could allow Bleu's behaviour where they were concerned, but he wouldn't tolerate it towards Olivia. Bleu nodded.

Olivia took a strip of rubber from the table and wrapped it around Loren's right upper arm. The feel of her hands on him was pleasurable until she tied the material and tugged it tight. He raised an eyebrow at the sensation of numbness that crept upwards from his fingertips. She tapped the inside of his elbow and then eased the needle into his vein and slotted the glass vial into place. Loren jerked in response to the feel of his blood flowing from him and filling the vial.

Strange.

It was almost pleasurable.

He had never allowed another to take blood from him, but all elves knew that it was an intense experience, one that could be used to heighten sex, bringing it close to a level of pleasure enjoyed by bonded mates.

His head turned hazy. His gaze drifted to Olivia. It slowly dropped to her lips. Soft. Rosy. Begging for a kiss. He wanted to kiss them.

He wanted to taste her.

Someone moved on his senses and they focused on the intruder. Bleu. The feel of his eyes on him, studying him, brought Loren out of the haze of lust and his desire to kiss Olivia.

Olivia was staring at him too. More specifically, she stared at the vial, her eyebrows pinned high on her forehead.

"Is something wrong?" Loren said and she shook her head, her eyes shooting wide as she quickly lifted them away from the vial and her cheeks flushing with colour.

She glanced away. "I was just thinking your blood is red like mine... which is stupid because you were covered in it when I met you. I was wondering what else is the same."

"I would imagine our physical composition is very much the same, with only a few key differences." He looked down at the vial. It was almost full. Olivia removed it from the contraption and then pressed a wad of white material to the point where it entered his flesh and slid the needle from his vein.

"Hold this," she said and he did as she had instructed, replacing her fingers with his, keeping the soft material in place. She took the rubber strip from his arm and feeling returned to his fingers. "Thanks."

She scribbled something on a label, stuck it on the glass vial, and placed it in a rack. Her gaze roamed back to him and down to his legs.

"If it's metal, I'm afraid it's going to have to come off. The machine I would like to use to scan your body doesn't like metal. It will interfere with it." She sounded nervous and felt it too. Loren could understand her apprehension. Bleu was already on the verge of issuing a protest.

Loren held his hand up. "Very well."

The piece of material fell off his arm, revealing the dark hole in his skin. Olivia had taken his blood. What would it be like to have her take his blood properly, as a mate should? He knew how to complete a bond. She would need to take his blood into her body, drinking from him. Just the thought of her wrapping her lips around a wound on his flesh and sucking had him hard beneath his armour.

He shifted uncomfortably and Bleu raised an eyebrow at him again and then looked over to Olivia where she stood beside a large white ring-shaped machine, pressing buttons on it.

Loren spoke with him in their tongue. "Are you concerned about the tests?"

Bleu shook his head. "I am concerned that for a male who claims to desire to be free of this bond, you are enjoying the female's attention rather too much."

A very blunt and very Bleu response.

"I am intent on undoing the bond, Bleu," Loren said, keeping to their language so Olivia couldn't understand their exchange. "You need not be concerned. My mission is still the apprehension of my brother."

Bleu's expression twisted into darkness. "Vail deserves death for the things he has done, not containment. You swore to the council that you would end your brother."

Loren closed his eyes and scrubbed a hand over his face. "I know. I will do what I must for my people... even if it will kill me."

"My prince..." Bleu started and Loren looked up at him, hiding none of the weariness invading his body, pressing down on him and crushing his heart. "I spoke out of turn without thought for your feelings. I apologise. It was cruel of me."

Loren shook his head. "No need to apologise, Bleu. I know what I must do. I have put it off for too long, giving my brother too many chances to hurt our people and those I care about, all because I cling to a ridiculous ideal that I can save him."

"It is because your brother is one of the people you care about that you desire such a thing."

Loren supposed that was true. He loved his brother, even after everything that had happened, and he didn't want to imagine a world without him, let alone make it real.

The hard edge to Bleu's expression softened. "I am glad I never had a brother."

Loren managed to smile but there was no trace of feeling behind it. "Your sister is trouble enough."

Bleu's face fell. "Do not remind me. She is off in the second kingdom of the demons, intent on uncovering some artefact that was lost millennia ago. She will get herself into trouble one day."

"One day?" Loren smiled properly now. "When is she not in trouble, and when is her big brother not having to go to her rescue?"

Bleu smiled too and Loren was glad to see his second in command relaxing again.

Olivia ruined it by speaking. "Our linguistics department would love to study your language, if you would let them? I'm sure they would find it fascinating."

Bleu scowled at her and then at Loren, keeping to their language. "The female seeks to allow her comrades to learn our language so they might infiltrate our species and bring them harm."

Loren shook his head. "She does no such thing. She is merely curious. It is the way of her species, and our own. Did we not seek to learn the mortal languages as they entered an age of great civilisations? We did not do so to find a way to bring them to their knees or harm them. We did so because we were curious and wished to communicate with them and understand them."

Loren rose to his feet and turned to Olivia, speaking in her tongue now. "I am sorry but that is not a good idea. No species outside of ours can speak our language and that is how we wish to keep things. Not even the demons can speak our tongue."

She looked crestfallen but rebounded quickly. "Their loss. At least I get to study you."

The glimmer in her brown eyes spoke of how much she was enjoying his presence for reasons other than merely studying him. It was a dangerous feeling, and one he shared too. He liked being around her, felt drawn to her even when he knew no good would come of it and that he could never allow his guard to slip. He had to resist her and couldn't get involved with her. He had to maintain his rigid control and his distance.

"Speaking of studying." She pointed to the ring-shaped machine and the bench that had slid out of it.

Loren called his trousers back to him and sent his armour away. He looked down at the two metal bands around his wrists.

"I do not think it wise to remove my armour completely. Will it be necessary?" He didn't think it wise because Bleu would probably try to remove Olivia's head if she attempted to force him to remove the bands containing his armour, leaving him completely vulnerable.

Olivia looked as though she wanted to say yes and then flicked a glance at Bleu and shook her head. Loren looked across at Bleu, catching his grim look and the way his fingers were curling around the hilt of his sword again, ready to draw it.

Loren went to her and followed her instructions, lying with his head at one end of the bench, closest to the entrance of the machine.

"It will make funny sounds but it won't harm you. We use it all the time. It's just going to give me a complete image of the inside of your body and then I'll do the same with Bleu and we can see if there are any physical differences." She smiled down at him and he had the sense that she was trying to reassure him. "Just keep your head straight, looking up at the top of the machine, and try not to move."

Loren nodded and she moved away, revealing Bleu. He didn't look pleased, or at all convinced that the machine wouldn't harm him. Loren wasn't either, but he trusted Olivia. If placing him into this strange machine would assist her in finding a way to break the bond between them, then he would place himself into it, proving to Bleu that it was safe so he would do the same.

Bleu moved closer, his clawed fingers flexing around the hilt of his black blade, his gaze tracking every move Olivia made.

"We'll need to leave the room," Olivia said and Loren realised she was speaking to Bleu.

"Why?" Loren looked down at her and then at Bleu.

"The machine uses radiation to take pictures of your insides. It's necessary for the operator to move to a safe room to avoid a dose of radiation themselves." She flicked a nervous glance at Bleu when he growled.

"I will not allow my prince to be poisoned by this machine." Bleu held his hand out to Loren. "Please leave the machine."

Loren shook his head and then looked at Olivia. "The scan is necessary?"

She nodded. "It would help me a great deal. I swear, it's a tiny dose of radiation. Harmless, really."

"Not harmless enough that you do not have to leave the room," Bleu snapped and his hand went to the hilt of his sword, his gaze darting back to Loren. "Please, my prince. Leave the machine."

"No, Bleu." Loren shook his head again. "If Olivia says it will not harm me, then it will not harm me. I am happy to place my trust in her."

Bleu grumbled in their language, "I am not."

Loren knew that, and knew that Bleu only desired to protect him. He sighed and turned to Olivia.

"Please proceed. Bleu will do as you ask and leave the room with you. Won't you, Bleu?"

Bleu huffed.

Olivia smiled shakily and pointed towards a door with a yellow and black triangle on it. Next to it was a thick glass window. She led the way through the door, appearing in the window with a very grim-looking Bleu, and began working on a computer. Loren settled himself again, trying to relax but finding it difficult now that he knew the machine was about to give him a dose of radiation.

He had heard of it and the devastating effect it could have. The mortals had built bombs that utilised radioactive substances in order to severely harm other mortals. He couldn't understand why a species was so intent on destroying itself.

Loren tensed when the bench began to move, easing him into the machine. He kept still as it whirred and chugged, and then the bench was moving him out again. Painless. Fast. He wanted to know what image it would produce. He had spilled many of his enemies' organs during battles, but had never seen any when they were in the right place. What did he look like inside? How similar was it to Olivia?

Bleu still looked displeased as he entered the room with Olivia, even when Loren sat up and rose to his feet.

"Nothing to be concerned about. It is painless and curious, and you will get to see what your insides look like," Loren said and Bleu tossed a vicious glare at the machine.

"It shows you?"

Loren stifled a laugh at his friend's horrified expression. "No. But I am sure Olivia will let us see the results."

He looked to her and she nodded.

Bleu shuddered. "I don't want to see my insides. I like not seeing them."

A soldier born and bred. If anyone had ever doubted it, they would have changed their mind on hearing and seeing Bleu as he pressed a hand to his stomach, the most vulnerable point on any elf. Bleu liked his insides hidden because it meant he wasn't gutted and bleeding out on a battlefield.

"Very well. You do not need to see them." Loren touched his shoulder, squeezing it gently to reassure him that no one would force him to look at the results of the scan, but making it clear that Bleu would be going through the scanner whether he liked it or not.

"I can take your blood now, Bleu," Olivia said, a slight quiver in her voice, a sign of her nerves.

Bleu took a deep breath and nodded. His armour receded, exposing his bare muscular chest, and he sat in the chair for Olivia.

Olivia took the seat beside him and picked up the rubber strip.

The moment she laid a hand on Bleu's arm, Loren saw red.

He flicked his armour back into place and launched himself at Bleu, slamming into the chair and him, and bending the stand. Bleu growled and called his armour back, but not before Loren had slashed at his exposed chest with his sharp black claws, cleaving into his flesh. Olivia shrieked and stumbled backwards, toppling her chair and landing in a heap on the floor.

Loren snarled, exposing his fangs, and his ears extended, flattening against the sides of his head. Bleu's eyes blazed purple and his lips peeled back, revealing his own large fangs. He grappled with Loren but it didn't stop him from hacking at the chest of his armour, trying to gouge through the tough black scales. His armour was weak against the same material. It was the only metal able to penetrate it. He would shred it with his claws and tear the male's heart out for daring to go near his female.

Bleu growled and bowed up against him, forcing Loren off him. Loren attacked again and Bleu evaded him, countering any strike he couldn't dodge completely.

"My prince," Bleu snapped, his anger flowing from him, inciting Loren's rage. The male was furious with him because he had dared to stop him from laying hands on the female. The female belonged to Loren. The male would pay for attempting to steal her from him.

Loren threw himself at him again.

Bleu smashed his right fist hard into Loren's face, the blow connecting solidly with his left cheek. Loren staggered right, his head reeling and the taste of blood filling his mouth. He stumbled into the wall opposite the table with the computers on it.

And his sword.

Loren stared at it and then at Bleu.

"You are not yourself. Do not do something you will regret." Bleu flexed his claws.

Loren would not regret removing this male's head from his body because it would mean this male could not attempt to steal his female again.

Loren reached for the weapon.

"Loren, no!" Olivia appeared between them, her brown eyes enormous, the racing beat of her heart echoing in his chest. Her fear crawled through him, subduing his lust for violence and bloodshed. She paled and he did too. She could feel his dark twisted hungers. They rushed through her blood just as her fear filled his.

Bleu stood a few feet behind her, his purple eyes locked on him and his armour still in place.

Loren lowered his hand to his side and stood down, horrified by how strongly he had reacted to the sight of Olivia touching Bleu, and how badly he had wanted to hurt his friend because of it.

Bleu cursed him in their tongue. "And you tell me that I have no reason to be concerned? Really? Because that little display of aggression had nothing to do with your ki'ara laying her hands on me, right?"

Just the words and the image they evoked were enough to have Loren flying into a rage again. He dodged past Olivia in a blur of speed and fury, and grabbed Bleu by the throat. He slammed Bleu down into the chair, pinning him against it, hissing at him as he tightened his grip to choke him.

"Loren!" Olivia grabbed his shoulder and hauled him off Bleu, her strength startling them both judging by the ripple of shock that ran through their bond. He clenched his teeth and growled at her, but her look of disgust mixed with horror was enough to ground him.

He took a few steps back, distancing himself from Bleu, disgusted at himself and disturbed by how driven he was to protect her and stop Bleu from being near her.

Bleu rubbed his throat and glared at him. "Maybe I can draw my own damn blood or just spit in the vial."

He grabbed the needle from the table near him, sent his armour away from his chest and arms, and carelessly stabbed himself in the soft flesh on the inside of his elbow, grimacing as the sharp metal punctured his skin.

Loren closed his eyes and lowered his head, feeling like a monster for the way he had treated his friend and driven him to harm himself. Bleu's lip was cut and bleeding, swelling too, and his chest bore deep claw marks. Bleu hadn't held back when he had struck Loren, but it wasn't payment enough for what Loren had done to him.

"I am sorry, Bleu." He lifted his head and looked across the room at his friend, his black eyebrows furrowed and his heart heavy. "I will wait outside while Olivia tends to you."

Loren didn't wait to hear either of their responses. He headed straight for the twin glass doors. They whooshed open, sliding apart for him to exit the room, and he moved down the corridor far enough that he couldn't see into the room so he wouldn't be tempted to look. He couldn't risk another outburst like that. Olivia needed to record Bleu's vitals and take his blood, and Loren had no doubt that he would try to kill him again if he saw Olivia touching him.

He leaned back against the wall and closed his eyes, seeking some calm amongst the raging storm of his emotions, needing it so his fangs would recede and his eyes would return to blue, masking their true colour from the humans using the corridor.

He could feel their eyes on him as they passed. Some of them even triggered his senses, warning they were a threat to him, but he didn't care. If they attacked him, it would be their death right now. He would kill them in a heartbeat to slake some of his thirst for violence. Rather them than Bleu.

Olivia wouldn't be pleased.

Her expression had cut straight through him and he never wanted her to look at him with such disgust and disappointment again.

Loren's fangs finally receded and he commanded his eyes to become blue again. He pushed away from the wall and took swift agitated strides along a short length of the pale cream corridor, fighting his desire to return to the room. Too dangerous. He wanted to see what they were doing but he couldn't risk it.

His mind supplied images of them, taunting him with visions of Bleu and Olivia. He ground his teeth and tried to shut them out, focusing on other things, anything to get his mind away from his friend and his female.

The more he tried to halt the images, the worse they became, until all he could picture was Bleu and Olivia, locked in a passionate embrace, his friend pleasuring her as Loren had in his dreams.

Loren couldn't take it, or how it made him feel, violent and on the edge, wild and lost to a feral need to claim Olivia as his and put Bleu in the ground.

He growled under his breath, earning a startled gasp from a young female hunter as she passed and a glare from her older male companion. The male's hand went to his weapon, a short blade hanging at his waist, and Loren silently urged the mortal to draw it. He wanted to fight. He needed it.

Loren dragged himself away, turning his back on the humans. This wasn't like him. He was normally peaceful, seeking diplomatic solutions whenever possible, even with his brother.

Vail.

He didn't want to end up like his younger brother but he feared he was already treading that dark path, and the bond wasn't even complete.

Loren stopped, turned towards the wall and banged his head against it. The humans passing by gave him a wide berth and he couldn't blame them. He was acting like a madman.

Driven wild by a female.

He pressed his palms against the wall, despair eating away at him, twisting his insides into tight painful knots. What was he going to do? He had been in Olivia's presence for barely more than a human hour and he was already close to falling over the edge and doing something terrible that he could never take back. The longer he spent in her company, the worse this hunger was going to become, and if he wasn't careful, it would end up controlling him. What if he hurt her? What if he killed Bleu?

He would never forgive himself.

Loren banged his head against the wall again, grinding his teeth and grimacing as it all became too much for him. The images of Bleu and Olivia still played out in his mind, pushing him ever closer to the edge, until he had to dig the claws of his armour into the plaster of the wall to keep himself anchored there, stopping him from bursting into the room behind him.

The doors swished open.

Loren forced himself away from the wall, a second apology to Bleu balancing on his lips.

It was Olivia.

Their bond spoke to him, telling him what he could already see in her expression and her soulful brown eyes that always showed him everything she was feeling. She was tense and wary, afraid of him now. He lowered his head, unable to look at her. He had frightened his female, shaking her trust in him.

"Loren?" she said in a low, gentle voice that curled around his numb heart, thawing the ice that had encased it.

He was afraid too. He had never felt so afraid. He didn't want to look into her eyes and see her fear of him, or her disgust, and he didn't want to hear how he had scared her by allowing her to experience such dark terrible emotions through him.

"Loren?" Her tone held a firmer note and he obeyed, unable to ignore a command from his ki'ara.

Loren looked down into her eyes. They filled with pity, softening more with each second that he dared to look into them.

"I'm done now," she said, casual despite the nerves he could sense in her. "I did my best not to touch him. That was what it was all about, wasn't it?"

Loren shut down the fury that curled through him on hearing that she had indeed touched Bleu while he had been out here pacing like a caged animal, refusing to let it own him. He was master of his body, not this wretched bond.

He hated to admit it but Olivia needed to know what he had dragged her into so she would know the cause of his outburst and could perhaps help stop it from happening again.

"I could not bear the sight of you touching him," Loren said, the tight gravelly sound of his voice shocking him. He had never sounded so dark and possessive before. He had never felt it either.

He wanted to possess Olivia. Body and soul. He wanted to claim the heart that was rightfully his.

His to own. His to cherish. His to protect.

His to love.

She belonged to him.

His fangs itched and the points of his ears began to extend. Loren fought the change but it was hard to suppress it and stop it from happening when he was thinking about Olivia, and also thinking about her touching Bleu. It was a one-two punch that knocked his senses reeling and had him back on the verge of losing control. A male doctor coming towards him eyed him, not a challenge but Loren felt it as one, and he wanted to rise to it and beat the male into submission.

The male's eyes narrowed. He had noticed Loren's eyes changing. Loren cursed beneath his breath and looked away, fighting to master his emotions. His gaze caught on Olivia's and he stared down at her, feeling lost and bewildered, tired of the constant battle against his emotions and the effects of their incomplete bond. He wanted a moment to breathe.

He needed a minute to rest, sixty seconds away from this world, alone with Olivia.

Olivia moved closer, raised her hand and touched his cheek, staring deep into his eyes. Bliss. Loren leaned into her touch, finding his balance in it, mentally stepping away from the edge and towards her. His ki'ara.

"It's fascinating when your eyes do that... and your ears. Why does it happen?" She brushed her palm across his cheek and a hot shiver went through him when she feathered her fingertips up his ear to the tip. He barely stifled a groan. He wanted her to stroke them. Lick them. His eyes began to change again.

"It is a response to my emotions. Certain ones trigger a change and it is difficult to stop it from happening." Difficult was the understatement of his extremely long life. Impossible. Especially when she was gently caressing his ear, brushing the pointed tip, her eyes filled with the fascination she had mentioned.

"Emotions," she whispered and then her brow crinkled and her brown eyes shifted back to his. "Such as anger?"

He nodded.

"And?"

Loren frowned. "And what?"

"What other emotion?" She tilted her head to one side, her fingers continuing their exploration of his ear, driving him mad with the emotion she was asking about. "You said emotions. Plural. What other emotions trigger this change?"

Loren stared at her, his gaze drawn to her rosy lips and his mind instantly leaping to recall his vivid erotic dreams of her. He wanted to sample her mouth and know her taste as he had in those fantasies. He wanted to explore every inch of her soft skin and show her what it was like to be loved by him. He wanted to slake his thirst for her.

His fangs grew long again and his ears extended, and he knew from the surprise in her eyes that his had changed and from the arousal darkening her irises that she had figured out the other emotion that would always make him lose control.

Loren claimed her waist with both hands, careful not to hurt her with his claws, and pulled her closer to him.

She wanted to know what other emotion fuelled this change in him and he would spell it out for her.

"Desire."

CHAPTER 8

Olivia swallowed hard, held captive by Loren's beautiful rich purple eyes and the passion in them, falling into them with no hope of stopping herself. The feel of his hands on her waist shattered her self-control, plunging her deep into dangerous territory, and her guard slipped. His gaze locked onto her lips, burning her with its intensity, stealing her breath away. Enough men had kissed her in her life for her to know that was what he intended.

He wanted to kiss her.

And by God she wanted him to do it.

She wanted to kiss him, had skirted around that desire several times in the past hour alone, pretending it didn't exist and that she didn't hunger for the feel of Loren's hands on her body, bringing her out of the dark loneliness of her life and awakening passion and pleasure within her.

Loren angled his head, his eyes hooded with desire, locked on her mouth.

Olivia panicked, unsure of her feelings. They tore her in two different directions, pulling her between shoving him away and letting him draw her into his embrace.

Her heart pounded.

His breath stuttered.

Olivia's gaze betrayed her and fell to his sensual lips as they parted, her pulse increasing as she subconsciously leaned towards him, rising on her toes to meet him.

The doors behind her opened, the sound startling in volume in the silent corridor. Bleu muttered something dark sounding in the elf language.

Loren froze, eased his hands away from her hips, and moved back a step, placing some distance between them.

Olivia came to her senses too and wished that she hadn't because she couldn't bring herself to look at Loren when her head was full of thoughts about kissing him, and she definitely couldn't bring herself to look at Bleu.

When they had been alone, Bleu had made no secret of his feelings. He had told her straight that Loren was off limits to her and that he would protect his prince by any means necessary. She had filled in the blanks for herself. Bleu would kill her if she made any attempt to steal his prince's heart.

It was a good job that she was only interested in him in a purely academic way then, wasn't it? She had absolutely no desire to grab Loren, pin him to the nearest wall and kiss him senseless. That would be stupid. She would probably lose her job and her head shortly afterwards.

It didn't stop the thought of going through with it from spinning around her head though.

Loren wanted to kiss her too. Bleu evidently knew that and had made it his personal mission to keep them apart. Would something as innocent as a kiss complete the bond between them?

She didn't think so. If it could, then Loren wouldn't be giving her heated looks that had her toes curling in her trainers, risking provoking her into planting one on him.

He wanted this bond broken.

Didn't he?

"Maybe we should test your stamina," Olivia said and blushed when both men quirked eyebrows in her direction, as if she had suggested a marathon lovemaking session. "On the treadmill."

Olivia scurried away, leaving them to follow her.

Loren said something terse to Bleu in their language and she glanced over her shoulder to see if they were following her. He looked across at her just as she did. His eyes met hers again and a flash of purple briefly coloured them.

Lust or rage?

He followed her, dragging Bleu along by the arm until the male shirked his grip and obediently followed, still muttering black things under his breath. Loren's handsome face twisted in a grim expression and he shot Bleu an irritated glare.

Perhaps it was a bit of both making his eyes switch.

Olivia turned away and led them down the cream corridor to the large room where they tested the hunters' fitness levels. The wall lining the corridor was mostly glass, allowing everyone to see inside. She didn't enjoy the thought of everyone being able to watch Loren while he ran, seeing his body on display. It caused a tight knot in her chest that was impossible to ignore, even though she did her damnedest to do just that.

She hoped for their sake that Loren and Bleu could control their emotions while she was testing them too. If Loren had another outburst like the one in the other room, when he had tried to strangle Bleu because she had dared to touch him, someone would see it through the glass. They would have hunters inside in an instant and the other doctors would be reporting them to her superiors.

Her superiors would probably order the hunters to catch and contain them, labelling them dangerous.

Which she supposed they were. Loren wanted to kill any male who went near her, including his friend. Bleu just wanted to kill everyone else.

What the hell had she gotten herself into?

Olivia reminded herself that this whole affair wasn't her fault. It was some elf called Vail's fault. He had orchestrated this to weaken Loren and have revenge on him, all because Loren had tried to take him down by harming his female. It sounded petty to Olivia, but if someone tried to harm Loren right now, when she was feeling a little bit possessive of him too, she would probably try to make them pay for it.

She went into the room and set about getting two of the treadmills ready for them. She wasn't sure what speed setting to use so she cranked it right up and then dialled it back a couple of notches. Many fae and demons displayed incredible stamina and speed. She had seen Loren cross a room in a blur to launch an attack on Bleu. Elves were most likely one of those fae.

Bleu said something gruff to Loren.

Loren came forwards and studied the two running machines, and the wires dangling from them. "What are these?"

"You run on them. I'm going to hook you guys up, and we'll monitor your vitals, and your breathing too. It will give me a better picture of your abilities and it's one of the tests I have to run for the other doctors." Olivia probably shouldn't have added that part about the other doctors. It caused Loren's black eyebrows to pinch together and his eyes to narrow.

Bleu bit out something she couldn't understand.

Was he going to talk in their language around her all the time now? It gave her the feeling that he was shutting her out and trying to make Loren do the same.

He was probably saying horrible things about her and Archangel.

"How long must we run?" Loren said and she moved away from the machines, went to the end of the room nearest the doors, and set up the computer.

"Thirty minutes." It would give her enough time to monitor the effects of the bond on Loren. If he were weaker because of their incomplete connection, then he would show signs of fatigue and elevated stress levels. Olivia caught his concerned look as he gazed at the machines and then at her. He didn't need to say it aloud for her to get the message. She was already aware of what she had proposed. She was signing up for the same fatigue and stress, and the same raised heart rate. "Believe me. I'm looking forward to it as much as you are."

"When we break the bond, you will no longer suffer this tie to me." Loren eyed the machine and frowned as he curled his fingers into fists at his sides. "The same will happen if we must complete it."

Olivia was going to pretend he hadn't just mentioned completing the bond again. It wasn't going to happen. If he tried to force it on her, he was going to have Sable and half of Archangel dragging him down to the cellblock for some very nasty jail time with the twisted ex-hunters who guarded the prisoners. They were notoriously heavy-handed and 'accidental' deaths of the inmates were common.

If he died, would the bond break?

She opened her mouth to ask but snapped it shut again before the words could leave her lips and slid a wary glance at Bleu. The elf would probably kill her on the spot to free his prince from the bond if she suggested they broke it via one of their deaths.

She finished setting up the machines, grabbed two sets of sweat shorts off the pile of clean clothes and held them out to Bleu and Loren. They both cocked eyebrows at them.

"You can't run in armour, and I need to place..." She really wasn't sure this was a wise thing to say. She pointed to the machines. "I need to stick those wires on you."

Loren unleashed a snarl and glared at Bleu.

Bleu backed off a step. "The female will put them on you and I will place mine on myself, following her instruction. I do not want her touching me."

Loren's shoulders relaxed. He rolled them and stalked to the nearest machine.

"You can change behind the curtain." Olivia indicated the one at the back of the room. Loren looked at it, and then down at the shorts, and curled his lip, flashing a hint of fang.

"I am not sure this is wise," he said, voice a dark growl, "You will see Bleu again."

Bleu huffed, rolled his eyes, and spoke in their language. Loren barked something back at him. Bleu countered, his tone gaining a sharp edge, his expression hardening with it. Loren shoved him in the chest and Bleu growled and stood up to him.

"What if I solemnly swear not to look at Bleu?" Olivia bravely stepped between the quarrelling men, forming a barrier she hoped would prevent Loren from slugging Bleu again. Or vice versa. The blow Bleu had landed on Loren's jaw earlier had left its mark. An ugly rich black and purple one.

Loren looked as though he wanted to tell her it wouldn't be enough but grated out, "Fine."

He snatched both pairs of shorts and went behind the curtain. Bleu followed. Olivia cringed when they began arguing again.

Loren was the first to emerge. His lip had a nice new split. Bleu came out next and she risked a brief glance at him. He sniffed and wiped his bloodied nose on the back of his hand, the action causing one of the long slashes across his chest to split open again. He huffed, picked up one of the towels from the stack on the bench, and dabbed at the wounds on his torso, wiping the blood away.

"Can you dial down the testosterone for the next thirty minutes?" she said to Loren and a flicker of something distinctly like guilt crossed his expression.

She kept her eyes on him and him alone as she hooked him up to the machine. Whenever she stuck one of the pads on his chest, his markings shimmered into being, chasing across his skin. She sneakily brushed his left pectoral as she placed the pad on it and felt him shiver beneath her caress, and her heart picked up. His doing. His gaze bore into her, intent on her face. She glanced up at him, her eyes briefly meeting his, just long enough to see that they were verging on purple again and his pupils had gobbled up his irises, turning them dark with passion.

Olivia trembled in response, the shivery hot ache returning, running through her and driving her to touch him again. She swept her fingers over his side as she placed the remaining pads on him. He leaned towards her and she looked up at him, anticipation swirling inside of her, cranking her so tightly that she was tiptoeing towards him, bringing her lips to his before she got control of herself.

Loren looked disappointed when she placed the mask over his mouth and nose and tightened it.

That feeling echoed in Olivia, and this time it wasn't a product of the bond. It was becoming harder and harder to resist her desire to know his lips and to feel his arms around her, gathering her close as he kissed her. She wanted it as much as he did and resisting it hurt her just as much too.

She stepped away from him, giving Bleu a clear view of him. She kept her gaze on her feet as she told him which pads to stick where and waited until he announced that he was done before she moved to the computer and checked his vitals to ensure he had followed her instructions correctly.

Both Loren and Bleu's vitals were coming in perfectly.

"What size feet do you both have?" She rummaged through the boxes of running shoes they kept on hand.

"Why is that necessary information?" Loren looked down at his bare feet. "It does not seem relevant."

Olivia held up a pair of orange and black running shoes. "For your feet."

Out of the corner of her eye, Bleu shook his head at the same time as Loren.

"We would rather run barefoot. How does this thing work?" Loren stepped onto the machine and grabbed the handlebars when the belt beneath his feet moved. "I see."

"Just start out slowly. Try to keep pace with each other," Olivia said but Bleu paid her no attention and picked up pace at a frightening speed.

Her eyes shot to the computer. He was going too fast. The machine was reading him at over twenty miles per hour already.

"Slow it down. This is about stamina. It's not a race, Bleu."

Loren growled. Olivia made a mental note not to use Bleu's name or speak to him specifically while he had his top off. The effect of the bond was fascinating though. Loren clearly regretted his actions whenever he attacked or threatened Bleu, as if he had no control over himself. Did the bond drive him to protect her from any male he viewed as a threat, whether it was a threat of physical harm or a threat of stealing her away from him?

She couldn't exactly ask him. If she did, he would think she desired Bleu and wanted his attention, or something equally as ridiculous. She didn't want to provoke him into attacking his friend again.

Olivia studied them on the computer, already feeling the effect of Loren's running, even though he had only been at it for a few minutes. His statistics were far lower than Bleu's, and she felt terrible as she watched them deteriorating. They were still above the levels of an extremely fit human, measuring high above Archangel's best hunters, but Bleu was in a different league. He showed zero signs of fatigue. His pulse was slow and steady, and his breathing was just as even and unaffected by his running.

She looked over her shoulder at them. Both men were keeping pace with each other, but there was a marked difference in their gait. Bleu had effortless strides. Loren was struggling with his and already a fine sheen of sweat coated his back.

Olivia lost track of time as she stared at his back, mesmerised by the way his muscles shifted beneath his pale skin. His markings flashed over his shoulders and down his back, and he growled, turning his head slightly towards her.

Did she make that happen?

Whenever the markings had done something similar back when he had taken her to his castle, he had glared at her as though she had caused them to flare. Did they irritate him?

They shimmered again and her heart picked up this time, pounding harder. A sudden rush of desire blazed through her blood and Loren frowned and ran faster, pushing himself. Olivia's head spun and she struggled to breathe.

"Slower... please?" she whispered and leaned over to clutch her knees. They trembled, her legs feeling achy and tired, as if she was the one running.

Loren slid her an apologetic look and nodded, decreasing his speed.

The effect of the bond was fascinating.

The moment he had disappeared from her apartment, she had felt different. Normal. When he had returned, the feeling of being linked to him had come back too. Did it increase when they were close together and decrease when they were apart? Was distance a factor in the strength of the effect of the bond?

The nerdy science junkie in her wanted to leave the room and go down the hall to see if the effect of the bond diminished as she moved further away from Loren, and so she wouldn't feel Loren's fatigue or his racing heartbeat as much. She couldn't leave him though, not even in the name of her research into his species.

One of the conditions of his stay at Archangel was that he would remain under her supervision at all times. It was bad enough that he had left the room earlier and people had seen him in the hall without her. If the doctors who had been present in the meeting caught her breaking the rules, leaving him unsupervised, they would be swift to file a report and take over. She didn't want to think about what would happen then. The image of Loren strapped down to an operating table disturbed her and her heart missed a beat.

Loren flicked her a glance and she cursed the concern in it and the way it soothed her, reassuring her silently that he was there with her and making her feel that he wanted to comfort her or discover the source of her momentary switch in feelings so he could make it go away.

"I still do not see why we must run for thirty minutes," Bleu said, his mask muffling his voice.

"Enough complaining," Loren snapped and misstepped, almost coming off the machine. He growled and found his balance again, regaining his rhythm.

It had been almost thirty minutes. There were seconds left on the clock now but she wasn't sure if Loren would make it. His heart rate was making her woozy and she could feel his fatigue, and that he was pushing himself to make it to the end of the session.

Bleu still showed absolutely no sign of fatigue or stress.

The effects of the bond to her were startling and she had a strange urge to apologise to Loren, feeling responsible for how much weaker he was now because of her.

Bleu bitched again and then fell silent. Olivia looked up to find him staring at the corridor. She frowned and shifted her gaze there, and found Sable peering in, waving at her.

A touch of purple entered Bleu's eyes, swirling amongst the green, and Olivia half-expected his ears to go pointy, and not because of rage.

Sable opened the door to the fitness room and smiled sheepishly, her golden eyes shining in that way that always told Olivia the huntress was up to no good.

"What is it now?" Olivia said, not giving her friend a chance to come up with some terrible excuse or flimsy lie. Sable loved bending the rules and often tried to get Olivia to help her push them as far as she could.

Sable brushed her long black hair back from her face and pulled her best puppy-dog eyes. "My old leg injury is acting up and I just need some meds. I know you have the good painkillers. Hook me up. Come on, Liv."

Sable always pulled out the big guns whenever her nightly hunts in the city were under threat. Innocent looks and pet names were her favourite weapons to use on Olivia.

"I don't want the bastards to take me off rota again."

Olivia sighed. "Sable, you're meant to rest an injury when it flares up, not aggravate it."

Sable scuffed the floor with her heavy army boots and shrugged. "I know, but I lost track of some prey last night and if I don't bag and tag him tonight, he might kill again."

The running machines beeped. Loren stopped and slid off the belt, barely keeping himself upright as his bare feet hit the floor without a sound. He panted hard and Olivia breathed slowly, focusing on levelling out her heartbeat and hoping it would help him, and would stop Sable from eyeing her suspiciously.

The sweat breaking out across her brow and her flushed cheeks probably looked weird to her friend. Could she say she was sick and running a fever? She would have to come up with a solid excuse if Sable asked what was wrong with her. Her friend wouldn't quit until she had confessed all otherwise, and she wasn't sure how she would react to the truth. She would probably try to kill Loren to free her from the unwanted bond.

Bleu casually slid off the machine, not at all out of breath and not a drop of sweat on him.

Olivia picked up one of the bottles of water on the desk and offered it to Loren. He curled his lip at it and took a white towel from the stack on the bench instead.

Sable stared at them.

Bleu rubbed a towel across his overlong black-blue hair and Olivia noticed his ears were slightly pointed.

He spoke to Loren again, using their language. They shared a deep, tense conversation as Loren dried himself off and then broke apart. Loren approached her, his heart steady now and breathing back under control.

"We will hunt the vampire." He used that commanding tone again, the one that brooked no argument. Olivia doubted it would work on Sable. She had a problem with authority. It was the reason she had joined Archangel.

"Excuse me?" Sable straightened to her full, but lacking, five feet nine inches. Loren ignored her. Bleu came to stand behind him, backing him up. Sable planted her hands on her hips. "It's my target. I tracked him for weeks... and how the heck did you know he was a vampire?"

Bleu grinned. "You reek of bloodsucker."

Olivia raised an eyebrow and shot him a you're-one-to-talk look.

Loren's gaze slid to her neck, landing on the point on the left side where he had bitten her, burning through the collar of her white jacket and making the marks throb in response. His eyes flashed purple and the tips of his ears turned pointy.

"What the hell are you?" Sable's hand went for the blade strapped to her thigh and Olivia grabbed her wrist, capturing her attention.

"You saw nothing," Olivia said, her tone firm, imitating her prince. "Swear on our friendship that you won't tell a soul."

Sable looked as though she would protest but nodded. "Only if I can get a closer look."

Sable was moving before Olivia could stop her, and a dark feeling opened inside her chest, a black desire to block her way to Loren. Olivia had never been jealous or possessive before, but she couldn't mistake the intense dangerous feeling for anything else.

Loren looked over Sable's head to her and their eyes met. An incredible sense of connection bloomed inside her, stealing her awareness of everything else in the room, leaving only Loren. Her heart thumped hard against her chest in response.

He was on her before she could blink, his lean powerful body caging hers against the wall near the door and his hands bracing her arms, pinning her wrists above her. His mouth claimed her throat, kissing and licking, nibbling but not biting, sending a hit of pure bliss rushing through her. Her knees weakened and she tilted her head to one side, the pleasure of his persuasive kiss and the feel of his tongue on her flesh scorching her and melting her bones, burning straight through the barriers around her heart and breaking them down.

"Fuck me," Sable muttered, shocking Olivia back to reality.

She froze midway through grinding the length of her body against Loren's, one of her legs still hooked around his backside, her moan coming out as a strangled sound.

Loren paused at her throat, his lips pressing against her, heavy breaths teasing her moist skin.

He slowly eased back and turned his head towards Sable. Olivia became painfully aware that Sable had made a terrible move.

She had drawn her crossbow and had it aimed at Loren, and her.

Loren's kiss-swollen lips peeled back off enormous fangs and he snarled at Sable, the sound dark and unholy. His armour glided over his body, his eyes changed to bright purple and his ears turned pointed. He snarled again and they flattened against the sides of his head, an action she had come to understand was a threat between elves.

There was such cruelty and viciousness in his black expression, violence that Olivia had felt in him before and witnessed firsthand. If he attacked Sable, he would kill her before she could loose the bolt to defend herself.

Bleu appeared between them, his black blade drawn and against Sable's throat before she could even twitch.

"Sable," Olivia said in a level voice and held her friend's golden gaze, hoping the huntress would do the sensible thing and listen to her. "Put the weapon away."

"No damn way," Sable spat out and glared at her. "They're fucking vampires. He was going to bite you."

Olivia shook her head. Loren growled lower, his body coiling and tensing. He was going to attack her friend because he thought Sable was threatening her. It proved her theory about the two reasons why Loren would lose control and attack someone, but she wished it hadn't been Sable in the firing line.

"They're not vampires, Sable." Olivia pleaded her with her eyes, keeping them on her. "He won't harm me... but he thinks that you will... you have to put the weapon away before this gets out of hand."

Sable again looked as though she would refuse. She eyed Loren and then Bleu, and then lowered the compact crossbow and collapsed it. She slid it back into the holster on her hip. Bleu eased his blade away from her friend's throat.

Loren didn't release Olivia.

He clutched her wrists, his grip too tight, hurting her bones and cutting off the blood supply to her hands. He wasn't relaxing. Why wasn't he relaxing? If anything, he felt tenser, closer to attacking. There had to be a way to bring him back before he hurt her or Sable. Olivia racked her brain. She had talked him down when he had attacked Bleu. Did the sound of her voice soothe him?

It was worth a shot.

"Loren?" Olivia whispered and wriggled, trying to get his attention. She steadied her heart, letting him feel that she wasn't afraid now, and she was safe because of him. "Look at me, Loren."

He glanced at her but then his gaze darted back to Sable and he growled.

"Loren? You're hurting my wrists." Olivia tried again and his grip on her eased enough that she could slip her wrists free. She lowered her hands, cupped both of his cheeks, and brought his head around so he was facing her. She kept his eyes on hers, looking deep into his and seeing the struggle in them, his fight to break the hold his instincts had on him. She brushed her thumbs across his cheeks, trying to steal his focus away from the other two occupants of the room. "Sable isn't a danger to either of us... you startled her, that was all. She's my friend and she wanted to protect me, not harm me. It's okay now, Loren. I'm safe. See?"

Olivia stroked his face, smiling at him, keeping calm and embracing the warmth his protective behaviour stirred within her, letting him feel that it pleased her.

His eyes slowly changed from purple to blue and the points of his ears shrank, until his ears resembled hers again. Loren stepped back, releasing her.

His blue eyes held hers, the warmth in them fading as new emotions formed in the link between them. Cold engulfed her. She could sense what he was going to do and she didn't want to let it happen.

Violet and blue light chased over his body, highlighting every sweep and curve of his muscles.

"Don't—" She reached for him but he disappeared. She turned to his friend. "Bleu—"

He teleported too.

Olivia sagged against the wall, conflicting emotions colliding inside her, leaving her in disarray.

Sable came to stand in front of her and huffed. "I thought you said he wasn't a vampire."

Olivia shook her head, eyes fixed on the ceiling in a thousand yard stare as she struggled to piece the barrier around her heart back together and cope with the sudden emptiness inside her that Loren's disappearance had caused. The more time she spent with him, the stranger she felt when they were apart.

The stronger she ached for him to come to her and hold her close to him.

"He isn't a vampire," she whispered, adrift on the turbulent sea of her emotions, riding the storm and wondering when Loren would return.

Sable pointed at her. "Then explain that bite mark on your throat."

Olivia's hand shot to her neck, her fingers going straight for the healing puncture wounds on the left side, and her eyes dropped to meet Sable's thunderous glare.

Olivia swallowed hard.

She was in trouble now.

CHAPTER 9

Loren's apartments in the castle appeared around him. For once, he was glad that Bleu couldn't teleport into them as he could and had to use the single access point in the courtyard like everyone else. He needed a moment to get his feelings back under control, crushing the ones that had ruled him back in the Archangel facility. A fierce physical need had come over him the moment he had felt Olivia's feelings through their bond, sensing her jealousy and then her desire, and then he had lost control when Bleu had mentioned the vampire.

The thought of biting Olivia, the memory of her sweet blood and the intense pleasure that had invaded every cell of his body when he had tasted it, had sent him careening over the edge. He had lost his mind and had been on her before he had been aware of what he was doing. It had been too late then. The feel of her body pressing into his and her soft flesh beneath his lips had triggered an explosive combination of desire, need and a dark hunger within him, driving him to taste her again and take pleasure from her, and give her pleasure too.

He had wanted to please his female.

Nothing else had mattered.

The whole of his focus had been on showing her that he was able to satisfy her every need, and that together they could experience the ultimate bliss reserved for only mated couples.

She had reacted so sweetly to him too, her body heating beneath his fingers and mouth, arching wantonly into his. Her hips had ground against his in a feral, desperate way, her actions beyond her control. She had been a slave to her desire too, unable to do anything except seek the pleasure she needed and embrace their mutual hungers to find it.

Gods, he wanted to return to her and finish what they had started.

Loren spat out a dark curse and paced his rooms. His armour bit into his groin with each stride. He palmed his hard length through the black scales and fire flashed through his veins. A groan left his lips and he dragged his hand away. Bleu would be here any second to give him hell about what he had done with Olivia. He would hardly be able to deflect Bleu's observations about him desiring the female if he was sporting an erection.

He turned on his heel and halted, his gaze on his bed. Images of Olivia laying naked and waiting for him there burst in his mind, taunting him. She would look divine tangled in the rich purple sheets, their colour contrasting perfectly against her pale smooth skin and her glossy chestnut hair. He groaned again, dug the heels of his palms in his eyes and rubbed them. He needed to get a grip.

He had thought he could handle being around her, but they had barely been together a few hours and he had attacked Bleu several times and had come close to biting her again.

Someone knocked at the door.

Bleu was being polite. That was never a good sign. Whenever Bleu was polite, it was because he was figuring out a way to berate him about something without overstepping the mark.

"Enter," Loren said and paced back across the room, buying himself time to get his body under control.

The arched wooden doors opened and closed. When he turned to pace back towards them, Bleu was leaning against the closed doors, looking casual. Also not a good sign.

"Do not start." Loren swept his hand out in front of him for emphasis. He didn't need Bleu pushing him right now, not when he was having difficulty locking down his emotions.

The distance between him and Olivia meant that they were less affected by each other, but he could still sense a fragment of her feelings. They were there in the background, drowned out by his own, but still there. If Olivia focused, she would be able to feel his too.

She felt as confused as he did, and as torn up by the distance between them. He hadn't anticipated this. He had thought only completed bonds would awaken this sort of connection, a link that tied them together so deeply that it felt as though part of him was missing now that he was away from her.

Bleu's steely purple gaze tracked him as he paced.

Loren could sense he wanted to say something about Olivia and how Loren had behaved tonight, acting very differently from the man he was used to being around.

He ached to return to her.

He couldn't give in to that need though, not until he felt less on edge and more like his normal collected and composed self. The time apart might weaken the growing bond between them too, keeping it under control. If it worked, then he would endeavour to spend short amounts of time in Olivia's company before retreating to be alone, stopping the bond from growing stronger.

Part of him rebelled against that plan, railing at him and crying out for Olivia.

Loren curled his fingers into fists, clenching his hands so tightly that the claws of his armour dug into his palms.

"You need to kill something." Bleu's deep voice lacked emotion.

He was right. He needed to kill something, and there was a rogue vampire on the prowl in London.

Loren had a deep dislike of all vampires. They were wretched, evil, cruel and an abomination. They were a constant reminder of the dark and terrible path an elf could tread, one that ultimately led to the destruction of everything noble, good and beautiful in them.

When the first elves had become tainted, their souls twisted towards the darkness so deeply that they had begun to lose much of their powers and their ability to withstand the light, Loren and his father had despaired.

His father had searched for a way to save them, to bring them back into the light, in harmony with nature, restoring their goodness and eradicating the evil in their souls. It had been impossible and they had lost so many elves to the darkness by the time his father had passed on that Loren had done the only thing he could to protect his people. He had withdrawn them from the mortal world.

The tainted elves had continued to lose their powers, gaining terrible new ones in their place, and for centuries they had ravaged the mortal world, spreading their wretched blood to others.

Loren, Vail and the council had discussed sending their legions to the mortal world to destroy the creatures they had termed vampires, but the vampires had bought themselves a stay of execution without ever knowing it. They had begun to form a society, complete with rules and a hierarchy.

The presence of this social structure and rules tempered his desire to eradicate them like the vicious pests they were and had saved them from his wrath over the past four thousand years. Vampire society didn't condone killing humans during a feed because it increased the risk of the general population becoming aware of them. Instead, those vampires chose to use their remaining psychic gift to place the host under a thrall, giving them pleasure through a mental link while they took only enough blood to satisfy their hunger. If a mortal were accidentally killed, they disposed of the body in a discreet way, keeping their kind under the radar of the mortal population.

There were other vampires though, a dangerous subset of the species, who didn't care about the rules and often drained humans to the point of death and left the body where it fell, or turned them and invariably left them to handle the transition from human to vampire alone, without instruction or support. Those vampires were a menace to mortal and vampire society alike, and had been present ever since the vampires and elves had evolved into two separate species.

Loren despised the vampires who sought to murder mortals, making them suffer and feeding off their fear and distress, eventually killing them or turning them against their will.

A long time ago, he had taken great pleasure in tracking and destroying such vampires. Perhaps it was time he rekindled that passion.

Loren focused and called his weapon to him from the Archangel facility. The air before him shimmered and his black blade materialised in his hand.

"Let us hunt." Loren tied the belt around his waist and settled the sword at his side.

Bleu smiled darkly. "May the best elf win."

He teleported. Loren followed him, appearing outside the Archangel facility. Bleu stood a short distance away across the wide square in front of the tall curved glass building.

Loren looked up at the towering height of it and then at his surroundings. There were other buildings similar to it nearby, and smaller buildings beyond them in a mixture of styles. Many of the lights in the buildings were still on, but others were off, speaking of the late hour. The square was empty too, not a single human moving around.

The city hummed around him, a thousand noises blended together, from vehicles, to electricity wires, to humans socialising. He could hear it all but couldn't discern anything from the jumbled sounds.

A gated park stood beyond a road, the Archangel building facing straight onto it. Tall trees swayed in the darkness on a gentle breeze and animals moved around in the safety of the night, free to roam without fear of humans.

Loren felt drawn to the green swath of land tucked amongst the tall harsh glass, steel and concrete buildings. A small slice of paradise amongst so much cold soulless architecture. Did Olivia visit the park? Did she enjoy nature and the feel of sunshine on her skin?

He had caught her look of fascination when he had announced that he had taken her from her world to his. She had wanted to see beyond his walls and take in the beauty of his kingdom. It was a small slice of paradise amongst so much fiery black unforgiving terrain. Vail had seen to that. It had been his ingenious idea, but together they had made it real, bringing light into Hell and allowing their barren land to bear seed and grow green and beautiful.

Vail.

Loren stared at the trees. Vail had been here. He had brought him to this place, unconscious and weakened, leaving him in this very square for Olivia. He had known she was Loren's fated female and had planned for Loren to bond them. Both Loren and Olivia had played their parts to perfection, doing exactly as Vail had expected, giving him a chance to have his revenge.

His brother wanted him to suffer as he had, bearing the pain felt by his ki'ara, and he couldn't allow that. He wouldn't allow it.

He would find a way to protect Olivia from his brother's sadistic game.

"Come. It has been many years since you've hunted in this world. Let me reintroduce you to the fun of slaying vampires." Bleu beckoned him and Loren shook his dark thoughts away and crossed the square to him.

Bleu led the way, no doubt tracking Sable's scent to discover her hunting route.

"We should not kill him immediately." Loren palmed the hilt of his sword and stretched his senses out to monitor his surroundings, unwilling to give a vampire any chance to sneak up on them. They were wily creatures, bent on killing, and often preferred to track their prey from the shadows before swiftly attacking, using speed to their advantage.

"You desire to toy with him?" Bleu glanced over his shoulder at him and Loren shook his head. He wasn't interested in playing with the vampire.

"I desire to speak with him." Loren scanned the lower brick buildings around them. Cars passed along a road ahead, little more than blurs of white and red lights. He had seen reports on everything of importance in the modern world, although sometimes those reports were lacking to a certain degree. For example, he had not known about computers and their importance in modern mortal society. When he had time, he would speak with those in charge of keeping him informed and would request they do a better job. It was imperative that he keep up to date on things, in case situations like this arose and he had to venture out into this realm.

"Then we kill him?" Darkness tainted Bleu's voice. Elves never had liked vampires, but vampires were related to them whether they liked it or not, born of elf blood and darkness. His second in command would do well to remember that, if only to guide him on his path through life and stop him from becoming a shadow of that creature.

"If we can get him to talk, then perhaps we could gain access to the demons and fae who live in this world. We could infiltrate the social places they have in this city and question people there about recent activity in the area."

Bleu looked back at him again, his dark eyebrows knitted together. "You mean to track your brother using this vampire?"

"I do." He wanted to question the local fae about Vail and whether they had seen him. Most fae travelled between this world and Hell, and many would know of his brother.

The mad elf prince.

Bleu nodded. "A good plan. I like it."

He stopped at the end of the road where it joined the busy four-lane affair that had cars whizzing along it and sniffed the air. People moved around on this street and those that passed eyed them with curiosity.

Perhaps armour was not the best choice of clothing for blending into this world.

"Bleu," Loren said and his second in command looked across at him. "We are not blending. How do we blend in this world?"

"Easy." Bleu closed his eyes and mortal clothing appeared over his body. Dark jeans like those Olivia wore covered the armour on his legs and a black t-shirt concealed that on his chest. He completed the ensemble with a long black coat that reached down to his ankles, loose enough that it hid the sword hanging at his side.

Loren owned no such clothing, therefore he couldn't call it from his apartments to him as Bleu could.

Bleu's green gaze gained an amused glimmer. "I swear they are clean."

Before Loren could ask what he meant, black jeans hugged his legs and an equally dark button down shirt covered his upper body. A long black coat similar to Bleu's flowed over him, falling down to just above his ankles. Loren had never worn anything so common.

"The clothing of a mortal barbarian suits you," Bleu teased and Loren pinned him with a warning glare. "Come. I think I know where our prey will be."

Bleu crossed the quiet road, heading left towards what appeared to be a neighbourhood still busy with people even at this time of night. Loren caught the sound of music coming from some of the illuminated establishments in the distance. He followed Bleu but paused before leaving the quiet road behind and looked back along it towards the Archangel facility, his gaze drawn there as well as his heart. It told him to return to Olivia.

It demanded it.

He had to find out everything he could about his brother though and needed time for the bond between them to fade in strength, and that meant leaving her alone for a few hours. Not alone. She had Archangel and her friend, Sable, to protect her. They were a powerful organisation whose hunters had proven themselves determined to take on any demon or fae they viewed as a threat, aiming their weapons at him several times in only a few short hours. Olivia would be safe with them.

Loren turned away and found Bleu watching him. He caught up with him and Bleu fell into step with him. Loren could feel him building up to saying something. His friend had been quiet too long, not mentioning everything that had happened. It wasn't like him.

"Spit it out." Loren couldn't stand the tense silence anymore.

Bleu raked his eyes over Loren. "What was that all about?"

Loren wasn't sure what to tell him. He wasn't sure what it had been all about. Was it a product of the bond? Or was it something else?

"Do you desire the female?" Bleu's light tone didn't lessen the gravity of what he had asked.

Loren sent his armour away from his hands and scrubbed one over his face. It was no use lying to himself, or to Bleu.

"Yes. I do desire Olivia." There, it was out in the open now. Bleu could talk some sense into him, reminding him of his duty and his mission, and he could get his head and heart straight.

"It's the bond," Bleu stated flatly.

Loren sighed. If only it were that simple. "It is not the bond."

"It's the bond," Bleu said it again, as though if he said it enough it would be the truth.

"No... it is not the bond. It is her... she is..."

Bleu growled. "Don't say it. I don't want to hear it. I just want to kill something."

Loren smiled at him, amused by his black scowl and the frustration flashing in his eyes. Loren's gaze shifted a few centimetres back, to the concealed tips of his ears.

"Are you sure that is all you want?" Loren's smile turned wicked.

Bleu shot him a black look. "What's that meant to mean?"

Loren lifted his shoulders in an easy shrug and then grinned. "I saw your reaction to the female slayer."

Bleu huffed. "I'm not interested in her in particular... but it's been a long time since I've been in this world, and with a female... and I know it's been ridiculously longer for you... so that's why you were all over that female today. Celibacy and a bond. A ticking bomb."

Loren let it go because he knew it was more than that. He hadn't been with a woman in four thousand plus years, but that wasn't why he desired this one so fiercely, and neither was the bond between them.

He had thought Olivia beautiful when he had come around to find her watching over him like a true angel.

Just thinking about her had his blood pumping and filled him with a dark need to return to her and sample her mouth, and taste her flesh again. He. wanted to run his lips down her throat to the marks he had placed on her smooth flawless skin and sink his fangs into her, drawing her blood into his body, strengthening the connection between them.

"Stop thinking about her," Bleu snapped.

Loren smiled an apology at his friend and dragged himself back to the hunt. They entered an area with many humans, some of them rather inebriated. Easy prey. If he were hunting for blood, he would look for such a place.

Bleu sniffed again. "You smell that?"

Loren closed his eyes and inhaled through his nose, taking the stale city air down into his lungs. One scent stood out amongst the thousands of others.

Blood.

Vampire blood.

He opened his eyes and looked at Bleu. Bleu took off, sprinting down an alley to their left, away from the humans. Loren tried to keep up with him but he still hadn't regained his strength after the torturous thirty minutes of running Olivia had put him through. When he lost Bleu, he tracked his familiar scent. It led him back to the park. The Archangel building towered in the distance off to his left. The park was larger than he had believed, a long rectangular tract of land in the middle of the buildings.

Loren followed Bleu's scent, vaulting the cast iron fence and landing silently in a crouch on the other side. A thick layer of leaf litter cushioned his steps as he wove through the trees surrounding the park.

Bleu cursed in their native tongue and Loren broke through the trees and stopped dead when he saw why.

Someone had beaten them to the vampire.

The male hung from the branches of a large oak tree, broken and lifeless, his clothes and flesh shredded. Blood dripped from his bare feet to land in a pool on the grass and path beneath him. He hadn't been there long judging by the fact that his blood hadn't coagulated yet. Whoever had done this atrocious act was still in the vicinity.

Loren knew who had committed it.

The male's flesh and clothes had been cleaved open, the method of the attack all too familiar to him.

Loren raised his right hand and called his armour. The scales swept over his hand, forming long serrated claws over his fingers.

Vail had been here.

He had left this vampire on display for the humans to find. It was a message. Vail was showing him that he had no qualms about exposing demon and faekind to the mortals, just as Loren and the council had feared.

A shiver skittered across the back of his neck and he turned, scouring the darkness for his brother.

"He's here, isn't he?" Bleu whispered from the shadows of the night.

Loren nodded, his heightened vision cutting through the darkness, revealing everything to him.

His gaze caught on something and snapped back to it. Vail. He stood in the middle of the park, as still as a statue, facing him.

Loren drew his sword and ran at his brother. Bleu followed suit, racing past him to engage Vail before him. Vail pulled his two shorter blades out of the air, his eyes flashed brilliant purple, and he slashed at Bleu. Bleu leaped back but it was exactly what Vail wanted him to do.

Vail grinned and flicked one hand out, using a blast of telekinesis to knock Bleu flying. Bleu sailed through the air and landed hard, rolling to a halt just in front of Loren. Loren crouched to check him.

"Son of a bitch," Bleu muttered and swept his hand over his blade, transforming it into a long double-ended spear. "I'm going to kill him."

For once, Loren didn't tell him that he couldn't. He caught the surprise in his friend's eyes and rose to his feet, coming to face Vail.

"Brother." Loren flexed his fingers around the hilt of his blade and drew in a deep breath, mentally preparing himself for the fight that lay ahead.

Vail grinned, a wild glint in his purple eyes, and disappeared in a flash of violet and pale blue light.

Loren easily predicted the move, bringing his sword over his shoulder to defend his back. Vail's blades clashed with it, the sound ringing out in the darkness. Bleu got to his feet and thrust his spear at Vail, catching him on the shoulder. Vail hissed and bared his fangs at Bleu, and knocked him back with a blast of power.

"Stay out of this, Lapdog." Vail threw another blast at Bleu, but Bleu teleported in a blaze of violet and green light, easily evading the attack. He reappeared behind Vail and Loren used the momentary distraction to attack his brother.

Vail growled at him, exposing his fangs again. Bloodied. He had fed on the vampire before butchering him.

"Come to kill me, Brother?" Vail smiled at him, cold and emotionless, countering each strike of Loren's sword with his twin blades. He led the dance, luring Loren forwards, always defending.

Buying himself time?

Loren withdrew when he realised that wasn't the case. Vail was trying to wear him out. Bleu leaped in and attacked in his place, the length of his spear giving him an advantage over Vail if he could dodge his telekinetic blows. Loren was glad all over again that Bleu had demanded to accompany him. Bleu could keep up with his brother, attacking and defending at incredible speed, landing several blows on Vail.

Loren couldn't.

He was already tiring and he was weak. It would be easy for Vail to injure him when he was in this condition. He had to rely on Bleu to weaken Vail and only then could he attack.

With a weapon.

He had other abilities at his disposal though, ones that could help Bleu.

Bleu growled and thrust his spear at Vail. Vail deflected it with one blade and attacked with the other, slashing at Bleu's chest. Bleu arched backwards, evading the tip of the blade, and swung his spear, smashing it into the side of Vail's head. Vail staggered left and bared his fangs, his ears flattening against the sides of his head. Blood crept down his right temple, black in the low light.

Vail roared and brought both short swords down in a swift arc towards Bleu. Loren flung his hand out and hit him with everything he had, sending him shooting across the grass. Vail slammed into the thick trunk of the tree he had hung the vampire in, splinters of bark and wood exploding outwards under the force of the impact. Everything was silent and still for a few long seconds and then his brother clawed his way out of the tree and snarled at him, blood covering the entire side of his face now.

His armour had borne the brunt of the damage though, protecting Vail.

Bleu rushed him, not giving him a chance to shake off the effects of the blow. He leaped at Vail, holding his spear in both hands and bringing it down hard. Vail clumsily blocked with his right forearm and the impact sent him to his knees. Loren's breath left him when Vail's gaze snapped to his and fear flooded the link his brother had long ago closed between them.

"Vail," Loren whispered and reached for him, unable to ignore his need to protect his flesh and blood.

Vail reached for him and disappeared in a bright flash of colourful light.

Bleu's spear hit the dirt and he growled. He swung around to face Loren, breathing hard, and Loren could sense his fatigue and frustration. The tree creaked ominously.

"Bleu, move!" Loren stared in horror as the huge oak began to fall towards his friend.

Bleu looked over his shoulder.

Loren used the last of his strength to teleport, grab Bleu and disappear again just as the tree crashed to the grass, the sound of branches snapping a cacophony in the night.

He landed hard with Bleu a short distance away and looked back at the tree as it settled on the grass, limbs swaying and swishing.

"You were foolish to leave your ki'ara alone, Brother." Vail's cold voice drew Loren's gaze up the height of the fallen tree.

His brother stood on one of the broken branches near the top, perfectly balanced in a low crouch, his feet together and knees splayed. He rested his elbows on his knees and cocked his head to one side, his wild black hair falling down over one eye.

Loren opened his mouth to say that she wasn't his female and she wasn't alone, but stopped himself when Vail casually checked his armoured wrist as if checking a watch that wasn't there.

"Time is up." Vail lifted his head and smiled down at him. "Boom."

A huge explosion rocked the ground, the shockwave from the blast sending Loren and Bleu to their knees on the grass. Leaves swept past them and Loren instantly pushed back onto his feet and turned away from the fallen oak, towards the other end of the park.

Fire rained down from the middle of the Archangel building and swallowed several of the floors in flame and billowing white smoke.

A chill ran down Loren's spine and his arms, and incredible pain engulfed him and then he felt nothing.

"Olivia."

CHAPTER 10

Olivia's ears rang as she clawed herself out from underneath a section of ceiling tiles. Red lights flashed and thick smoke swelled from fires dotted around the large open-plan room. She covered her mouth with the bottom of her white coat and squinted, her eyes stinging. She sat in the middle of chaos, struggling to take it all in, staring at those less fortunate than her as their lifeless eyes looked off into eternity and unable to hear anything above the ringing in her mind.

Her heart thundered, spreading acid through her veins. Her left hand rested limp in her lap, the burning in her fingers telling her at least two of them had suffered severe trauma, possibly broken.

Sable.

She had been talking with Sable away from the lab when the explosion had happened.

Olivia tried to move and cried out as her right leg blazed with white-hot pain. She dropped the cloth from her nose and mouth and clutched her shin with her good hand.

"Olivia!" Sable's voice cut through the damned ringing and relief surged through her when she spotted her friend coming towards her, nursing her arm. A huge gash down her forearm oozed blood in thick rivulets.

"Sable." Olivia pushed the word out, alerting her friend to her location. Sable's golden eyes shot to her and she hobbled over, struggling to keep her footing on the debris.

"We have to get out of here. The whole place might come down." Sable released her arm and held her bloodied hand out to Olivia.

She shook her head. She couldn't leave. There were injured here who needed her help. Sable included.

She grimaced and used her teeth and her good hand to tear a strip of material from her jacket.

"We have to help as many as we can. Starting with you," Olivia said and held the white material out to Sable. "Help me with this."

Sable nodded and crouched before her, and together they managed to bandage her forearm, tying it tightly to slow the bleeding.

"What happened?" Sable helped her to her feet.

Olivia didn't dare put any weight on her injured leg and she didn't want to look down to see what sort of state it was in. She had to help the others first. She would worry about her own injuries later.

"Don't know." Olivia thanked her friend with a smile when she slung her arm around Olivia's waist and helped her over a section of the ceiling.

More doctors came through the thick black smoke. Among them was one of the smug doctors from the meeting. He looked like hell. Blood coated the left side of his face and saturated his white coat.

"What happened?" Olivia said to him and he lowered his hand from his mouth.

"The whole laboratory is gone. Wiped out in the blast. God knows what happened up there. We're taking the injured down to the square." He covered his mouth again and moved on, pausing to check the vitals of everyone he came across. The other two doctors did the same. Judging by the fact that only smoke and blood dirtied their skin and coats, and they showed no sign of injury, they must have been on the lower floors at the time of the explosion.

"I'm getting you out of here," Sable said and Olivia wasn't in a position to argue with her. "You'll get these wounds checked out and then you can help anyone waiting in the square. This place is a death trap."

Just as she said that, the floor shook and a second explosion rocked the building, this one feeling more distant than the first. Higher up?

The laboratory levels were towards the centre of the building. If only those levels had blown up, that meant hundreds of Archangel staff were trapped above them.

Mark's office was up there, and so were all the staff quarters for those who lived in the building.

Sable had tried to convince her to go up to her apartment in order to spill the beans about the situation with Loren, but Olivia had refused. If she hadn't, they would have been trapped up there too.

Sable helped her to the emergency stairwell and down to the next level. It was a different world. No fire or smoke touched the rooms on the other side of the glass wall. Sable pulled her away and they continued down to the bottom floor of the building, and out into the square.

Glass and debris from the building covered the stone slabs. Sable adjusted her grip on Olivia and they hobbled together away from the building and towards the park. Doctors were working on the injured there, using whatever they had on hand to patch up their wounds, and there were already Archangel ambulances on site, ferrying the worst affected staff members to one of the other facilities in the area. How long had she been unconscious?

Olivia took in the chaos and the carnage, the fifty plus victims of the explosion as doctors fought to save them, and the bodies that lined the square just metres away from them. Who had done this to them?

She looked back up at the building and covered her mouth, biting back a sob as she saw the state of it. The floors above the laboratory levels were in darkness until around three from the top. The second explosion had destroyed those levels and they burned, sending smoke and sparks of fire high into the night sky.

A deliberate attack.

They had taken out the laboratory and then they had taken out the roof so they couldn't use helicopters to rescue everyone trapped in the upper part of the building.

Olivia's knees gave out and Sable crumpled with her to the ground.

"Pull it together." Sable gently shook her. "These people need you. I'm going for a doctor, we're patching that leg and that hand, and then you get on your feet and you help these people. You hear me?"

Olivia nodded, staring blankly at the burning building, numbed by the sight of it and the thought that someone had done this. It hadn't been an accident.

A female doctor she didn't recognise came to her and bandaged her right calf up. She placed the little finger and ring finger of Olivia's left hand in a plastic cast and bandaged them up too. Olivia took the meds she offered and swallowed them, her eyes still locked on the building, her vision blurred with hot tears.

Awareness of her surroundings slowly dawned on her and a sense that she was being watched crawled over her skin.

Olivia looked away from the building, over her shoulder towards the park.

There was a man there.

Loren.

Olivia stood and corrected herself as her vision cleared. He looked like Loren, wore armour like Loren, but it wasn't him.

He stared at the blazing building with a wild look in his purple eyes.

Four male hunters approached him and she gasped as two short blades appeared in his hands and he cut them down before they had a chance to draw their weapons or defend themselves. His gaze slid to her and he smiled, sending a chill tumbling through her, and disappeared in a burst of light.

"Olivia!" Loren's voice rang out over the noise of the building, the wail of sirens as the fire engines arrived, and the cries of the injured, and she hated the way it wrapped around her and warmed her, making her feel safe.

She wasn't safe.

A homicidal maniac had blown up a building just to hurt her.

Loren rushed towards her, dressed like a goth and looking like hell, his eyes gradually changing to blue but retaining a corona of purple around the outside of his irises, as if he wasn't in full control of himself.

She turned away from him, limped to the nearest person in need of medical assistance, and used what the female doctor had left with her to start patching them up. She diligently sewed the gash on the female hunter's arm, ignoring Loren as he ground to a halt right next to her, Bleu hot on his heels.

Sable was right. She was going to do everything that she could for the injured and wasn't going to flake out now that they needed her. This was her fault after all.

No. This was Loren's fault.

Fury turned her blood to wildfire and she tried to be gentle with her patient, not wanting to take out her anger on her. She was going to store it up and unleash holy hell on Loren once she had made sure everyone who had a shot at survival did just that.

"Olivia?" Loren said and she continued to pretend he didn't exist, rage simmering in her veins.

She cut the thread, covered the stitches with some steri-strips and then gave the huntress some painkillers.

Olivia struggled to her feet, her right leg protesting as she put her weight on it. Loren caught her arm to help her and she smacked his hand away.

"Don't touch me!" She shoved him in the chest for good measure and hobbled off, heading to her next patient.

Loren grabbed her arm again, his grip firmer this time, and pulled her to a stop.

"Olivia," he whispered and she couldn't hold back her anger anymore. She turned on him.

"Someone was here who looked a whole damned lot like you. He went through those hunters like..." She pointed towards the bodies that someone was taking care of near the park and closed her eyes, not wanting to remember just how easily the man had cut them down. "They hadn't stood a chance, Loren. They hadn't stood a chance. None of us had."

She pushed away from him again, shirking his grip, and eased down to kneel beside a young male doctor with a head injury. The gash was deep, cutting across his forehead and into his hairline, and bleeding profusely. She swabbed the blood away to reveal the extent of the wound.

"This is going to hurt, but I have to stitch it," she said softly, and he nodded and swallowed hard.

Olivia took another needle, threaded it, and carefully began stitching the wound closed, occasionally pausing to give the young man a moment to gather himself. Loren hovered over her, Bleu his perpetual shadow.

Glass exploded from the building, showering the square. Olivia tensed and curled into a ball as quickly as she could. People screamed and she screwed her eyes shut, not wanting to think about everything that was happening. Because of Loren.

Because of that maniac she had seen.

She uncurled and realised that Loren had wrapped himself around her, using his body to shield her from the glass. Olivia hated that the self-sacrificing action warmed her even a fraction of a degree. She was supposed to be mad at him.

Olivia jerked back, dislodging him, and continued her work. The fingers of her left hand ached even though she did her best not to move them and her leg was killing her, but she kept going, stitching the wound on the man's head. He needed her help. She couldn't flake out now. She couldn't, no matter how tired and weak she felt.

"You need to rest," Loren said in that commanding snarl of his and Olivia ignored him.

She finished stitching the wound, cut the thread and then bandaged the man's head. She checked him over for other injuries and Loren growled. Olivia knew why. She was touching the young doctor, feeling her way over his body. Her patience snapped again.

"Don't take that tone with me," she barked at Loren and his irises flashed purple.

Bleu's eyes widened and he gave her a look that asked if she had lost her mind.

She had. She had lost it the moment Loren had come into her life. It was the only reasonable explanation for the insanity that had occurred in the few days she had known him, both in her world and where her feelings were concerned. She had to be crazy to have felt attracted to him.

He was rude, inconsiderate, treated everyone as though they were liable to attempt to bed her or kill her, and she'd had enough of him.

"Get away from me." She shot to her feet, regretting it the moment the dizziness hit her and she almost collapsed.

Loren caught her and she wanted to punch him, but she didn't have the strength. She tried to knee him in the balls instead but he blocked her and smiled softly.

"Olivia, you need to rest." He cradled her against his chest and righted her, and she cursed herself for leaning into him, seeking his warmth and how safe he made her feel. "You are injured and need proper medical attention."

"No." Olivia wouldn't let him coddle her. It would be the last straw. She didn't need a man to take care of her, especially not Loren. He only wanted her to rest because she was in pain and that meant he was in pain too, because of this ridiculous bond. She pushed out of his arms and looked around her at the blood and the glass, the fire and the chaos. Olivia calmly brushed her hair from her eyes, wiping her tears away at the same time, and faced Loren. "I can't take a break... because people are dying. My friends are dying."

Regret shone in his blue eyes. "I should have anticipated this. I shouldn't have left you here alone. It made you an easy target and I am sorry."

"Save your apologies for them and them." She pointed to the injured and then the row of covered corpses, and then swung her hand behind her and pointed at the building. "And them... Loren. Apologise to them... trapped in there... afraid... dying because of you."

Olivia turned away and scrubbed the heels of her hands across her eyes, sniffed back her tears and focused on the people who needed her.

"Olivia, please," Loren called after her but she didn't slow down.

Sable left a group of hunters who had been helping the injured out of the building and glared beyond her at Loren and Bleu. "Want me to kill them?"

Olivia smiled and shook her head. "No. There's been enough death today... and I do think he's honestly sorry for what happened."

"What did happen?" Sable drew her collapsible crossbow anyway and played at pointing it at the two men who hadn't dared to move after her.

Which was Sable threatening?

It had to be Bleu. If it had been Loren, he probably wouldn't have hesitated to attack her.

They had both been injured though. Had they been fighting the man who had blown up her world?

"His enemy just became our enemy." Olivia trudged towards her next patient.

She focused on taking care of the injured with Sable's assistance. The night wore on, the fire department put the blaze out and more were rescued from the building, many of them from the floors above the laboratory levels, including Mark and others she thought of as her friends. Olivia found it increasingly difficult to concentrate through the pain but she soldiered on, unwilling to give up while there were still people who needed her.

The sky lightened and the sun broke the horizon, painting ribbons of cloud in pinks and gold, but she found no warmth or beauty in it today.

The last of the injured were ferried away to one of the medical facilities used to tend to wounded hunters.

Olivia sat in the middle of the square, surrounded by blood and glass, tired to her bones.

Sable patted her shoulder. "I think he's about to lose patience."

Olivia could feel it in him. He had kept away from her, but had never been further than a few metres, and his eyes had constantly been on her. He had protected her from a distance, ignoring Bleu's suggestions that they return to their world, determined to watch over her.

She lifted her heavy head and looked across the square to him.

He wobbled in her vision and darkness loomed up and swallowed her. The world came back a heartbeat later and she slowly opened her eyes and found him looking down at her, his blue eyes flooded with concern and his anxiety mixing in with her weariness and the pain throbbing deep in her bones.

"No more arguing," Loren whispered and she nodded, too tired to resist him. He gathered her closer and she leaned her head against his cool hard chest and shut her eyes.

The scent of smoke and blood disappeared, replaced by a crisp fresh breeze that carried the scent of blossom.

He had taken her away from her world again, back to his.

She opened her eyes and looked up into his, and he softly stroked her cheek, his crystal blue eyes warm with tender concern.

"You will rest now?" he said in a low gentle voice and lifted her in his arms. Olivia curled into him, battling the call of sleep, and clung to his long black coat. He laid her down on the rich purple covers of his soft bed and she didn't let him go. Her fingers clutched his coat lapels. Loren smiled but there was no warmth in it and covered her hands with his. "I am sorry, Olivia."

She nodded. He didn't need to tell her that he was sorry about what had happened. It was there in his eyes and in the connection that linked them. She could feel his sorrow and his suffering as if it were her own.

"What sort of freaky ass shit did you just do to me, you weirdo?" Sable's voice echoing in from outside drove some of the sleepiness from her and she frowned at Loren.

A distinctly Bleu growl came next.

He must have teleported Sable with him.

"Back off... back the hell off, vampires!"

He also must have forgotten to remove Sable's weapons first. Olivia thought she heard a few disgusted mutters about vampires and mortals.

"Excuse me." Loren eased her hands away from his coat, released her and disappeared.

He reappeared a moment later with Sable, who promptly threw a right hook at him. Loren dodged it, held his hands up, and stepped aside. Sable's golden-brown eyes instantly shot to her and she raced to the bed.

"They took you too?" Sable said and Olivia tried to sit up. Pain shot up her left arm from her fingers and she grimaced.

Loren was by her side in an instant, helping her up and arranging his pillows behind her. A little more of her anger towards him melted but she clung fiercely to the rest.

"I've been here before," Olivia said to her friend and Sable's eyes widened. "No... no... not like that. It's not what it looks like. I told you... we're just bonded and we're breaking that bond. Loren doesn't want me, and I definitely don't want him."

Much.

She kept her eyes on Sable, resisting the pressing desire to look at him and see if his expression matched the feelings flowing through their bond. Loren did want her, and his increased heartbeat and elevated hormone levels said the sight of her on his bed had him thinking about wanting her right that moment.

Bleu burst into the room.

"You want another round?" Sable raised her fists.

Bleu wiped the back of his hand across his bloodied lip and narrowed his purple eyes on her friend. He definitely wanted a second shot at Sable's title.

"Bleu," Loren said, and Bleu's gaze drifted to him. "I require a moment alone with Olivia. Please show Sable around the castle and answer any questions she might have."

Sable smiled viciously at Bleu. "There's only one room I want to see and only two questions I have."

Bleu straightened, his eyes flashing dangerously as Sable sauntered up to him.

She prodded his chest. "Where's your sparring room and do you want me to whip your butt in it?"

She tossed Olivia a good-luck wink and dragged Bleu from the room. Loren stared at the closed arched doors.

"Your friend is trouble. It is not wise to challenge Bleu." Loren slowly looked across at her and Olivia forgot her pain and her anger for a moment as she smiled at the thought of Sable taking on Bleu. That was the huntress she knew. She was sporting an injured arm but she just couldn't resist the opportunity to fight a new species.

"I think Bleu will find it's not wise to challenge Sable," Olivia said and then her smile faded and she looked down at her ruined dirty white coat and her ripped jeans. Blood had soaked through the bandages around her lower right leg. Here in Loren's castle, she felt as if she were thousands of miles away from what had happened tonight and it would be so easy for her to just shove it aside and forget what she had lived through, and why.

She looked up at Loren and his expression turned sombre, the light that had been in his purple eyes fading to reveal the sorrow she had witnessed often in them.

"Who was he and how did he plant the bombs in Archangel?" she whispered. "No more dancing around this... Loren... I need to know what I'm dealing with. He's not just your enemy anymore. He's our enemy now."

Loren sighed, sat on the edge of the bed and scrubbed a hand through his black hair, tousling the longer lengths on top and revealing the pointed tips of his ears.

"Vail is... my younger brother."

Olivia stared at him, waiting for that to sink in. Loren had been at war for all these centuries with his younger brother.

That was why he had talked of containing him and capturing him. That was why he hadn't killed him before.

Ice formed in her veins, engulfing her heart, dragging up memories she had fought hard to suppress. She drew her left leg up and held on to it, resting her chin on it as she realised that she and Loren weren't so different after all. They came from different worlds but both of them wanted to save their brother. She had lost hers. Loren still had a chance with his.

"Olivia?" Loren whispered and she dashed away the tears lining her lashes. "Are you feeling unwell?"

She nodded. She hadn't felt right since the night she had fallen into a parallel world full of monsters and mayhem.

She didn't want to think about it so she focused on Loren and his brother, locking away the memories of her one.

Loren moved closer to her, his proximity comforting her, stealing away some of her pain.

"Tell me... what happened to make you go to war with your own brother?" She stared down at his hands on the bed, pale against the purple sheets, afraid to look at him because she feared she would give in to her need to feel his arms around her if she did. She wanted to lose herself in him and forget everything, even if it could only be for a handful of hours.

Her gaze betrayed her and drifted up his arms, and she pulled it back to his hands. It was strange to see him in a shirt and jeans, and the long coat. They didn't suit him at all.

He shifted again and heaved a sigh.

"Vail had been away with his legion of our army, scouting the borders of our lands that join it to the area we know as the free realm. Many different species live there, with no one king or queen to rule them. He sent back word stating that he had found something and he couldn't wait to show me." Loren's deep voice held a sombre note and Olivia felt his pain. She reached out and placed her hand over his, hoping to give him some comfort, knowing what it was like to think back to happier times that were now tainted by one terrible moment of darkness. Loren shifted his hand beneath hers, moving it so their palms pressed together and his fingertips grazed her wrist. "Months later, the remains of the legion returned, a young Bleu amongst them. Many of them were savagely injured and I feared my brother dead until Bleu and other men had the courage to speak out, revealing that it was Vail who had turned on them. They said he had become crazed by the presence of a magic bearer."

"Kordula," Olivia said. "His ki'ara."

Loren nodded. "I believe their completed bond triggered this change within him."

She lifted her eyes to his and saw in them that he also believed that if he completed his bond with her, that he would follow his brother into madness.

Loren looked away, turning his noble profile to her and staring at one of the arched windows lining the dark stone wall behind her. "I dispatched my finest soldiers to track and capture Vail, but he fought and slew them all before disappearing. Over the centuries after that, he attacked other kingdoms, mainly the demon ones, bringing their wrath down upon my kingdom and my people. The number of my kind dwindled, our might diminished, and I was kept busy trying to carve out peace with the kingdoms who wanted to see me dead and my people destroyed."

"That's terrible." Olivia brushed her fingers against his palm and felt his shiver race through her. "You never stopped trying to save him though."

He shook his head. "No. I searched for him whenever I could, and fought him close to every other century, always failing to capture him. The council grew weary of my desire to imprison Vail rather than kill him, and I reluctantly agreed to seek my brother's head in our next battle. I have to put the safety and wellbeing of my people before my own desires."

Loren's purple gaze filled with weariness that she could feel in him. The constant war against his brother had drained him and now all he had were tainted memories and a heart filled with regrets.

He didn't even have his fated female.

He was giving her up too. She could see it now. He was placing his people before his own desires, and that meant sacrificing his one ki'ara and his brother.

Her heart ached for him and she curled her fingers around his hand, squeezing it gently, trying to show him that she was here even if she couldn't understand what he was going through. He was giving it all up for his people. It made her feel cold, and sorry for him.

He had been alone for millennia and now this council of his and his own sense of duty to his people had him cementing that loneliness, seeking to shatter the bond with her and destroy his brother.

"Loren," she started but he slipped his hand from under hers and stood.

"Rest, Olivia. I will take you home by nightfall." He turned his back on her, blue and purple light flashed over his body and he disappeared.

She was beginning to tire of his tendency to do that but she couldn't blame him for running away from her whenever things got too intense for him. He was trying to save himself from suffering more than he already was.

Olivia pulled her leg closer and stared at the spot where he had sat beside her, holding her hand and taking her comfort, until she had dared to voice the feeling in her heart.

He shouldn't have to give up everything.

It wasn't right.

He had already been through so much pain because of what had happened with Vail and now he was supposed to kill his only brother.

She hadn't been able to kill hers.

She had wanted to save him too.

She hadn't wanted to be alone.

And neither did Loren.

Olivia touched the marks on her throat, focusing on them, seeking Loren through their connection. He felt agitated, upset, and in pain. She ached to go to him and take that hurt away, to tell him that just because he was a prince, it didn't mean he should have to live his life alone.

What was she doing?

She was supposed to be mad at Loren but she couldn't blame him for wanting to save his brother, and she couldn't blame him for what had happened at Archangel. She had demanded he let her stay there, even though he had told her it would be dangerous. She had ignored his warning and Vail had done exactly what Loren had said he would, targeting her in order to make him suffer.

Punishing him for the attempt he had made on Kordula's life.

Olivia was as much to blame for the explosion as Loren was, but the true culprit was Vail. Vail was to blame for everything. He had turned on Loren and his people. He had driven his brother to war with him when all Loren wanted to do was save him and his people. He had forced this bond between Loren and her, all for the sake of revenge, stealing his brother's only ki'ara because Loren felt too damned guilty about desiring her above the safety of his people and was too damned noble to say screw his duty and take a shot at winning her.

Olivia groaned. Did she want Loren to win her? She vaguely recalled feeling offended at one point by the fact that he wanted to break the bond, but that was before she had come to know him and know how attracted he was to her. He craved her as much as she craved him, and she was too tired and hurt to lie to herself anymore. It wasn't the bond. Loren was six-feet-six of gorgeous with a heart of solid gold. Any woman in her right mind would want him and she was not certifiably crazy yet.

Did she want to win Loren?

Her heart tore her in too many directions until she wasn't sure which one was the one she wanted most of all. There was one thing she kept coming back to though.

The last non-human she had trusted with her heart had broken it and her trust, and had destroyed the world she had carefully constructed for herself after her brother's death.

She couldn't go through that again. She couldn't risk her heart. She wasn't brave enough to do it, and that left her with only one direction.

She wanted this bond broken.

Didn't she?

CHAPTER 11

Loren stood on the rooftop of the large complex of sandstone buildings in central London, his gaze on the night sky, studying the stars but not really seeing them. His thoughts were elsewhere, two floors down and five rooms to his left, where Olivia worked in her new laboratory in the Archangel headquarters.

Things had been tense between them since the attack on Archangel and he could understand why she was keeping her distance from him, and why Archangel were blaming him for what had happened. The deaths of many of their people were his fault. He should have ended Vail centuries ago, before things had gotten this far. He could have met Olivia under different circumstances and as a different man from the one who had left her open to attack, and had brought death and suffering to her people. All because he had panicked. His guard had slipped and he had realised it too late to stop Olivia from capturing his heart.

She had stated her feelings quite clearly to her friend.

Olivia didn't want to be his mate.

So there was little point in considering what his life would be like if she were his, yet thoughts of a future together had plagued him for the past two days, and fear she would reject him stole his voice whenever they were alone.

Olivia's friend Sable had taken to sparring with Bleu whenever Olivia didn't need him for the tests she had needed to run again due to losing all of her data in the fire. Loren thought that Sable was doing it to keep Bleu occupied, giving Loren time alone with Olivia, but he couldn't understand why she would do such a thing. It didn't make sense. She had offered to kill both him and Bleu several times since they had met. Sable would never desire to help him with Olivia.

It was a lost cause anyway.

Olivia was working harder than ever to find a way to break their bond and had demanded he order his men to do the same. She wanted it broken.

That left him hollow inside.

A cold space opened behind his breastbone whenever he thought about Olivia succeeding in finding a way to undo what had happened and parting ways with him.

What future awaited him if that happened and if he killed Vail?

A colourless, cold and empty one.

Loren had the terrible feeling that Olivia would take his heart with her, leaving him hollow and dead, drifting through his existence without feeling anything ever again.

He pressed his bare hand to his chest, the black scales of his armour cold beneath his palm, and focused there, using his abilities to strengthen the connection between him and Olivia so he could feel her clearly.

She was still on his senses, her heartbeat level and her emotions stable. Sleeping. She had probably worked herself too hard again and had fallen asleep on her desk. It had happened last night too, after she had worked for almost two days solid on gathering the data she needed from him and Bleu, refusing to take even five minutes to rest.

Her injuries still hadn't healed yet.

He could feel them as a dull ache on his body, something he took as a sign that despite the current distance between them, they were growing closer and their bond was growing stronger. He could sense her more easily too, pinpointing her location with more accuracy without expending as much psychic energy.

When he had offered to heal her injuries for her, she had refused. He had pressed her for a reason why but she had given him none. Did she feel as though she should suffer the pain of her injuries as payment for what had happened? Or was she clinging to them as a reminder of what had happened so she could hold on to her anger?

She was angry with him, and with herself.

Loren could distinguish the difference between the two emotions if he focused when he was around her. He didn't need to focus to know she was angry with him though. She made that perfectly clear whenever she had to take blood from him or go anywhere near him. She had stabbed, jabbed, prodded and poked him, all with gusto that warned her rough treatment of him was meant as a form of punishment.

She had also taken to touching Bleu, placing the pads on his bare body with deliberate care and lingering a second too long with her fingers on his skin.

She was doing it on purpose. He had warned her several times not to push him but she didn't listen. Whenever she had an opportunity, she did something that wound him tight inside and drove him close to attacking Bleu. It took every ounce of his willpower to stop himself. Bleu didn't deserve his wrath when he had done nothing wrong.

Loren only wished he knew why Olivia punished him so cruelly. He could understand it if she lashed out at him, or shouted at him and laid the blame at his feet. He couldn't understand this torment though. What did she expect of him?

Did she want him to hurt his friend?

"Here you are," the soft female voice cut through the silence of the night and he brought his gaze down from the stars and looked over his shoulder at Sable.

She stood near the roof exit, her black combat trousers and t-shirt causing her to blend into the darkness and the breeze blowing her black ponytail across her shoulder. She could be an elf with hair like that.

"Here I am," he countered and turned to face her. "Is there a problem with Bleu?"

"Oh, hell no." She waved her hand dismissively. "He's resting from the latest can of whoop-ass I opened on him."

Loren smiled indulgently. Bleu was most likely giving the human female time to catch her breath, feigning tiredness to save her from having to swallow her pride and admit she was beaten. He had come to understand Sable at least. The female had an admirable sense of determination about her. She refused to let anyone best her. If someone beat her, she got right back up and tried again to defeat them.

"I am sure he will be ready to lose to you again soon enough." Loren had wondered often over the past few days whether Bleu was interested in Sable in an intimate way. His second in command seemed content with sparring with the female, but sometimes he had a look in his eyes that said he wanted more than an exchange of physical blows with her.

Sable shrugged. "It's not the reason I fight him. I've been trying to give you two time together to talk but all you do is mope around and all she does is hide in her work. So let's get to business."

"Business?" Loren didn't recall desiring to discuss any business with the female and he certainly didn't recall moping at any point over the past few days.

She nodded and crossed the roof to him, peered over the edge towards the street several storeys below, and then up at the stars.

"It sure is quiet tonight. If I was your psycho brother, I'd be busy plotting something bad. It's a good night for bad shit to happen."

Loren scowled at her, his fangs descending and his ears changing, the pointed tips appearing.

"Dial it back a notch, big guy. Your brother is a special case." She tapped the blade sheathed at her waist. "Liv told me about him. I can see why you want to break things off with her. It's not because this whole bond thing weakens you now, is it?"

Loren looked away from her.

"Yeah, you've got that noble thing pegged, but don't pretend you haven't thought about being with her. What's the difference? You break the bond and you get stronger... you complete it and the same thing happens. Right?" Sable leaned into his line of sight. "Right?"

Irritating and interfering little mortal. She had been playing with him and Olivia, distracting Bleu so they would be alone together, and now she was annoyed because her plan to push them together hadn't worked. Olivia didn't want him. Couldn't her friend see that?

"The same things happen, but the consequences are vastly different." Loren shifted his gaze to meet her golden one. "If I complete the bond with Olivia, she is still a target. If Vail captured her, or killed her... I could not bear it. He would seek to do just that. Breaking the bond will free her. She will be safe."

She frowned. "But I don't get it... I see the way you look at her, Loren. You can't bear not having her."

"This is not true." He turned to face her fully and she peered over the edge of the building again, the light from the street below softly illuminating her face but casting shadows around her eyes.

"Liv has a tendency to work late... she's always working... and when she gets like that, you have to understand she does it for a reason." Sable stared down at the people walking along the street below them, her tone distant. "You can deny your feelings if you want... but if you decide to admit to them... everyone at Archangel has a reason they're here, even Olivia. If you want to get to know the real her, the one she hides behind the white coat, then ask her about the scars on her right inside forearm. Maybe then you'll understand her behaviour... and both of you will stop dancing around your feelings."

Loren stared at her in disbelief. Sable was matchmaking? She glanced at him, shrugged and smiled, and took off towards the roof exit, leaving him alone with his thoughts.

Why would Sable want to give him a shot at winning her friend? Olivia couldn't stand him. Her behaviour the past few days had made that painfully clear.

His eyes widened.

She had a reason she was treating him like this and Sable's words gave him the feeling that he was wrong about Olivia. Olivia did want him. She was trying to push him away to protect herself for some reason. She was trying to make him jealous not because she wanted him to hurt Bleu.

She wanted him to drop his guard again and show her that she didn't have to be afraid because whatever she was feeling, he was feeling it too.

He wanted her.

Loren focused on her and discovered she was still in the laboratory. He closed his eyes and teleported there.

Olivia sat on the high stool where he had left her an hour ago, her microscope in front of her with the slide still in place, and her body twisted at an angle so she could lay her head on the long white table top. She had her cheek pressed against her notepad and right hand tucked under her temple.

Some of the glossy waves of her chestnut hair had fallen down and snaked across the white top or brushed her pale face.

Her left hand rested on the table beside her, her little and ring fingers still wrapped in bandages and tape.

Sleeping here wasn't going to do her any good. She needed to rest in a bed and for longer than a few snatched minutes.

Loren approached her silently and carefully lifted her into his arms. She murmured in her sleep but didn't wake. He held her close, staring down at her beauty as she slumbered in his arms. His female. He wanted to stroke the strands of hair from her face and take care of her, doing all he could for her. She was his to claim, destined for him, and he had waited too long for her to give up now. Sable was right. He couldn't stop thinking about Olivia and he had never felt anything as strongly as he did this desire to have her.

Olivia belonged to him.

His gaze lowered to her right forearm. Would she tell him if he asked about the scars her white coat concealed? Would it give him the insight into Olivia that Sable believed it would, explaining her reasons for keeping her distance from him and giving him a chance with his ki'ara?

Loren hoped that it would.

He focused on the small two room apartment that had become Olivia's quarters in the building and took them there.

She stirred as they reappeared, her lashes lifting to reveal sleep-filled brown eyes that lit upon his, their softness awakening his desire to keep her safe.

"What happened?" she whispered and blinked slowly, fighting the fatigue he could sense in her.

"You fell asleep at your desk again. I thought it would be better you sleep in your bed." He carried her to the double bed and gently laid her down on the pale blue covers.

Olivia sat up, rubbed the sleep from her eyes and looked around her. "No. I can't be here. I have work to do."

Loren shook his head. "You will rest, Olivia. You were asleep at your desk. I do not think that constitutes working."

She frowned at him and went to leave the bed. Loren caught her shoulders and held her in place.

"Please, Olivia. Rest." He could see what she was going to say. "I do not desire this because I hurt or am tired because of our bond. I desire this because I am worried about you."

She blinked at him, her eyes lingering on his, a distant look in them, and then relaxed. She dropped her gaze to her hands where they rested in her lap and picked at the bandage around the two injured fingers on her left one.

"Do they still hurt?" He sat beside her on the pale covers and she went to shake her head and then nodded. At least she was learning that there was little point in lying to him when he could sense things in her.

Loren took her hand, closed his eyes, and focused on their bond. He had read all about the link between eternal mates and the benefits, but knowledge was vastly different to experience, and he wasn't sure this would work when the bond was incomplete.

He let himself fall into the connection and experienced a strange sense of flowing through his body and into hers, travelling from her heart to the broken fingers of her left hand. He willed the bones to fuse, his own aching in response as he transferred the injury to himself. Olivia gasped and Loren grimaced as the bones in his fingers shattered.

"Stop it! You're hurting yourself." Olivia pulled her hand free of his but her act of compassion came too late.

Loren looked down at his fingers. "I may need to borrow your cradling device until I can source some blood."

Her right hand went to her throat, her eyes wide.

"I will not take yours, Olivia. I have done enough to hurt you already." Loren straightened his two broken fingers, biting down on his tongue to hide his pain from Olivia. She gave him a dark look that reminded him that there was little point in him lying to her about this sort of thing too. She could feel his pain echoing in her own fingers.

"Why did you do it?" She removed the bandage and plastic cradle from her left hand, marvelled as she flexed her healed fingers, and then frowned as she moved closer to him.

A hot shiver bolted up his arm when she took hold of his hand and it had absolutely nothing to do with pain.

"I naturally heal faster than you. What would have taken you weeks to heal, will take me barely a day. A day of discomfort is preferable to weeks of watching you suffer in silence. That pains me more." He studied her hands as she set about bandaging his fingers, her actions gentle, and slowing.

Her hands lingered on his. "You didn't have to do this."

"I would take all your pain if I could." He lifted his head and looked at her as she stared at their joined hands, her brown eyes reflecting the hurt he could feel in her. He didn't know the source of her feelings and suspected he never would unless he did as Sable had suggested and asked her. "Olivia?"

"Hmm?" She looked up at him, her gaze distant again. She was miles away from him, as lost in thought as he had been on the roof. He wanted to divine her thoughts. He wanted to know the woman behind the white coat.

He kept hold of her hands with his injured one and used his other one to push back the right sleeve of her white coat. She started, trying to pull away from him, but he caught her bare wrist, refusing to let her hide anymore.

He would know his female.

She would not deny him this.

He carefully turned her arm so he could see the underside.

His blue eyes widened and turned purple, his fangs descending at the sight of the marks on her wrist.

"Who bit you?" They were unmistakable. Twin puncture wounds, ragged and vicious, as if someone had ruthlessly torn at her flesh with fangs. Further up her arm was a long thick ridge of scar tissue that cut diagonally from inside her elbow down towards her wrist. His gaze locked on the bite mark though, fury burning through his blood, causing the points of his ears to extend.

Olivia tried to pull her arm back and cover the scars.

"Who did this, Olivia? Tell me." He wouldn't let her go and he couldn't take his eyes off the marks on her pale skin.

Sable's words echoed in his head, taunting him. Everyone at Archangel had a reason they were there. Olivia's was branded on her wrist, a vicious scar from an attack that had no doubt left her wounded psychologically as well as physically.

And he had bitten her.

Olivia managed to twist her hand free of his grasp and held it against her chest, shrinking away from him.

He stared at his empty hand, reeling from what he had seen and the knowledge of what he had done.

"Olivia, I..." He wasn't sure what he wanted to say to her, or whether she would even listen to him. He met her eyes, losing himself in their rich dark depths and cursing himself as he noticed the tears that lined her lashes. He had hurt her. "I am sorry... I bit you against your will... I did not know—"

"You couldn't have known," she interjected softly and cast her gaze down at the pale blue bedclothes beside her.

"That is why you fought me so... because you thought I would kill you. Like this vampire tried to kill you?"

She refused to look at him but she nodded.

Loren reached over and settled his palm against her cheek, hoping to reassure her. She didn't flinch away from his touch and he took it as a good sign.

"I would not have killed you, Olivia. I was hungry, but I was in control. I knew how much to take without hurting you... but it is no excuse for what I did. It is no wonder that you despise me. I am no better than the vampire who attacked you." He lowered his hand away from her face and she surprised him by catching it before he could fully withdraw.

"I don't despise you, Loren... and I don't hate the vampire who did this to me."

He frowned. "Why ever not?"

She looked up at him, her soulful brown eyes filled with tears and sorrow. "Because he was my brother."

Gods. Her brother had turned vampire and had attacked her. He couldn't stop himself from clutching her hand, holding it tightly in his, needing to feel her and needing her to feel him, and know that he would never let anything bad happen to her ever again.

"You want to save your brother, Loren... I wanted to save mine... and I couldn't... and I have to live with that every day."

Was this confession what Sable had anticipated when she had told him to ask Olivia about the scars? Her friend knew her history and had known that it would bring him closer to her somehow, but he still didn't understand how. They shared a common desire, and Olivia had failed to save her brother. Loren couldn't see how it would help him win Olivia's heart and understand her recent behaviour.

Unless the two scars on her arm weren't related. What other terrible things had Olivia endured in her short life?

He pushed aside his curiosity about the other scar and focused on the one she seemed willing to talk about.

"What happened to your brother?" Loren said, keeping his tone soft and gentle, hoping to soothe the hurt he could feel building within her. "Is he the reason you joined Archangel?"

Olivia nodded and toyed with Loren's fingers, her focus fixed on them.

"I went through med school before joining a local hospital in London. I used to see my brother all the time, even when I was really busy with studying." She ran her fingertip along the length of his index finger and pressed it against the tip. A distraction. Not just for her from her dark memories, but for him. If she kept toying with his fingers, he was going to have trouble focusing on her and shutting out the desire she stirred with each caress.

"It sounds as though you have always worked yourself too hard," Loren said and she shrugged.

"He would come by and force me to take a break, dragging me out to dinner somewhere close to the hospital." She glanced up at him. "It seems you both have a tendency to interrupt my work."

Loren didn't like her comparing him to her brother, who had attacked her, but he let it go, knowing she didn't mean it in a bad way. "You were sleeping, not working."

She shrugged again, released his hand and unbuttoned her white coat. She slipped her arms out of it and let it pool behind her on the bed. Her dark blue t-shirt hugged her breasts, another distraction he didn't need. He tried not to stare at them, because his body was already getting the wrong idea, and it was impossible to conceal the effect she had on him when he was wearing his armour. If she noticed, she was liable to demand he leave and then he wouldn't know what had happened with her brother.

Olivia turned her right arm around and held it out to him, so he could see the scars.

"Daniel didn't contact me for weeks and I was worried about him, so I went to see him. I found him in his flat, sitting in a corner, rocking. I thought it was a medical problem... drugs or something. He looked so gaunt and pale. Sick."

"Starving." Loren had seen enough starving vampires to know what they looked like when their bodies began to fade away and they lost their mind to their hunger.

She nodded. "I tried to help him... and he..."

"He bit you." Loren curled his fingers around her wrist and brushed his thumb over the scars. "Savagely."

She swallowed and lowered her head again, as if she couldn't bring herself to look at him or the scars. Loren's heart went out to her when tears raced down her cheeks and he realised he was wrong. She was trying to hide her tears from him. She didn't want him to see her crying.

Loren moved next to her and gathered her into his arms, holding her with her cheek against his chest but giving her space so she didn't feel stifled. She leaned into him, one hot palm pressing against his left pectoral. He focused and sent his armour away from his chest, partly because he wanted her to be comfortable and resting against cold metal scales was not going to achieve that, and partly because he wanted to feel her against him, skin-to-skin.

He stroked her hair, keeping his caress light and slow, not wanting to startle her.

"I thought he was going to kill me. He almost did." Her voice was hoarse, quiet, and he could feel her struggling with her emotions, battling to gain control of them and stop the tears from coming.

"What happened?" He leaned down, closed his eyes, and pressed his lips to her hair. Her soft fragrance filled his lungs, warming his heart. His female. He would make her feel better if she would only let him. He would give up everything to have her.

"Archangel." She rubbed her eyes, her voice gaining strength now. "They burst into the flat and pulled me away from him. They thought I was a victim."

"You were."

"No," she snapped and he expected her to shove away from him, but she remained in his arms, leaning against his chest. "I was his sister. I tried to stop them but I couldn't... I told them he was just sick and he wasn't a threat. I thought they were police or some government drug squad. They refused to listen to me and dragged me from the room, and then they—"

"Shh," Loren whispered and stroked her hair, keeping his breathing and emotions level, giving her an anchor of calm to hold on to if she needed it. She curled against him, burying her face against his bare chest, her tears hot against his skin. She didn't need to tell him what had happened. He could fill in the blanks.

Archangel had killed her brother.

Olivia was silent for long minutes, her uneven breathing loud in the quiet room. Loren held her, keeping up the motion of his fingers against her hair, giving her time to collect herself and refusing to rush her to satisfy his curiosity.

He focused on the motion of his hand and the feel of her in his arms. He had never comforted someone before, had never even considered doing it or what it would feel like, or even how one went about it. It seemed to come naturally to him where Olivia was concerned. He knew to hold her like this, to keep her close but give her space, room to breathe. He knew not to rush her, and to let her set her own pace. If she needed it, he would sit like this with her all night, never moving and never speaking, just giving her comfort and expecting nothing in return.

It fascinated him.

Olivia sighed and shifted, resting her cheek against his chest again. "Archangel questioned me about Daniel. I didn't understand any of what had happened until they explained what he had become, and even then it had been difficult for me to believe."

Understandable. She was a scientist. A doctor. She had sought a medical explanation for her brother's behaviour and Archangel had given her one that must have sounded crazy to her.

"What made you believe?" He looked down at her and she frowned and brushed her fingers over the scars on her wrist.

"They had a vampire in captivity. They showed her to me and I saw her fangs and her red eyes with their strange elliptical pupils, and... she looked like Daniel had." She paused and closed her eyes. "After that, Archangel told me that there were other creatures out there, and that they needed more staff to research them. They told me I could help."

She drew out of his arms and looked up into his eyes, her dark ones lined with tears.

"I signed up because I wanted to promote a better relationship between the fae and demons and mankind." She wiped the last of her tears away.

"You are very noble, Olivia." He brushed his knuckles across her flushed cheek, staring deep into her eyes. "There are few humans in this world who could live through what you have and still seek to help the demon and fae species. I admire your compassion."

She had been through a lot though, not just what had happened with her brother but what had happened to cause the other scar on her arm and the deeper one on her heart. An event that had made her heart fragile and made her fiercely protect it. He could see now that she would never give it to him, even when he had begun to desire it.

"Loren?" Her eyes flickered with nerves that he could feel in her, but there was determination and other emotions flowing through the connection between them too. What was it she desired to ask, but feared he wouldn't answer?

"Yes, Olivia?"

She glanced down at her hands, frowned, and then raised her gaze back to his. "You mentioned that elves were a forefather of vampires... did you mean... did vampires stem from elves?"

He nodded. "Long ago, our species divided. A faction of elves had turned dark, losing all good and becoming tainted."

"How?" She snuggled closer and her breasts pressed against his chest.

He bit back a groan and commanded his body not to respond. His cock twitched regardless, ignoring his order. He ground his teeth and focused on what Olivia was asking, using the distasteful topic of conversation to extinguish his desire.

"Elves can survive on blood alone for extended periods, but—"

"You mean you can eat too?" Olivia jerked back, her eyes wide and filled with fascination that he could feel in her.

Loren felt fascinated too. He had never had a female interrupt him as often as Olivia did. In his world, she would have been punished severely several times already. He smiled to himself. The council weren't going to know what to make of her and her treatment of him, her disregard for his position as a prince and ruler of a kingdom, when they met her.

His smile dropped from his face. They would never meet her. He had to stop thinking that there was a future for them, that this would somehow end in the way he wanted it to, with her forever in his arms as she was now.

He nodded. "Elves require food for sustenance. We eat mostly fruits and vegetables though, nourishing foods. Blood gives us strength and the energy we need to boost our abilities, such as healing and our psychic capabilities."

"Wow. I figured you were like vampires and just survived on blood."

He smiled at the twinkle in her eye, the one that told him she was cataloguing everything he said, filing it away in her mind. He had no doubt that she would be writing it down later. The council would be angry with him if they discovered he was giving knowledge on their species to a female aligned with demon hunters, but she had asked him a question and he could see in her eyes and feel in her heart that she needed to know the answers. She needed to know how vampires came to be, and how his species now differed from them.

"Elves can survive on blood for extended periods if absolutely necessary, but it is dangerous. It is very easy for us to feel the pull of darkness if we rely on blood too much. We only use it sparingly now, and it is because of the vampires." Loren stroked her cheek, using the soft feel of it beneath his fingers to ground himself and calm his emotions. He didn't want her to feel the anger and disgust he felt because of vampires, not when her brother had been one of the unfortunate ones, left to fend for himself and driven mad by what he had become. "Many millennia ago, some elves began to drink too deeply, killing hosts and surviving on blood-only diets. It changed them and we tried to find a way to undo what had happened because of their excess consumption of blood, but found we could not. As more and more of my people succumbed to this sort of bloodlust, I withdrew the untainted from the world of mortals, severing ties with those infected by darkness."

He paused and stared deep into Olivia's eyes, feeling her compassion and softer emotions flowing through the link between them. She felt sorry for him. She could feel his pain even though he had locked it deep within his heart, hoping to hide it from her and the world.

"Vampires became a separate species and with each generation, the dark took more of their talents and gave them terrible new ones. They gained the power to spread their wretched blood, poisoning mortals and turning them. But they lost many of their psychic powers, and the ability to eat food and walk in the sun."

"So elves can't make other elves?" Olivia said and he shook his head and then smiled.

"Only through procreation. Vampires can procreate with other vampires, but not with any other species, not to my knowledge at least."

"And vampires can turn mortals, and procreate with those?"

He nodded.

"Can elves only procreate with other elves?" Her voice trembled the tiniest amount, betraying the nerves he could sense in her.

She knew he would think in terms of them and whether they could make children together. Was she thinking the same way, wondering if she could bear his child? The thought that she might be gave him the courage to dare hope that he could break down her defences and make her his.

"While elves can love other species, they can only produce offspring with other elves or with their mate after the bond has been completed and their mate has become immortal."

A touch of colour climbed her cheeks and she looked down at their laps.

Loren's heart thumped against his chest. She had been thinking in terms of them.

Olivia cleared her throat. "You don't seem to like vampires."

"No, but the feeling is mutual. Vampires do not like elves, either. We view them as tainted and evil, and they harbour deep resentment towards us because they don't have the powers of their ancestors. Us."

"Understandable." She fiddled with the bandage around his broken fingers and then glanced up into his eyes again, and quietly said, "Could there have been hope for Daniel?"

Loren didn't want to pain her by answering that question truthfully but he couldn't lie to her either. He captured her hand, holding it gently in his, forging a connection between them that ran deeper than ever so she would know he was there for her and she didn't have to face her pain alone.

"Your brother was a rare case. I have no love for the vampires but they have integrated into mortal society and do not normally turn humans against their will. It was likely that a rogue vampire, one who flouts their society's rules, turned your brother. They are the worst kind of vampire, despised by their own species. Most vampires live in a civilised society, divided into classes—" he started but she interrupted again.

"I know that," she whispered and frowned down at their joined hands. "I've studied the data Archangel has collected and I know the vampire who turned my brother was considered rogue by vampire society... and that made Archangel and the vampires consider him as rogue too. It wasn't fair. If they had only given him a chance, he could have... I know I could have... if Archangel hadn't..."

He couldn't bear her pain. It burned like acid in his blood, destroying him. He clutched her hand, trying to give her the comfort she needed.

"You were not able to save your brother, but there are others you can save—"

"Have saved," she corrected and toyed with his fingers again. "It's the only reason I joined Archangel. I saw that female vampire and I wanted to help her. I wanted to find a way to… I don't know what."

"You didn't want others who could live in harmony with humans to suffer the same fate as your brother. It is a noble cause you have taken up. It speaks of your compassion. You could have turned against all fae and demon species, desiring to eradicate the vampires as an act of vengeance, embracing all that Archangel stood for… but you did not. You chose the better path… desiring to enlighten the hunters and change how Archangel operated so the many fae and demons sharing your world who mean it no harm could continue their lives in peace."

She nodded but looked uncomfortable with his praise and fell silent for long minutes before finally speaking again.

"Loren… have you met many vampires?" She sounded more uncomfortable now, more nervous about her question and how he might respond.

"I have." He stroked her palm, his focus on it so he could control the dark feelings in his heart, not wanting her to sense them.

"But you've been in your realm for thousands of years… are there vampires there too?"

"There are." And he hated that fact. "The vampires who consider themselves purebloods, those who have only born vampires in their families and no turned members, have a small army in the lands around my realm. I have had many encounters with this army known as the Preux Chevaliers as they often involve themselves in the demonomachies… the demon wars."

She looked fascinated again and he could almost see her filing away the information. "I would love to see all these realms you speak of."

Loren shook his head.

"You, dear Olivia, will not be visiting any demon realms. They are too dangerous and I do not want my—" Loren cut himself off, cursing himself for still thinking of her as his to have and hold forever, when she was never likely to become his mate.

His precious and beloved ki'ara.

Thinking of her that way only brought him pain and made him suffer, and if he felt it keenly now, it would kill him when he finally broke the bond and she left him.

He averted his gaze, trying to escape the way hers bore into him, intent and focused, as if she sought to discover the words he refused to voice and knew the way to divine his thoughts.

"Rest now, Olivia. I will make sure nothing happens to you."

He went to stand, but she caught his arm.

"Loren?"

"I will not tell anyone what you told me, if you swear not to tell anyone the information I have given you about my species." He turned back to her, sure that was what she had meant to ask him, and she shook her head.

"I... thank you for... just thank you." She leaned across and pressed a kiss to his cheek.

Loren's heart galloped and he stared beyond her, unsure what to do. Olivia lingered, her lips against his cheek, burning him and igniting a need he had been fighting from the moment he had come around to find her watching over him.

He wanted to kiss her.

"Olivia," he whispered, surprised by the gravelly dark sound of his voice.

She eased back and he fought to voice what he wanted to tell her.

She didn't give him a chance to get the words out.

She burned them and all reason away with a kiss that scorched him right down to his bones.

CHAPTER 12

Loren stared wide-eyed into the distance, the world around him blurring as Olivia's lips claimed his, her ferocity startling him. Before he could bring himself to believe this was really happening, and begin to respond, she jerked away. Her enormous brown eyes and her emotions warned that she was going to bolt, and his very soul cried out in protest. She had kissed him. She couldn't undo what she had done and he wasn't going to let her run.

He was going to kiss her.

He had her in his arms before she could blink, pulled her awkwardly against his body, and claimed her mouth. She resisted at first and then she was kissing him again, her lips clashing desperately with his, driven by the same need that echoed within him. He groaned and deepened the kiss, tangling his tongue with hers and tasting her. Sweet, intoxicating, Olivia.

Her hands pressed against his bare chest, burning his flesh, and her kiss branded her name on his heart, an indelible mark that he would bear forever.

She owned it now.

He was a slave to her, lost in the pleasure of their kiss and how incredible it felt. It overwhelmed him, bringing forth emotions so intense that he shook from them, barely able to control himself. He needed her now, needed to satisfy his soul-deep hunger to claim her as his female and to give her pleasure the likes of which she had never known. He wanted to make her belong to him, steal the heart she guarded so well, shake her to her very foundations as she stripped him down to his.

Olivia moaned, the sound bliss to his ears, guiding him and telling him that she enjoyed the fierce way he kissed her, mastering her mouth and giving her no quarter.

He hadn't kissed in over four thousand years, but he could remember the times he had been with a female, and it hadn't felt like this. Olivia created feelings in him that were beyond powerful, emotions that detonated and rocked him, and that were addictive. He wanted more. He needed more.

Loren laid her down on the bed, across the white coat that she had dropped on the pale blue covers, and pressed his hands into the mattress, keeping himself off her. He feared he would lose control with her if their bodies came into contact now. He had been alone too long, and she felt too good.

"Loren," she whispered and arched towards him, her hands clutching his bare arms. She slowed their kiss, teasing him with bare sweeps of her lips across his that sent shivers through him and lightened his insides.

He couldn't take it.

He growled, the points of his ears extending, and swooped on her mouth, his kiss aggressive and hard, reclaiming her lips, designed to let her know that she was his now and he would have her.

No more dancing.

She writhed beneath him, her frantic actions bringing her body into contact with his as she clutched his biceps and raised her hips. Her thigh brushed between his legs and his fangs sharpened in response, his hunger for her spiralling ever deeper. He wanted to bite her again.

He wanted her to bite him.

He needed to complete this bond.

Loren tore away from her and breathed hard, kneeling on the bed astride her left leg.

"Loren?" she said, her soft voice edged with hunger that he wanted to satisfy.

He held his hand up and continued his struggle against his deepest desire. "A moment."

He had bitten her against her will, bonding her to him. He couldn't forcibly complete the bond, sealing it for eternity, changing her irrevocably. She would hate him for it. He had sworn to break this bond and only complete it as a last resort. He wouldn't go back on his word.

Olivia sat up and reached for him, sliding one warm hand around the nape of his neck. "Come back to me."

He read between the lines to the feelings she hid in them. She needed him to kiss her again before she changed her mind. She wanted him but she was fighting her desire, driven to push him away. Why?

She wanted him. He wanted her.

Why would she fight their mutual attraction?

Her brown eyes gained an edge that warned she was close to bolting, her fear getting the better of her. Her fingers tightened against his nape and he was powerless to resist her. She drew him back to her, her lips seizing his, driving all reason back out of his mind. Olivia wanted this. He would give her what she needed, but no more. He wouldn't overstep the line again.

Olivia leaned back, bringing him with her, and he covered her body with his, bracing himself on his elbows above her. He kissed her harder, taking the lead again, and she writhed beneath him, rocking her body into his. He groaned and rubbed his hard length against her thigh, losing himself in thoughts of being inside her, their bodies intimately entwined, sharing a moment of bliss.

He needed that.

She moaned and he kissed along her jaw, curled the tip of his tongue around her earlobe, and then moved to her neck. He picked up her split-second tense and didn't linger at her throat, not wanting to frighten her with the thought he might bite her after everything she had told him.

He wouldn't even if she asked, because he was too far gone to control himself and if he sank his fangs into her throat and tasted her blood again, he wouldn't be able to stop himself from trying to complete their bond.

His ki'ara.

She felt good beneath him. Right. He loved the way she moved, the desperate undulations of her body that spoke to his, calling him to press against her, to give her what she needed. The feel of them skin-to-skin at last.

Loren moved back and grasped the hem of her t-shirt. Pain shot up his left arm from his broken fingers, a reminder of their condition. Olivia gasped and he gritted his teeth, cursing the weakness. He wanted nothing to interfere in this moment. Not her injuries or his.

Olivia's hand curling around his and bringing it away from her clothing and up to her lips swept away his anger. He stared at her, fascinated as she pressed light kisses over the bandage and his two broken fingers, as if her kiss alone could heal his pain. There was a beautifully solemn yet tender look in her eyes as she inspected them, kissing them from time to time, and the pain did begin to fade. His female's touch was magic, more powerful than any he commanded.

He had brought light to his people, but she had brought light to his dark world. She had given him something incredible, the wondrous bond between them that made him feel whole and gave him the strength to do what was right. He would never let her go. He would find a way to make her see that they belonged together. They were fated, destined to love each other, each born for the purpose of completing the other.

He wanted to say all this to Olivia but if he spoke these things aloud, they would scare her and she would run from him again. She wasn't ready to hear that he had fallen for her, heart and soul, and would wither and die without her now.

"You look too serious," she whispered and he shook his head, caught her hand with his good fingers, and lured her up to him.

Loren kissed her, a gentler exploration of her lips, building up the heat between them again and trying to deny his softer emotions, fearing they would colour his actions and she would sense them and bolt. He was wise to her now. She needed this to be about lust and satisfaction of carnal desires—aggressive, fierce and passionate. She needed to hide her softer feelings and deny her heart because she feared the outcome.

He was in no position to make love to her anyway.

Over four thousand years without sex meant that this first time would be about satisfying his dark need for her, to claim her body and soul, and ruin her to all other males.

He grasped the hem of her t-shirt and pulled it off over her head, breaking the kiss for only as long as it took the garment to pass between their lips. He kissed her harder, pouring out his desire and his need, letting her feel what she

did to him. She made him crazy and wild, made him feel lost in his passion
and ruled by his desire.

Loren dropped the t-shirt on the bed and went to palm her breasts. Material
greeted his hands, soft and satiny beneath his fingers. He drew back and
frowned at the garment she wore. Elf females wore corsets over their dresses.
Human females appeared to wear a smaller version of that supportive garment
beneath their clothing.

"What is this?" he said, eyeing the garment.

Olivia smiled and reached around behind her. "I'm not waiting while you
fumble with your first bra."

Fumble? He had intended to cut the unholy thing off her not fool around
with whatever held it in place on her body.

She tossed the bra aside and he groaned, his gaze drawn to the dark dusky
buds of her nipples and the creamy swells of her breasts. Touch. He went to do
just that and grimaced as his broken fingers protested. He cursed them in his
tongue and Olivia's smile widened.

She reached for the belt of her jeans and he growled. He wanted to undress
her. She shot him a frown.

"Your fingers are broken. You'll hurt yourself trying to remove them and I
want you naked against me."

Naked against her.

Loren growled low in his throat.

He might have broken fingers, but there were other methods of undressing
her at his disposal.

She was his, and that instinctual drive that told him that she belonged to
him was strong, encompassing all of her, and therefore all of her belongings,
rendering them as belonging to him also.

He mentally commanded her trainers and jeans to enter the portal to his
room and she gasped, her eyes shooting wide when she was suddenly left in
only a pair of cream satin knickers.

Loren didn't give her a chance to indulge her inner scientist and ask how he
had done such a thing. He threw another mental command at the rest of his
armour and the scales shifted over his body and disappeared into the bands
around his wrists, leaving him naked.

Olivia floundered, her mouth hanging open, eyes raking hotly over him.

His female liked what she saw. He grinned at the dark desire in her eyes,
the mark of her approval, and kissed her again. She sank back onto the bed,
taking him down with her, and he settled his weight on his elbows, shifted his
legs between hers, and groaned as their bodies came into contact.

She was hot and soft beneath him, and the feel of her thighs cradling his
hips combined with the satin stroke of her underwear over his hard length was
almost too much for him. He ground his teeth until they hurt, focusing on the
pain to dull the pleasure so he wouldn't make a fool of himself.

Olivia didn't help.

She rolled them over, landing astride him, and rubbed her core along his shaft, ripping a groan from his throat. Her hands glided over his torso and his markings flared, sensitising his flesh until even the barest caress was too much. He moaned and screwed his face up, unable to control his reactions to her touch, driving his hips against hers.

"I like these markings," she whispered, fingers tracing them, pushing him closer to the edge.

Loren clutched the bedclothes and his broken fingers sent pain burning up the nerves of his left arm. Pain. Good.

He embraced it this time, trying to conceal it from Olivia so she wouldn't know how close he was to coming just from her touching him.

Just from the hot moist feel of her against his aching shaft.

His dreams came crashing back to him, filling his head with replays of everything he had done to her in them. He wanted to take her hard as he had in his dream, when she had been on the inspection table. He wanted to see the pleasure on her face and feel it drenching the connection between them.

Olivia leaned over and swept her lips across the markings that curled around his left pectoral, eliciting another husky moan from his throat. She kissed downwards, worshipping every inch of him in a way no woman had before her.

Her lips brushed the string of symbols that curved over his hip but the feel of the caress was lost on him, his focus elsewhere. Her breasts were against his erection, resting either side of it. All he had to do was thrust. He couldn't help himself. He ground his hips, rubbing himself between her breasts. Olivia smiled wickedly, a look that plainly told him that she was going there soon, and nothing would stop her.

She teased him by lazily sweeping her fingers over the marks on his hip. "Do all elves have these?"

Loren growled at her, his fangs punching long from his gums, and his ears flattening against the sides of his head. She dared speak of other males when they were like this?

He had her on her back before she could even gasp and caged her beneath him, grinding his cock against her and clutching her wrists above her head on the pillows. She moaned and arched into him, pressing her breasts against his chest.

He growled again, dipped his head, and kissed them, sucking her right nipple into his mouth and rolling the bud with his tongue. His fangs scraped her sensitive flesh and she shuddered beneath him, a darker moan escaping her. Loren tried to ignore the hunger it sparked within him. Her pleasure wasn't permission to bite her.

Loren shifted aside and cupped her mound with his right hand, keeping his left against her wrists. He stroked her through the damp satin until she tipped her head back, frowned and worked her body against his.

"More," she uttered and he gave it to her.

He slipped his hand into her underwear and into her plush petals. So wet. She wanted him fiercely. His female needed him.

She moaned and rocked her hips, riding his fingers, rubbing her pert nub against them. He shoved her knickers down enough that he could reach lower and groaned as he probed her entrance. Her wet heat lured him and he couldn't deny his need to know the feel of her. He eased a finger into her sheath and she bucked wildly, her harsh moan loud in the room and dripping with pleasure. Her body clenched his, drawing his finger in deeper.

Loren growled.

He couldn't wait any longer.

He withdrew and she moaned, her eyes opening, and then stilled when she saw him sit back. Her eyes darkened and she shifted on the bed, calling to him like a temptress. He yanked her underwear off, covered her body with his and reclaimed her mouth with a passionate kiss that had her rocking against him in an instant.

Loren leaned on his left elbow and gripped his cock in his right hand. He teased her with it, rubbing the soft head up and down, from her sheath to her nub. Her face screwed up and she clutched his biceps again.

"Loren, please," she murmured and he gave her what she needed.

He nudged the head of his cock inside her, raised her hips off the bed with one hand and eased into her. Her body gloved his, tight and hot and wet, and he groaned as he inched in, savouring their first connection.

Olivia moaned, her fingers tightening against his arms, her face a picture of bliss as he joined them.

The bond between them deepened, entwining their bodies and souls, threatening to undo him before he had even thrust into her once. He had never felt anything like it. Every inch of him was on fire, burning at a thousand degrees. He withdrew and plunged back into her, letting her feel every inch of him, stroking her slowly and deeply. Pleasure so intense that it blinded him sparked along every nerve in his body, rippling in waves with each measured thrust he made.

Olivia grabbed him around the back of his head and dragged him down to her, kissing him hard. Her teeth clashed with his, her breathy moans drawing out his own. She gasped and moaned with each thrust of his cock into her body, quivering beneath him, her thighs trembling against his. Their hearts raced in unison, the rapid beat of Olivia's driving his, making his head spin.

"God," she uttered and he cursed too, the mind-blowing pleasure of being with his female, his Olivia, far more incredible and consuming than he had ever imagined it would be.

He could feel all of her as if they were one. The ecstasy that flowed in his veins also flowed in hers. The bliss that sent him rocketing towards his climax pushed her ever upwards towards hers too. It ruled them both, filling them with pleasure they would never find with another, and Loren knew he was ruined.

He belonged to Olivia now.

"Loren," she whispered against his lips, the sound of her sweet voice filling his mind, adding to his bliss.

He clutched her hip and drove into her, as deep as she would take him, determined to satisfy her before he found his own release. His female needed release. He could sense it in her, a dark consuming need that bordered on painful to her. He wanted to give her pleasure. He wanted Olivia to belong to him too.

His ki'ara.

He thought it as he rocked into her, giving her the pleasure she needed. She wrapped her legs around his hips, her feet pressing into his backside, guiding his thrusts as she had in his dreams, roughening them. He obeyed his sweet female, pumping her harder but withholding much of the strength he was still capable of, afraid that he would harm her in his quest to please her. The incomplete bond weakened him, but he was still far stronger than a human male, capable of breaking her if he wasn't careful.

She moaned and held on to him, her nails digging into his flesh, her lips clashing with his. He broke the kiss, pressing their foreheads and noses together, and breathed with her, his heart thundering against his chest.

"Loren." She breathed his name so sweetly, a command that he would forever obey. She was close, her body gripping his with each thrust he made, flexing around him as she sought her climax.

He drove harder, plunging deeper, tearing moans from her with each thrust. Her feet pressed him downwards each time, forcing him back inside.

She pressed her forehead to his, dug her fingers into his arms and gasped.

Olivia arched into him, her hot sheath clenching his shaft as he thrust into her, and cried out her climax. Her body throbbed around his, milking him and drawing him deeper. Her ecstasy flooded the link between them, swirling through him, pushing him over the edge.

Loren shattered a heartbeat later, jerking into her and spilling his seed in hot jets of pleasure that robbed him of his breath and had him quivering all over, every cell in his body claimed by a warm haze of bliss.

They breathed together, locked in each other's arms, linked by their bond.

Olivia's heart pounded against his chest as he lay on top of her, struggling to catch his breath. Her hands trembled against his arms, her body still quivering from her release. His was too. He didn't even have the strength to roll off her. His muscles were liquid, his bones like rubber.

"That was..." Olivia whispered, her breath skating over his face. "I think someone needs to invent a new word for what that was because they all seem quite inadequate."

Loren smiled and relaxed, bracing his weight on his elbows so he didn't crush her. His female had enjoyed it. He had given her pleasure and had satisfied her needs.

He pressed a soft kiss to the tip of her nose and then drew back and looked down at her. Crimson touched her cheeks.

"Is it always like that for you?" She looked beautifully awkward about asking that.

Loren shook his head. "Never."

"A bond thing?" A trace of wariness entered her eyes now.

He nodded.

She frowned. "What am I missing here? You knew how good this would be... did you want to make me see what I'll be missing when you break the bond?"

"No." Loren withdrew from her but kept her caged beneath him. Her frown hardened. He stroked her cheek and looked deep into her eyes, his expression resolute and serious. "I have no intention of breaking this bond, Olivia."

She stiffened beneath him. "You dare."

He shook his head. "I will not force it upon you... but I will not let you go so easily. I cannot, Olivia. I will fight to make you see that we were meant for each other. We were born to be together. I will fight until I hold your heart in my hands, and I can only hope you will be gentle with the heart you now hold in yours."

CHAPTER 13

Sleeping with Loren had been a huge mistake. A monumental one. The sex had been fantastic, mind-blowing, but then he had changed the game. He had turned what should have been purely about scratching an itch into something that she couldn't think about without wanting to scream.

How dare he say those things to her with such an earnest look in his beautiful purple eyes?

She held his heart? He wanted to win her? What the hell was she meant to say in response to that?

Her guard had been down and he had taken full advantage of it, ruining her resolve to keep her distance from him. She had foolishly kissed his cheek and her fight against the attraction she felt towards him had crumbled, leaving her vulnerable and stupid enough to act on her desires.

She had done her best to avoid him over the past two days. She had hidden out in a few meetings, some of which she had arranged to fill the gaps between the official ones on her schedule, but avoiding Loren had proved impossible. Whenever he came across her, he tried to speak to her, and she couldn't take it. She remembered what had happened the last time she had let a demon into her heart.

He had destroyed her world.

She couldn't let that happen again. Her bond with Loren had already done enough damage, destroying the lives of many of Archangel's staff, and she had to break it. Unless she broke the bond, Vail would be coming after her and he would end up hurting the people she knew again. She couldn't live with herself as it was.

A demon had duped her and Archangel had paid for it in blood.

Now a fae prince had forced a bond on her and Archangel had again paid in blood.

She might hold Loren's heart, but she could never give him hers. She hadn't asked for this and she couldn't deal with it either. She had to protect her heart from him. She couldn't fall for him. She couldn't give in to her desire.

Olivia stared through the microscope at the slide, but it was out of focus, and she didn't care. She kept staring at the fuzzy image of her blood, afraid to move because Loren had found her again. He had been standing just metres from her for the past five or possibly ten minutes, staring at her, waiting for her to come out of hiding.

"Olivia," he husked and a shiver tumbled down her spine, the lush baritone of his voice heating her bones. "I know you are not working. You have been avoiding me. You refuse to speak with me... why?"

He damned well knew why. He had shaken her when he had told her that she already had his heart. Another demon had said such pretty things to her once and it had all been a lie. She couldn't trust that Loren spoke the truth. She couldn't go through that pain again.

She pushed away from the white desk, turning on the stool at the same time, and hopped down. She hurried for the door.

Loren blocked her path, forming a wall of black.

Olivia tried to go around him but he was there wherever she went, getting in her way, sparking her anger and then stoking it. She kept trying to get around him, edging closer to the glass doors, convinced that if she just kept her head down, she could avoid the confrontation she could feel coming.

"Olivia," he whispered, an edge of pain in his voice now, cutting her deeply and making her want to lift her head and look at him.

She didn't want to hurt him, but she didn't want to be hurt either.

Couldn't he see that?

She couldn't stand it anymore. She ducked past him and raced for the door. He was there before she could reach it, his eyes bright purple and his ears pointed. His fangs showed between his lips when he snarled a dark oath in his own language.

He grabbed her arms, his bare hands cool against her overheating flesh, and refused to let her go when she wriggled.

Olivia felt his frustration mounting, the bond between them relaying his emotions clearer than ever. It was growing stronger. It wasn't fading at all.

"Olivia, tell me why you are avoiding me." He held her firm and she glanced up at him, her fight leaving her when she saw the hurt in his striking eyes.

She wanted to hold him whenever he looked at her like that, a wounded male, still too damned beautiful for his own good. He wanted to fight for her. He wanted her heart. He was both warrior and prince as he stood before her, dressed in tight black trousers, leather boots, and a long jacket similar to the one he had been wearing the night they had met.

A dangerous aura surrounded him, warning her not to test him because he was already at his limit. He needed her. She had wanted him to fight for her, hadn't she? Now she was running scared because it felt as though he had gone to war on her defences and she was destined to lose her heart to him.

"Your brother is not the reason," he muttered, his eyes narrowing with the frown that married his black eyebrows. "Sable said I would understand your behaviour towards me if I understood your past... but how am I to understand it if you will not let me in and tell me what happened to you?"

Sable? That matchmaking little... Olivia checked herself. Sable probably meant well, and she did know all about what had happened to Olivia, and had clearly recognised it was the reason she was afraid of Loren and their bond, and the feelings he awoke in her.

Loren eased his grip on her arms and lowered his left hand to her right forearm. He stared down at it, a glimmer of concern and hurt in his eyes. She looked there too and noticed that he had removed the bandage from his left hand, and that his fingers looked healed now. She couldn't feel any pain in them. It was strange how she had grown used to the bond and how it linked them, and had learned how to deepen the connection and use it to discern things about Loren.

Like the fact his heart was racing, spreading hurt through him that began to feel a lot like hopelessness. Was he giving up on her?

Wasn't that what she wanted?

The thought of him turning his back on her caused a physical ache in her chest and a desperate desire to catch hold of him and not let go.

Loren stroked his fingers over the white sleeve of her coat. "Who sunk his claws into your heart and made you like this, Olivia? Tell me and I will hunt and will not stop until I slay your demons. I swear it."

Olivia covered his hand with hers, holding it against her forearm. Was she really going to do this?

She lifted her gaze back to his and took a deep breath. "You swear you'll slay him?"

He nodded. "I am an exceptional hunter, and I will not allow anyone who has hurt my ki'ara to live."

She believed him. He would probably hunt the demon to the ends of the earth, or whatever realm they lived in, to take him down.

"He's already dead," she said, "But thank you for the offer."

He smiled. "Perhaps I can hunt his kin and kill them instead?"

Olivia shook her head. "I'm not the sort to blame a whole species for the actions of one individual. I also don't think it would be good for you. You have a kingdom to think about, you know?"

His expression darkened a shade. "Do not remind me. I have rather enjoyed being away from there... but that is not what we are talking about. Tell me, Olivia. I want to know you... I want to know the woman behind this coat."

He stroked the lapels of her white lab coat, a distant look in his eyes. She could read him through the connection she had to him and knew his feelings. He was enjoying being away from his kingdom because he felt free with her. He felt like the man he had been four thousand years ago before Vail had turned on him and their kind, driving him to war with him. He didn't need to say it for her to know it.

They were the same in a way.

She was enjoying being with him because he made her forget all the bad things that had happened to her, stopping her from dwelling on her past, and made her think about her future for once and her life. She had spent too many years thinking about only her work and it had become her life, who she was.

She had lost sight of the woman behind the white lab coat, but Loren had brought her back to the fore, and she felt like the woman she had been before she had joined Archangel, when her life had been full of hope and she had lived in a world filled with possibilities.

"Tell me, Olivia." The low husk of Loren's voice sent a hot shiver through her and she absently stroked his hand.

"I'm not sure what species of demon he was... I thought he was human. Maybe I was just blind or naive." She focused on his hand and how warm she felt where it rested, even though her coat formed a layer between their bodies. "I met him in a club when I was out with Sable and a few of the other hunters, and he was really... hot."

Loren growled low and she cast him an apologetic smile.

"You did ask, remember?"

He huffed. "It does not mean I have to like what I hear. I do not like the thought of you with another male, especially one you found hot."

Olivia held her smile inside when he looked himself over, blatantly wondering how she viewed him. She had thought he was sex on legs before he had given her the most incredible orgasm of her life. Beauty, brains, brawn and bloody incredible sex. The man had the whole package.

She kept her face straight and didn't say anything, but the sly smile that curled the corners of his sensual lips told her he had picked up on her feelings and knew her thoughts.

"There was some heavy petting and then we started seeing each other. He was attentive, supportive, sweet and a demon in the sack." That earned another dark growl from Loren and he muttered something about tracking and killing the male's entire race anyway. She patted his hand and he glared at her. "Don't shoot the messenger."

"Tell me I was better," he said and the wild yet vulnerable edge to his purple eyes had her going against her better judgement.

"You were better."

He looked as though he wanted to kiss her but stroked her arm instead, his gaze holding hers. She wanted to keep this conversation light so she didn't begin to dredge up the details about what had happened and didn't risk dropping her guard again, but it became impossible as she stared into his eyes, remembering everything he had said to her. He wanted her heart. He wanted to complete their bond.

A bond that would unite them forever, making her immortal.

What if she went along with that and it turned out he was just like the bastard demon and he had used her, playing her for a fool?

Eternity of living with herself and that betrayal? She didn't think she could take it. It was hard enough living with the hurt that burned inside her now and she only had to bear it for a finite number of years.

"Olivia?" Loren smoothed his palm across her cheek and she closed her eyes, unable to look at him while she was trying to get her emotions in check and back under her control, and kick her heart back into line.

"I fell in love with him, Loren... I fell for him and I thought what we had was real, and then he used everything he had learned from me and my clearance... and he infiltrated this building." She opened her eyes and stared at the purple embroidery on the breast of Loren's black jacket, replaying that terrible night. "He went on a killing spree... there was so much blood. My pager went off and I rushed to answer the call, and ran into him. I couldn't believe what I was seeing... but I knew it was my fault. I had been foolish enough to fall for a demon, and he had played me like the weak human female I was. All to infiltrate and destroy Archangel."

"And then he attacked you?" Loren closed his fingers around her forearm and she nodded.

"I tried to stop him." Her voice squeaked and she coughed to clear the tightness from her throat. "I fought him, trying to distract him so hunters would have a chance to kill him."

Loren's grip on her tightened, his voice a dark thick growl. "You tried to sacrifice yourself."

She jerked out of his grip. "What else was I supposed to do? People were dying because of my stupidity. They were all going to die because I had been stupid enough to trust a demon with my heart."

Loren reached for her but she evaded him, stumbling back a few steps, needing the space or she was going to end up giving in to her fierce need to feel Loren's arms around her and hear him say the words that would somehow fix her broken heart and make it new.

She shook her head and clenched her fists. "I can't do this, Loren. Can't you see that?"

"I can see that you were hurt, and you feel betrayed still... and you think all men are out to hurt you and use you like that."

"Not all men... just demons."

"I am not a demon, Olivia." He tried to reach for her again but she kept shaking her head and backing off, keeping the distance between them even.

"Demon... fae... the similarities are there... and I can't pretend they don't exist. You were dumped on our doorstep and I felt so attracted to you, even when I knew I shouldn't, even when I kept thinking about him and what he had done. Then this whole crazy bond thing happened because you bit me and then you demanded to come to Archangel... and then the building that had become my home is bombed." Olivia struggled to breathe as the weight of it all pressed down on her, the force of it crushing her. "And I can't stop thinking you're out to do the same to me."

Loren snarled, flashing his fangs at her. "I am not using you, Olivia. Look into my eyes and tell me you honestly believe that this is a farce and I have no feelings for you."

She couldn't, because part of her already knew that this wasn't fake. This was real for both of them, but that didn't mean it would have a happy ending.

"I did not come here to infiltrate Archangel or hurt you... or anyone you care about, Olivia, and you know that in your heart, because you know my feelings. I should not have left you alone that day, allowing Vail to attack you and your people. It was a mistake, and I wish I had the power to turn back time and undo it... but I do not." Loren stepped towards her, his black eyebrows furrowing as he raked his fingers through his hair, clawing the black-blue strands back. "I swore to keep you safe and I will do just that, and I will not let Vail hurt anyone else here at Archangel. I will do all in my power to prove myself worthy of your trust... but I will not give up now that I have decided to fight for you. You are my ki'ara... and I would do anything you commanded of me."

"Break this bond," she whispered and regretted it when she felt the pain it caused him.

He lowered his head. "Anything but that. I cannot do that. I will not do it. I cannot force you to complete the bond with me, and cannot stop you from searching for a way to break it... but I will not give up on finding a way to pierce your armour and claim your heart."

"Stop it." She turned away from him and wrapped her arms around herself, rubbing her right forearm. "I can't..."

He came up behind her and gently settled his hands on her shoulders. The weight of them comforted her and she could feel him close to her, aware of every inch of his body that hovered near to hers, feeling it so clearly that it was as if he were already against her.

He lowered his head and his cheek brushed her left ear, and his breath skated down her collar. The marks he had placed on her throat tingled and she closed her eyes.

"Olivia," he husked and she told herself to fight, to break free of his hold and keep pushing him away. She couldn't let him shatter her armour and claim her heart as his victory. She couldn't. "I am not that male. I would never hurt you like that. To hurt you would be to hurt myself."

"Because we're linked," she stated flatly.

"No." He leaned closer, bringing his body into contact with hers, and she relaxed into him, losing awareness of the world around them. "If I hurt you, it would hurt me because I have fallen under your spell. You have brought light to my dark world, Olivia. You have captured the dead heart of this prince and given it new life. I live for you... and I would gladly die for you. I—"

"Stop... please, Loren... just stop." She couldn't take it anymore. Whenever he talked like this, she melted inside, warmed by his words and the feelings that flowed through her in response. She ached to hear him speak to her of his feelings, wanted to believe they were real and not a lie, but there was always that shadow of doubt at the back of her mind and the dark memories that haunted her heart. They told her not to trust him. They told her this was too good to be real, that a gorgeous powerful man like Loren could never truly desire a workaholic weak human female like her.

Loren rubbed her arms and sighed. "You can tell me to stop all you want, Olivia, but that word will not change my feelings and it will not alter yours. It will not make me give up the fight for you... it will only make me fight harder."

She knew that. She did.

Olivia placed her hands over his on her arms and focused on the feel of him behind her, his heart steady and feelings calm, a rock that she could cling to in the storm of her conflicting emotions and desires.

Her anchor.

"Loren..." She wasn't sure what she meant to say because she wasn't sure of her feelings, not like he was. She didn't know whether to turn in his arms to kiss him or to shove him away. She didn't know whether to smash the heart he had given to her or to draw it close to her breast and cherish it. The heart of a prince. A heart he hadn't given to anyone in five thousand years and now she held it in her hands and it frightened her. It was too much, too soon. "I can't take this. Nothing can happen between us, Loren. Can't you see that?"

"No," he barked and his grip on her arms tightened, his frustration flooding the link between them, warning of his mounting anger. "It is too late for that sort of talk, Olivia. Something has already happened and there is no going back now. I will not let you."

She opened her mouth to snap at him and he twisted her in his arms and kissed her, his mouth capturing her words as a moan as bliss shivered through her again. She melted into the kiss, drowning in the connection that sizzled between them, setting alight to every nerve in her body until she buzzed from head to toe. He pulled her closer, angling his head and mastering her mouth, claiming dominance over her that thrilled her too much for her to fight it.

She kissed him back even as she told herself this wasn't happening and she had to stop it before it got out of hand again. Her body and heart weren't listening to the fragment of her mind that was telling her to break away from him, to sever the connection that had her falling into his arms and moaning as they wrapped around her, caging her against his delicious body.

Loren growled. "I want you."

Sense said to deny him that want. The rest of her moaned in agreement.

"Here," Loren husked and grabbed her backside. He lifted her feet from the ground and kept kissing her as he walked her to the long white bench table where she had been working.

"Here?" Her eyes widened when she realised what he meant. "We can't... not here. People will see."

"People will not see." His voice darkened and the blinds across the windows that lined the corridor side of the room closed, a shower of sparks exploded from the sliding glass doors, and the lights went out. "Mine now. No one will see my female but me."

Dangerous words. She was giving him completely the wrong idea by letting him do this. She had to stop him.

He kissed down her throat, nibbling persuasively, and she forgot what she was meant to be doing and dug her fingers into his thick black hair, holding him to her.

Curse him. He said she had him under her spell but it was the other way around. Her dark elf prince had some sort of black magic at his disposal and had worked it on her, enslaving her body and her heart, making reason flee her mind whenever he touched her.

She had to stop him.

"Loren." She had meant it to come out firm and resolute, not as a pleasure-drenched whisper that tore a moan from him in response and had him popping the buttons of her white coat.

She fumbled for his shoulders in the darkness, the loss of one sense heightening all her others. She gasped as she found his biceps. They were bare, his muscles tight and trembling beneath her touch as he rushed to undo her coat. A second gasp escaped her when he cheated again, using his powers to make everything under her coat disappear.

"Dreamed of having you like this," he growled against her throat, kissing it, and then drew back as he parted her coat to reveal her bare body. "You are so beautiful, my ki'ara."

"You can see in the dark?" That wasn't fair. She wanted to see him too. She wanted to rake her gaze over every perfect, delicious inch of him.

He chuckled. "My female is hungry."

Olivia realised she had been clawing his biceps. The marks on them shimmered, bright and colourful in the darkness, illuminating his face and his torso.

"Do I make them do that?" she whispered and traced them with her fingertips, following the curve over his shoulder and under his collarbones to his chest. He groaned as she tracked the lines of symbols downwards, around the shape of his pectorals to his nipples.

"You bring them out," he murmured and leaned in to kiss her throat again. Olivia gave up the fight and tipped her head back, savouring the feel of his mouth on her flesh and his tongue laving her, pressing in hard one moment and then softly the next. He nipped at her with blunt teeth again and moulded his hands around her bare breasts.

"Loren," she moaned and he shushed her.

"I will satisfy you, ki'ara. Let me savour you first."

Savouring sounded good. She loosed another groan when he thumbed her nipples, sending sparks shooting outwards and heat pooling in her belly.

"You never answered my question." She twisted the longer lengths of his hair around her fingers and guided him downwards, aching to feel his mouth on her breasts.

"Do not mention other males." The sound of his dark commanding snarl cutting through the inky black room thrilled her. He groaned as if he had picked up on her excitement and yanked her coat open, exposing her. He swooped on her left breast, pulling the nipple into his mouth and tugging hard on it, and tweaked her right nipple between his finger and thumb.

Olivia tilted her head back and lost the power of speech as he teased her, sending more fiery heat racing around her body and pooling between her thighs.

Loren released her breast and growled into it. "Princes have markings. No common male bears them."

She smiled in the darkness, aware he wanted to make a distinction between himself and every other male. He wanted her to see that she had an important and powerful male for her mate.

A prince.

Olivia admitted that it did thrill her, but not as much as that thing he was doing with his fingers. Oh. My. She rolled her eyes back in her head and groaned as he stroked her plush petals, dipping in occasionally to tease her aroused nub.

She wriggled closer to the edge of the table and hooked her legs around him, and decided two could play at his game.

She had a wicked need to satisfy her whatever he was to her.

CHAPTER 14

Olivia wrapped her fingers around Loren's hard length and he groaned and muttered something foreign under his breath. His hands shook against her and he shallowly thrust his hips, driving through the ring of her fingers. She released him and palmed the full impressive length of him as she moved her hand downwards. He bucked and groaned when her fingers curled around his balls and she gently rolled them.

"Ah, female... cannot... take it." He thrust again, his shaft rubbing her wrist, his heart beating wildly in her chest. "Too long."

She cocked an eyebrow. "What's too long?"

He groaned and didn't seem as though he was going to answer, so she brought her other hand into play, swirling her fingertips around the soft crown of his length in time with each roll of his balls.

"Since I... nothing." He grunted and jerked against her, his breath washing across her chest as he braced his hands on the table edge on either side of her thighs.

She wasn't taking that for an answer. "Loren... when were you last with a woman?"

He huffed, hips curling towards her, heart pounding. "The other night... with you."

He was evading. She gave his balls a slight squeeze and he groaned her name, his cock pulsing beneath her other hand.

"And before that?" she said and brushed her thumb over the crown, teasing his slit. He grunted and the table shook as he tensed.

"Wait... wait..." He breathed harder and she heard him swallow. "Wait."

Olivia refused and he grabbed her wrists, forcing her to stop.

"No... a second." Because he was going to climax if she didn't give him a moment to catch his breath.

"And before you slept with me?" she repeated, determined to know now that she had realised that the slightest touch had him close to coming undone.

"Centuries," he bit out and released her hands, only to claim the one around his shaft. He wrapped his hand around it, keeping it on his flesh, making her squeeze him tightly. He groaned, the sound low and guttural.

"How many?" Vague answers weren't going to satisfy her.

He muttered black things at her in his language and moved her hand on his length, forcing her to stroke him. That was cheating. She tried to take his hand away from hers and he swore again, and then sighed.

"Forty-five."

"Wow... seriously?" She wished she could see his face now. She remembered that she could and swept her free hand over his chest, causing his markings to shimmer into life. They illuminated the hard planes of his face. He was serious. "Why?"

"Wanted you," he whispered and kissed her again, and she tried not to melt at that thought. He had given up on women because he had wanted his fated female. She couldn't imagine how lonely he had been in those four thousand five hundred years, his only family at war with him for most of them.

No wonder he had changed his mind and wanted to convince her to complete their bond now rather than break it.

"Touch me," he murmured, moving her hand on his length. "Like you were before. I liked it."

He was new to it. She could tell that much. She lowered her other hand to his balls and fondled them as she stroked his hard cock, alternating between palming it and swirling her fingers around the sensitive crown. He groaned whenever she did something he really liked and she wondered what else he had never experienced with the women he had been with before.

She pushed against his chest and he growled, clearly getting the wrong idea.

"I'm not leaving, just switching tempo." She stroked her palms over the defined muscles of his torso and then traced the markings over his hips with her fingers. They shimmered in rainbow colours beneath her touch. "I love these. Like living ink."

She followed the twin lines that skirted his nest of dark curls and he moaned breathlessly, his length twitching and beckoning her.

Olivia slipped off the bench table, kneeled before him and licked the length of his cock.

Loren made a strangled noise and the lights in the room flickered. Olivia hoped that if he got wild and lost his focus, the lights weren't going to come on and expose their naughtiness to everyone in the corridor. There were voices out there sometimes, murmured conversations about broken doors and dark rooms.

She shoved away her fear, embracing only the part of it that excited her, and wrapped her lips around Loren's length. He grunted and his hands seized her shoulder and the top of her head. His fingers tangled in her hair, tugging it loose of her pins, and he tensed as she took him into her mouth and began to suck him with long, slow strokes.

"Olivia," he growled and she worked her hands into her play, using one in time with her mouth on his shaft to increase his pleasure and the other to toy with his balls again, rolling and kneading them. He grunted and began to thrust shallowly, using his hands to guide her on his length at the same time. "Gods... ki'ara... I..."

She could feel him growing thicker, his pleasure running in her veins as well as his, becoming so intense that she moaned as she licked and sucked him, enjoying it as much as he was. He pumped into her, his movements jerky and tense.

"I... Olivia," he gritted out and breathed hard, his heart pounding as he climaxed, making hers race too as she swallowed around him, licking and teasing him down. He shivered and pushed her away, and she sat back on her knees and smiled up at him, wondering what he looked like as he stared down at her. She could feel his eyes on her as he struggled to come down from his release. He growled. "Need to taste you too."

She gasped when he grabbed her and had her on the bench table in a flash. She tried to pinpoint him in the darkness but it was impossible. His hands claimed her hips, he pulled her to the edge, and then he was on his knees before her, her legs over his shoulders. She threw her head back and groaned at the first sweep of his tongue over her most sensitive flesh. He parted her with his fingers and delved deeper, swirling his tongue around her nub, sending her out of her head.

"More." She was already wound tight from pleasuring him and feeling his bliss in her veins. It wasn't going to take her long to find her own release. He spread her legs further apart and eased two fingers into her sheath, pumping her slowly as he explored her with his mouth. She leaned back and breathed hard, electricity dancing along her limbs with each sweep and lick, every swirl and thrust. "Loren."

"My female likes this." He was making the understatement of the century. She loved it. She rocked her hips against his fingers, riding them and his tongue, and tunnelled her fingers into his hair. She clung to him as he tormented her, sending her soaring higher and higher, pushing her towards the precipice.

"Close," she whispered, her heart thundering and legs quivering. He rubbed her with his fingers, each stroke making her moan. She tensed, tried to relax, and tensed again, unable to help herself. He laved and suckled her nub, thrusting his fingers into her at the same time, and her backside came off the table as wildfire heat shot through her and she climaxed.

Loren growled against her, tickling her, and withdrew his fingers. He delved lower, lapping at her, tasting her just as he had said he wanted to. Another growl rumbled through him and his markings blazed brightly, and then he had risen to his full height before her.

"Want you again."

She wasn't about to protest but he didn't give her a chance. He entered her in one swift hard stroke and grasped her hips as he pumped into her, holding her at the edge of the table. She looped her arms around his shoulders and held on to him as he took her, his thrusts deep and hard, rattling the beakers and equipment on the table.

Olivia moaned, blazing through the haze of her first climax and spiralling towards a second as he laid claim to her, his long shaft filling her up and striking deep within her. She moved her hands to his hair as he kissed her and brushed her fingers over the pointed tips of his ears.

Loren jerked hard and grunted, the sound wild and animalistic. He definitely liked that.

Olivia kissed across his jaw and licked the length of his left ear. He pumped harder, his movements frantic and rough, their combined heartbeat off the scale. Incredible pleasure blasted through her and she couldn't resist nibbling the tip of his ear. Loren snarled close to her ear, his fingertips pressing into her hips as he leaned over her, forcing her backwards.

"Want..." he muttered and she was about to ask what he wanted when he licked her throat.

She shivered, a mixture of ice and fire shooting through her veins. He wanted to bite her.

God damn her, but she wanted it too.

He must have sensed her desire for him to do it because he groaned and thrust more frantically, hips pistoning, bringing them together in a hard blissful joining. He brushed his lips down her throat to where he had bitten her before and she panicked.

"Wait... this won't..." She couldn't get the words out. Loren wanted to complete this bond and had sworn not to do it against her will. She should have trusted he meant that and that this wouldn't seal the bond between them, that it was only about blood and pleasure.

"It will not," he whispered, his thrusts slowing and lengthening, driving her out of her head as pleasure rippled through her with each leisurely stroke. "Will make it feel good this time. Give me permission, sweet ki'ara... my Olivia."

She did. She tilted her head to one side, exposing her throat to him.

He groaned as he eased his fangs into her throat and she flinched at the slight sting as they cut into her, but then he withdrew them and began to draw on her blood, and Olivia's whole world exploded in a burst of colour, feelings and the most incredible pleasure she had ever experienced.

This is what he felt when he bit her.

It awed her.

Loren sucked harder, quickening his pace again, building the pressure between them until Olivia couldn't take any more. She wanted to feel it again. She needed it. She raked her nails down his back, through his hair, and stroked his pointed ears, and he snarled into her throat and sank his fangs back into her at the same time as he thrust his cock as deep as she could take it.

Olivia shattered and only Loren's strong arms around her held her together.

His hips jerked as he drank from her, pumping his seed into her, his cock throbbing discordantly to her body. He stilled but didn't let her go. He cradled her against him, holding her off the table and keeping her on his softening length. She slowly pieced herself together and realised he had stopped drinking and was licking her neck, his strokes gentle and his feelings overflowing with affection and tenderness.

"My Olivia," he murmured softly against her throat and she stroked his black hair, too afraid and uncertain to say the words aloud.

Her Loren.

Her eternal mate.

Could she trust him with her heart?

Or would Loren succeed where the demon had failed and completely destroy her?

CHAPTER 15

Loren held the door to the club open for Olivia and she thanked him with a small smile and passed him. His gaze tracked her, his heart heavy as she moved away from him. Not just physically, but emotionally. She had been drifting away from him since their moment in her new laboratory. He had been convinced that it would bring them closer, not drive them further apart. More than ever, he felt he was going to lose his ki'ara. She would find a way to break the bond between them, he would kill Vail, and he would be truly alone.

It weighed down on him, souring his mood. Even Bleu had noticed it during their meeting with Olivia and Sable about the club they had visited the night that Olivia had met a male who had torn her heart and her body to shreds.

He curled his fingers into fists and the armour he wore beneath his mortal clothing of black jeans and a black shirt automatically covered his hands, turning his fingertips into long serrated black claws. If the demon hadn't already been dead, Loren would have been on the warpath, determined to hunt him down and butcher him for what he had done to Loren's fated female.

Bleu cast him a concerned glance as he followed Sable into the club, and held back as Loren entered behind him. His long black coat, jeans and t-shirt made him blend into the near-darkness at this end of the large warehouse-style club.

"This is not wise," Bleu said over the continual thump of loud music. If you could call it music.

The patrons of the club seemed to be enjoying the cacophony, grinding to the heavy beat on the expansive dance floor to his left, their movements stuttering in the flashing coloured lights. Other patrons watched from a balcony that ran around the rectangular room, forming another floor. Dark velvet curtains covered the spaces between the supporting steel pillars in places. Private boxes? What sort of club was this anyway?

The image of Olivia in one of those boxes with another male ran through his mind, tormenting him.

The constant flickering light and pounding volume only worsened his mood.

He knew that Bleu wasn't talking about coming to the club being a bad move. He thought bringing Olivia and Sable was unwise, but Loren refused to go anywhere without her now, even if it meant bringing her somewhere that most likely pained her.

And pained him.

He didn't want to see her here, where she had attracted the attention of another male and begun a relationship with him, not when there were many males on the prowl for a female in the area and he felt as though he was nearing the end of his relationship with her. Would she torment him as she had with Bleu, seeking the attention of the males? He couldn't bear it.

His eyes changed and his ears extended, becoming pointed beneath the wilder strands of his black hair. He growled and Bleu placed his hand on his chest.

"Perhaps you should have remained at Archangel." The lights flashing across Bleu's face changed the colour of his skin and his eyes. His irises were green though. For once, Bleu was in better control of himself than Loren was.

Loren shirked his grip and sought Olivia, needing to see her and look into her eyes. He had to know if she was planning to seek the attention of other males or whether she had moved past such low methods of torturing him.

He spotted her a short distance away, talking animatedly to Sable. Olivia was beautiful with her chestnut hair cascading around her bare shoulders, a dark purple halter-top clinging dangerously to her breasts and the flat plane of her stomach, and her delicious long legs encased in black jeans.

He had never seen her dressed so provocatively. She had been embarrassed when he had visited her apartment to collect her and had set eyes on her. Perhaps the fact that he had growled, drawing the attention of a passing pair of hunters, had made her awkward. They had stared at him, and then Olivia, and then whispered about them as they had moved on down the corridor.

They knew that Olivia had given herself to him and they knew her history, and he had wanted to kill them for daring to insult his female behind her back.

It had been difficult to stop himself, and only Olivia moving closer to him, her eyes on his face, had drawn him out of his dark rage.

She hadn't stopped being shy around him since then, and he hadn't stopped staring at her like a boy wet behind his ears who had experienced his first spark of desire for a beauty.

Olivia's dark eyes drifted across to him, the coloured lights playing across her skin, highlighting just how beautiful she was. Mine. He had never desired anyone so fiercely, so completely. He had never needed anyone as he needed her.

She caught Sable's hand and moved towards him, the crowd seeming to part for her. He couldn't take his eyes off her, transfixed by her beauty and the way she looked at him alone, even though she passed many males, and several of them turned to watch her.

Mine.

He wanted the world to know it, beginning with every male in this club.

She halted before him, a shy edge to her expression, and he breathed hard as he wrestled with himself, torn between pulling her into his arms and kissing her and keeping things on a less intimate level.

He feared that if he tried to kiss her, she would pull away from him, increasing the distance between them. He wanted her closer, and that meant he had to figure out how to show her that she could trust him and he wouldn't betray her as the other male had. He was not that male. If she gave her heart to him, he would cherish it and keep it safe forever. He would never allow anything to happen to her.

He lifted his hand, drawn to touching her cheek, knowing it would reassure her. His black armour peeled back to his wrists. Her awkwardness wasn't only because of the things that had happened between them and the events of her past. It was because she felt self-conscious without her white coat, her armour. It was because she feared that he might lose control in the club and draw attention to them.

She didn't need to fear in that respect. Demons or fae ran this club, and most of the people sharing the room with them were non-human. The staff behind the bar and clearing the tables were a mixture of demon and fae, including some rarer species.

He had spotted the blond jaguar shifter male serving drinks behind the bar. They had a unique scent. All shifters did. This one was different though, unlike any jaguar he had encountered before. He smelled not quite right. Stronger somehow. Darker.

All feline species of shape-shifters were highly territorial, but that wasn't the only reason there wouldn't be another jaguar male amongst the crowd or staff. They were rare now when once they had flourished. Demons had decimated their species, driving them back into the rainforest.

Loren was surprised to find this one living in a large urban area.

Normally, jaguars preferred to surround themselves with expansive dense green forests or wide open fields, places where they could let go of their mortal form and unleash their natural cat one. Unlike other species of shifter, cats had difficulty keeping control of their animal instincts and felt driven to transform on an almost nightly basis so they could run wild and hunt. Was this male's strength the reason he could live in such a built up area and work during the hours of darkness without losing control and revealing himself to mortals?

"Stay close," Loren said over the noise of the music and Sable tossed him a bored look. She would get herself into trouble if she ignored his warning.

He scanned the crowd and the more he looked, the less he liked the situation. Olivia and Sable were two in only a handful of humans in the club, and many of the demons and fae were already eyeing Sable with suspicion. She had left her combat gear at home, dressing in tight black leather trousers and an equally tight black t-shirt that had dragon wings in gold on the back. Like Olivia, she wore her straight black hair down, and she had no weapons on her.

Or at least none that he could see.

"Chill out. We've been here before." She tossed her hair over her shoulder, revealing a stylised tribal cross on the inside of her wrist. "I need a drink."

Olivia caught her arm before she could leave. "I think we should listen to Loren and stick together."

Sable took Olivia's hand off her arm. "I'll bring you back a beer."

Olivia looked lost and then rebounded, plastering on a smile. "She has been here quite a lot. I'm sure she'll be okay."

She didn't sound sure, or feel it. Loren moved closer, wanting to reassure her but unable to bring himself to lie.

"I count six humans total in this club," Bleu said, shattering Loren's chance of breaking it gently to Olivia.

She gasped and turned wide eyes on Bleu. "Are you serious?"

He ignored her and leaned closer to Loren. "I'm going to tap a siren."

"Be careful, and do not go too far." Loren didn't like the thought of Bleu placing himself in the firing line of sirens, but it was a good strategy and would be beneficial if Bleu succeeded.

He nodded and drifted into the crowd, standing a good four inches taller than most of the males. A string of female heads turned to follow his progress, curious murmurs rippling through the crowd. Speculation. Loren smiled at some of what he could hear. They were wondering what species he and Bleu were, and many were miles off the mark. He was definitely not an incubus, although the way Bleu prowled through the throng of people, his gaze seeking out females, was the way one of that species would behave.

Olivia sidled closer. "Did he mean tapping like for information or like a keg, but with blood in it not beer?"

He shifted his gaze down to her and she didn't look sure whether she wanted to know the answer.

Loren took hold of her bare arm. A shiver arced along his nerve endings and set them alight as his fingers closed around her soft flesh and his markings shimmered into life beneath his armour. He lured her away from the main thoroughfare and towards a quieter corner near the end of the long bar to his right that occupied nearly the entire wall opposite the dance floor.

He was sure Sable would be able to find them there, and he wanted Olivia away from the curious and sometimes heated gazes of the males skirting the edge of the dance floor. He was reaching the limit of his patience already and was calculating the outcomes of either kissing Olivia to show the males that she was mated and belonged to him or killing them all.

Olivia would not be impressed either way.

"Sirens are telepathic." He brought his mouth close to her ear so he didn't have to shout for her to hear him over the volume of the music. There were humans in the club and alerting them to the existence of non-humans would bring not only his council down on his head, but the main demonic and fae council too. "Elves gain short term use of the abilities of a blood host if they are demonic or fae."

"Bleu wants to use telepathy to listen in on everyone and see if they've heard anything about Vail?" she said and he nodded. "Fascinating. You can do this with all fae and demons?"

Loren nodded again. "We drink a small quantity of their blood and gain those abilities, but it lasts only a limited time. We have to find another of that species and take more of their blood to renew the ability."

"Why not just bag the blood? That way you'd have it on hand whenever you needed it. You could carry a package of vials around with different types of blood in it."

He shook his head this time and drew her closer when a passing male glanced her way. He growled and flashed his fangs at the young demon, whose eyes flickered turquoise in response to the act of aggression. Loren held his ground, his own eyes vivid purple, warning the demon what he was. The young male snorted and took off, preening the small horns curling behind his ears and concealed by his wild blond hair.

Loren turned back to Olivia to find her staring after the male. He snarled and she gasped, tensing beneath his fingers, and her eyes shot back to him.

"I was just wondering what he was," she snapped and he felt as though she had rekindled the dying hope in his heart with those words.

Olivia wasn't interested in the males here. She stared up at him, her brown eyes almost black in the low lighting, and he forgot what they had been talking about before the male had interrupted them.

She had painted her lips a dark shade of pink and had run black kohl around her eyes, bringing out their intricate colour, awakening every thread of gold in the rich brown. He wanted to kiss the paint from her lips and see them flushed dark pink from it.

"Loren?" she said and he shook his hungers away, aware that she was picking up his desire and it was putting her on edge.

"We can only gain abilities from blood taken from the source. It must come from a living creature."

She looked away from him, her eyes turning glassy, and he moved closer to her, concerned the jumbled feelings he could detect in her were the result of fear of the demons, or perhaps something else.

"Olivia?" he whispered and touched her cheek, and she jerked her head up, her eyes meeting his.

What was his female thinking to make her look so sorrowful?

He brushed his fingers across her cheek, his black eyebrows furrowing as he stared down into her eyes, trying to discern the source of her feelings so he could remove it and make her smile again.

Her gaze darted away from his, fixing on the bar to her left, and she quietly said, "Why don't you tap a siren too then... if it would help with the search for your brother?"

Loren frowned at her suggestion and then sighed and pulled her into his arms, gathering her close to his chest. "I have no interest in tapping a siren for blood, or anyone for that matter."

She looked up at him. "Because you're not hungry?"

An instant replay of taking Olivia's blood caused an instant hardening in his trousers and Olivia's eyes widened. He shifted his hips away from her.

"No, not because I took your blood." He smoothed his palm across her cheek, holding it, and holding her gaze too. "I do not want to drink from another female. I only want you."

"For blood?" Her voice shook, her uncertainty adding an edge to her shyness that warmed him.

She wanted reassurance. She wanted him to tell her things she had tried to stop him from voicing before. She desired to know his feelings. It was a good sign.

He shook his head. "For everything."

Her blood had revitalised him though, restoring his strength. He felt more powerful now, and more like his former self. Was it because of the bond between them? Was there something special about her blood now?

She looked at his arms around her and her air turned awkward again, and he had the feeling she was desperately trying to change the subject when she next spoke.

"What will happen if Bleu goes too far? You didn't mean that as 'don't wander off now' did you? It was a warning."

"We can permanently take on the abilities of a host if we kill them. It is dangerous because we do not know the full list of abilities a host might have. All fae and demon vary, with only a base set of abilities in each species. Each individual has differing strengths in their key abilities, and can also have abilities that others do not. If we are not careful, we could end up negating some of our own abilities with those we took from a host we had killed, and there is no way to reverse the effect." He lowered his hand from her face and thought about all the elves who had been foolish enough to go too far, and those who had become addicted to stealing the abilities of others by drinking them to death.

There were many corrupted souls in his kingdom, spreading their poisonous ways and encouraging others to follow their lead. He and the council had been trying to extinguish the practice of such a dark art for centuries with little effect. It seemed every year more of his people succumbed to an addiction to power.

"You don't kill people then?" Olivia said, her soft voice bringing him away from the darkness that awaited him back in his own world to her in this one. Her world.

Would she ever consent to leave this place and live with him? She lived for her studies and her science. She wouldn't want to leave it and her mission at Archangel behind. Perhaps he could convince her by offering to allow her to study his world.

"I have never killed a host."

"Have you had many... forget it... you must have had thousands, probably hundreds of thousands in your life." Her voice took on a bitter edge and he frowned at her, and the feelings that flooded the link between them.

She turned her profile to him and stared at the feet of the crowd to her right.

Her pain beat in his heart, telling him what she was thinking.

Loren gently cupped her cheek and brought her eyes back to him. "I am a prince, and as a youth I was given donors but I also needed to be protected. I have survived for the most part on donated blood, not from the vein. I will not lie and say I have never bitten someone. There have been times when I have had to take blood from the vein... when I have bitten humans and some other species... but only when I had to replenish my body and had no other choice."

"Like me?" She held his gaze, hers as steely as her tone had been.

He sighed. He didn't like where this was going. She was trying to drive a wedge between them again and force them apart. She was searching for a reason not to trust him and not to fall for him.

"I am sorry for what I did to you, Olivia. I was sick and weak from blood loss, and I had little control over myself. It is no excuse for my actions though, and I wish you would see how sorry I am that I hurt you." He lowered his hand from her face and turned away, pressing his back against the bar top and resting his elbows on it as he stared out into the crowd, searching for Bleu.

Olivia's gaze burned into the side of his face.

Males flicked glances at her as they passed, running daring eyes down the length of her body and lingering in places they shouldn't.

He clenched his fists, his fingers becoming claws again, and gave up trying to keep himself in check. These males needed to learn whose female they dared to look at. They would learn not to gaze upon his ki'ara.

His eyes changed, his ears altered to their normal appearance, and his fangs lengthened. He shirked the mortal clothing Bleu had given him, revealing his armour beneath. The males looked at him then rather than Olivia, their gazes losing the dark taint of desire and picking up one of aggression.

Whispers went through the club and before long, almost everyone had glanced at him at least once.

"What are you doing?" Olivia whispered and tugged on his arm.

He didn't look at her.

He grabbed her around the waist as he mentally commanded his armour to complete itself, forming his helm that swept back into jagged spikes on top of his head, dragged her against his body, and kissed her.

She wriggled against him at first, her hands pushing at his chest, and then she yielded, going soft in his arms and lifting her hands to grasp his shoulders, clutching him so hard that he felt it through the black scales of his armour. The murmurs running through the crowd grew in volume.

Mad elf prince.

That one had him growling against his female's lips.

Others hit the right mark.

Not the mad elf prince.

The sane one.

Someone dared to grab his shoulder and he turned on them with a vicious snarl, and then froze when he saw it was Bleu who gripped him. His second in command scowled at him.

"And you had the audacity to warn me not to go too far?" he said in their language.

Loren looked down at Olivia as she panted in his arms, and then beyond her to Sable who stood in a puddle of glass and liquid with a shocked look on her face and her empty hands held in front of her, and then around him.

Bleu was right, and he had gone too far, and it hadn't stopped the males from staring at his sweet Olivia.

Darkness curled through him, rage burning up his blood like an inferno, and he unleashed a roar in their direction.

"Newly mated?" A male voice came from behind him, calm and cool, not a trace of fear coming from his scent.

Loren scowled over at the owner of the voice.

The male jaguar shifter set a shot glass down on the black bar top and grinned to reveal short fangs. "On the house. You need it."

Loren drew in a deep breath to stop himself from killing the male and sent his helmet away, keeping the rest of his armour in place. He released Olivia and lifted the proffered drink to his nose, and sniffed. It burned all the way down to his lungs.

"What is this?" he said with a frown and the male scrubbed a hand over dirty blond tousled hair, his bright golden eyes filled with amusement. The colourful club lights flashed over him, changing his white shirt to match each hue.

"Hellfire," the male said with another grin and winked at him. "The only known cure for the bitch of a bond."

This male didn't seem to place much importance on a sacred bond and it irked Loren. An eternal mate was something to seek out and cherish.

"I am expected to drink this?" Loren raised an eyebrow at the black liquid in the small glass.

"It would be rude not to drink it and it will stop you from scaring customers away from my club." The jaguar's expression turned serious.

Bleu's black blade was against his throat a heartbeat later and Bleu was growling at the male. "You seek to poison my prince?"

Several males of different species melted out of the crowd behind Loren, triggering his senses to high alert. They formed a loose crescent around Bleu and Loren. Come to protect their boss, presumably. The jaguar wielded more power than Loren had given him credit for. Loren calmly placed the glass down on the bar and pushed it across to the jaguar male.

"So you are an elf prince then?" The jaguar casually placed two fingers against the razor-sharp edge of Bleu's sword and eased it away from his throat. The heavy scent of his blood filled the air around them and he placed his fingers into his mouth and sucked thoughtfully. He pulled them out with a pop and quirked both sandy eyebrows. "Not the crazy one, I hope."

Loren lost his patience again. "I remind you that is my brother you speak of in such a foul, disrespectful way. I am in no mood for this. Tell me what you know of Vail, or you will have no customers in need of service. I will kill them all."

Olivia tensed and he thought she would say something, but she remained mute beside him.

The jaguar waved around him and Loren sensed the gathered males backing away and blending into the crowd. He pushed the shot glass back across the tacky bar top to Loren. "You really need to drink this. It will take the edge off your temper if nothing else. Drink enough and you won't even remember that collar around your neck."

"I do not desire a cure for my predicament." Loren pushed it away again.

"I'll take it." Sable leaped in before he could stop her, grabbed the glass and drank it down in one go. She gasped and her eyes watered, and then she was coughing and smashing her fists against the bar top.

"Poison," Bleu muttered and was beside Sable in an instant, one arm around her and the other clearing her black hair from her face as she wheezed. "You dare poison the female."

"Human?" The jaguar glanced at Olivia, his voice weak. Loren snarled at him for daring to look at his female, grabbed the collar of his white shirt, and dragged him over the bar.

He growled at the male, his face mere centimetres from his and his black claws shredding the male's shirt.

The jaguar growled back at him, the sound feral and strange, and his fangs lengthened. Fur rippled over his body.

"Water," the male spat out.

He wanted water? Loren frowned, confused by his request considering his predicament.

"Water!" Olivia called out and one of the female bartenders rushed over to her with a glass. She helped Sable drink the liquid down, Bleu holding her steady in his arms.

Loren released the male shifter.

The jaguar backed off beyond arm's reach and straightened out his ruined shirt. "You need to leash that temper if you want to stay in this club."

"Do not look at my female then." Loren was trying to keep a 'leash' on his temper but it was hard when there were so many males in the club and he viewed all of them as a threat.

"Noted." The jaguar poured another shot of Hellfire and drank it down, following it with a second one.

Sable finally stopped choking but her eyes still watered, her face flushed red.

"You okay?" Olivia said and she nodded and then seemed to realise that Bleu was holding her.

Sable jerked out of his arms and buried her face in her hands. When she emerged, the dark mess her tears had created under her eyes was gone and she made a strange awed-sounding noise. "That was some drink. Can I have another?"

Olivia gave her an unimpressed look. "No."

Bleu muttered something and returned to Loren. "I couldn't find a siren."

The jaguar male shook his head. "You won't. Not around here. Too many nymphs. Those ladies hate them. The males mess with their mojo. I think they cancel out each other or some crazy shit like it."

Bleu gave him a disinterested look but Loren could see that his second in command was already trying to figure out the best way to tap the shifter for information. They hadn't gotten off to a good start but Loren would find a way to smooth over the rough beginning and convince the jaguar to talk more about his club and those who frequented it.

"Bathroom," Olivia shouted just as the music faded to change songs and everyone nearby looked at her. A blush burned up her cheeks and she grabbed Sable and rushed away from him.

"Interesting female you have there." The jaguar male stripped off his ruined shirt.

Loren was thankful that the male had waited until Olivia was out of sight before revealing his muscular bare chest. Scars slashed across his golden skin. Claw marks. He had fought a lot in his years. It was impossible for Loren to tell his age from his appearance though. Most shifter species could easily live to over a thousand years old without appearing beyond forty in mortal terms.

"Are all elves as aggressive when it comes to protecting their females?"

Loren nodded. The jaguar didn't need to know that part of Loren's aggression was because his bond with Olivia was incomplete. Until he convinced her to seal their bond, finalising it, he would be permanently on edge and convinced that all males were attempting to steal her from him.

He had heard rumours once, when leading a regiment of his army, that it was extremely rare but possible for a female to have two males as her fated ones, and that she could bear an incomplete bond with both until she completed it with one of them, at which point the bond to the other would shatter. He had never seen or heard any solid evidence to prove it was nothing more than the idle talk of marching soldiers trying to wind each other up, but the thought that Olivia might have another potential male in this crowd sent a shiver through him and chilled his blood, and he wanted her back with him.

The jaguar opened two slender brown bottles of something and set them down on the bar top in front of Loren, and then began mixing something in two glasses.

"Name's Kyter." He poured several different liquids into the two glasses and then tossed ice in with the mix, and glanced up at Loren. "I take it you came here looking for your brother?"

Loren nodded. "Vail. His name is Vail, and it would be wise you contact me should you see him. He is extremely dangerous. He may have a female with him, a dark witch known as Kordula."

"We get a few witches in here and it can be hard to get a bead on them because of their spells, but I'll keep an eye out. You got a number we can contact you on if your guy comes walking into the joint?" Kyter poured the mixes into a tall metal container, plugged the end with one of the glasses and shook it.

"Olivia will have a number for you." Loren hoped Olivia didn't return while he was mixing the drink. The action of shaking the contraption in his hands showed his muscles off and was drawing attention from several females lining the bar.

Kyter didn't seem to notice them. He set the metal container down, cracked the glass off the end, and poured the mixed liquid out into two clean elegant glasses with long stems and a wide curved bowl.

The female bartender came over and handed a fresh shirt to the jaguar and he teasingly flexed his muscles, earning a roll of her eyes but gaining an eruption of giggles from the females waiting at the bar.

Kyter put the shirt on and buttoned it. Loren's gaze followed the female bartender and then settled on the women at the bar. Did the jaguar male like the attention from all the women?

His earlier words about bonds left Loren feeling that he was a devoted bachelor like Bleu, determined to avoid finding his mate.

A prickle of awareness ran down Loren's spine and a blast of anger followed it. He shifted his gaze away from the females at the bar, to the point behind them where Olivia stood staring at him.

"Busted," Kyter muttered and Loren glared at him.

He held his hand out to Olivia. She came to him, leading the way with Sable ambling along behind her, but didn't take his hand. She sat on the stool beside him and settled against the bar, her profile to him. Kyter pushed the glass of coloured liquid to her and then slid one over to Sable when she finally reached the bar.

Loren barely leashed the growl that rumbled through his chest.

Bleu moved, grabbed one of the bottles of alcohol in front of them, and took a swig from it, and then another. Was Bleu irritated by the attention Kyter showed Sable?

Loren was more than irritated by the attention the male jaguar showed to Olivia.

But Olivia was annoyed with Loren too. He had been looking at those females and she had seen him, and she thought he was attracted to them. He could feel it in her.

What could he do to show Olivia that she was the only female he desired?

Being in the club with her, where she had been with that other male, a male who had hurt her and made it hard for her to trust another, and seeing so many other men looking at her was driving him crazy. He wanted to erase the demon from her heart and wanted to stamp his mark on her in front of all these males.

It was becoming impossible to resist touching her, even though he knew that she was still fragile and was still intent on fighting him, and that things were still precarious between them.

He hadn't won her yet and this evening had made him feel he wasn't even close to achieving the victory he fiercely desired.

Perhaps Kyter was right, and Bleu had chosen the best recourse.

He needed to dull the edge of his temper. If he were lucky, it would dampen his need for Olivia at the same time.

Loren picked up the bottle of beer, brought it to his lips and drank it down in one go.

CHAPTER 16

Olivia wasn't sure what happened. One moment Loren was standing beside her and the next he was on his knees, growling dark things in his language. She looked past him to Bleu, who stood frozen with his beer in one hand and his eyes locked on Loren.

"Holy fuck." Bleu awkwardly slammed his bottle down on the bar. It rocked and then fell, spilling the contents.

The nice man behind the bar swore too.

Loren's ears went very pointy and just as Bleu stooped to help him up, he shot to his feet and shoved his hand into Bleu's face, sending him flying backwards into an unsuspecting group of people. The two males pushed their females behind them, their eyes flashing red at the same time. Vampires.

The blond male in the group shoved Bleu aside and bared his fangs at her. A corona of gold fire and blue ice edged his crimson irises and elliptical pupils.

Olivia stared into his eyes, lost in the strange sensation of falling and the growing haziness that swept through her, heating her from head to toe.

A feral growl shattered the hold the male had on her and she shook her head, trying to recall where she was and what was happening.

Loren stood before her, his gaze locked on the blond male. A vampire or something else?

The two females had moved out from behind the males, their dark gazes narrowed on Loren and her. The one closest to the brunet male muttered something about taking Loren down with a kiss.

Succubus.

Olivia growled now. No succubus bitch was going to sink her claws into Loren when she was around.

Bleu got to his feet and faced the vampire males, his black blade at the ready. The males stared at him for long tense seconds and then flashed their fangs and moved on, guiding their females away.

"Loren." Olivia reached out to touch his arm and he whirled to face her, his fangs enormous as he growled and knocked her hand away.

He said something she didn't understand, grabbed her cocktail and drank it in one go. He staggered forwards and dropped the glass, and she saw Bleu behind him, his hand on Loren's arm, as if he had tried to reach for the glass. It smashed at her feet and she leaped back, bumping into a huge man who caught her and tossed her a wicked grin.

That did it.

Loren erupted, launching himself at the immense male and shoving her towards Sable. Sable caught her and they banged into the other women sitting at the bar. Olivia pushed out of Sable's arms and tried to grab Loren before he could attack the man, but she wasn't quick enough and neither was Bleu. Loren slammed a right hook into the man's face and followed it with a left uppercut.

The dark-haired man snarled, all of his teeth sharpened and ram-like horns curled from behind his ears. He huffed and smoke curled from his nostrils and she swore he grew a few inches.

The man from behind the bar leaped over it and shot his hands underneath Loren's arms, hooked them over his shoulders and pulled him back. Bad move. He had left Loren completely exposed to the demon.

Olivia rushed forwards to intervene but she was too slow again. Something collided with her cheek, the taste of blood filled her mouth, pain stabbed like a million hot needles across her skull and the room faded to black.

Cool.

Warm.

Hot.

Her cheek was hot. Her brow was cool. Her body was warm.

Noise. Disjointed. Pain. Fragmented. Intense.

Her cheek was hotter.

"Liv?" Sable.

"Olivia?" Loren. Warm. Sweet. Violent. Loren.

"What?" she murmured, wondering what they were doing annoying her when she had been having a really good dream about Loren.

"She's coming around." Sable again. Coming around? Had she not been sleeping?

Olivia opened her eyes and frowned at the three familiar faces hovering above her, and the one vaguely familiar one.

Loren looked, different. His purple eyes lacked focus and he had a really big bruise on his cheek. The same cheek as her hurt one. His fingers pressed against that cheek and the pain faded as he touched it, caressed it. The wound on his cheek worsened. The riot in her skull quieted.

"Loren?" she whispered.

"I am here, ki'ara." He smiled at her but he didn't look happy.

"What happened?" She looked at the four people and realised she was in Loren's arms but was on a floor, in a loud flashing room.

"Turns out that Loren has never had booze before and there's a bloody good reason for it." Sable grinned when Loren and Bleu scowled at her, and then Loren's face fell and she could feel his shame flowing over her.

"You were hurt because of me... again. I am sorry, ki'ara. I do nothing but hurt you." He released her and stood, and she reached for him on instinct, afraid he would disappear again if she let him. She wrapped her hand around his ankle and held on to it, and he looked down at her but remained with his back to her.

She refused to let him go. It was coming back to her now and he wasn't solely responsible for what had happened this time, just as he hadn't been solely responsible for all the other times.

She had been the one who had acted like a child when she had seen him looking at those other women. She had been so jealous and angry, and they had been so beautiful. She had felt that he hadn't been interested in them. There had been a marked difference in the constant quiet flow of feelings that came through the link between them when he had gone from looking at them to looking at her. She hadn't been able to get it through to her heart that he hadn't been lying when he had said he only wanted her though and didn't want any other female, and had ended up shunning him and drinking instead.

And he had done the same.

If she had known he would react as he had, she would never have pushed him. She would have done things differently.

"Loren," she said and lost her courage.

He looked back at her again and then sighed, stooped and helped her onto her feet. She closed her eyes when he gathered her into his arms and wrapped one hand around her head, holding it to his chest.

The pain was gone but she could feel it in him. He had taken it from her again and that was why he sported a bruised cheek now. Olivia drew back and swept her fingers over the dark mottled flesh.

"You didn't need to do that," she whispered.

"No, what he really didn't need to do was make a mess of my joint." The man from behind the bar sounded as pissed as hell and she looked back at him and then around the busy club.

Oh. My. Loren hadn't frightened away all of the patrons but he had done a rather nice job of rearranging everything within a few metres radius. Broken barstools littered the area around her and there was a huge dent in the black bar top that looked as though Loren had tried to drive the demon's head through the thick wood, and had succeeded.

She looked for the demon and found him sitting on the floor a few metres away to her left, leaning against the black wall. The female from the bar tended to the wounds Olivia could see beyond the slashes in his black t-shirt. Olivia looked back at Loren.

He diverted his gaze to the floor off to his left. It still lacked focus and he didn't seem completely stable on his feet. Because of the alcohol? He had never tasted it before.

"Bleu." Olivia turned a scowl on him. "I thought it was your duty to protect your prince? You knew what would happen if he drank, didn't you?"

He looked sheepish and raked his fingers through his overlong black hair, confirming her suspicions.

She still wasn't sure what had happened. She looked back at Loren, staring up at his handsome face until he finally brought his eyes back to her.

"How come the beer made you crazy and not Bleu?" She touched his cheek again and he flinched. She gentled her touch, lightly caressing the bruising.

"I have had no exposure to it." He didn't look as though he was going to elaborate.

Olivia looked back at Bleu.

"It is something we have to become accustomed to slowly because of our metabolism. It took me many years to handle more than a sip," Bleu said and Olivia pieced the rest together for herself.

Loren had drunk a whole bottle of beer and then the remains of her rather potent cocktail. It explained the unfocused look in his eyes and his lack of balance, and also his earlier outburst.

"You're drunk," she stated it in a voice that left him no room to argue.

Loren shrugged and smiled, and it hit her straight in the middle of her chest and made her heart miss a beat. The twittering of females drew her attention away from him and she glared daggers at them all. They scurried into the crowd and Olivia grabbed one of the remaining barstools, set it down where Loren had been standing before getting instantly drunk, and manoeuvred him onto it.

He was still almost as tall as she was.

"Idiot," she muttered and smoothed his black hair back. He had a few nasty cuts in his hairline that were bleeding and his lip was split too. Someone needed to take care of him, and her heart said to let it be her.

Loren parted his knees and she didn't resist him when he claimed her waist and pulled her closer. His purple gaze turned hooded, focused on her lips. He leaned towards her and she pressed her hands against his chest.

"No. I'm not kissing you when you're drunk." It seemed like a reasonable excuse.

Sable arched an eyebrow at her. "So you have been kissing him before tonight then?"

A fierce blush surged up Olivia's cheeks but she ignored it and continued checking Loren over. The demon seemed to have come off worse than he had, but she couldn't see the rest of his body. His armour hid it from her eyes and she wasn't going to ask him to let her see his chest because the irritating women hadn't gone very far and he was liable to do something stupid when under the influence of the booze. The thought of other women seeing him in all his glory had her squeezing his shoulders and glaring at him.

His black eyebrows rose and a confused edge entered his eyes. Now he thought she was mad at him. That probably wasn't a bad thing.

He tried to kiss her again.

"Loren!" She pushed him back and Bleu stepped in to help her. He shoved Loren a little too hard, or Loren was more drunk than they had thought, because he ended up falling off the stool and landing in a heap in the broken glass and spilled drinks.

Bleu growled something dark in their language, picked Loren up and set him back down again. Bleu's black armour peeled away from his arm and she gasped when he turned his wrist towards him and sank his fangs into it. He released his wrist, his lips and fangs bloodied, and shoved it against Loren's mouth.

Loren tried to get away from it but Bleu held firm, forcing it past his lips. When it became clear that Loren was going to refuse to drink, Bleu snarled at him, grabbed the nape of his neck and tipped his head back. Blood dripped down into Loren's mouth. His eyes shot wide, the edges of his purple irises flashed brightly, and his torso violently arched forwards.

Bleu snatched his hand back and licked the puncture wounds. "Keep an eye on him."

Before she could ask where he was going, Bleu disappeared. Olivia stared at Loren, her heart racing in her chest as he breathed hard, leaning backwards over the bar with his wide eyes locked on the grotty ceiling.

"Never seen that before," the man from behind the bar said and scrubbed his dirty blond hair. "Are they, uh, involved?"

Olivia shook her head.

He shrugged, leaned forwards and peered down at Loren. His heart still rushed, driving hers wild too. What had Bleu done to him?

Finally, Loren blinked, sat up and looked around him in a way that left her feeling he wasn't sure where he was or how he had gotten there. His eyes eventually fell on her, he groaned and buried his head in his hands.

"Loren, are you okay?" She rubbed his back and he shook his head. "Do you feel sick?"

He shook his head again and she caught a single muffled word. "Hangover."

Bleu reappeared holding a small elegant blue glass vial. Loren lifted his head to look at him, dragging his fingers down his face.

"You might need this." Bleu held the vial out to him and Loren slowly reached for it, took it, and popped the leaf-shaped lid off with his thumb.

He drank it before she could ask what it was and crushed the bottle in his fist.

"Feeling better?" Bleu said and Loren nodded.

"What did you do to him?" Olivia couldn't hold her tongue any longer. She kept rubbing Loren's back, the pain ebbing and flowing through him calling her to action and her heart wanting to soothe him.

Bleu shrugged. "Kick started his body into healing. The medicine was for the hangover."

Olivia gaped. It made perfect sense. Loren used blood to replenish damaged cells and heal himself. Bleu giving him blood had triggered that instinct in Loren's body, forcing it into healing mode not just because of the injuries he had picked up in the fight, but because of the damage the alcohol would have done to his organs. Loren's heightened healing ability had dealt with the effects the alcohol had on him, pushing him from drunk to sober in a matter of seconds.

Why hadn't she thought of that?

Her shoulders sagged.

Bleu must have noticed it because he offered her a rare smile. "You'll remember it for next time."

Loren groaned.

"No next time." He looked around him at the damage and groaned again, pinching the bridge of his nose. "Olivia?"

"Yes?" She moved closer to him in case he was feeling ill after all and needed her. He looked up into her eyes, his striking purple ones filled with a mixture of pain, embarrassment and something else she didn't want to name.

"Never let me drink again."

She nodded before she realised what she was doing and the way he smiled at her melted her heart. She hadn't meant it as a sign that she intended to stay with him, but he had taken it as just that.

"You're paying for this mess."

Loren looked away from her to the blond man who she was beginning to suspect owned the club. He had a feral look about him and was only a couple of inches shorter than Bleu, but he was broader built, and had rich golden skin and equally golden eyes. Her inner scientist shoved to the surface, demanding she ask him what he was because he definitely wasn't human.

"Agreed, Kyter. I will have funds sent to you." Loren raked his black hair back again and his purple gaze scanned the club. "I do not suppose anyone here will talk to me now about my brother."

Kyter laughed. "You'd be surprised. I think they developed a healthy respect for you."

Loren didn't look so sure. "I think they believe me to be my brother."

Olivia leaned in and rested her head on Loren's shoulder, unable to resist her need to comfort him and reassure him that he was nothing like his brother. Their bond wasn't turning him crazy. It was just making him possessive, and protective, and it was doing the same to her. He stiffened and then relaxed when she ran her right hand down the length of his right arm and settled it over his.

"They might talk to Bleu," she offered.

"Bleu, take Sable and see what you can find out." Loren sounded far more like his usual self, the commanding edge back in his voice. Bleu pressed his hand to his chest, motioned to Sable, and led her away. Loren looked at the man called Kyter. "I have seen cameras around the Archangel facility. Do you have cameras like those?"

Kyter's mouth fell open, he leaned closer, and then whispered, "You're with Archangel?"

Olivia nodded.

Kyter spat out a black curse and rubbed the back of his neck, tossing a wary look around the room.

"Best you keep that under wraps. We get plenty in here who have a problem with you people," he said to Olivia and then slapped Loren on the shoulder. "Man, fate really dealt you a bum hand."

"Hey," Olivia barked and Loren growled.

"That is my female you speak about. Watch your tongue, before I remove it." Loren's arm shot around her and he pulled her close to him, his eyes dark and locked on Kyter.

"Just saying." Kyter held his hands up and then smiled, flashing short fangs.

What was he?

Olivia was itching to know. He couldn't be a vampire because he was far too tanned, and she didn't think Loren would associate with vampires anyway.

He wasn't a demon, because she hadn't spotted any small horn protrusions behind his ears when he had tunnelled his fingers through his hair. Some species of demon could control their appearance, making themselves human to the untrained eye, but others couldn't completely conceal their small horns and their fangs and their nails permanently resembled short dark claws.

She had read that young demons found it impossible to hide their horns as it was an ability that came with age when they matured. Then there was the older generation demons. They didn't hide their horns on principle. They were proud of them and found it shameful to conceal them in order to blend in with mortals.

Kyter didn't have dark claws either.

He was something else.

A fae?

Archangel had labelled everything without horns and a tendency to shift into a truly demonic appearance that included wings, and breathing fire in some varieties of demon, as fae. Sirens were in that genus, so were elves. There were around fifty other creatures in it too, including a large number of shape-shifter breeds.

"Why is your female staring at me?" Kyter said and she grimaced. Was he stupid or what?

Loren's top lip curled back off his fangs and he aimed a growl at her. Olivia thanked Kyter with a glare that promised he would be getting a visit from a hunter if he kept annoying Loren.

"I was wondering what you were so I knew how to dissect you." She smiled sweetly at him.

"You hunters and your big talk." Kyter grinned at her and picked at his nails.

"I'm not a hunter," Olivia said, her own smile wicked as his fell away and he looked at her. "I'm one of the doctors... I'm sure you've heard the stories. The ones the hunters hand your kind over to."

He paled and looked to Loren for confirmation. Loren nodded and his arm around her waist tightened, drawing her closer. He was enjoying watching Kyter dream up horrible images in his head and she had to admit that she was too.

"I have camera footage," Kyter rushed out. "In the back... we record feeds from the ten cameras situated around the club. If your guy has been in here in the past week, we will have him on camera."

Bargaining. A very wise fae.

Loren nodded regally. "Show us to this footage."

"This way." Kyter jerked his chin towards the other end of the black bar top and loped away, his gait that of a predator. A rather sensual predator. The man moved as though he was on the prowl, drawing all eyes to him, but he didn't seem to notice any of the women who stared as he passed.

"What is he?" Olivia whispered it in case he was a species with heightened hearing.

Loren drew her even closer, pressing her against his side. "Jaguar."

She looked back at Kyter as he paused at the end of the bar, waiting for them. Jaguar shifter. She would kill to study him. Loren chuckled and her gaze whipped back to him.

"You have that look again." He stroked her cheek and the warmth in his eyes combined with his light caress to heat her right down to her soul. "I like that look."

"What look?"

He smiled and she melted from her feet up to her knees, her legs turning to jelly. Damn him for being irresistible. She kept trying to maintain and even create some distance between them, and he kept undoing all her hard work with just a smile or a stolen glance, or a sultry stare that scorched her and made her ache to kiss and touch him again.

"The one that I find reassuring. You look at Kyter as if he was a science experiment, not a potential lover."

She nudged Loren's shoulder. "I looked at you like that once. Things can change."

He shook his head, his smile holding. "No, my sweet ki'ara. You never looked at me like that. You have always looked at me with desire in your eyes."

She blushed and tried to look away but he wouldn't let her. He held her steady, forcing her to look into his eyes, and she felt she couldn't hide anything from him. His unwavering gaze stripped the layers of her defences away, her guard crumbling under the intense heat of it, and she couldn't do anything to stop it from happening.

He brushed his thumb across her cheek. "Sweet Olivia... your heart tells me through our bond what you refuse to voice... it speaks of your emotions... your desire when I kissed you earlier... your jealousy when you thought I looked upon those females with lustful eyes... your concern when I was drunk and injured... your relief as I say these words and you realise that I desire no one but you. I know your feelings even if you do not."

She covered his mouth with her free hand. He caught her wrist, removed her hand from his lips and pressed a kiss to it.

"You need not fear. They are not my feelings to voice. I will wait as patiently as I can for you to say what is in your heart, Olivia. I will not rush you, even when I desire to hear you tell me that I am your mate. I am not a fool." He pressed another kiss to her hand and then held it to his face, leaning into it and closing his eyes. "I want us to be together, but there are things in your heart you must come to terms with before that can happen. I understand, and all I can do is hope that somehow you will come to see that I am not like that man who hurt you and I would never betray you."

Olivia hoped for that too.

She wasn't sure yet whether she wanted to complete the bond with Loren, but she did want to be with him. She wished things could be normal between them, a human relationship, without a deadline looming over it. She wanted things to progress at a natural speed, not sweep her along like a flash flood. It made her panic whenever she thought about it.

The incomplete bond weakened Loren and there was no knowing when Vail would attack him, or her, and no telling whether Loren would survive such an attack. Vail was stronger, his bond to his female complete, and that female was a dark witch. What if they both attacked Loren?

Icy claws squeezed her heart, threatening to pierce it.

Loren wouldn't stand a chance. He might die because she had hesitated, too afraid of the past repeating to embrace a future with him. She panicked now as she stood looking down into Loren's beautiful eyes and knew he had sensed it in her when he rose to his feet.

She expected him to draw her into his embrace and hold her, but he pressed a kiss to her brow and released her instead.

"Let us speak with Kyter." He walked away from her and she ached, her legs weak again, fear and hurt combining to press down on her as she watched the distance growing between her and Loren.

He could only discern her feelings. He couldn't decipher them. He thought she was going to reject him again and was distancing himself before it could happen, not giving her a chance to voice things he believed would be hurtful.

"You look like someone just sucker-punched you." Sable came up behind her and nudged her left shoulder, and then looked beyond her to Loren. "Ah... what did he do now?"

"Nothing." Olivia dragged her gaze away from Loren as he talked with Kyter.

"So why the long face?" Sable cocked her head to one side and frowned at her. "Don't tell me you're still going in circles because of what happened before?"

Olivia jerked her chin up. "It's not that... it's... it's... that."

Her shoulders sagged and she flagged the bartender. If she was going to have a dumb heart to heart with Sable, she at least wanted another cocktail to dull the pain.

The female who had been tending to the demon came over to her. "Nice catch you have there. What'll it be?"

Olivia's lips compressed into a hard line and she slammed her palms down on the bar top, making the brunette jump. "I want one of those drinks the nice jaguar made me and your eyes off my male."

She couldn't believe she had just said that. She had never threatened a woman over a man in her past and she had done it several times tonight. She felt possessive, territorial. The bartender was right. Loren was a good catch. The best. He was gorgeous, powerful, protective, and he really cared about her. He had nursed her injuries, taking the pain into himself so she didn't have to suffer it.

Sable was grinning when she dared to look at her.

"Don't look at me like that." Olivia slumped onto the barstool Loren had occupied and rested her arms on the bar top, and her chin on her arms.

The bartender said nothing but Olivia could feel that she wanted to, just as Sable did.

Once they had paid for the cocktails and the brunette had gone away, Olivia sighed and twirled the silver umbrella in her drink, staring at the rich purple liquid. The colour of Loren's eyes and just as intoxicating.

Sable sipped her drink and then set it down. "Listen, Liv... I've known you a long time and I know what you've been through... but I also know Loren. He isn't here because he wants to hurt you. He's here because he wants to protect you. He isn't here because he wants to bring down Archangel... he's here because he wants to protect his people from a maniac. He is nothing like the demon who screwed you over."

"He's a fae," Olivia said and took a gulp of her drink. Yup. Just as intoxicating as Loren. It warmed her just as fiercely too, making her head fuzzy and heart pound.

"I'm not listening to your excuses." Sable downed her drink and slammed the glass onto the sticky bar top. She pulled Olivia up and frowned at her. "I can't believe you're going to pass up on eternity with a gorgeous, noble, immortal prince because some arse broke your heart years ago."

Olivia played with her drink again, withering under her friend's glare. Sable knew her history but that didn't mean that she knew her feelings, or her fears, or could stand there lecturing her about Loren. She didn't know what it was like to face the prospect of becoming immortal and entering into an eternal bond.

Sable took her drink from her. Olivia snatched it back and held it closer to her, scowling at her friend.

Her golden eyes turned cold and serious. "Liv, I know you're scared... and I know it's hard for you... but love isn't easy and I don't want to be sitting here with you in one week or two week's time because you found a way to break the bond. I know you'll regret it when it happens, and Loren is gone, and there's no way of getting him back. *Ever.*"

Olivia stared blankly at her drink, Sable's words sinking in and making her heart and head spin more than the potent cocktail. The chill of dread replaced the heat of it in her veins and she blinked slowly.

She hadn't really thought about it before and she didn't want to think about it now. She had grown used to Loren being around, encouraging her when she was tired and near the end of her rope, taking care of her when she was hurt, protecting her when she was scared, and standing by her through everything.

It hit her hard.

She couldn't imagine her life without him in it now.

She didn't want to imagine it.

Because she loved him.

She didn't want to go back to microwave meals at three in the morning and spending every hour in her lab because she hated being at home because it reminded her that she was alone. She didn't want Loren to leave and go back to his world.

She didn't want to break the bond.⁻

She wanted to complete it.

CHAPTER 17

Loren turned away from Bleu and Kyter when the door to the small back room of the club burst open. Olivia stood there, hands braced on the doorframe, breathing hard. The wild look in her brown eyes unsettled him and he was moving towards her before either Bleu or Kyter had even looked away from the bank of monitors they observed.

"Olivia?" Loren looked beyond her to the corridor that led back to the club, sure he would find his brother or another male after her. "What happened?"

She shook her head and fought to catch her breath, and then she was in his arms, kissing him senseless.

Loren's wide eyes slowly closed and he gathered Olivia against him, wrapping his arms around her and settling his hands in her upper and lower back. He leaned into her, bending her to his will, seizing control of her frantic aggressive kiss.

Bleu grumbled, "I have a sudden urge to kill something."

"I told you not to look. That female is throwing off pheromones that any shifter within three miles will be able to smell." Kyter chuckled. "If you're lucky, we'll find a clue as to your other elf prince's whereabouts and you can go kill him. If you're not, I'll give you a bottle of Hellfire to dull the pain in your thoroughly seared eyeballs."

Loren broke the kiss and growled at them. Olivia grabbed his hand and pulled him out into the grim dimly lit corridor.

"I can't find a way to break the bond." She rushed the words out in one stream and he frowned at her, confused by the sudden announcement and her emotions.

She had been melancholy when he had found her in the laboratory before, but she hadn't mentioned that she had failed her mission. There had been times this evening when he had felt she was keeping something from him and perhaps this was it. But she looked happy. That didn't make sense at all. Unless.

Loren held both of her hands and ventured a brave step forwards. "I am sorry my blood did not give you the key to undoing our bond. I know how much you desired to be free of me."

Olivia shook her head, her chestnut hair shifting across her bare shoulders. "I didn't finish my research."

Loren arched an eyebrow.

She gripped his hands and moved closer to him, until only a few inches separated them, and looked up into his eyes. "I can't find a way to break the bond because I don't want to break it, Loren. I want to complete it."

A shiver ran through his body, cascading over his arms and down to his toes. His markings flashed beneath his armour in response, spreading heat across his skin in a rippling wave.

He stared at her, sure he was mistaken. His heart beat steadily, a sign that hers did the same, and her emotions felt stable, showing no trace of the distress he would expect her to feel if she feared there was no way out of the bond and she still wanted it broken.

Loren still couldn't bring himself to believe what he had heard.

He shifted his hands to her face and held both of her cheeks, tilting her head back so he could peer into her eyes. He searched them but they revealed only positive feelings to him, and he couldn't detect a lie in them.

Olivia grabbed his shoulders, tiptoed and kissed him again. He groaned and couldn't help kissing her back for a handful of hard heartbeats before he got hold of himself and pushed her away again.

He had to be sure.

"Swear you are of sound mind and know what you are saying." He clutched her face, his gaze searching hers for a flicker of doubt. "You are committing to centuries together. You are talking about completing a bond and making it unbreakable, Olivia."

A touch of nerves entered her eyes and her heartbeat, and her fine eyebrows furrowed. "Are you trying to ruin the moment?"

He shook his head, meaning it with all of his heart. "No... but I must know that you understand what you are entering into."

Olivia smiled and his breath caught in his throat. She settled her hands against his chest, her soft touch burning him through his armour, causing his pulse to quicken and his blood to heat.

"I know," she whispered, sincerity and tenderness in her sweet voice. "I'm getting a future with the man I've fallen in love with."

Loren knew that it took a lot for her to say those words after everything she had been through. He drew her into his arms and kissed her, and opened the portal to his rooms in the castle at the same time. Bleu would have to handle scouring the video footage with Kyter for a sign of his brother. His second in command would understand Loren's need to leave with Olivia and complete their bond straight away, even if he would make a fuss about it later.

Olivia ran her hands over his shoulders and then his chest, causing his markings to trigger, heating his skin. She mewled and he obeyed her silent command, sending his armour away. The black scales swept over his body, cascading up his legs and torso and down his arms to the twin bands around his wrists.

She moaned then and her hands scorched him, blistering his skin and burning him with a desire to have her naked against him. He broke the kiss and hastily peeled her purple top up, pulling it off over her head and freeing her bare breasts. He groaned and tossed the garment onto the dark stone floor, and cupped her breasts, weighing each of them and thumbing her nipples.

Olivia loosed a low moan and arched into his caress, her eyes turning hooded and the connection between them speaking of her desire. She wanted him, and he ached for her, but he refused to rush this. This time when they made love, they would complete their bond, forming an eternal cycle between them, an unbreakable link.

He would take her blood and she would take his.

Loren groaned at that thought and kissed her again, devouring her mouth and aching to possess all of her. He had never been bitten before. No one had ever tasted his blood. The thought of Olivia taking it, becoming his first and his only, made him want to rush just as she did.

Olivia tangled her fingers in his hair, kissing him deeper, her soft tongue playing with his and teasing his lips. She flicked the tip over his canines and his fangs emerged, drawn out by her touch. She caressed them again, from root to pointed tip, driving him crazy with need. He wanted to bite her again, to sink his teeth into her sweet flesh and drink of her blood.

Loren swept her up into his arms, carried her to the bed in the middle of the room and kneeled on it. He laid her on the dark purple covers and kissed along her jaw to her throat, and followed the smooth column downwards, his lips brushing her flickering pulse. He growled, saliva pooling in his mouth at the thought of biting her, and forced himself to move onwards, trailing his lips over her collarbone. She arched her breasts towards him and he obeyed her again, kissing his way down to them and then swirling his tongue around her left nipple.

"Loren," she husked and he sucked the puckered bead into his mouth

She cried out and grabbed his shoulders.

He groaned at the feel of her short nails digging into his flesh, clutching her to him, speaking of her need and how her desire already had her skirting the edge of madness. He rocked his hips, thrusting his hardening shaft against her thigh, and frowned when he encountered denim and not her soft warm skin.

Loren tore himself away from her breasts and kissed down her stomach, his desire to get her naked gaining a new reason behind it as he kissed and licked her supple flesh. He wanted to taste her again.

He tugged the belt of her black jeans open and unbuttoned them as he kissed ever downwards. She lifted her backside off the bed. He gathered her jeans and underwear, and kissed the length of her long legs as he drew them both down to her ankles. She quickly toed her shoes off and Loren removed her jeans, underwear and then her stripy socks.

He sat back and raked his gaze over her. His female lay on his bed, her milky skin a delicious contrast to the rich purple covers, and her chestnut hair spilling around her bare shoulders. Her eyes lingered on him, dark with desire, passion that he stirred in her. She ran them over him, mimicking his own actions, and nibbled her kiss-blushed lips. Her cheeks coloured and her gaze darkened further. The way her teeth sank into her lip, tugging at the soft flesh, called to him.

Loren moved onto all fours and crawled up the length of his beautiful Olivia, each brush of their bodies sending a hot shiver through him. He covered her body with his, bringing them slowly into full contact, and she moaned. He swallowed the end of it in a kiss, aggressively claiming her lips and tunnelling his fingers into her hair to hold her against him. He wouldn't let her escape him. She had sworn to be his and she would be.

Forever.

Olivia skimmed her hands over his shoulders, the action stirring his markings again, their emergence heating his skin as fiercely as her touch did. She swept her fingers upwards over his shoulders to his neck and claimed the nape of it, one hand curling around it and the other raking through his hair. He groaned and kissed her harder, grinding his shaft against her core at the same time, ripping a low moan from her throat.

Her left hand claimed his shoulder and he didn't resist her when she pushed, rolling him onto his back. She straddled his hips and kissed him, her hair tickling his chest and her hands pressing into his shoulders with force that he enjoyed. He had never met a woman like Olivia. She took command when the urge struck her, unafraid to force him into submission, dominating him in a way that he found pleasurable because it spoke to him of the fierce desire she held for him, a need that echoed within him.

She kissed his lips and then his chin and along his jaw, moving downwards towards the left side of his throat. Loren's instincts kicked in, commanding he give his neck to her, exposing it for her lips, and her teeth. He wanted to feel them in his flesh even when he knew that was impossible. Olivia was not of the fae or demon breed. She had no fangs to satisfy his dark needs.

He still needed to feel her lips on his flesh though and his blood flowing into her, forming and then forging a permanent bond between them.

The black and silver metal bracelets around his wrists heated and his armour swept over his hands, turning his fingers into razor-sharp claws.

He clutched Olivia's shoulder with one hand, careful so as not to cut her, and gently pushed her away from his throat. He curled the fingers of his other hand around, leaving only his fore and middle finger extended.

His ki'ara had no fangs of her own, so he would make the marks for her, twin puncture wounds that he would proudly wear on his throat for all to see, and all would know this female had claimed him.

He brought his hand up to his throat and pressed the tips of his claws in, but Olivia caught his hand and stopped him.

Cold slithered through him and he frowned at her, fearing she had changed her mind and didn't want to complete their bond now that she knew what it entailed.

Blood.

She held his hand in both of hers and he stared up at her, afraid to speak in case he prompted her into voicing words that he didn't want to hear because they would shatter him completely.

Olivia stroked the black scales covering his left hand, her brown eyes fixed on it, her fingers trembling. What internal war was she waging as she sat astride him?

She finally lifted her eyes to his, her fine eyebrows furrowed, and spoke softly. "I want to do it."

His heart missed a beat and it took him a moment to comprehend what she was saying.

His ki'ara had no fangs of her own but she wouldn't allow that to stop her from making her mark on him. She wanted to be the one to puncture his flesh with the tips of his claws, and the look in her eyes and the way she held him firm said she would accept no argument about this matter.

Loren nodded, his fangs aching with the need to bite her too. He sat up on the bed, the action causing his erection to slide against her most intimate place and she gasped and moaned, tensing in his arms.

He needed to be inside her when they exchanged blood. He couldn't do this any other way and the dark hungry look in her eyes and the way she rocked her core against him said that she couldn't either.

He sent his armour back into the bands around his wrists and clutched her backside, drawing her closer to him. She kissed him again and circled his neck with her arms, and rocked her hips against him, sliding her moist core up and down his aching length. Loren moved her too, guiding her actions and making sure her heat stroked every inch of him, all the way to the sensitive head.

She moaned and deepened the kiss, her tongue playing with his and her fingers clawing his hair. He held her tighter, his fingertips pressing into her buttocks, and lost himself in the feel of her against him, rubbing herself along his body. He couldn't take much more but he couldn't bring himself to make her stop either. It was bliss to have her in his arms like this and to know what they were about to do.

"Loren," she murmured against his lips, the hard peaks of her breasts rasping his chest. He lifted her higher, bent his head and captured one nipple with his mouth, pulling the bud between his lips. She moaned and arched into him, and he shifted one hand to her upper back, supporting her as he licked, suckled and teased her breast. "Loren."

He dipped his other hand lower, curling under her buttocks to touch her most sensitive flesh, and she jerked and moaned, her body quivering in his arms. He circled her entrance and she arched further, pressing her backside higher, allowing him to ease his fingers into her. She groaned as they slid into her wet sheath and she flexed around him.

His shaft pulsed, aching to be inside her and feel her contracting around him, drawing him deeper into her heat. He wanted to take her hard and fast, a rough coupling that would have her crying his name in bliss and feeling all of his strength.

"Loren," she moaned again, husky and pleading, driving her hips upwards and taking his fingers deeper inside her. He couldn't take any more.

Loren released her breast and withdrew his fingers. Before she could complain, he had flipped her over onto her front before him. He rose up behind her, pressed her shoulders down into the mattress, and shoved his cock deep into her body. She gasped at the sudden intrusion and it melted into a groan as he withdrew and slid back into her, letting her feel every inch of him and how hard she made him.

How wild.

He released her shoulders and grasped her hips, holding her firm as he thrust into her, hard and fast, causing her to rock forwards with each powerful pump of his hips. She moaned and curled her hands into fists, clutching the purple covers. Her hair spilled around her shoulders as she rose onto all fours and pushed back against him, driving him deeper into her wet heat.

"Loren," she gasped and flexed around him, and he grunted at the feel of her clenching him tightly, gripping him hard as he drove into her over and over again, a slave to his dark need.

Olivia spread her knees further and sank back onto the bed, moaning each time he entered her. Loren couldn't help himself. He clutched her hips, pumping her faster and taking her harder, driven by his need to possess her. She groaned and writhed, tipping her head up and forcing herself onto him, her actions as wild and untamed as his own.

He buried one hand between her thighs and fondled her bundle of nerves, earning another high gasp and groan from her. She shuddered in his arms, breathing hard, her heart hammering in time with his. He curled his hips, raw animal need at the helm, commanding he take her harder and make her find her release in a shattering climax.

His cock thickened, semen rising to the base of his shaft, his balls tightening as he took her and she moaned and writhed before him. He squeezed her nub and she convulsed upwards as she came, throbbing around his length, drawing him into finding release with her. He pumped harder, rougher, risking using more of his strength to take her in a wild coupling that had their bodies slamming together. She moaned again and her bliss shimmered through him, pushing him closer to the edge and taking him higher.

Loren growled, his lips peeling back off his fangs, and then grunted as he shot his seed into her quivering heat, thrusting shallowly into her as he fought for breath.

Olivia moaned with each pulse of his length and their ecstasy combined, ebbing and flowing through the link, making him hazy.

He pulled out of her and she rolled onto her back, a lazy smile winding its way across her flushed face. She looked down the length of her body at him with hooded eyes that spoke of her contentment and satisfaction. His female was sated.

He was not. He still wanted her. Needed her.

She held her hand out to him, as if she had sensed that need, and he pulled her to him, bringing her to kneel before him again. She kissed him, her fingers mussing his black hair further as his sank into hers, their long lengths tangling around the chestnut waves, anchoring her to him.

Olivia broke away and gave him a wicked smile as she pushed his chest. He took the hint and moved backwards, towards the head of the bed, and sank down against the pillows there. Olivia crawled onto him, straddling his thighs, and kissed him again, slower than before. The tempo between them changed with that kiss, the edge taken off their need, bringing them both down onto a more even keel.

Loren wrapped his arms around her and savoured her kiss and her taste, his body still quivering from his climax, hot and hazy. He wasn't sure how long they remained like it, exploring each other's mouths, but the haze of his climax began to lift and he grew hard again, aching to be back inside her welcoming heat.

She drew back and stroked her fingers over his chest, causing his marks to shimmer to the surface in rainbow colours. They flushed brightly, illuminating her hands, and she looked fascinated as she caressed them, tracing some of the symbols with her fingertips.

She bent her head and kissed the marks on his left deltoid, and followed them over his shoulder to his collarbone. She paused there and his focus honed in on her until he lost awareness of the world around them.

"Loren," she whispered and he knew what she desired because he desired it too.

He withdrew his hands from her hair and called his armour to them, changing his fingers into claws. She took hold of his right hand, curled all but two of his fingers over, and stared at his throat. His heart pounded, the pace nauseating, and he breathed hard, struggling to steady himself.

"Inside you," he murmured and she nodded in agreement and rose off him.

Loren carefully curled his armoured hand around his cock and positioned it beneath her. He groaned as she took him back inside her, their combined juices from their first time making it easy for him to slide in as deep as he could go. She moaned and wriggled, ripping another groan from his throat.

"Love the feel of you inside me." Those words almost pushed him over the edge and it was hard to deny his urge to take her hard and fast again, making her feel all of him.

She rose off him and back down again a few times, slowly riding him, making him tremble. He wanted to drink from her as they made love this time. He wanted to sink his teeth into her and mark her forever.

"Olivia," he husked, voice thick and deep, dark with his desire.

She bit her lip and nodded, her brown eyes verging on black. She moved his hand to his throat and he tipped his jaw up, giving her clear access.

Olivia inhaled slowly and a flicker of concern came through the link between them, and he knew she didn't want to hurt him.

"Do it, please... I need you to do it, Olivia... now."

She pressed the points of his two claws into his skin on the left side of his throat and then pushed down. He flinched at the fiery sting as they punctured his flesh and then groaned as that heat swept through him, filling every inch of him and making him jerk his cock inside her. She moaned and clenched him, eliciting a growl from him, and pulled his claws out of his throat.

"Drink now, ki'ara," he whispered and she swallowed hard and then leaned in, her breath hot and moist on his throat.

Loren held his breath, sent his claws away and held her, guiding her towards him, refusing to let her back out now that they had come this far.

The first touch of her lips on his throat sent a shiver through him. The feel of her wrapping her mouth around the two puncture marks and clutching his shoulders turned that shiver into a fiery wave of tingles. The first pull she made on his blood obliterated them, causing wildfire heat to savagely race through his body, burning him to ashes.

Loren had been mistaken. This was bliss. This was heaven.

His ki'ara was taking him into her body, forging the unbreakable bond between them. She was giving herself to him, forever.

He would give himself to her too, and he would never let her go.

Loren swept the hair from the left side of her throat, angled his head so he could reach her, and sank his fangs into her flesh. She gasped, spilling his blood, her body contracting around his hard length. He withdrew his fangs, clutched her backside, and drank deep of her as he moved her on his shaft.

She writhed her hips, rotating them with each downwards thrust that drew him into her, driving him further out of his mind, and drank harder, sucking ferociously on his blood.

Loren's head lightened, spinning as she took his blood into her. The feel of it racing towards her as hers raced towards him was incredible and he was lost in it and in Olivia. His strength surged through him, his heartbeat levelled, and he felt the connection between them as it tied them together, unbreakable now.

They were one.

Olivia moaned, shuddering against him, her mouth working furiously to take his blood even as the flow of it slowed, his body healing the marks she had made on his flesh. The marks on hers healed too, stealing her sweet blood from his lips. He wanted more but contented himself with licking the marks, catching every last drop of her blood, as he moved her on his cock, driving slowly into her.

The feel of her soft tongue caressing his flesh made him shiver and he groaned, aching to have her drink from him again already, even when he was too weak to allow it. His body raced to absorb the blood he had taken from her, and he knew that hers was doing the same. He was part of her now, and forever. His blood would make her stronger. Immortal.

"Ki'ara," he whispered and licked her throat.

She rode him faster, her hot breath skating over his sensitised flesh, sending another achy shiver through him.

"Loren," she murmured and then kissed him again. She tasted like his blood, hot and strong, laced with magic. He groaned and deepened the kiss, laying claim to her mouth as he laid claim to her body, moving her on him and tensing his backside to drive himself into her each time she bore down on him.

"Ki'ara." He groaned as she clenched him, her body tightly gloving his, choking him in her heat.

Olivia mewled and he felt her restlessness and her frustration. He was close too, standing on the edge, unable to push either of them over it into the waiting sea of bliss below. She broke away from his lips and returned to his throat, and did something that propelled him firmly over the edge.

She sank her teeth into his neck. The healing puncture marks burned as they reopened and she moaned, her body convulsing against his as she climaxed, her pleasure blasting through him.

Loren growled and bit her again, slicing deep into her flesh and pulling hard on her blood. His own pleasure claimed him, burning up his veins and melting his bones as he pumped into her, filling her with his seed.

Olivia moaned and relaxed into him, sagging against his chest. Loren gathered her close to him, leaned back into the pillows, and gently lapped at the wounds on her throat, savouring her blood and the connection between them. He could feel all of her, every last drop of her feelings, as if she was part of him.

She released his neck and curled up against him, her head against his shoulder, her heart steady and breathing soft. Loren held her closer and pressed a kiss to her forehead.

"Your heartbeat is slower than mine," she whispered and he smiled and nuzzled her forehead with his cheek. "Does that mean we did it?"

"We did it," he said and she looked up at him, a sleepy edge to her brown eyes. His smile widened when he saw the blood on her lips. His blood.

He slid his right hand along her jaw, tilted her head back, and softly kissed the blood away. She kissed him at first and then her movements began to slow and he could feel her drifting away, their lovemaking and the change coming over her because of their completed bond combining to steal her strength.

Loren gathered her into his arms, lifted her off him, and drew back the covers on the bed. He laid her down and settled beside her, and covered them both with the purple bedclothes.

Olivia cuddled up to him, settling with her head on his chest, her breasts pressing against his ribs, and one leg hooked over his thighs. He placed his arm around her and closed his eyes, and held her as sleep claimed him too, his thoughts on protecting the female in his arms.

His ki'ara.

He was no longer alone in the world and neither was she.

They had each other now and he wouldn't allow anything to separate them. Not even his brother.

CHAPTER 18

Loren woke alone but he could sense Olivia nearby without needing to use his psychic abilities to strengthen his awareness of her. It flowed just beneath his skin now, a permanent link that would guide him to her no matter how far she travelled from him, and would drive him to go to her. He closed his eyes, enjoying how easily he could sense her presence and her emotions. She felt content and happy, and fascinated.

He rose and pushed the purple covers back, and swung his legs over the edge of the large bed. He stretched, scrubbed a hand over his black hair, shoving the longer strands back, and stood. With a simple mental command, one of the black doors of his long row of wardrobes opened. He padded across the dark stone floor to it, took down a pair of tight black trousers, and tugged them on.

Loren fastened them as he crossed the room to the tall arched doors of his apartments. The morning breeze blew in through them, the scent of blossom stronger today, signalling a period he had come to think of as summer. The long sheer blue curtains danced in the breeze and he walked through them, the soft material caressing his skin.

Olivia stood on the wide balcony that ran along the length of the main room of his apartments in the castle, her back to him and her palms pressed into the elegant dark stone balustrade. Tall columns carved with ivy leaves and animals spiralled upwards on either side of her, supporting the roof of the balcony. It wasn't a solid structure. The columns supported stone arches resembling a flying buttress on a mortal cathedral. Laced between each stone arch were fine filaments and curled around those strong threads were a plant native to this land, a creeper with heart-shaped green leaves and stunning blue flowers that were just beginning to bloom.

His mate straightened as if she had sensed him behind her and was waiting for him to speak. She would be able to feel him now, just as he could her, their bond allowing her to pinpoint his location to within a few metres.

She wore one of the rich purple sheets from the bed wrapped around her like a long dress and the early morning light caught her chestnut hair and threaded it with gold. She turned her head slightly, her beautiful dark gaze on the world stretching out below them.

Her world now.

Her kingdom.

She would be a good princess for his people, her compassion and caring nature driving her to find ways to protect them. They would adore her, just as he did.

Loren felt drawn to her as she stared out at their world, her beauty hitting him hard and stealing his breath. He didn't resist the pull of her, never would be able to, and drifted towards her, coming to stand behind her.

He wrapped his arms around her and an incredible sense of bliss and contentment filled him, tugging a sigh up from his heart.

He had lost faith that he would ever find his fated female and now his ki'ara was in his arms, her back nestling softly against his front, warming him.

Loren lowered his head and pressed a kiss to her throat, on the marks he had made last night during their bonding.

Olivia reached over her shoulder and fondly tangled her fingers in his hair, and then dropped her hand to the left side of his neck and stroked the marks there. Marks she had made to take his blood into her body, completing their bond and triggering a change in her that would make her immortal like him, granting them an eternity together.

Loren sighed again, feeling at peace for the first time in countless centuries. Whole at last.

"Can I see your world, when all this is over?" She stroked the nape of his neck, sending a shiver down his spine that turned from hot to cold as her words sank in.

They brought him down, reality closing in again to crush the peace inside him, setting him on edge. He had to deal with Vail, because he couldn't let his brother take Olivia from him. His brother's revenge would be brutal, unbearable. He couldn't lose Olivia.

Loren kissed her cheek and drew her closer, needing to feel her in his arms and know she was safe for now at least. "Our world... and I will show this realm to you, when all this is over."

She smiled. "It's beautiful here."

He could hear the wonder in her voice and feel it inside her. He looked out at the vista before them. The grounds extended for almost a mile, dotted with dark stone garrisons for the section of the army stationed permanently at the castle, but leafy and green too, with pale stone paths running between all of the buildings and the main gates. The dark stone walls were high, designed to protect everyone within the grounds. He and Vail had wanted a fortress that would prove difficult to penetrate in a battle, and that could house all of the elves from the nearby villages beyond the walls.

His gaze drifted there, to the collections of buildings scattered around the undulating landscape, paler patches in a sea of green and bright jewel colours. Beyond the walls were farms and woods, and rivers of crystal clear water that fed the land and were as necessary to its life as the sun filtering down from the darkness above.

Olivia leaned into his chest and he could feel her desire simmering in her veins, her need to explore this world and see everything with her own eyes. She wanted to explore it with him, studying it like the scientist she was. He could easily imagine her poring over every plant and animal, and marvelling at their use of what she probably deemed magic.

Loren tipped his head back and stared up at the dazzling light that shone down on his realm.

"There's darkness in the distance, but your world is full of beauty and light. How is it possible?" She turned in his arms, her gaze on his face.

Loren looked down at her and then beyond her to the distance. The reach of his lands were limited in several directions, and he could see the black lands beyond, glowing orange from the rivers of lava that flowed through them.

"You know how I travel via portals?" he said, trying to find a way to explain what they had done without making it either too complicated or too simple. If he went too simple, she would be angry with him, feeling as though he was treating her like a child when she had a brilliant mind. She nodded and looked up, and his gaze dropped to the marks on her throat, a bolt of heat striking like lightning in his veins. Her lips curled into a smile.

"I can feel you staring." There was a teasing note in her voice that he liked. His female knew him well. She caught his chin and raised his head, bringing his eyes away from her throat and up to the artificial sky. "Back to the portals."

"It is possible for us to project portals away from our bodies, but it uses a vast amount of energy to do such a thing. We constructed a permanent portal to bring light to our land from above... from your world. Every elf in my kingdom works in cycles to keep it functional, focusing all of their power on it from a special room within the west tower of the castle, the highest point in my lands." He glanced towards that tower, barely able to make out the top of the conical roof through the blossoming flowers shading the balcony. "When they tire, new elves take their place. The cycle allows for everyone to have long periods of rest between the times when they must help with the portal, meaning they can live their lives and attend to their farms or their businesses. All of the kingdom works to bring light into the darkness of Hell, so our land can thrive and grow, bearing life as our lands back in the mortal world had before we had to leave. We do the same to bring clean water into the land. It flows in via one portal and then out via another, re-joining the same undiscovered river in the mortal world."

"Wait... Hell? We're in Hell?" She stared at him in disbelief and he nodded.

"This realm is what many in your world would consider Hell. A place filled with demons and darker creatures, and even fallen angels in some areas."

"You moved your people to Hell from the mortal realm... because it's better here?" She frowned at that and he could see she was having difficulty grasping it.

"Here open warfare is rare and we do not come into contact with many dark species who would seek to harm us. In fact, since Vail went to war with me, many species living in this realm believe us to be the most violent and dangerous in all of Hell." He had always hated that. His species were not warmongers, unlike many of the demon species who were always involved in a demonomachy with at least one of the other demon realms. "Most species in this realm prefer to remain within the borders of their own lands and only venture out to trade with another species in theirs."

"I see. Like countries."

He nodded. "If you would prefer that term. This country shares borders with two of the demon countries, and others. There are countries here run by gods and goddesses, and even the being you would know as the Devil."

"Hell, no... he exists?" Her eyes shot wide and a tremor of fear went through her.

"I would never allow him near you, Olivia, and he has little interest in mortals. Mere speculation by your kind." He drew her closer anyway, wanting to reassure his female that she was safe in this land with him. No one would dare harm her here. Well. No one except his brother.

Loren's heart slowly sank, thoughts of Vail weighing it down in his chest, and Olivia raised her hand and smoothed her palm across his cheek, the action soothing him.

"What's that look for?" she said softly and he tried to wipe it off his face and shut down his feelings, but it was hard when he was standing on the balcony in the spot where he had often stood with Vail, discussing matters and looking out over their kingdom.

"The portal was Vail's idea," Loren whispered, a twinge of sorrow causing his heart to clench. He missed Vail and how things had been once, and would have given anything to have his brother back, had tried so hard to achieve that, but he had finally realised that it was impossible. He couldn't save Vail, just as Olivia hadn't been able to save her brother.

Olivia's eyebrows furrowed and she sighed as she stroked his cheek, looking up at him with her back pressed against the balustrade.

"Is there a king and a queen in your kingdom?" Nerves laced her voice.

Loren shook his head and her fear melted away. "There hasn't been a king since my father died over forty-eight centuries ago. We moved to this world after that, and I ruled together with Vail."

"What about your mother?" Olivia said.

Loren looked beyond her to the distant green lands, struggling to bring forth any memories of his mother. "She died giving birth to Vail. I was around a century old at the time, too young to remember her clearly. Our father died around fifty years after that."

"How old would you have appeared in human terms?"

"I would have looked like a young teen, perhaps sixteen or seventeen in your terms. Vail had looked half my age." He caught her frown, smiled and tucked her hair behind her ear, curling his fingers around it. His own ears were pointed, marking a difference between their species that he hoped wouldn't come between them. He was sure his people would love Olivia, regardless of their differences. "Elves age quickly during their first two hundred years, reaching adulthood by the end of them. Our aging slows dramatically after that, until we reach a point where it halts completely. Your aging will do the same because of my blood in your body and the changes the bond has caused, granting you immortality and increased strength and senses."

"You were very young when you took control of your kingdom then?" She cast her dark eyes out over the castle grounds below them, her gaze flickering around and following the people in the courtyard as they went about their business.

"Vail and I had good advisers, but we also had our father's blood in our veins and had been raised with all the knowledge we needed to run our kingdom." Loren's smile faded again as he thought about how difficult things had been though. Many of their kind had broken away from them, unwilling to follow the lead of what they considered children. They had remained in the mortal world, their souls becoming increasingly corrupted until they had become something as dark and wretched as vampires, straddling the gap between the two species but belonging to neither.

Olivia shifted around to face the courtyard, pressing her back into his front again. He wrapped his arms around her and held her as she studied his world, her feelings flickering through their link, entertaining him.

She was desperate to go down and interact with the elves she could see. He wasn't sure they were ready to meet her. He needed to make a formal announcement and then give them time to become used to the fact that he was mated to a human, and then she could meet her people. If she went down now, they would notice her marks and the council would be demanding a meeting with him.

He didn't have time for such matters, and he didn't really have time to linger here at the castle with Olivia. Vail was still on the loose back in the mortal world and Loren wouldn't be able to live with himself if something happened to Bleu or Archangel, and he knew Olivia wouldn't be able to either.

He pressed a kiss to her bare shoulder, lingering with his lips against her warm skin, breathing in her soft scent. "We should return. Bleu will be worried... and he tends to end up scolding me if he is worried. I do not want to face an angry Bleu the moment I return. It would rather spoil the moment."

She giggled. "He just cares about you. You must have been together a long time. I've never seen someone act so protective of someone as Bleu does of you."

Loren smiled against her. "We have been together since Vail went to war with me. Bleu was in his regiment and one of the survivors. You should have seen him. A scrawny, reckless and disobedient two hundred year old. He had a fierce temper and set me to rights without caring who he was speaking to. I had never met a male like him."

"Sounds like Bleu," she said with a smile in her voice. "I bet he's been setting you to rights ever since too."

He chuckled now, the weight pressing on his heart lifting as he thought about Bleu and all the years they had shared. "He has learned a modicum of respect, or at least learned to show it around others for the most part. If we are alone it is a different matter... and I admit it is nice having someone who is unafraid to speak his mind to me and who treats me as a friend."

Olivia looked across at him.

"He doesn't treat you as a friend, Loren. He is your friend... I'm sure he will be able to find a way to occupy himself in your absence though... he hasn't taken his eyes off Sable since he met her." Olivia turned in his arms, her expression fading to one of concern and then seriousness. "Is Sable Bleu's ki'ara?"

Loren shook his head. "I do not think so. I think Bleu desires Sable, but I am not sure she is his fated female. Bleu has had many females in his time and more than one at a time for some of those."

Olivia's right eyebrow arched. "He's a player. No wonder he and Kyter seemed to get along. Sable can handle herself, but I don't like the idea of Bleu trying to get into her knickers if he isn't serious about her. Can fae and demons fall in love with people other than their mates?"

He nodded now. "It is possible. My parents were not fated."

She looked relieved to hear that and he admired how much she cared about her friend, although he seriously doubted Bleu had any intention of falling for Sable. Bleu clearly desired her, wanted to bed her, but he had often spoken of his easy conquests in the mortal world, and Loren had the feeling that he saw Sable as a challenge and liked it. A female who hadn't immediately thrown herself at his feet. Loren could almost guarantee that if Sable succumbed to Bleu's charms, his friend would be content and then return to his bachelor life. He could be wrong though.

"Are you a player?" Olivia said, teasing him. She knew the truth about him, but the sparkle in her eyes said that she wanted to hear it again and liked knowing that he had been alone for a long time before he had met her.

"I am not a player... as you put it. I never have been. I began searching for you a very long time ago, Olivia, and now I have you." He grasped her waist, pulled her against him and kissed her.

She leaned into it, her hands coming to settle against his bare chest, and then pushed back, breaking away.

"Is there a difference between a normal female and a ki'ara?" There was his little scientist, her eyes gleaming with interest and curiosity.

Loren stroked her sides and nodded. "A vast difference. Being with you... my ki'ara... is bliss, wonderful, like being complete for the first time in my life. What I have experienced with you is a thousand times more intense and satisfying than what I have experienced with other females." He ignored the way she frowned and pressed her short nails into his chest, secretly enjoying the jealousy that coiled through her. "It is the reason many fae species and demons place such importance on our mates. Nothing compares to being with them. Everything else is a shadow of what we would have with our fated one."

She loosened her grip on him and relaxed again, but sombre feelings flowed through their bond and her eyes reflected them. "It sounds romantic... and I feel sorry for Bleu then."

Loren brushed the backs of his knuckles across her cheek. "Bleu will find his mate one day. He is not in any rush though. He is a male born for battle and war, not tending to a mate."

"A devoted bachelor and a player." Olivia sighed. "We should definitely get back before he tries to seduce his way into Sable's pants then, because if he hurts her, she will probably kill him."

Loren couldn't help smiling at that, easily able to picture such an event occurring. Sable would certainly go to war with any male who dared to hurt her, and Loren had the feeling that Olivia would be there fighting at her side.

He gathered her to him and she tiptoed and kissed him. They would return to Archangel and find out if Bleu had discovered anything about Vail at the club, but first he had another pressing matter to attend to.

He wanted to turn his bathing pool fantasy into a reality.

CHAPTER 19

The portal shimmered in multi-coloured hues before Loren, as tall as he was and twice as broad, slowly draining his energy. It took a lot of power to teleport in this way, forcing his ability to manifest itself away from his body, but Olivia had asked to see a portal like the one they used to bring light into his kingdom.

He took Olivia's hand and guided her towards it. Her wide eyes darted around as they approached, her curiosity bouncing through their bond to him. She reached out with her free hand and gasped when it made contact with the portal and then disappeared. Loren smiled and led her into it and the moment they appeared in her apartment at Archangel, she turned to look back and frowned.

"Where did it go?" She glanced at him.

"Portals do not show on the other side. It would rather give away our approach." It wasn't just a matter of stealth either. While portals could be used for sneak attacks, they were more readily used as an easy method of transportation between his realm and this one. If a portal was visible at the destination, there was a chance that someone there could use it to cross over into his realm, or they could ambush him.

A shiver went through him and he tightened his grip on Olivia's hand, his fingers pressing into the back of it.

"Something is wrong." He cast his blue eyes around the room, his senses stretching beyond the walls of the small apartment, spreading through the building as he tried to pinpoint what had him suddenly on edge.

Was it Vail?

His heart rate picked up and he sent a mental command to his armour. It rippled over his skin beneath his formal black coat and trousers, and he was careful not to cover his hands so he didn't hurt Olivia with his claws.

"What is it?" Olivia curled her free hand around his arm, drawing closer to him.

Her fear trickled through the link, but she was experiencing other emotions too. Fight and not flight. She felt her friends were threatened again and she wanted to seek out and eradicate the source of that threat.

"I do not know." Just as he said that, alarms wailed and the lights dropped. Red flashing lights replaced them, hurting his sensitive eyes.

Olivia flinched, pressing her face against his arm. "Bloody unholy sound!"

She was still growing accustomed to the changes in her body and her heightened hearing and vision was probably causing her pain.

"Come," he said and pulled her with him. He broke out into the corridor and several hunters rushed past, Sable and Bleu among them.

Olivia's friend stopped and stared at her. Olivia blushed deeply, awkwardness written across her face as well as her emotions.

"What is it?" Olivia said over the constant screech of the alarm system.

Sable loaded her compact crossbow, a vision of dark menace in her combat gear and with her hair tied back into a long ponytail. "Something just popped into the cafeteria, and it is big. Like huge."

Loren's heart pounded now. "Take us there."

Sable ran on ahead and Loren followed with Olivia, struggling to maintain the slower pace. It was good to have his full strength back. If he wanted to, he could be down at the cafeteria in a heartbeat. He didn't know where it was though and it was quicker to follow Sable than it was to follow his senses.

Olivia kept pace beside him and Loren dared not look at her. She still wore her sexy halter-top and tight jeans, and he needed to concentrate. If he set eyes on her running in that dark purple top, he was liable to forget what he had been doing and want to kiss her, and more.

Evidently completing the bond did not lessen the ferocity of his need for her.

They ran down several flights of steps and along another pale corridor, and then he spotted the cafeteria ahead. The doors were jammed open, held in place by a broken table on one side and a collapsed hunter on the other.

Sable rushed forwards and checked the condition of her comrade.

Loren burst into the room and froze, pulling Olivia behind him to shield her. His armour completed itself, forming claws over his fingers and his spiked black helmet, but leaving his face mask open.

He growled and drew his black blade out of the air, bringing it to him from his rooms in the castle, and mentally commanded the alarms to cease. The lights in the room came back up, startlingly bright, hurting his eyes and those of the enormous male battling in the middle of the room. The male growled at the lights and continued his fight against the hunters.

Bleu teleported to the other side of the room, his black armour in place and his eyes bright purple in the slits left open on his horned helmet.

The immense demon battling between them paid them no heed and lashed out with one meaty muscled arm, sending half a dozen hunters flying across the room. He took the human males down with ease but he wasn't killing them. Had his brother sent the male to harm Archangel and increase the unease between Loren and the hunters?

The male was enormous, broad and thickly muscled, his torso bare and his lower half clad in tight leather trousers that matched the colour of his wild russet-brown hair. Blood streaked his dark golden skin from several wounds on his torso, some of which still had the crossbow bolts sticking out of them. He snarled, flashing large fangs at the hunters, and swung wildly again, bashing several of them together and sending them crashing into a heap on the floor.

Other hunters called out commands and the demon turned crazed red eyes on them. The dark brown ridged horns that curled from behind his ears grew and the tips of his ears began to grow pointed.

This was not good.

As it was, the male stood taller than Loren and Bleu, his formidable strength making him a threat to both of them. If the male went fully demonic, he would grow several feet taller and become infinitely more dangerous. Loren had to stop him before it happened.

Loren moved forwards, his blade at the ready.

The demon swung to face him and, rather disturbingly, the wild look in his eyes grew clear when they settled on Loren.

No, not Loren.

Sable.

She stood beside him, her crossbow held at the ready, looking tiny compared with the male but furious too. She wouldn't back down. She would take on this demon who stood almost a foot taller and two foot wider than she was.

The demon's horns shrank and he was savage as he shoved his way towards them, snarling and growling at any hunter who dared to get in his way. Bleu skirted the edge of the room, his gaze locked on the demon, his blade ready. Three arrows stuck out of the demon's left shoulder, and the itchy trigger finger of a young female hunter embedded a fourth in his deltoid. It didn't even slow the demon.

He halted two metres from Loren, straightened and preened his horns as if nothing out of the ordinary had just been happening.

"You are a hard man to find," the male's deep voice rumbled through the room, a dark growl, his thick accent making it difficult to understand his English.

Strange that a demon would choose to speak that language to him. It was almost as if he wanted these hunters to know that Loren was the reason he was here.

Had Vail sent the demon to kill him after all?

"State your business." Loren swept his blade out, aiming it at the male's throat, and tipped his head back, holding his gaze. With his other hand, he kept Olivia close behind him. She refused to remain hidden, but at least she only moved far enough to peer past him, and ended up between him and Sable.

The demon grinned. It might have been a smile. It was always hard to tell with demons. They had rough masculine features and fangs that didn't fully retract. A smile looked like a grin most of the time.

"I was not sent by your brother."

That didn't ease Loren at all and he only grew more unsettled when three other demons appeared behind the male.

Bleu eased forwards and Loren could sense the arrival of more demons had set him firmly on edge. Loren held his hand out to Bleu.

"All is good here," he said to him and then turned to the demon. "Is it not?" The immense male's eyes darkened to a rich shade of crimson and he nodded. His gaze darted down to Sable and then back to Loren. It did this several times in the space of a few seconds and Loren had the impression that it wasn't because she had her crossbow aimed at him and it was unsettling him. No. The way a corona of scarlet flared around the edges of the male's eyes whenever he looked at her, and his horns grew larger and more pronounced, said it was a very different emotion commanding his gaze to leap to her and study the little human female.

He desired Sable.

"I need your assistance," the demon said and Loren arched an eyebrow.

He had come here, to Archangel, to ask Loren for help with some matter? No wonder he hadn't killed any of the hunters, but still. It was highly unusual for a demon to approach him directly about such a thing. Normally, they would send their messenger to the elf council and they would deal with negotiations between the two species, and come to some form of agreement.

Unless.

Loren moved a step closer and stared at the huge demon before him. He spoke English, had three subordinates standing behind him, all with their heads bowed, and had the audacity to speak to Loren directly as though they were equals.

A demon king.

Red eyes didn't give him much to go on though. Several of the demon species had red eyes when enraged, although this demon's eyes had failed to change back to a different colour. They had merely darkened to a deeper shade of crimson. What king was he?

Loren glanced at Bleu to see if his second in command had figured it out. Bleu mouthed the elvish word for three.

The Third King.

Loren knew little about him. He had become king long after Loren had gone to war with Vail. If rumours were to be believed, Kordula had killed the previous king of the Third Realm, placing this male into power.

Were they working together after all? Was this all a trick?

Why else would this demon appear now, asking for his assistance, rather than working through the normal channels?

The male huffed and plucked the bolts from his left shoulder and arm, gritting his teeth as they pulled free of his flesh.

Their clang as they hit the floor cut through the silence.

"I will help you in return for a favour. I need your men at the battlefield. I need to settle a war in my kingdom." The demon crushed the last bolt in his huge fist.

Help him? Loren frowned. Did the demon mean to help him with his battle against Vail in exchange for Loren leading his army to war with his enemy?

Loren shook his head. "I have no interest in your demonomachy. The elves have no reason to join your fight."

One of the males behind the demon king moved forwards, an uneasy edge to his dark red eyes as he looked beyond Loren. He spoke to his leader in the demon tongue, a language that Loren had mastered many millennia ago.

His words sent a chill sliding down Loren's spine and turned his blood to icy sludge in his veins.

"We were too early. The female has not yet been taken."

Loren spun on the spot to face Olivia and reached for her at the same time, but he was too slow.

Vail appeared behind her, his armour covering all but his vivid purple eyes, his helmet matching the crown of spikes that Loren wore, and grabbed her around the waist. Loren swung his blade, aiming for his brother's head, but it cut through empty air as his brother disappeared.

Loren bellowed in rage, his fangs punching long from his gums and his ears growing pointed, flattening against the sides of his head beneath his helmet. He turned on the demon king and roared as he attacked, catching the male off guard.

The tip of his blade sliced across the demon's broad chest and the other three demons rushed Loren, colliding hard with him and almost taking him down. Bleu leaped into the fray, his dark sword a black slashing arc as it cut down the back of one of the demons, sending him to the floor. Loren thrust forwards with his clawed left hand, using a powerful blast of telekinesis to throw the remaining two demons off him. One hit the ceiling, punching a hole in the plaster tiles, and the other flew across the room, slamming into the wall.

The demon king growled at him, his eyes flashing dangerously and his horns growing, curling around in front of his pointed ears.

Loren discarded his blade and flexed his claws.

The huge male's dark short claws grew in response to the threat, becoming deadly talons.

"Do not do this," the demon snarled and hunkered down, preparing himself to attack even as he spoke words that said he wanted to avoid a fight. "I swear on the life of my future fated one that I am not allied to your brother and had no part in this."

Loren reined his fury in on hearing those words, clawing back control over his ragged emotions and his dark hunger to shed blood.

A demon would never make such a vow lightly.

They valued their eternal mate just as the fae did. His soul cried out for Olivia and he reached for her with his senses, needing to feel she was safe and discover her location so he could rescue her from Vail and Kordula before it was too late.

Cold emptiness greeted him. The other end of the link was gone, severed. His brother's female had concealed Olivia, just as she had somehow clouded the link between him and Vail.

Bleu moved beside him, flanking him with Sable.

The demon closest to them picked himself up off the floor and grunted as he reached around behind him, touching the wound slashing down his muscular bare back. The two other demons were pulling themselves together too, all of them casting dark angry looks in Loren and Bleu's direction.

The Third King held his hand up. "Leave us."

The three demons looked unwilling to follow that order until the king growled at them. They glared at Loren and Bleu and disappeared one by one.

The king's order strengthened his position, giving Loren reason to believe he spoke the truth and hadn't come here because Vail had sent him.

"How did you know?" Loren bit out, finding it hard to speak as he struggled with his feelings, the crushing weight of losing Olivia too much to bear. His knees weakened, threatening to give out, and it took all of his willpower to stop himself from collapsing and crying out for her.

His heart plagued him, torturing him with images of Olivia held at the mercy of Vail and his worst nightmares coming true, all because he had again failed to protect her. He should have kept one hand on her. He should have kept her safe.

He had vowed to do that and he had failed again, and now his brother had her and it was only a matter of time before he realised that Loren had completed the bond. When Vail discovered that, he would act out his vengeance.

He would destroy Olivia and in turn destroy Loren.

He couldn't allow that to happen. The demon had information and he would give it to Loren, at sword point if necessary.

The hunters around the room closed in by a few inches, their weapons at the ready, all aimed at the demon king.

Sable flicked Loren a glance that asked whether she could kill the demon and he shook his head. He could feel her pain on his senses and see it in her eyes. She was hurting because of the disappearance of her friend and wanted to hold this demon to blame, just as he did. If the demon king didn't manage to convince him completely that he wasn't working with Vail and Kordula, Loren would turn the little hellion loose on the male. The demon's desire for her would force him to hold back and that was a weakness Loren had no qualms about exploiting.

Loren growled and picked up his sword. He stalked across to the demon male, set his jaw and narrowed his eyes on the demon's red ones.

"Speak of what you know and how you came to know it." Loren flexed his fingers around the hilt of his sword, his desire to retrieve Olivia before she came to harm shortening his temper and wearing down his patience.

"We met with a magic bearer, seeking to see the future of my kingdom. She had a vision, but not of my war. She saw your future and that is why we knew what would happen to your fated female," the demon king said and Loren snarled at him, exposing his fangs.

"Describe this witch." It had to be Kordula. She had tricked the demon king into creating a distraction that had left Olivia open for Vail to capture her.

"The female is small, of pale skin and white-blonde hair, with large blue eyes. She is young and lives near this city. Her people call her Rosalind."

Sable immediately rushed around the room, drawing the demon's gaze to her. It brightened again and his breathing turned laboured, his horns growing at an alarming rate. He definitely desired Sable, and it was making Bleu twitchy. His friend was on edge, his purple gaze pinning the demon with a murderous glare as the male's eyes followed Sable around the room.

She picked up something silver and rectangular, and came hurrying back to Loren. It was some sort of monitor or computer, but none like he had seen before. It was thin and had no wires attached to it. Merely a small flat screen no bigger than his two palms side by side. She flicked her fingers over the bright display and images of people appeared. She skimmed down them, her gaze darting around the screen, and then tapped one of the pictures.

Sable turned it towards him and the demon king. "Is this her?"

Loren peered at the image of a young, blonde woman. The information beside her picture stated her name and last known address, and other details such as her documented powers and her threat level, which was apparently green. Did green mean not a threat?

"This is her." The demon king stared at Sable with blatant heated desire in his eyes and flexed his fingers. Loren knew the feelings running through this male. He had experienced that undeniable need to touch Olivia when they had first met and had barely leashed it himself. Sable would probably rip the demon's arm out of its socket if he dared to touch her.

The female in the picture was not Vail's ki'ara.

Loren focused on Olivia again, desperate to feel her. It took all of his power to form a fuzzy connection between them, but it relieved him nonetheless. Olivia was alive, for now.

"I can help you, Elf," the demon said, his deep voice gaining a hard edge. "If you agree to help me."

Loren nodded. He would do anything to retrieve his ki'ara, even lead his people to war with another demon realm.

The Third King slid his crimson gaze towards Sable again and Bleu twitched beside Loren, his sword rattling as he tightened his grip on it.

The demon looked back into Loren's eyes. "I can find your fated female, but only if your brother returns."

Loren stared at him, fury burning like acid through his veins, and clenched his fists, causing the points of his serrated claws to press into his palms.

"Vail will return, and when he does, I will kill him."

CHAPTER 20

Olivia came around to find herself at one end of an elegant eggshell blue room with a beautiful woman with very long dark red hair and icy blue eyes looking down at her. Her lips matched her hair and the dark make-up around her eyes made her irises appear almost white ringed with dark blue, and her flawless pale skin gave her the appearance of a doll, too perfect to be real.

She planted her hands on her curvy hips, drawing Olivia's jealous gaze to the perfection that continued to her figure. Full breasts rose high on her chest, supported by elegant silver metal curls and points that formed a sort of corset over her long black strapless dress.

"What does your brother see in such a bland female?" the woman said in a silken tone that did nothing to hide the haughtiness from her voice.

Olivia frowned at her and sat up on the wooden floor. Bland female? Just because she wasn't the goth version of a Barbie, it didn't mean she was bland. Loren didn't seem to think so. He had murmured to her several times over the past day alone that he thought she was beautiful, although she had found his announcement that she was the most beautiful female in the world to be a stretch.

She was certainly not bland though.

She would have told the woman that if she hadn't been able to sense the danger radiating from her in waves stronger than Loren had ever emitted.

Kordula.

It had to be Vail's female, which meant that he had been the one to snatch her from the cafeteria.

Olivia's thoughts turned to Loren. He would be frantic. There had to be a way to let him know she was safe. She focused her thoughts on him, all of her concentration, shutting out the bright and elegant period room around her that looked like it belonged in a fancy country house hotel.

Loren.

She pressed her hands to her chest, her heart aching with the need to feel him. The link between them felt clouded and weak. Was it the distance causing the static in the line or was it something else?

Olivia looked up at the woman standing before her.

A witch. Olivia had researched a few in her years at Archangel and all of them had incredible powers, able to weave spells and concoct potions capable of causing great destruction or infinite good.

There were three different castes of witch. Those born of the rare bloodlines capable of calling on the light or the dark sides of nature, were always of the light or dark themselves. Those born of a common coven witch were neutral, unable to connect with the power the light and the dark held without using spells beyond the level of most neutral witches. A light or dark bloodline could never bear a neutral witch or warlock, and vice versa. It was a calling, passed by blood to their offspring.

They could harness the power of nature and the world around them and tended to live in solitude, never acting as a coven. All light and dark magic bearers bore core abilities but some had rare talents, such as the power to gaze into the future.

The light tended to focus on life and their connection to that side of nature, harnessing it to heal and do good for others.

The dark had a connection to death and destruction, and forces from beyond the grave.

Kordula looked as though she dealt in the darker side of sorcery.

A male prowled into view behind her, hands clutching the sides of his bent head, fingers buried in his tousled black-blue hair. He growled, his agitated strides eating up the parquet floor, his bare muscular chest heaving with each laboured breath.

Vail.

What was wrong with him?

"Stop that infernal pacing!" Kordula snapped and Vail halted mid-stride, frozen in position, as if the witch had aimed her deadly powers at him and forced him to halt. "Come to me."

Vail turned on his heel and glared at Kordula's back as he stalked towards her, his eyes wild and vivid purple. He eased his hands away from the sides of his head and his black armour emerged from the bands around his wrists, jerkily covering his hands and forming his fingers into ragged, stilted black claws. He flexed them but it seemed to take him great effort, as if he had to fight his own body to make it move. He reached for Kordula, dark menace in his crazed eyes.

"Vail," Kordula said in a voice that was all sweetness and smiled over her shoulder at him. "What have I told you about behaving nicely?"

Olivia gasped when the armour covering his hands began to recede but then swept forwards only to recede again. Was Kordula controlling Vail's armour? They were mated, forming a powerful bond between them. Just as Loren had taken Olivia's injuries into himself, using the link between them to make it happen, Kordula was using it to keep Vail's claws sheathed.

He bared his fangs at her.

"Watch the female while I prepare." Kordula turned imperiously away from him and swept out of the room, slamming the door to an adjoining one behind her.

Vail stood before Olivia, staring down at her, as tall as his brother but the insane twist of his lips and dark dull edge to his eyes stole something from his beauty.

He didn't move a muscle, was barely breathing now.

Olivia swallowed and kept perfectly still too, even though her backside was going numb from sitting on the floor and she didn't like having to crane her neck to look up at the madman standing before her.

He looked too much like Loren.

Was this what Loren had feared would happen to him when they had completed their bond?

"Loren will be looking for me," she whispered, afraid to raise her voice any louder in case Kordula heard her or it triggered Vail into attacking. "I know he hurt your ki'ara... but hurting me won't solve anything."

Vail's lips twisted in a snarl and he shoved his fingers through his hair, clawing it back. He grimaced and mouthed something, a lost and desperate look entering his eyes.

"Loren still loves you, Vail. He wants to help you. Let him help you."

Vail shook his head and screwed his eyes shut, and his armour swept over his body, covering him from toes to neck. His claws dug into his scalp and his hands shook. He mouthed something again and she shrieked when he suddenly knelt before her, the force of his knees hitting the parquet jolting her.

He struggled to bring his hands down and they trembled as he held them out to her, his black claws glistening with blood that he had drawn from his scalp.

"Loren is sorry for what he did to your ki'ara," Olivia whispered, her heart pounding now that Vail was so close to her.

She didn't dare attack him. He looked crazed, as mad as everyone said that he was, and Loren had told her that he wanted to make her suffer in order to hurt him and have revenge for what Loren had done. Olivia didn't want to end up as a victim of Vail's claws.

She eyed them and swallowed hard.

Vail edged them closer to her.

She glanced at the wooden antique chair off to her left. Could she reach it and hit Vail with it before he cut her to shreds? If she did hit him with it, would it affect him at all? He might be insane, but he was still at full strength as far as she knew, and that meant he could easily defeat her.

Vail mouthed something again, the desperate edge to his eyes growing more intense.

"Can you not speak?" It was a possibility. Kordula might have commanded he not speak to her.

Why would she do such a thing though?

He shook his head and reached for her, and she scurried backwards, keeping some distance between them. Vail frowned and lowered his hand, his shoulders sagging, and then his eyes lightened.

He used his claws to scratch the dark wooden floor. Olivia peered closer when she realised he was writing. Her heart rushed in her ears and she ended up on all fours, crawling closer so she could read what he had clumsily carved into the wood.

Her eyes widened. "Not ki'ara. Tricked. Slave."

Her head shot up and she stared into Vail's haunted eyes.

"She isn't your fated female?" Olivia struggled to grasp that, even when he managed to nod. "She has you under her spell... she can control you."

He looked away and raked his claws over the words he had scratched into the wooden floor, as if he couldn't bear the sight of them or her now that she knew what had happened to him. He kept scratching the parquet until he had obliterated the words, leaving no evidence behind.

"Do you have any control over yourself?" she whispered and he nodded, and looked back at her, the hollow and haunted look in his eyes hitting her hard.

Vail hadn't gone mad because of the bond. He had gone mad because of the things Kordula had done to him, and the longer Kordula was gone from the room, the more sane he began to look. Did her power over him weaken as the distance between them grew?

"Have you ever gone against Kordula's wishes?" Olivia's gut said that he had, and he had paid dearly every time he had tried to do something not on her agenda.

He nodded again and pain filled his eyes, and he dropped his gaze to his knees and shuddered.

Olivia had talked to Loren about Vail during their time together, wanting to know what had driven his brother to go to war with him. Loren had spoken about how Vail seemed to change before his eyes during their fights, and was almost sane one moment and then completely crazed the next. Were those changes in him because he was fighting Kordula's hold over him? Was he trying to resist her commands and not harm his brother?

It was a possibility, and if her speculation was right and Vail was under Kordula's command, then he wasn't fighting against his brother, he was fighting on the same side.

Someone moved in the room behind her and she tensed. Vail tensed too and moved away from her, scooting back a few inches, as if he feared Kordula finding him close to her. He frantically pressed his hand to the ruined section of parquet and glared at it. The wood bowed and creaked, and began to repair itself.

Olivia's heart went out to him. She had seen the demons and fae that Archangel held in a containment facility, and had seen how scared they had been whenever they felt one of their captors would discover they had done something bad and would punish them. Vail feared Kordula would see the scratched floorboards and become suspicious, and she would make him talk somehow.

Olivia didn't want to imagine how.

Vail threw a desperate look at her and then jerked around, his gaze darting to different points around the room but constantly flickering back to the door Kordula had exited through.

Kordula had tricked Vail and bound him to her, and had probably commanded him to do the terrible things that Loren had spoken to her about. He had been under her spell for forty-two centuries, and God only knew what Kordula had made him do in all that time, and how she might have used him in order to break his mind. He was broken. She could see it in his eyes now as he panicked, fearing the return of the sorceress and her retribution.

"Are you going to kill me?" Olivia whispered, afraid to know the answer to that question but needing to ask it.

Vail's purple gaze shifted back to her and he shook his head with considerable effort.

"Will Kordula?" That question hung in the air between them for what seemed like forever before he finally nodded.

A sorrowful look entered his eyes and he settled his hands on his thighs, his shoulders sagging again. He mouthed something and she didn't know what he said, not only because she couldn't read lips, but because she could tell he was speaking his own native tongue. It was a strange language, with mouth movements far different from English.

"Loren will fight you," Olivia said and the harrowed edge returned to his gaze, and then he nodded very slowly.

He reached forwards and scratched into the floor.

Kill me.

Olivia's gaze leaped back to his, her eyes enormous as she stared into his and realised the true depth of his pain and his suffering. The corners of his lips tilted up into something akin to a smile, but it held only hurt and hope.

He wanted to die.

Something terrible dawned on Olivia.

"Was it Kordula's plan to bring Loren to me and have us bond?" She instinctively reached for Vail and caught his wrist before he could withdraw, holding his fingers poised above the words he had etched into the floor.

He stared into her eyes, blinked once and shook his head.

Her stomach turned, her insides flipping with it.

Vail had brought Loren to her, his fated female, not because he had wanted to weaken his brother, but because he knew that Loren had been seeking his female for so long, and he would need her now to fill the void Vail would leave.

Because he was going to get himself killed somehow.

He wanted death as an end to his suffering.

The doors opened and Vail scrambled backwards, purple gaze flicking between Kordula as she entered and the words he had scratched into the floor.

Kordula raised an eyebrow at his behaviour, came to them and looked down at the words. She scowled at Vail.

"I command you not to communicate with her and this is what you do?" Black and red ribbons twirled around her hands and she raised them. "On your feet."

Vail rose as ordered, his movements jerky, telling Olivia that he hadn't been given a choice. Kordula was using her power to force him to do as she bid, controlling him. He cast a fearful look down at Olivia and then his demeanour changed, losing the sorrowful and haunted edge, and gaining a dark and violent one.

His lips peeled back off his fangs and he growled at Kordula, the pointed tips of his ears extending and his eyes flashing dangerously.

"You dare attempt to protect her?" Kordula was on Vail in a heartbeat, her slender hand closing around the front of his throat. She easily lifted him off the floor despite the vast difference in their height and build. The ribbons of black and red that curled around her arms all rushed at Vail and burrowed into his flesh. He threw his head back and cried out, the sound so harrowing that Olivia covered her ears, unable to bear hearing it because she knew that Kordula would turn that incredible power on her before long.

Vail thrashed and snarled, clawing at Kordula's arms and spilling her blood. It rolled down her bare forearms to her elbows and dripped onto the floor. It turned black and writhed before Olivia's eyes, like a living thing.

"You will return to Archangel and we will finish this. Do you understand?" Kordula tightened her grip on Vail's throat, the last of the ribbons crept into his flesh and his struggling ceased. He stared at her, docile and calm, his purple eyes hazy and unfocused.

Kordula set him down, caressed his cheek and placed two fingers under his chin. She caught it with her thumb and lowered his head, so he was looking at her. The redheaded witch rubbed her body against the full length of his and kissed him. Vail didn't move but his eyes lost their calm edge and darkened. The pointed tips of his ears flared back and Olivia knew it wasn't because he felt lust and desire.

It was because he felt rage.

Vail was locked in his body as Kordula kissed him and worked her body against his, and Olivia had a dark urge to stand up and lash out at the bitch. She almost went through with the ridiculously stupid idea that would end in a very swift death when Kordula ran her hand down Vail's stomach and cupped his groin, fondling him.

"Play nice, my love, and I will reward you later." Kordula kissed across his cheek and curled against him, and looked down at Olivia, her arms draped around his shoulders. Vail continued to stare forwards, motionless, the only sign he was alive the dark edge to his eyes, the hunger to maim and kill.

Not his brother, but the witch-bitch draped all over him like a lover.

Kordula pressed her cheek against Vail's and ran her fingers down his other one. "Now go, my love, and end your brother."

Darkness flickered across Vail's expression, that same black emotion curling through Olivia's veins in response to Kordula's order. He tried to shake his head, and then his demeanour changed again, turning feral and savage. He growled, flashing enormous fangs, and the points of his ears flattened against the sides of his head, and then he was stepping back from Kordula.

Violet and pale blue light traced over his black armour, growing in speed as he stared at Kordula with hunger for violence in his eyes.

"Go." Kordula pointed at him.

Vail disappeared.

Olivia kept very still, suddenly aware that she had just lost her one unlikely ally and was now alone with a psychotic witch hell bent on making Loren suffer for what he had done to her.

"I don't know why you want me—" Olivia started but Kordula whipped around to face her and cut her off.

"Save it, sweet thing. I know you belong to Loren. His fated one. Vail had some nerve throwing you two together. I had wanted to do things peacefully and merely capture you and take you down to see Loren." Kordula moved to tower over her again and made a noise of disgust as she eyed the words Vail had scrawled on the parquet, her lip curling and her pale blue eyes turning glacial. "Vail's disobedience might have changed the plan but the objective and the outcome remains the same."

"What plan is that?" Olivia said casually and Kordula tossed her a wicked smile.

"You think I have lived this long, come this far, to tell you my plan like one of those villain clichés?" Kordula laughed, the sound raking down Olivia's spine, and dark ribbons swept over her arms again, fluttering upwards towards her shoulders. "You will not live to foil it, and neither will Vail if he dares to go against me again."

"I wasn't calling you a walking cliché." Although it had crossed her mind. The woman looked and acted as though she was going for the wicked witch or evil sorceress of the year award. "I just can't understand what drives a talented, beautiful woman to go to war with the elves."

Kordula eyed her with suspicion and then moved past Olivia to one of the antique wooden armchairs that formed a crescent with a couch around the fireplace and settled herself on the padded dark blue seat.

Perhaps flattery really could get you everywhere and playing on Kordula's desire to be adored and obeyed was the way to sneak through her defences and discover what she was up to.

If Olivia could find out, then she might be able to find a way to tell Loren. Their connection was fuzzy now but it might grow clearer if Vail led Loren to her. She still wasn't sure how the link worked or if it could be used to communicate with Loren in some way.

Kordula crossed her legs, revealing a long split up the side of her black dress and flashing a lot of pale toned thigh. It probably hadn't taken the witch much effort to convince Vail to let her close enough to him to cast her spell on him and ensure he was firmly under it. Most men in this world and the other one would probably throw themselves at the feet of such a beautiful woman.

She had used that beauty to gain Vail as an ally and had gone to war with his brother. Why? What did Kordula hope to gain? Only two possibilities came to Olivia. Either Kordula wanted revenge for something, or she wanted to gain power.

Olivia had read that many warlocks and witches born with darker magic were easily seduced by the power it gave them, strength far superior to neutral witches and even those who bore light magic.

"Did you ever love Vail?" Olivia couldn't hold that one in. She had thought Loren's brother insane and evil, but now that she knew he was a puppet belonging to the woman before her, she almost felt sorry for him.

Kordula laughed again, giving Olivia the answer to her question. She hadn't.

"Princess Kordula has a nice ring to it, don't you think?" She leaned back into the armchair and smiled down at Olivia. "You must admit that you were rather enchanted that your elf was a prince, in control of a whole kingdom, were you not?"

Olivia couldn't deny it, because it was partly true, but she hadn't desired Loren purely because he was a prince and ruled a kingdom. That hadn't mattered to her heart. It had only mattered to her head. She had been enchanted by the thought that a prince desired her, but she had moved past such shallow feelings when she had discovered the man behind the title, and how wonderful he was.

Kordula hadn't moved past it at all. That was clear. She had done as many women in Olivia's world did, seeking to gain power by capturing the heart of a male who had power. She had targeted Vail, and Vail had believed her to be his ki'ara and had fallen for her trick.

"Why Vail? Why not one of the demon kings?" Olivia glared at Kordula, hiding none of her hatred. She despised this woman and all who sought to sleep their way into power, using their beauty as a weapon to enslave a man.

Kordula's smile faded, her pale blue eyes turning frosty once more. "Loren did not tell you of Vail's prediction? It was well known in Hell, and I heard of it when I was a young girl, living in squalor in an adjoining kingdom. Prince Vail had been told that his fated female was a sorceress."

Olivia frowned. Kordula had played on that, using it to her advantage. Luring Vail into her trap.

"I grew up in a wretched land, with little food and even less light. It was rotten and festering, and I saw my chance to elevate myself to a position I deserved." Kordula curled her lip again, the disgust in her voice telling Olivia just how much she had hated where she had grown up. Still, Olivia wouldn't accept it as an excuse to use a man, to drive him insane and torture him.

Olivia stood on trembling legs and clenched her fists at her side. "You could have done something about it."

Kordula smiled, her red lips curving slowly. "I did... I ventured to the edge of the realm where I knew Vail to be with his army and threw myself on his mercy. He took one look at me, a filthy, starving, wretch, and turned his back on me. I cursed him and used the last of my strength to hit him with a spell that sent him flying through a score of his men. When I came around, Vail was tending to me."

And the evil edge to her smile told Olivia that she had known she had succeeded. But Kordula's desire had been gaining power, not just gaining a male and a war. Something must have gone wrong, and Olivia had a feeling she knew what had happened.

"Vail wrecked your plan... you asked him to do something that sent him mad and he attacked his own people to stop it from happening. He made an enemy of himself in order to protect Loren and stop you from seizing power over his country."

Kordula shot to her feet, the air around her darkening and crackling with red bolts of energy. Her lips twisted into a sneer and her eyes bled into crimson. "He ruined everything!"

The witch launched her hand forwards and a bolt of red energy struck Olivia hard in her chest. Heat ricocheted through her body and she flew across the room and slammed into the wall. A cry of pain ripped from her lips, lightning arcing across her back and burning through her bones, and she dropped to the floor, hitting the parquet hard.

Olivia expected the agony to render her unconscious but the pain faded as she breathed, and she swore she could feel her bones mending and damaged flesh knitting back together. The bond had made her stronger. It had made her immortal.

She lay on the floor, buying herself time to recover fully and fearing another blast of that power might just test the limits of her new regenerative abilities and knock her out.

Poor Vail. He had done the only thing he could in order to stop Kordula from killing Loren and establishing herself as ruler of the elf kingdom, turning on his own beloved people and turning his brother against him, and he had been paying for it ever since. Kordula had been using him to attack the elves, and other kingdoms, and Olivia had no doubts that he had fought Kordula every step of the way too, only bringing more of her wrath down upon him.

Vail had done all he could to stop Kordula from fulfilling her plan to seize the elf kingdom for her own.

"Now you want to use me to make Loren suffer because he almost killed you." Olivia pushed herself up and got to her feet, coming to face Kordula.

"Not just Loren."

Olivia frowned at that admission. She wanted Vail to suffer too, and he would if Kordula made him hurt Olivia and in turn destroy his brother.

"Why?" Olivia said and wondered if Vail was with Loren now, fighting him or fighting Kordula's command to kill him. "Loren told me you attacked the kingdom after he almost killed you, and you caused vast devastation and a huge death toll. Isn't that vengeance enough?"

Kordula's red lips compressed. "I used the power of the blood of almost forty warlocks to give me the strength to bring hell down on the elves and your bastard prince, and it would have worked but the battle left me depleted, and Vail used that as his chance to teleport me away. He sacrificed much of his power to seal the access points in the elf realm to me and he learned his lesson... he paid in blood for what he had done to me."

Olivia repeated everything Kordula had said in her head, piecing it together with what she had read about sorcery. Kordula could gain power through drinking blood. How much of Vail's blood had she drunk in order to restore her strength and punish him for daring to seal the elf kingdom to her?

No wonder Loren hadn't seen his brother for centuries before the night that had brought them together.

"It was your idea to find me." Olivia stared at Kordula, reading the fluctuations in her expression and her body language, and using her new super senses to detect even the most minute change in her heartbeat.

"I had wanted to find you but had thought it impossible, as there was every chance you were an elf, locked in a kingdom I could not enter." Kordula moved a step forwards and then she was right in front of Olivia, her hands closing around Olivia's throat. Kordula drove her backwards, into the pale blue wall behind her, pinning her against it. "Imagine my joy when Vail discovered your location."

Kordula's eyes burned red around the edges and ribbons of crimson and black rushed up her arms towards Olivia's throat. Her heart leaped in her chest, pounding wildly, and she grabbed Kordula's arms and kicked with all of her might, trying to break free before the magic could touch her.

Olivia cried out as the first thread burrowed into her flesh, searing her, the pain so intense that darkness crowded her mind and she could no longer feel even a hazy connection to Loren.

She screwed her eyes shut and tears streamed down her cheeks as another spear of Kordula's power penetrated her skin and whipped through her, the pain debilitating, stealing all of her strength and leaving her unable to fight back.

Kordula's voice broke through the darkness pulling Olivia under.

"Imagine my joy when I make you bleed before your bastard prince and watch him suffer."

Olivia desperately clung to consciousness as fear of what might happen if she succumbed to Kordula's terrible power rushed through her and focused everything she had on Loren and her love for him, determined to re-establish the link between them.

It was hazy but she felt him.

He was in pain too.

Vail had found him.

Before she could figure out a way to strengthen the link, another barb pierced her skin and darkness flooded her mind.

CHAPTER 21

Loren led Bleu and the demon king, Thorne, away from the Archangel facility where Vail had snatched Olivia, concerned that his brother would attack again and kill the hunters and staff. Archangel had no part in his battle with his brother and didn't deserve to end up dragged into it because Loren had lingered there. He would lead his brother somewhere away from humans and take him down.

Although, escaping one human had proved impossible.

Sable had insisted that she come with them, pointing out that Olivia was her friend and a member of Archangel, and someone from their company should be with them to act on her behalf. Loren considered himself as acting on Olivia's behalf, but Sable had refused to listen. She had practically forced him to agree to bring her with them by turning to Bleu and demanding he teleport her.

That had sent Thorne into a dark rage that had simmered below the surface of his red eyes, but hadn't gone unnoticed by Loren. The male felt protective and possessive of Sable. It was not a good sign.

Demons were notoriously violent and aggressive when it came to their fated females, worse than elves, and with good reason.

There were no female demons in the world and a demon could only produce offspring with his mate.

It was a method born of a blood curse placed on the heads of all demons by the Devil when the demons had dared to rise up against him, claiming a large expanse of land in Hell for their own and forming kingdoms. The Devil had made them pay for their insubordination by wiping out all female demons and making it difficult for the males to keep up their numbers because they would have to seek out their fated female in order to procreate, and it was hard for demons to move around in the mortal world. Their horns, fangs, claws and size tended to draw attention.

Loren still wasn't sure whether Sable was Bleu's fated female, meaning there was a possibility she was one of the rare fabled females who potentially had two eternal mates. The last thing Loren needed right now was Bleu ending up in a competition with Thorne for her affection.

He had a brother to kill, a mate to rescue, and had agreed to side with Thorne in a war against another demon kingdom. That alone meant that Thorne and Bleu would be around each other for days or weeks. Loren didn't want to imagine how dire things would be should they both be Sable's mate.

Thorne stood opposite him and Sable, his eyes glowing faintly in the near-darkness of the rectangular park, the wrecked Archangel building where Loren had met Olivia as his backdrop.

Bleu stood a short distance away, close to the larger male, his gaze on Sable as she checked her crossbow and the assortment of blades and other weapons strapped to her body over her black combat clothing.

Loren wanted to remind both males that the huntress was not the reason they were here and felt like warning them that if they allowed Olivia to come to harm because of their mutual desire for Sable had led them to bicker over her, he would murder them both.

Sable finished checking her weapons and kept her crossbow handy, the loaded bolt gleaming wickedly in the light from the surrounding buildings.

"You think he'll show?" she said, her black eyebrows pinned high on her forehead as she looked up at Loren and her golden eyes a dark shade of amber.

He nodded and formed his armour over his fingers, arming himself with his claws, and then held his hand out before him. The air shimmered and his black blade appeared in his grip.

Bleu did the same with his sword and then swept his hand over it, his purple gaze focused on the blade. It transformed into his favoured double-ended spear and Sable stared in fascination. It was probably the first time she had seen Bleu perform that trick.

Thorne snorted and held his hand out, his palm facing the grass. The glowing red pommel of a sword rose out of the ground, followed by a long leather-bound hilt, and a wide steel blade. It edged upwards towards the demon king's hand and seemed endless as it rose. Bleu arched an eyebrow. Sable looked stunned.

Loren wondered just how big the demon's sword was.

The blade showed no sign of tapering to a point.

The pommel reached Thorne's large hand and he turned it, running his palm down the length of the black hilt, and then pulled the point free of the earth. The broadsword stood almost as tall as Thorne's shoulder, the height of Sable. A formidable weapon.

Bleu did not look impressed when Thorne grinned at him, revealing fangs, a cocky edge to it.

Loren could almost see the mood between the two deteriorating and turning into a competition to gain Sable's attention.

The Third King shoved the tip of the huge sword into the ground and casually leaned on the guard, his grin holding.

Until Sable went back to checking her weapons, a disinterested look on her face.

"I'm bored of waiting." Sable scowled at Loren. "Isn't there something you can do to make your brother show up?"

"Not really. He will come, and when he does, I will make him pay for taking Olivia."

"Not until we have her, big guy. Remember that. If Vail pops in for a chat, we have to find out where she is before we cut off his head. Okay?"

Loren didn't need the reminder, not the one about his need to find Olivia's location because he could no longer sense her, and certainly not the one about the fact he was about to kill his only brother. He had finally lost all hope and desire of saving him. Vail would pay for what he had done and if he had harmed Olivia in any way, Loren would extract that payment slowly and painfully.

A familiar shiver went down Loren's spine.

"He comes." Loren readied his blade and turned on his heel, his gaze seeking Vail.

Vail stood where the oak tree had fallen during their last fight, dressed in his black armour, a crazed glimmer in his purple eyes. He crouched and touched the sawdust-littered scarred earth, a frown on his face. Loren felt the pain too. It echoed within him, a thousand hot needles that pricked his bones and dulled his senses. They had both harmed nature in this park and she still bore her teeth at them, her wrath yet to fade. The oak had been ancient, several hundred years old. It would be a long time before nature forgave them for their sin of felling it.

His brother rose to his feet and met his gaze across the tract of dewy grass.

"Where is my ki'ara, Vail?" Loren bit out, unable to keep his anger and pain from his voice.

Vail looked away, a sombre air about him, a marked difference from how savage he had looked when he had taken Olivia from the Archangel cafeteria.

It was times like this, when Vail looked much as he had done before meeting Kordula, that Loren felt he stood a chance of getting through to his younger brother.

"I need her back, Vail. Please. What I did was wrong, but it does not make what you do now right." Loren flexed his fingers around his blade, preparing himself.

"Speaking with him isn't going to solve anything," Sable spat, aimed her compact crossbow and loosed the bolt.

It flew directly at Vail's head.

Loren's heart hitched.

Vail calmly raised a hand and deflected it at the last second, using his telekinesis to divert its course. The bolt zipped into the bushes and trees lining the edge of the park.

"Give me my friend back you bastard!" Sable drew two vicious-looking long knives from the harness around her shoulders and ran at Vail.

Fool.

Vail gave her a bored look, flicked his wrist and sent her flying through the air. She shrieked and flailed, dropping her blades. Bleu growled and sprinted, moving in a blur of speed. He pressed down hard on his final step and pushed off, leaping high into the air and catching Sable. He landed safely and Sable stopped shrieking, and instantly pushed out of his arms.

"I'll kill him for that," she barked and Loren signalled Bleu, silently instructing him to hold her back before she got herself killed. Olivia would never forgive him if that happened, and she would never forgive herself either.

Loren looked over his shoulder at Thorne. Would the Third King's plan really work? There was only one way of finding out.

Thorne nodded, his wild dark chestnut hair shifting with the action and falling down to caress his brow. His irises glowed red around the edges, he pulled his sword free of the earth, and wielded it with both hands. He roared, the sound shaking the earth and drawing Vail's focus to him.

Vail scowled at the demon, snarled and held his hands out. The air before them shimmered and his two shorter blades appeared in his grasp.

Thorne charged him, each heavy footfall rocking the ground beneath Loren's feet, his sword held at his side, pointed behind him, ready for him to swing when he was close enough.

Vail hissed, his ears flattening against the side of his head.

Thorne lashed out in the demon tongue. "You will pay for what you did, little wretch."

Those words confirmed the rumours. Vail and Kordula had been the ones to kill the previous Third King and his queen. Thorne's father and mother.

Thorne swung hard and Vail blocked with both of his swords. The demon king's broadsword crashed into them and Vail grunted as the force of the blow drove him backwards, his footing slipping on the damp grass, leaving long muddy tracts in it.

Vail shoved forwards and Loren didn't give him a chance to recover or attack Thorne. He launched himself towards his brother, throwing his free hand forwards at the same time, using a telekinetic blow to send him tumbling across the grass. Vail lost his weapons and eventually came to a halt over twenty metres away, covered in grass and mud. He shakily pushed himself up and growled as he came to his feet.

Vail called his blades and they whipped into his hands. He stared across the dimly lit park to Loren, breathing hard, his eyes laced with pain that Loren could feel in him as the connection they shared via blood grew stronger again.

Loren held his head high, completely unaffected by the expenditure of psychic power it had taken to toss Vail that far.

Vail wrapped one arm around his middle and spat blood out onto the grass. He looked back at Loren and Loren swore that he smiled before he came blazing towards him. Vail flipped his two swords in his hands so they pointed downwards from his grip and growled as he attacked.

Loren matched him blow for blow, easily predicting his brother's attacks. Vail was holding back. Why?

Was his brother toying with him?

Did he want to give him hope of saving Olivia only to take it away, increasing his suffering?

Loren shoved his questions away and focused on the fight, not giving Vail a chance to best him. He could keep up with him now that he was back at full strength, his bond with Olivia completed. Vail flipped his blades again and attacked with both, forcing Loren to defend.

Bleu came out of nowhere and thrust forwards with his spear, catching Vail in his side and cutting through his armour but only nicking his flesh, barely drawing blood. His aim had been off. Not good, but not a disaster.

Only a weapon made of the same material as the armour could cut through it, negating its effect. Vail could heal his armour but that meant sending it back into the bands around his wrists, leaving himself vulnerable.

Or more vulnerable than he already was anyway.

Vail turned on Bleu and hissed.

Loren seized his chance and swung at Vail. Vail desperately lashed out with a blast of power, forcing Loren to teleport to avoid it. He landed a short distance behind Vail and continued his attack, aiming for his brother's back.

Vail swung one sword over his back, blocking Loren's blade, and deflected Bleu's spear with his other blade.

He couldn't defend against three blades though.

Thorne's aim was impeccable. He drove his sword through the slash in Vail's armour and deep into his flesh.

Vail bellowed, dropped his blades and grabbed Thorne's broadsword. He yanked it from him and staggered backwards, towards Loren. Blood pumped from the wound in Vail's side, the scales of his black armour glistening with it as it ran down to his thigh.

Loren stared at his brother, hesitating when he should have struck a vicious blow, injuring him further.

He couldn't move.

All he could do was breathe hard, battling the debilitating pain that seared every inch of him and blazed in his heart like an inferno, threatening to burn it to ashes in his chest.

Vail.

The link between them was wide open for the first time in forty-two centuries and all that flowed through it was crippling pain, dark and devastating, born not of his injury but of something else.

A red and black vortex appeared behind Vail and pulled him into it.

Loren collapsed to his knees and Bleu raced to him, coming to a crouch beside him.

"My prince, are you injured?" Bleu's concerned expression turned to one of relief when Loren shook his head.

Loren grasped his knees, his hands shaking. Vail's pain faded, the connection between them severing again, but it left him weakened.

A different feeling surfaced in his heart and he closed his eyes and pressed his hands to his chest, focusing on the faint link, nurturing it. Olivia. He could feel her and she was hurting. He had to find her before Kordula and Vail could have their revenge on him.

Loren lifted his head and looked up at Thorne. The immense male stood before him, his eyes shining bright like coals in the near-darkness. Bleu helped Loren to his feet and Sable joined them, flipping one of her knives, a black look on her face.

Thorne raised his broadsword with one hand and rested the blade on his free palm. He closed his eyes, licked the blood from the end that had punctured Vail's side and swallowed it.

Loren's heart pounded. This had to work.

"Well?" he said, his patience leaving him as fierce need to find Olivia claimed his heart. "Can you track him?"

Thorne opened his red eyes and they met Loren's. "I have him."

Relief beat swift and fierce through Loren. Only a few demon species could track someone via their blood and he was thankful that Thorne was the king of one of them.

He would be with Olivia again soon enough.

All they had to do was follow Thorne's senses and Loren would see her again, and he would stop at nothing to save her from his brother's grasp. He couldn't save both of them, no matter how much he desired it deep in his heart. He had to sacrifice one dream to achieve another.

"Take us to them," Loren said to Thorne and the demon king nodded, turned on his heel and stalked towards the Archangel building at the other end of the park, his bare muscular back shifting with each heavy step that pounded the earth.

Sable started after him, muttering dark things to herself about taking Vail apart when she next saw him. Loren took a deep breath.

He had felt Vail's pain.

What had happened to his brother to make him hurt that much? There had been so much darkness in the link between them, when once there had always been light. Vail had always had a zest for life, had been outgoing and compassionate, forever in search of fun. That part of his brother was gone now and Loren was no longer sure that it was his bond to Kordula that had turned him mad and crushed his spirit.

"Is something wrong?" Bleu said in their language and Loren stared ahead at Sable and Thorne, and the Archangel building beyond.

He shook his head, shaking away his thoughts at the same time. It was too late now to consider what had happened to his brother. It was too late to save him. His brother had taken Olivia. His brother had brought death down upon his people. He had made thousands suffer and he would pay for it.

Vail was no longer his brother.

He was just another enemy to kill.

Loren moved off and Bleu fell into step beside him, his spear held down at his side, his gaze fixed ahead on Sable. Loren lost himself in thought as they followed Thorne, unable to completely shut out Vail and his suffering, torn between wondering what had happened to him and focusing on Olivia to keep the hazy connection between them alive.

Thorne left the park, crossed the road to the wrecked Archangel building, and turned around to face him.

"Have you lost him?" Loren feared that the demon had and he would fail to save Olivia.

Thorne shook his head and spoke in his demon tongue. "Still tracking. It was strange. He moved closer. I wondered if he was coming back, but he has returned to where the portal took him now."

Erratic behaviour, but Loren didn't have time to ponder why his brother had been returning to them before he had gone back to wherever they were holding Olivia.

"Thorne." Loren looked at Sable and Bleu, and then at the large male demon. "How powerful are your portals?"

Thorne squared his broad thickly muscled shoulders. "More powerful than elf ones."

"Can you teleport three with you?" Loren could manage to teleport one other beside himself and that often took a lot of focus and could weaken him depending on the situation. He didn't feel weakened when he teleported Olivia or Sable, but he had teleported elves before and the drain on his powers was intense then. The theory went that the more powerful the creature you wanted to transport with you, the more power you needed to make it happen.

He was asking Thorne to teleport two powerful elves and a human.

The Third King lifted one shoulder in an easy shrug. "It would not be a problem."

He had his arm slung around Sable before she could move, pulling the slender female against his broad frame. Sable squeaked and tried to break free, but the demon's large hand settling on her hip made her still and a fierce blush stained her cheeks.

Bleu frowned and tightened his grip on his spear.

"You want me to stab you?" Sable said and the demon looked down at her.

"No." His rough gravelly voice held a confused note. "Why would I desire that?"

"Because it's what's going to happen if you don't stop manhandling me." She pushed again and the demon reluctantly loosened his grip on her, allowing her to break free.

Sable smoothed her black t-shirt down, neatly arranging the hem along the belt of her combat trousers.

Thorne still looked confused. Loren didn't have time for this.

He grabbed Thorne's arm and then grabbed Bleu with his other hand. "Sable."

She looked up, a hint of colour lingering on her cheeks, and stared at all three of them before she stepped forwards and took hold of Bleu and Thorne's hands. Both males shot deadly glares at each other and then Thorne's eyes burned red and a vast black hole opened beneath them.

"Hold on," Thorne growled and Loren hoped to the gods that Sable did as he said because a portal was no place to get lost. If she let go, she could end up anywhere, in this world or the demon one.

Darkness swirled around them and then lifted to reveal a decrepit manor house illuminated by floodlights. The hum of a nearby generator filled the silence, obliterating the softer sounds of the nature all around them. Shadowy silhouettes of trees speared the sky, swaying in the cool night breeze.

Scaffolding covered the sandstone three storey façade of the manor house and there were no lights on inside. Several of the windows had been boarded up.

Loren ran a calculating gaze over the building and released Thorne and Bleu. It was falling apart and looked as though it hadn't been lived in for at least fifty years. Vail could have been hiding here with Kordula for all that time, or possibly longer.

How long had Vail and Kordula been in the human world?

Sable broke away from them and flipped open her small crossbow. She loaded a bolt and looked over her slender shoulder at Thorne. "So, Demon, where's the bastard who took my friend?"

Thorne arched a dark slash of an eyebrow at her biting tone and pointed towards the house. "I thought it was rather evident, little female. He awaits yonder."

"Yonder? Who the hell says yonder anymore?" Sable hooked her crossbow on her belt and turned away, missing the black scowl Thorne directed at her back.

Loren thought yonder was a perfectly good word.

Bleu called his helmet, the black scales forming it over his cheeks and his forehead, and then flaring back into twin curved horns.

Loren followed suit, mentally commanding his black spiked crown and helmet to form but leaving his face mask. He needed to be able to speak with the others without it hindering him.

Sable stalked off. Bleu followed with Thorne.

Loren focused on the building, his senses mapping every floor. He could hear three heartbeats. One far slower than the other two. Olivia. She wasn't inside the building. She was outside somewhere. The link between them was as hazy as ever, but it was dull and calm too. Combined with her slower heart rate, it left him in no doubt that she was unconscious.

He closed his eyes as he walked towards the rundown manor, focusing all of his power on enhancing his senses so he could pinpoint the locations of the owners of the three heartbeats.

"They are outside." Loren frowned and felt Bleu, Sable and Thorne halt and turn their gazes on him. "Olivia is unconscious. Higher than the other two. Vail is bleeding. I can smell his blood. He is weakening. Kordula is..."

"Here."

Loren's eyes shot wide and he quickly shifted his sword, gripping it in both hands before him.

Kordula threw her hand towards him and black ribbons shot at him like spears. Loren ducked and rolled, came to his feet and growled as he brought his sword down in a swift arc aimed straight for her chest. She fanned her fingers out and more thick black bands blocked his sword. They curled around it and Loren quickly withdrew it and distanced himself. He didn't have time to dance with Kordula. He had to get to Vail and end him before his brother could harm Olivia.

He looked to Bleu and Thorne.

Both males nodded and readied their weapons.

Loren called a portal as Bleu and Thorne attacked Kordula in unison, drawing her attention away from him. The purple and blue light flashed over his body and he leaped forwards and appeared right beside Sable. She gasped and attacked with her long knife, and he blocked with his left forearm. The blade struck harmlessly against his armour and Loren grabbed her and called another portal.

He came out on the other side of the manor, close to the scaffolding that covered it too, and growled when he saw Vail and then froze when he spotted Olivia. She hung from chains near the top of the scaffold, suspended with her arms out beside her and a loop of chain around her neck. The chains were precariously loose and if her hands slipped free of them, the one around her neck would strangle her.

Or worse.

His heart stopped when he realised a chain wasn't the only thing around her neck. A fine filament caught the glow of the floodlights illuminating the gravel drive and the lower floor of the house.

If Olivia fell, it would decapitate her.

Loren snarled at Vail where he stood several metres away in the large clearing between three floodlights, clutching his side. Blood glistened on his hand and down his leg, and Loren could see the pain written across his pale face and in his dark eyes.

Sable cursed viciously, reached under her arm and sent three throwing knives flying at Vail. Vail easily deflected them with a wave of his hand, sending the blades firing back at them. Loren pulled Sable behind him and blocked each knife with his black sword, knocking them to the ground.

"Get her down," Loren tossed the words at Sable before he released her, readied his sword in both hands and rushed his brother.

He had to be careful. It would only take a few blasts of telekinetic power to shake the scaffolding and cause Olivia's death.

Kordula appeared off to Loren's right as he clashed with Vail, bringing his sword down hard to strike Vail's twin blades. Thorne appeared swinging his broadsword at her and the tip sliced across her upper left arm. Blood streamed down it and she shrieked at the demon king, who merely grinned at her.

Bleu appeared behind Vail and thrust forwards with his black double-ended spear. Vail disappeared and Loren had to dodge Bleu's blow, shifting his hips to the right and clumsily knocking the spear away with his black blade. Bleu's horrified expression was apology enough but the prickle of hairs across the back of Loren's neck and the way his senses screamed in high alert said it hadn't been meant as an apology.

Loren swung to face Vail, bringing his sword up at the same time. Too slow. Vail slashed down Loren's chest, cutting a long gash in his black armour, a savage twist to his expression.

It faded a moment later, turning as horrified as Bleu's had been, and then Vail growled and stumbled backwards, dropping one of his blades. He pressed his hand to his forehead and screwed his face up as he dug the points of his claws into his scalp, drawing blood.

Kordula shouted something that Loren failed to catch and Vail's demeanour changed, turning vicious once more. He attacked again, striking hard and fast, driving Loren backwards towards Bleu. Bleu shot past him and engaged Vail, and Loren was thankful for the brief respite.

Bleu ducked and dodged, thrusting and parrying with his spear, keeping Vail on the defensive. Loren turned to check on Thorne and his eyes shot wide as he saw thick black and red bolts flying directly at him. Loren called a portal but wasn't quick enough. The powerful spell hit him square in the chest, some of the spear-like bolts striking the gash in his armour and sinking deep into his flesh, and he shot backwards.

No.

Loren's whole body reverberated with the force of the impact as he struck the scaffolding, causing the metal to bend and twist under the strain.

Olivia screamed.

CHAPTER 22

Olivia shrieked as pain tore through her and she came awake, her vision blurring and distorting, making the drop to the ground below her shrink and grow. It focused and she struggled and then wished she hadn't when her left hand slipped free and she dropped.

Something cold tightened around her throat, cutting off her air supply, and she shot her hand up and reached for her other secured arm. Chains. Olivia stretched and grabbed the ones holding her other arm just as her wrist slipped free. The chain around her neck tightened further, making darkness encroach at the corners of her mind, and something sharp cut into her throat.

"Olivia!" Loren bellowed and her gaze darted to him. He stood below her, a wild panicked look on his face.

Bleu and Vail fought nearby, and beyond them were the witch-bitch and the huge man from the Archangel cafeteria. He fought like a demon, swinging an enormous sword with no visible effort.

She kicked her legs and tried to pull herself up to relieve the pressure on her neck, but the chain slipped through her hands and she skidded further down. A hot sting slashed around her throat and she gasped, her eyes shooting wide.

Olivia's hands slipped again.

Loren roared below her and his fear flooded the link between them, forcing it back to full strength somehow.

She was going to die.

She lost her grip on the chains and dropped.

Warm hands grasped her forearms. "Got you."

She had never been more glad to hear Sable's voice. Never again would she moan about her friend's requests for painkillers so she could go out and hunt when she should have been resting her injury or how she liked to tease Olivia whenever she was bored.

Olivia looked up to find her laying on the scaffolding boards above her, her hands locked tightly around Olivia's bare forearms. Sable growled with effort and pulled, and the pressure on Olivia's neck lessened.

Olivia held on to her friend's arms as she slowly raised her.

"Do you have her?" Loren shouted from below.

"I have her," Sable hollered, steely determination in her golden eyes. She added quietly, "Only bloody thing I'm good for is saving your arse. Go get the bastards, big guy."

No. Olivia panicked and grabbed the edge of the wooden board as soon as it was within reach. She hauled herself up on trembling arms and Sable grasped the belt of her jeans and pulled her awkwardly onto the scaffolding.

Olivia quickly removed the makeshift noose from around her neck and ground her teeth to bear the pain as she pulled the thin wire away from the groove it had cut into her flesh.

"You okay?" Sable said and Olivia nodded, pushed to her feet and looked around. "Take it easy. The guys have this one. I pretty much failed to make an impact and bloody Bleu had to save me."

Olivia could tell how much that had irked Sable but she didn't care right now.

"I have to get down there, Sable." Olivia didn't want to see what was happening below them but she couldn't stop her eyes from drifting to the battle.

"No way."

"I need to get down there now." Olivia spotted a ladder off to her left, towards the end of the scaffolding, and started for it.

Sable grabbed her arm and stopped her, and she went to snap at her friend but lost her voice when she saw the fight below them.

Loren and Bleu were battling hard against Vail, all of them bleeding from gashes in their black armour. The demon was changing, his horns curling around his pointed ears now and his eyes glowing like the fires of Hell as he attacked the redheaded witch and did his best to block her spells. Wounds from where Kordula's attacks had hit covered his broad muscular chest and he seemed to be moving more slowly than before.

Kordula hit him hard with a left hook that was impossibly strong for such a frail looking female. It knocked the demon backwards, sending him stumbling and struggling to keep upright.

"Damn. Thorne's going to get himself killed at this rate. Bloody idiot," Sable muttered and unhooked the crossbow from her belt. She opened the quiver-pouch there and danced her fingers over the bolts in it. She pulled out one with a thick pointed tube secured to the end and grinned at Olivia. "Let's see the bitch dodge this."

Sable loaded the explosive bolt, aimed and fired. It whizzed towards Kordula and the demon Sable had called Thorne. The demon's pointed ears perked up and he shot Sable a glare and then disappeared.

The action distracted Kordula and Sable's bolt hit her shoulder and exploded on impact, sending her spinning through the air and crashing to the ground in a blaze of fire and smoke. Had it killed her?

The smoke cleared to reveal the sorceress lying on the gravel, blood covering the right side of her body and pooling beneath her, black in the bright floodlights. The slinky material of her dress was shredded and smouldering, and the top right side of the metalwork corset had blown open, the silver curling outwards in places.

A dark snarl came from behind Sable.

Sable tensed and her eyes edged towards her shoulder. Olivia's gaze leaped to the demon towering over her friend.

Thorne's eyes burned bright crimson, his huge body hunched over in the small area between the two levels of scaffolding, his broad shoulders almost spanning the width of the frame.

"You seek to harm me, little female." His deep voice vibrated through Olivia and Sable slowly shook her head and pointed towards Kordula who lay in a smoking heap on the drive.

"I seek to kick that bitch's arse," Sable said calmly but Olivia could see past her false smile to the fear it hid.

Thorne scared her for some reason.

He took a step closer and ran his gaze over Sable's body, his expression unconvinced at first and then gaining a decidedly hungry edge. Oh. My. No wonder Sable was on edge around Thorne. Olivia glanced back at her and caught the almost imperceptible touch of colour on her cheeks.

The demon's red eyes slid to Olivia and she seized her chance.

"Take me down there," she said and he looked below them at the raging battle. She didn't want to look now because she feared she was going to be too late and was beginning to consider the outcome of grabbing the chain and sliding down it to reach the ground. She had to stop Loren.

Thorne nodded and held his large left hand out to her.

She grabbed Thorne's arm and he grabbed Sable, tucking her against his bare chest despite her protests and blushing, and then darkness opened below them.

Olivia dropped into it, clinging to Thorne, regretting her decision to ask him for assistance. She had expected him to use portals in the same way Loren and Bleu did. There was something disconcerting about plunging into a black hole.

The darkness receded and Olivia instantly broke free of Thorne and Sable, running towards Loren and Bleu where they battled Vail.

Loren's handsome face was a picture of determination, his black spiked helmet making him look formidable as he struck hard at Vail with his blade, murder in his eyes. A chill went through her when he managed to slash across Vail's shoulder and turned his blade to deal another blow while his brother fought to recover from the first.

"No!" Olivia screamed and Loren froze mid-swing but Bleu didn't.

He drove his spear through Vail's side from behind and Vail cried out in agony, the force of the blow causing him to arch forwards.

"No," Olivia shouted again and raced towards them. She had to stop them before they killed Vail. He was just a pawn, used against his will by Kordula in her insane quest for power.

Olivia slowed as Kordula rose to her feet behind them, her flesh knitting and mending before Olivia's eyes, becoming perfect and smooth once more. The metalwork of her corset repaired itself and the threads of her dress wove together. Her hair floated around her shoulders and her black dress fluttered around her long legs.

The witch's eyes blazed crimson and bright arcs of red energy crackled around her.

Olivia threw herself forwards as a bolt of crimson lightning struck at her and grunted as she hit the gravel hard, skidding across it.

Loren peeled away from his brother and was at her side a split-second later, pulling her onto her feet and shielding her with his body. A bolt of red energy hit him in the back and drove them both forwards. They smashed into the crumbling sandstone wall of the building beneath the scaffolding, Loren's arms and her backside taking the brunt of the blow, and dropped together to the ground.

"Olivia?" Loren said and released her. His hands claimed her cheeks and he pushed back, his purple gaze warmed by concern and the fear she could feel in him.

"I'm fine," she muttered and arched her back, cracking everything into place.

Loren's gaze fell to her throat and the slash that cut around the front of it and darkened. He growled and went to turn away and she grabbed his wrists, stopping him from launching himself at his brother.

"No." Olivia held firm when he tried to break free of her and he looked back at her, his black eyebrows knitted into a dark frown and his gaze narrowed and bright with the fury she could sense in him. "Listen to me."

She glanced beyond his shoulder to the fight. Thorne had joined Bleu in his battle against the witch and Vail, and Sable was doing her best to help but her speed couldn't contend with theirs and Bleu and Thorne had to save her more than once when she came under fire from Kordula's red lightning.

Vail was still fighting, slashing at Bleu and Thorne with his twin black swords. He was paler now than he had been just minutes before, bleeding out from multiple wounds, but was feral and wild as he fought, a contrast to the man she had seen when they had been alone.

"Kordula is controlling Vail somehow." She looked back at Loren and her heart sank when she saw in his eyes that he didn't believe her. "Loren... your brother told me. Kordula is not his ki'ara. She tricked him. She is using him because she wants your kingdom. It's a sick and twisted game to her and Vail is caught in the crossfire, a pawn that she is using for more than just fighting."

Loren's gaze darkened again and he looked back at his brother.

"You have to listen to me, Loren. Please. We can save him somehow." She hadn't realised how much she wanted that until the words left her lips. She had failed to save Daniel from Archangel but she had a chance to help Loren save Vail from Kordula, and she wouldn't give up until she had gotten through to Loren and made him believe her.

Vail engaged Bleu, drawing him away from Kordula and Thorne. The red lightning struck Thorne in the thigh and he bellowed in pain and growled as he clutched it. Sable gave a war cry and attacked Kordula with her two long knives, using close quarters manoeuvres to hinder her ability to attack with magic. She landed several blows with the wicked blades, ripping through Kordula's black dress and tearing through flesh beneath. The dark witch slammed the flat of her hand against Sable's chest and she hit the gravel, spraying it everywhere.

Thorne bared huge fangs at Kordula and attacked, swinging his broadsword at the woman's head as she raised her hands to fire a spell at Sable while she was down. Kordula shifted to aim the attack at him and huge leathery wings erupted from his back and he shot upwards, dodging the spell. It blasted into the ground and threw gravel high in the air, leaving a smouldering crater behind.

A male cried out and Olivia's gaze darted back to Vail and Bleu.

Bleu pulled his spear from the side of Vail's chest, spun it in the air and brought it down again, aimed directly at Vail's head. Vail barely managed to block the attack with his twin black swords and the force of the spear clashing with his blades drove him to his knees. Bleu grinned, victory flashing in his eyes.

She had to stop him. Her gaze darted around and landed on a small blade with a ring at one end on the gravel just a few metres from her.

Olivia pushed away from Loren, launching forwards towards the small throwing blade. She scooped it up in her right hand and threw it with everything she had at Bleu, sending it shooting towards him at incredible speed.

She really hoped her aim was as bad as she thought it was. Loren would hate her if she hit Bleu.

The knife zipped harmlessly over Bleu's left shoulder but it did exactly what she had planned. He paused and frowned at her, forgetting his attack. Vail used the distraction to escape from Bleu's reach.

Loren snarled and grabbed Olivia, dragging her back against him on the ground. "What in the gods' names do you think you are doing? Have you gone insane?"

"Saving your brother," Olivia snapped and jerked out of his grip. "I'm not crazy... Vail is. Kordula has done things to him that have... he isn't right, but that doesn't mean he doesn't deserve to live, Loren. Kordula is making him do this. Can't you see that? You said he acted weirdly sometimes and seemed to be different. This is why. He's fighting her hold over him, but sometimes he isn't strong enough. Sometimes he can't stop himself from doing terrible things."

Olivia turned on Loren, her anger getting the better of her. She wanted to hit him and rail at him until he listened to her and saw that she was telling him the truth.

Loren stared beyond her, his eyes wide, filled with conflicting emotions that ran through her. She knew she was asking a lot but she also knew in her heart that Vail hadn't lied to her.

"Vail is being controlled by the witch, Loren. You have to believe me. Your brother is fighting her but she's too powerful," Olivia said, loud enough that she was sure everyone must have heard her.

Vail broke past Thorne and Bleu and ran at them.

Loren pulled Olivia onto her feet and faced his brother.

Olivia curled her fingers around Loren's hand, drawing his attention down to her, and couldn't stop the words from leaving her lips, even when she knew they would wound him. This was her last chance. Vail couldn't withstand another attack. Loren would grant his wish and then he would discover that she had been telling the truth and he would hate himself for what he had done.

"He wants you to kill him, Loren. He brought us together because he wants to die... and he didn't want you to be alone when that happens."

Vail ground to a halt, dropped his blades and threw her a pained look as he clutched his head, curling his black claws around it. He tossed his head back, forcing his elbows high into the air as he held the sides of his head, and snarled, baring his fangs. Fight it. She knew he could. He was weak from the blood loss but he could still fight Kordula's spell. He had to.

His purple eyes shifted down to Loren and he mouthed something.

"Brother," Loren whispered and took a step towards him, and then shoved Olivia behind him when Vail's demeanour changed again, his eyes growing dark with violence.

Vail lowered his hands and his blades shot back into them, but he made no move to attack.

He stood before them, his chest heaving with each hard breath, his head still tipped back and eyes on Loren. The lights from the generators cut across him from behind and his left side, forming two shadows on the gravel.

"Kill him, Vail." Kordula's voice rang out over the sound of her battle against Bleu, Thorne and Sable.

Vail's lips compressed and he lowered his head, staring at Loren. Olivia could see the war in his eyes, the fight between carrying out Kordula's command and resisting her order, and she knew he was going to lose even when she desperately hoped he would win.

Vail's blades clinked as he shifted his grip and then he was right in front of them, bringing his two swords down in black arcs towards Loren and Olivia's necks.

CHAPTER 23

Loren swept Olivia into his arms and instantly teleported with her, narrowly avoiding Vail's blades. He reappeared behind his brother with Olivia. Vail's swords clashed, he snarled viciously, and spun on his heel to face Loren.

Olivia was right and Loren couldn't believe he had failed to piece it together for himself before now when the evidence had been there all along.

Vail had never been out to kill him. He had always tried his hardest to pull his punches and never once had he dealt a mortal blow.

Loren pushed off, leaping backwards, placing more distance between himself and his brother. Vail growled, flashing his fangs, and swept his blades down in two swift arcs at his sides.

Guilt crawled through Loren's gut as he gazed upon his brother, all of the signs he had discarded over the four thousand years flickering through his mind and tormenting his heart. He had always believed his brother to be evil and had never seen what was really happening. He had allowed Vail to suffer enough that he now longed for death when he had once been all about living.

Bleu appeared beside him, Sable tucked against his side. The female hunter was injured, bleeding from a long gash up her left arm. She clutched it to her, breathing hard through the pain he could sense in her.

"Bleu, keep Vail busy but do not kill him," Loren commanded and Bleu nodded, released Sable and went after his brother, clashing hard with him.

Loren released Olivia and brushed a kiss across her forehead when she looked up at him, her fear resonating in his blood.

"I will free my brother. You must take Sable and tend to her. Be careful, sweet Olivia. Do not drop your guard. Understand?" He stroked her cheek and held her gaze, his tone soft and laced with all the love he felt for her.

She nodded but looked reluctant to leave his side. He knew what she wanted to hear him say but he couldn't bring himself to speak the words that would reassure her when he wasn't sure whether he would survive the fight against Kordula. The witch had taken some severe blows but she was still powerful and she had abilities at her disposal that could cost him his life if he wasn't careful.

"Go." Loren nudged her towards Sable and she burst into action, hurrying to her friend and leading her away from the battle and towards the edge of the lighted area.

Loren wanted her completely gone from the grounds, whisked away to safety, but he knew she would refuse if he suggested it. He took one long glance at her and then straightened his shoulders, shut down the pain echoing through his body, radiating from the wounds he had sustained in his fight against Vail, and turned to face Kordula.

Thorne dived at the witch, coming out of the darkness like a missile with his large dragon-like wings pinned back and his sword held to one side, pointed towards Kordula. He rolled in the air as she blasted him with several bolts of red lightning, avoiding them all, and spread his wings when he was close to the ground. He landed hard at an angle and broke into a sprint, coming around behind the sorceress and swinging his broadsword at the same time.

The heavy blade connected hard with Kordula's left hand as she produced a black disc a few inches in front of it but she failed to block the blow completely. The tip sliced through her hand, shearing three of her fingers at a diagonal, and she shrieked and thrust her other hand forwards, unleashing a crackling blast of red energy.

It struck Thorne hard in the side, spinning him in the air, and he landed in a heap on the gravel.

Loren called a portal to him and leaped forwards, appearing beside Thorne. "Are you alright?"

"Not dead yet," Thorne grumbled and pushed himself onto his hands and knees, growling at the same time. Blood pumped from the ragged wound in his left side and he covered it with his right hand, grunting and grimacing.

Loren swallowed hard as he assessed the damage done to the demon king. He had hoped to have an ally in the fight against Kordula, but the wound was bleeding badly. Thorne cast him a dark glare that dared him to try to stop him from fighting. Loren knew better than to coddle a demon, especially when they were injured. Demons could bear the pain, and some only grew more savage and deadly when they were in danger of losing their life.

Loren couldn't risk using Thorne in the fight against Kordula, but he had another more important task for the noble demon king.

He clasped Thorne's right shoulder and looked deep into his red eyes. "Protect the females."

Thorne's features set into a hard scowl and his eyes glowed like the fires of the underworld. He nodded, shoved to his feet, and took up his broadsword.

"Kill the wench." Thorne tossed the words on a black snarl and loped off towards Olivia and Sable, his wings shrinking into his back at the same time.

Olivia would be safe now and so would Sable. Thorne wouldn't allow anything to happen to them. He would protect them with his life. It eased Loren's mind and he turned to face Kordula.

She stood a short distance away, working her dark magic on her fingers. The bones grew out of the severed ones and then muscle, vein and tendon covered them, and skin formed. She raised an eyebrow at them, turning them this way and that to inspect them, and flexing them.

Her red gaze sought Thorne but landed on Loren. Her scarlet lips twisted into a sneer and she looked across at Vail where he battled Bleu.

"Release my brother, Kordula," Loren said.

She smiled wickedly. "Never. I utter one command and he will kill himself... and what will you do then, noble prince?"

Olivia had been right and Kordula had just confirmed it for him.

Loren growled, gripped his black sword in both hands before him, and focused on it. He hadn't fought like this in countless centuries, not since before Vail had gone to war with him because of Kordula's twisted scheme, but he would return to his roots now and hope it would give him the advantage he needed over the dark witch.

He closed his eyes and released the hilt of his sword, holding it between his opened palms and keeping it from falling with his telekinesis. He drew his palms apart and felt the shift and the drag on his power as his blade succumbed to his mental command, splitting in two.

Kordula's gaze burned into him.

Loren closed his fingers around the hilts of his twin blades and opened his eyes, fixing them on Kordula.

She made a low unholy sound and attacked him, sending bolts of red lightning streaking towards him. Loren blocked the first four, rapidly becoming accustomed to using two swords at once, and dodged the remaining three, strafing to his right. They struck the gravel drive and sprayed dirt and stone into the air. He used all of his speed to come around behind Kordula and lashed out with the blade in his left hand.

Kordula swept her healed hand out and deflected it using one of the black discs of power. She failed to notice his other blade as she worked her spell and he thrust forwards, burying it deep into her shoulder. She cried out and swung her left fist, catching him hard across his cheek and sending him smashing into the ground.

Olivia called out to him.

Loren refused to heed her or look her way, unwilling to risk giving Kordula a chance to attack and land another blow. He rolled away from the sorceress and called a portal, and sank into it.

He reappeared above Kordula, dropping out of the night air, and brought both of his black blades over his shoulders and then swung forwards with them. They sliced through the darkness towards Kordula and she looked up, her red glowing eyes shot wide and she dropped to her knees, holding both hands out above her. A black dome formed over her and his blades struck it hard, the vibrations from the blow numbing his hands through his armour.

Loren kicked off from the dome, flipped in the air, and landed in a crouch nearby. The moment Kordula lifted her spell, Loren sprang at her, thrusting forwards with the sword in his right hand and preparing to bring his left one around in a sharp arc from below.

She grinned and Loren barely avoided skewering Vail as he appeared before him and lashed out with his own twin blades.

Bleu roared something dark and vicious in their language and teleported into the fray, knocking Vail out of the way and rolling across the ground with him.

Loren attacked Kordula again, weaker this time as fear of accidentally killing Vail played on his mind.

Kordula stood her ground and flicked her left hand out towards him, and he dodged right as thin black streaks like long needles shot from her fingers. He failed to evade them all. Fire seared his left shoulder and the impact spun him around, the world whirling across his eyes in a blur. Not magic. They were made of the same metal as his armour, able to penetrate it.

The ground came at him fast and he dropped one blade, pressed his hand into the gravel, and flipped himself over onto his feet. He growled and called his sword back to him, and grinned when he spotted Sable's throwing knives on the ground just ahead of him.

He spun to face Kordula, sweeping his right arm around at the same time and using a telekinetic wave on the blades. They shot towards her. She deflected the two he sent at full speed and moved too early to block the third, her mistake in thinking he would send all at the same speed costing her. The short ringed knife grazed her neck, slicing through her flesh and her dark red hair. Blood cascaded down her throat and chest and she covered the wound with her hand.

Vail growled and hit Bleu with a powerful blast of psychic power, sending him tumbling through the air and landing hard on the scaffolding. Bleu crashed through it, hitting each floor and some of the steel poles, flipped and landed on his front on the gravel.

Loren threw his hand out towards Vail and sent him flying through the darkness across the grass.

He sensed Olivia move, saw Kordula's gaze dart to her location as she ran towards Bleu, and kicked off as the witch sent five black needle-like shards at her. He threw himself into their path and two struck him hard in the left side of his chest.

The remaining three embedded into the stomach of the man standing before him, shielding him.

Vail.

Loren hit the ground, the force of the impact causing every one of his injuries to blaze with pain and the two long needles to burn fiercely.

Vail collapsed to his knees, his back heaving as he breathed hard, his right hand shaking as he reached for the long black spikes that punctured his stomach and came out of his back.

Loren yanked the two in his chest out, grunting as each pulled free of his flesh, and discarded them as he rushed to Vail's side.

Vail wavered and fell backwards, and Loren caught him. Blood coated his brother's lips and formed rivulets down his chin.

"Vail," Loren whispered and looked down at the three spikes in his stomach. He silently apologised to his brother for the pain he was about to cause him and threw a mental command at them, pulling them out of Vail's flesh. Vail cried out, bowing forwards in his arms, the sound cutting Loren to his heart as his brother's agony tore through him.

Loren growled and looked up at Kordula through his lashes, his gaze narrowing on her and his lips curling back off his fangs. His ears flattened against the sides of his head beneath his helmet and he snarled as he flung his bloodied right hand forwards and sent the five spikes flying at her.

She smiled wickedly as she dodged each one, taunting him with how easily she evaded them.

Loren grinned, flashing his fangs at her.

And teleported just as she dodged the final spike.

He appeared before her, his right hand flattened to form a point with his vicious black claws and shoved it upwards before she had even noticed him.

His claws ripped through the metal corset and the black material of her dress and plunged into her flesh just below her ribcage. He grabbed her shoulder with his left hand and drove his other one hard into her, until his claws punctured her twisted black heart and she gasped, her vicious grin becoming a look of horror and disbelief.

Loren closed his claws around her heart and stared down into her eyes as the red faded from them, revealing pale icy blue, ensuring he was the last thing she saw as he tore the vital organ from her body, spraying her blood across the gravel.

She dropped to the ground.

A huge broadsword came out of nowhere and severed her head.

Loren raised an eyebrow at Thorne.

"Just to be sure," the demon king said and nodded towards the heart still clutched in Loren's hand. "My kind would eat that."

Loren grimaced and dropped the black heart. "My kind would not."

He turned away and bright red light flared across his eyes, searing them. He raised his hands to shield them from it and squinted in search of the source.

Vail arched off the ground, a collar of markings blazing around his throat, his agonized bellow ripping through the night. Birds fled their perches in the trees and nature herself trembled in response to the harrowing sound.

Loren pushed forwards, driven to soothe his brother and help him somehow.

The markings disappeared and Vail looked at him, his purple eyes verging on black and rapidly filling with a wild and crazed but sorrowful look that Loren had seen too often in the past forty-two centuries not to know what it meant.

"Bleu!" Loren shouted and rushed to grab Vail before he could escape.

Bleu managed to reach him before Loren could but Vail fought him, vicious and savage despite his injuries. He clawed at Bleu, snarling and growling like a beast, his visage that of an animal as he bared his fangs and gnashed them. Bleu blocked as many blows as he could but others struck, Vail's serrated claws cutting easily through Bleu's armour and into his flesh.

Loren used all of his remaining strength to cross the distance between them in a blur of speed but even that wasn't fast enough.

Vail leaped backwards, pressed hard into the ground and propelled himself upwards, flipping heels over head to land on the remaining scaffolding.

"Vail... stay. I can help you get better." Loren reached for his brother and Vail hesitated, giving him hope that he would do as Loren bid.

Vail paused only long enough to look down at Loren with regret and a dreadful sense of finality in his eyes, the emotions flooding the restored link between them both speaking of his pain and issuing a silent apology, and then swan dived off the scaffolding towards the collapsed section.

"No!" Loren rushed forwards, heart beating wildly in his throat as his brother plummeted towards the ground and the mess of steel pipes that rose at jagged angles from it.

Purple and pale blue light burst across Loren's eyes and Vail disappeared.

Loren's knees gave out and he hit the dirt, the impact robbing him of his breath. He stared at the air as it shimmered, still reaching for his brother, and then threw his head back and roared until his throat burned and he ran out of air.

He collapsed forwards and pressed his hands into the gravel, hanging his head between his arms.

Vail was gone. He couldn't sense his brother at all, meaning he had closed the connection between them again, severing them once more.

Why?

Loren clawed at the gravel, refusing to believe it was because Vail intended to end his life. If he had wanted to kill himself, he wouldn't have called the portal. The force of hitting the broken scaffolding from such a height would have caused some of the steel poles to impale his body. He would have bled out before Loren could save him.

Olivia's warm hand came to rest gently on his back and he closed his eyes, the softness and tenderness of her touch soothing some of the pain from his aching heart. He had been determined to kill his brother and only she had stopped him from making a terrible mistake, but he had failed to save him in the end.

"Loren?" Olivia whispered and he lifted his head and looked at her. She crouched beside him, blood ringing her throat and dirt covering her pale skin, her gaze showing none of the pain he could sense in her. It showed only concern and affection, and something that worked to reassure him. "Archangel will help you find him. We have resources that can help you track Vail and then we can help him. We won't give up on him."

Loren nodded, heart buoyed by her words, grateful to his mate for her support and her confidence.

He sat up and looked over his shoulder at Bleu. Sable was tending to him and Thorne watched over them, his gaze tracking every move the huntress made. She glanced across at Loren and rose to her feet, grimacing as she clutched her injured arm.

"I'll help any way I can," Sable said, the offer unexpected and touching him deeply. Sable had no reason to get involved. Neither did Archangel, but the determination in Sable and Olivia's eyes said that the organisation would be helping him whether they liked it or not.

Loren looked back at Kordula's body.

"I will search for Vail and I will not stop until I have found him." Loren pushed himself up and Olivia helped him stand, holding his arm and then wrapping it around her shoulders and bearing his weight. He breathed through his pain, every laceration on his body burning and stealing his strength, but it wouldn't shake his resolve. "I vow I will never give up on Vail, even if he has given up on himself."

Olivia smiled up at him.

"We will never give up on him," she said and his heart warmed at her words. "We will find a way to save him."

He nodded and gathered her close to him, and pressed a gentle kiss to her lips, forever grateful to have such a wonderful, understanding, caring and stubborn ki'ara.

Loren pulled away from her and brushed his knuckles across her cheek, and then grimaced when the side of his chest burned as though someone had poured poison from the river of the seventh demon kingdom on it.

Olivia's brown eyes filled with concern and her eyebrows furrowed. "We need to get these wounds fixed up."

Loren nodded and looked at Bleu, Sable and then Thorne. "Care to test the limits of your teleportation ability?"

The Third King grinned cockily, exposing bloodied fangs and reopening the vicious split on his swollen lower lip. "One more little female is hardly going to test it."

Bleu caught Loren's arm and Sable's. Olivia looked wary about taking Thorne's hand and Loren nodded to let her know that he wouldn't see the male as a threat to him. She was his now and no one could take her from him, although he would kill any who tried.

She placed her hand on Thorne's and he grabbed Sable's, and then a black vortex swirled outwards from the centre of their rough circle.

Loren glanced back at the point where Vail had disappeared as he dropped into the portal and swore again that he would find Vail, no matter how long it took.

He would achieve the dream he had dared to give up on.

He would save his brother.

Thorne landed them in the cafeteria of the Archangel headquarters in London, causing a dozen hunters to leap to their feet and throwing the place into pandemonium again. Sable calmed the situation before the alarms blared and lights began flashing, and Loren almost thanked her for sparing him the pain of having to use his powers to silence them.

"You have one cycle of the moon, Prince Loren. I expect your assistance then." Thorne released Olivia, his dark red gaze pinned on Loren, and Loren nodded.

"Thank you for everything... for helping me save my ki'ara. I am forever in your debt." Loren held his hand out to Thorne and the demon clasped it and nodded. He released Loren's hand.

And lingered.

Sable slowly raised her eyes from Thorne's hand on her arm to his face, her eyebrows creeping up her forehead at the same time. The demon king stared down at her and, for a moment, Loren thought he would attempt to teleport with her, even though Bleu still held her other arm, and then he huffed, let go of her hand and stepped back. It looked as though it had taken Thorne considerable effort to place even that small distance between them.

The Third King frowned, opened his mouth to speak, and then growled and disappeared into a portal.

Sable stared at the shrinking black patch on the floor and then looked over at Olivia and blinked.

"Maybe we should get these wounds looked at now." Olivia didn't sound sure and Loren could see she had noticed the demon king's desire for her friend and was struggling with how to deal with it, just as Sable was.

And Bleu.

He growled something about killing and suffering, released Sable and stalked over to Loren. "My prince, we should return to the kingdom and inform them of our success."

Loren nodded and stopped to look at Olivia. They had never talked about where she would live and his heart told him that she would want to continue her work with Archangel. It meant a lot to her and he wouldn't stand in the way of her achieving her dream of promoting a better understanding between demons, fae and mankind when she sought to help him with achieving his own dream of saving his brother.

Olivia smiled. "You don't need to look so nervous. I'm going wherever you go. I have a whole new world to explore and hopefully document."

She stepped up to him, tiptoed and pressed a kiss to his lips. Loren growled and gathered her into his arms, slanted his head and claimed her mouth, ignoring the fierce ache as his wounds protested.

Violet light outlined his body and then chased over Olivia, bringing her with him to his apartments in the castle. A moment later, Sable's voice rang out from the courtyard below, scolding Bleu for kidnapping her again. There was going to be trouble ahead for Sable.

In one lunar month, Loren would lead his army with Bleu and Olivia to the Third Realm and Thorne's aid, and something told him that when that happened, Sable would be leading her own team to the same location under the banner of Archangel.

All hell was going to break loose in the Third Realm.

Loren smiled against Olivia's lips, his pain forgotten as he relished the feel of his female as she leaned into him, her mouth dancing with his, her sweet taste intoxicating him.

He focused on their connection, forging a stronger one and using it to seek out her injuries and steal them away before she could notice what he was doing. His back hurt and his throat blazed, but he didn't care. He would heal these new wounds and his old ones soon enough.

Olivia sighed and broke away from his lips, her dark gaze serious as she looked up at him. "I thought I told you not to do that. I'm immortal now... I can heal my own wounds."

Loren stared down at his beautiful ki'ara and shook his head, grazing his fingers across her soft dirty cheek at the same time. "I will never allow you to endure pain when I have the power to take it away."

She pressed her cheek against his palm and smiled, her kiss-swollen lips taking on a wicked look. "And I will never allow you to endure pain when I have the power to take it away."

Olivia brushed her wild chestnut hair away from her throat and drew the strap of her ruined purple halter-top aside, revealing the marks he had placed on her.

She tilted her head to one side and Loren half-groaned half-growled, gathered her against him and bent his head. His cheek brushed hers and he swept his lips across the healing marks on her skin, and she moaned and clutched his shoulders. Pleasure flowed through their link and he closed his eyes, opened his mouth and obeyed her silent command.

He eased his fangs into her and the first drop of her blood sent a shiver through him, bringing his tired body back to life and erasing his pain as he swallowed it down and pulled more of her sweet blood from her.

His ki'ara.

He had thought he would end this tumultuous journey alone, having sacrificed both of his dreams in the name of duty.

Now he had one of his elusive dreams nestled in his arms, her blood revitalising his body and speeding the healing of his injuries, and the pleasure she took from his bite flowing through him like ambrosia in his veins.

And the other he would chase until the end of time and he would never give up on it again because the delicate, beautiful female in his arms would never let him.

She would stand by him, supporting him, driving him onwards and giving him the strength to keep fighting to save his brother, even when he lost hope or his spirits were broken. She would always be there for him and he would always be there for her, and they would never be alone again.

His beautiful ki'ara.

His sweet Olivia.
His eternal mate.

The End

ABOUT THE AUTHOR

Felicity Heaton is a USA Today best-selling author who writes passionate paranormal romance books. In her books she creates detailed worlds, twisting plots, mind-blowing action, intense emotion and heart-stopping romances with leading men that vary from dark deadly vampires to sexy shape-shifters and wicked werewolves, to sinful angels and hot demons!

If you're a fan of paranormal romance authors Lara Adrian, J R Ward, Sherrilyn Kenyon, Gena Showalter, Larissa Ione and Christine Feehan then you will enjoy her books too.

If you love your angels a little dark and wicked, Felicity Heaton's best-selling Her Angel series is for you. If you like strong, powerful, and dark vampires then try the Vampires Realm series or any of her stand-alone vampire romance books she writes as Felicity Heaton. Or if you're looking for vampire romances that are sinful, passionate and erotic then try Felicity Heaton's new Vampire Erotic Theatre series.

If you have enjoyed this story, please take a moment to contact the author at **author@felicityheaton.co.uk** or to post a review of the book online

Connect with Felicity:
Blog – http://www.felicityheaton.co.uk/blog/
Twitter – http://twitter.com/felicityheaton
Facebook – http://www.facebook.com/felicityheaton
Mailing List – http://www.felicityheaton.co.uk/newsletter.php

FIND OUT MORE ABOUT HER BOOKS AT:
http://www.felicityheaton.co.uk

5000197R00120

Printed in Great Britain
by Amazon.co.uk, Ltd.,
Marston Gate.